SHENA MACKAY

Dancing on the Outskirts

virago

VIRAGO

First published in Great Britain in 2015 by Virago Press
This paperback edition published in 2018 by Virago Press

1 3 5 7 9 10 8 6 4 2

A CIP catalogue record for this book
is available from the British Library.

ISBN 978-0-349-00705-2

Typeset in Goudy by M Rules
Printed and bound in Great Britain by
Clays Ltd, Elcograf S.p.A.

Papers used by Virago are from well-managed forests
and other responsible sources.

MIX
Paper from
responsible sources
FSC® C104740

Virago Press
An imprint of
Little, Brown Book Group
Carmelite House
50 Victoria Embankment
London EC4Y 0DZ

An Hachette UK Company
www.hachette.co.uk

www.virago.co.uk

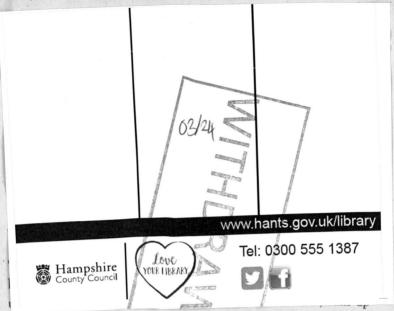
entire lives . . . A triumph!' Michèle Roberts, *Independent*

'A collection of exquisitely observed stories . . . Mackay will introduce us to the apparently trifling thoughts of a host of solitary characters and show us, with wonderful imaginative power, interior lives that are expansive, wondrous and tender. And even when her subjects are sad, the great power of her noticing, and her frequently piercing prose, transforms them into something vibrant and tender: her worlds are illuminated by glistening colours, busy wildlife, tactile skies, sibilant seas and responsive flowers. Mackay sees life in excruciatingly vigorous detail. Hers are lands in which it can feel as if everything is in bloom' *Telegraph*

'Shena Mackay's radiant short stories are skewering, funny and utterly original. *Dancing on the Outskirts*, a selection drawn from more than five decades of writing, was a high point of the year' Susannah

Also by this author

For Celeste Ondine Ouroussoff

Acknowledgements

My heartfelt thanks through the years go to my beloved sister Frances Loveday (1942–2015). Also to Deborah Rogers, wonderful agent and friend from 1963 to 2014, and the incomparable and much missed Ilsa Yardley (1928–2015). Enormous thanks, too, to David Miller and all at Rogers, Coleridge and White. Special thanks to Lennie Goodings who welcomed me back to Virago, and to Tamsyn Berryman and everybody who worked on this book. Last but far from least, as always, I thank Christie Hickman and all my dear family and friends for their unfailing support and love.

Contents

Dancing on the Outskirts

Awesome Day

Rick looked up at the clock above the counter. A quarter to three. It was always a quarter to three at the Wooden Nickel. In the bar with dark wood panelling halfway up walls hung with chipped enamel advertisements and brown photographs, a zinc counter, tobacco-stained flowers on the tin ceiling and a loop of coloured light bulbs reflected in the mirrors behind the bottles, it would feel like quarter to three even if the hands of the clock had not decided to stop there years ago. Rick checked his watch. It showed exactly the same time as the clock, until its slender second-hand flicked onwards. It had been quarter to three when he and Meriel first came to the Wooden Nickel and it was still quarter to three when they left. He knew she wouldn't show up here today. Especially in the middle of the afternoon. And yet he still hoped she might. She knew that he was leaving in the morning, on the eight o'clock flight to London. He flipped a coin. Heads she would, tails she wouldn't. Tails it was.

They had met on Broadway in a sudden snowstorm. What could be more romantic? Actually, they collided in the doorway of the down-town Duane Reade pharmacy where they had both dashed to buy an umbrella. Meriel's was large and bright green, his stubby and black, the last two in the rack, as if they had been waiting for them.

'Have an awesome day,' the girl behind the counter said to Rick, handing him his change.

Most of the previous snowfalls, except for a few persistent frozen lumps, had gone from the city and this blizzard came out of the blue. The snowflakes were too blinding for them to venture on to the street, so they got talking as they sheltered. Rick told her that he was in New York on business. Meriel was an actor, appearing in a double bill of early Tennessee Williams one-act plays in a tiny off-off-Broadway theatre. *The Case of the Crushed Petunias* and *A Perfect Analysis Given by a Parrot*. Snow stars melted on the green and black nylon, and a soft rain began to fall as they parted. Meriel left a ticket for him at that evening's performance and after the show they joined a handful of members of the company in the Wooden Nickel. The Wooden Nickel was one of those Lower East Side bars which had once been at the heart of New York bohemian life but the party had long since passed on. Meriel was as tall as he was, both dramatic and fragile-looking, blonde, with the inkiest blue eyes he had ever seen, and red, red lips. He would discover that she had a rose tattoo on her upper arm.

Rick's main impression of Serge, the company's director, and an actor called Eloise, who stuck around when the others had left, was that Serge was arrogant and Eloise snarky, and he couldn't wait for them to go. Eloise kept feeding the jukebox which bulked at the back of the room, a step up from the bar, refulgent with chrome and neon, behind the cluster of tables where they were sitting. It seemed to Rick that the two of them had some sort of hold over Meriel but he couldn't put his finger on it. At last, Serge shrugged on his enormous fur coat and Eloise wriggled into a skunk-like garment which had been tainting the air with the scents of mothballs, pizzas and old powders and perfumes, and they disappeared into the night. The bartender was making signs that he was anxious to close. Meriel and Rick were the last ones there.

Five weeks on from that awesome day, which turned to an enchanted night when he kissed Meriel on the sidewalk outside the Wooden Nickel, and thereafter to a series of enchanted nights, Rick, gazing into the mirror glass behind the bar, watched a string of little kids passing the window. They were in pairs, holding on to either side of a rope, with a teacher at each end. In their yellow sweatshirts under slick yellow tabards printed with the name of their school, they looked like ducklings being guided to a pond by a duck and drake. Or by two ducks. A blur of yellow like a lost Spring, and they were gone. His eyes filled with tears.

'Stick another one in there, Joe,' he said, draining his glass. 'You know what? I really thought it was the real thing with Meriel. I genuinely thought we had a future.'

'Something you should know. My name's not Joe.'

'Are you sure?'

'Mmm, hmm.'

'Another illusion shattered. I always thought it was Joe.'

'A lot of people want to think that.'

'What is your name then, if you don't mind me asking?'

'Cornelius.'

'So, Cornelius. I don't suppose you'd like to put another nickel in that there machine. I'm feeling so bad – something easy and sad . . .'

Cornelius picked up a cloth and began polishing a glass.

'I got other customers to take care of, in case you hadn't noticed.'

Rick glanced around. There was a cadaver in a hoodie in one of the booths, a horse, a couple bickering at the table where he had sat with Meriel on that first night, a lady with a little dog wearing a pink track suit and scarlet shoes on its tiny feet, and a construction worker shouldering his way through the door.

I'm outta here, he thought.

'Have an awesome day,' he said, picking up his coat which was trailing on the floor from the stool beside him.

But where to go? He didn't want to go back to the sublet in the East Village where he'd been staying. He couldn't go to Meriel's place. He could go to the theatre, for old time's sake, but it would be locked. Or some other company would be rehearsing there. For the duration of the run of Meriel's play, that shabby, rickety little theatre had become his world, and he had loved hanging out there, waiting for Meriel after the performance, buying flowers, taking her out to dinner. They always went back to Meriel's apartment, surprisingly spacious for a girl living alone, with dark little rooms cluttered with voluptuous vintage clothes. His sublet was above that of a dog-walker who boarded some of her charges, and the slightest noise set off a barking and howling. The smell in the hallway wasn't too pleasant either, and the light didn't work. He had bought a little torch to guide himself up the stairs.

Spring had arrived late, and gone, and come back. The skies were tender and blossoms opened on the trees, and flowers which had shivered in freezing winds opened their petals to the sun. Rick sat in Washington Square watching the nannies pushing their charges home in strollers, the squirrels chasing each other, the grandma and child feeding them nuts, the sparrows, all the people talking on cell phones. He had nobody to talk to. Even the barman didn't want him bending his ear.

If Cornelius had shown any interest he would have told him that his big mistake had been in telling Meriel the truth. Not at first, of course, but when he was sure of their love. He'd explained from the outset that he was divorced with a couple of kids, but they were doing okay. He was a good dad. That evening he'd come to pick her up at her place and they were having a drink before going on to a party given by one of her friends. Rick would have preferred to stay in, just the two of them. And there was the likelihood that Serge and Eloise would show up at the party. They always seemed to be hanging around. Taking both Meriel's hands in his, he told her that his business at home had failed and the deal he had hoped to make in New York had fallen through. He'd said that with her by his side he would pick himself up and start all over again.

There was a look of utter horror on her face when he suggested he move in with her, temporarily, until he was back on his feet. He could apply for a green card, he said, or they could live part-time in London, part-time in New York.

'I bet the London stage would just snap you up!' he told her.

'Snap me up? Are you insane? Do you know anything about anything at all?'

'Meriel, Meriel – we love each other. Anything is possible if we're together. I love the theatre too. I've written plays, you know – I've got a drawerful of them at home! I just haven't had the breaks – but the two of us together . . . '

Then she spat out at him that she'd thought he would put money into the company.

'You're just a sad old English grifter,' she said. 'I think you'd better leave.'

She locked herself in the bathroom.

It was true about the plays he'd written, all his rejected manuscripts. 'You'd never know it, but, buddy, I'm a kind of poet, 'he might have informed Cornelius. And then he could have told him about the worst thing of all. When he opened Meriel's closet. But here he was, in the park, and it seemed that everybody else had a life to go to. It was time to face the music. And not dance. He had come here in despair, taken on the sublet from a friend of a friend, hoping that something would happen to change his fortune. And it had, and it hadn't. Falling in love with Meriel, he had fallen in love with her city – and she had taken away not only herself but the whole of New York. He pictured the ride to the airport, past the clapboard houses, Rockaway and Queens, all the landmarks in reverse, all the sights that so excited him on his arrival.

What to do? Where to go? Against his better judgement Rick rang Meriel's cell phone. To no avail of course. He took a cab uptown and bought an enormous tiger and a panda and a thousand jellybeans in FAO Schwarz. Out on the street he realized they wouldn't fit in his case and would have to travel as guilty-dad hand luggage. He tried Meriel's number yet again and left another message. He found himself back down-town, with the hours to his check-in at the airport yawning ahead of him. He called in at the Ear Inn and the Lucky Strike, hoping against hope that Meriel might be there. He had no choice but to go back to the Wooden Nickel clutching two huge soft toys.

'Hey Cornelius.'

'Hey.'

'I don't suppose Meriel's been in?'

'Nope.'

Cornelius moved to the far end of the bar to serve a guy who had just come in.

Rick stared into his glass, and up at the clock. Quarter to three. The end of a brief episode. There he sat, identifying with a loser in a song. He wanted to tell Cornelius how he'd banged on Meriel's bathroom door and paced dementedly round her apartment. 'Here's the thing,' he'd say, if only Cornelius knew how a proper barman should act, 'I noticed a weird, unpleasant smell that I somehow recognized. I traced it to Meriel's closet and I opened the door, and there I saw Eloise's skunky old coat hanging. Stinking the place out. What was Eloise's coat doing there?

Well, I slammed the door quickly. But then I opened it again, because I'd glimpsed something else. It was Serge's fur coat. The motion of the door rattled the coats on their hangers, the fur trembled – it was like they were alive. As if Serge and Eloise had been there all the time watching us.'

Somebody had left a newspaper on the counter, folded back to the crossword. Rick, a bit of a crossword buff at home, studied it. The clues defeated him, his answers didn't fit the grid, he just didn't understand the idiom. He couldn't get those two coats – like moth-eaten predatory animals – out of his mind. And Meriel. If only she'd walk into the bar right now, he'd jump up and grab her and never let her go. The words of the song played in his head:

> But this torch that I found,
> It's gotta be drowned
> Or it soon might explode,
> So make it one for my baby
> And one more for the road.

The little torch he'd bought to guide him to his door was in his pocket. He pulled it out and dunked it in his glass, watching a bubble rise to the surface, waiting for it to burst.

Babushka in the Blue Bus

The 196 bus is elusive and blue and plies between Norwood and Brixton, painted with advertisements for Italy and the Caribbean, and seems to those who ride in it to have been stamped out of tin or constructed from rusty Meccano. It shudders and judders, the windows rattle in their sockets and are assaulted by branches of chestnut trees. On the afternoon of Good Friday, just about the time when there should have been darkness over all the land, the lower deck of the bus was taken over by a gospel choir whose minibus had broken down. Their crimson dresses and blazers packed the seats like a consignment of Papa Meilland roses that had escaped from a garden centre in full bloom, and almost immediately a melodious hum, as if bees were at work among the petals, drifted upstairs and swirled in the cigarette smoke.

Reginald Winchester, not his real name, sitting in the front left-hand seat of the upper deck, turned up his coat collar to protect himself from 'When I Survey The Wondrous Cross', the exhalations of righteous roses whose scent pierced him like thorns. The camel-hair was ringed with grease where his thinning plumage rested on it and the buttons hung from shanks of mismatched thread, but that coat had been a star in its time, acting, with a pair of caddish suede shoes now as smooth as leather, its wearer off the screen. His tightly buckled trench coat, his Homburg, his Trilby, his gun and his sneer had done their best to edge full black-and-white B-features into film noir, but at most his appearances evoked tired nudges of 'It's 'im, whatsisname, you know, that one that was in that film ...' Unopened bluebells in a garden blurred his eyes like unripe asparagus bluish with cold, and then, outside a church, a jaundiced poster spiked with a black crown of thorns. 'It's all your fault,' he muttered, 'for nearly two thousand years we've had Sunday licensing laws on a Friday, thanks to you. Bank holidays, who needs them?'

He had a One Day Travelcard in his wallet, and he was travelling to nowhere.

Subliminal tinned asparagus tips brushed his memory and he felt a queasy desire for a Sunday tea of lettuce in a cut-glass bowl, with canned salmon drowning a greenfly in salty water and beetroot tingeing the tinned Vegetable Salad with pink; apricots in Carnation milk and the pink and yellow windowpanes of Battenberg cake. He had been twenty-two when he had discovered that Battenberg cake was common. He wondered now if he would have been happier if he had never been disabused of the notion that it was posh. He jerked uneasily in his seat, noting and dismissing instantly two young women three or four seats behind him.

Terry was not sure how it had been her fault that they had passed that dead frog on the way to the bus stop, but Holly's white averted profile made it clear that she was to blame. She touched her friend's hand and offered a cigarette, and was answered by a shift of the shoulder.

'Don't be so prickly, Holly.'

Holly moved into the seat across the aisle.

'Well, I see this is going to be one of our memorable outings,' Terry said to the window, and lit a cigarette. A little breeze sneaked in and blew her smoke across Holly's stricken face. The day had started badly, with Holly faking a stomach-ache to postpone once again the long-promised visit to Terry's family, and when Terry had responded with two aspirin and an effusion on the restorative air of Woodside Park, Holly had waved away her breakfast tray and dressed bitterly in her least becoming clothes, combat fatigues appropriate for a saboteur. She had refused also to eat any lunch. Terry inhaled grey disappointment and imagined shoving her friend's head through the glass; but then how to introduce her to Mummy and Dad ... 'This is Holly, who I accidentally decapitated on the bus ... she's much prettier really, and those trousers don't do her justice ...'

'No, thank you.' Holly, staring through the window, unaware of its violent impact and of her head rolling down the hill, dismissed the plate of sandwiches held out by Terry's mother. A frog squatted on a wholemeal triangle. She shivered. She hated cucumber anyway. She hated Terry's mother, whom she had never met. It had just sat there, dead, pretending to be alive, on the pavement outside the Doctor's, as if it had been about to hop into the surgery, and hadn't made it in time. Terry would have stepped on it if she, Holly, hadn't screamed. Typical of her insensitivity. It was disgusting, and somebody should have cleared it away.

'I've heard so much about you,' she said to Terry's brother, 'and if I hear one more word I'll throw up.'

Teresa and Terence, the twins. Terry and Terry. She really did have a stomach-ache now; dread gripped her like a hungry octopus.

'Oh dear, I am being awkward, aren't I?' she smiled. 'I do apologize. I thought Terry would have warned you about my food allergies ... No, it's only a little scratch, please don't worry.'

She pulled up her trouser leg to reveal long reddening welts where the dog's claws had raked her skin. Lambert, the lovable Bedlington terrier, was dragged yowling from the room. She knew that sheepish poseur too well from the snapshots pinned above Terry's bed.

'I hate you, I hate you, I hate you!'

Terence's four-year-old daughter was on top of her, pounding her with tiny fists. She was smacked too, and put outside the door, her shrieks mingling with the dog's howls.

'You okay, babe? You look quite flushed.'

'I told you I wasn't well. I was just thinking about your family.'

'It'll be fine, I promise. We'll probably go for a walk after tea – you won't even have to talk to them much. It'll be easy – they're all dying to meet you.'

'I've got a blister,' she said.

Pushing whiny kids on rusty swings. Lambert, forgiven, pursuing Canada geese across a lake, grinning and shaking droplets of muddy water over her, and everybody laughing. She had detested Canada geese ever since boring wild-life documentaries at school.

'O sacred head, sore wounded . . .' swirled up the stairs.

'Jesus wept!' said Holly.

The man in the front seat whirled round to confront her. That was the one blasphemy which he could not countenance. His eye was caught, however, by an old woman lunging from the top step with a heavy shopping bag. She made her way to the long seat at the back. A warm, spicy smell of cinnamon and yeast and candied peel began to tantalize the noses of her fellow passengers. Reginald's eyes prickled in memory of an Easter garden of primroses and grape hyacinths in damp starry moss and a pebble rolled away from the mouth of a miniature cave. Baby leaves unfurled from fat reddish buds at the window; he took refuge from their freshness in a cigarette.

The tip of Terry's tongue licked her lips, luxuriating in an anticipation of buttery crumbs on a plate wreathed in convolvulus. The juddering of the bus was giving her a slight headache, and she knew from experience that concentrating on food was the best remedy for motion sickness. She saw the amaryllis, white, tipped with palest pink, flaunting against the bay window, the rosewood piano, the hot cross buns, the butter in the green glass dish. She had looked forward for such a long time to taking Holly to her childhood home but now she saw her hopes flushed away in an anorexic excess in the bathroom papered with fading peacocks.

Holly was regretting her rejected breakfast and lunch. 'What's that smell?' she demanded. 'It reminds me of something . . .'

Terry looked round. 'I think it's coming from that old lady,' she whispered.

'The Urals, or the Ukraine,' thought Reginald. The bright cotton scarf tied round her high-cheekboned face, the black stockings – she should have held a wicker basket on her lap covered with a snowy napkin, instead of that splitting plastic hold-all, and perhaps a drowsy hen clucking reassuringly over a clutch of warm eggs, an aromatic bunch of rough green herbs, a string of dome-shaped onions, black bread and sour red wine.

There was a scuffle and the scrape of claws, panting and swearing, as a dog dragged a boy, on the end of a lead, upstairs, followed by a girl. The humans slumped into a seat and the boy dropped the lead. The dog sashayed down the aisle, jumped on to the long seat at the back and flopped down beside the babushka, fixed her eyes on the black shopping bag and started to whine. The greasy dust that filmed every hair made her coat appear to be grey; black dragged nipples were evidence of puppies in her past. A wisp of rainbow chiffon twined in her studded collar was a festive or paschal touch at odds with her hang-dog mien. Her whines grew more persistent, and were ignored by the youth with a crooked swastika tattooed on his forehead, and the girl with a draggle of dried blood on her thigh under the torn mesh of her fish-net stocking. Terry was distressed. She thought of Lambert, and how she would have liked to have him to live with her, but the flat was no place for a dog. This was Rottweiler and Dobermann country. Pit-bull territory where dogs were kept as guards and weapons. She turned her head as the old woman succumbed, groped in her bag, and broke off a piece of something and slipped it to the dog. She almost lost her fingers. Then the dog was standing over her, yelping for more.

'Hey,' exclaimed the youth, 'that dog's eating a hot cross bun!'

Two more pairs of hungry eyes bored into the black bag.

'That's not fair,' said the girl.

'What about us then?' the youth accused.

With a smile of defeat or graciousness, the old woman held out a paper bag. They lurched down the bus.

'What about us then?' asked Holly.

'Holly!'

Holly was leaning over the back of the seat extending a hand.

'Mmmm, this is brilliant!' she sighed through crumby teeth. 'Homemade, and still warm! Terry, you've got to try one!'

Thus commanded by her friend, who seemed to be her friend once more, what could Terry do but sidle sheepishly after her?

'Are you sure you can spare another?' she said, biting into her bun. 'If only we had some butter . . .'

The old woman either could not oblige, or did not understand.

'Mind if I join you?'

Reginald, unable to maintain detachment as the dog embarked on, and swallowed almost whole, a second bun, gave a little bow as he sat down.

'Please.'

The babushka passed the paper bag, now holding one last bun.

The fat kid was right; it bore no resemblance to the cellophane-wrapped objects which, with no sense of occasion and brittle pastry crosses, had stocked the supermarket shelves for weeks. As he chewed, looking out of the window at an ancient cherry tree veiled in heartbreaking white, he had a shaky notion that there might even now be redemption by natural and human agencies.

'Herne Hill, Herne Hill, so good they named it twice ...' he said.

'Didn't you used to be whatsisname, you know, the one who was in those old films on telly?' asked the boy.

'Not really,' replied Reginald.

He half rose, in half-gentlemanly fashion, as the babushka stood and began to make her way towards the stairs.

'Happy Easter!' called Terry and Holly, to her disappearing headscarf.

Terry looked down and saw her standing on the pavement, a bent black figure engulfed by crimson gospellers, outside a closed supermarket.

'Most unorthodox,' mused Reginald. 'I thought Russians observed the Julian calendar.'

The Day of the Gecko

When the official part of the trip, at the World Book Fair in Delhi, was over, Alicia and her assistant Natasha flew to Goa. The road from the airport wound downward to the sea through banyans, trailing creepers and banana trees, passing grazing cattle and marshes of small white water lilies standing erect on their stems. The taxi hit a bump and in her mind's eye Allie saw her suitcase flying from the boot, spilling books and business clothes, and submerging with a splash and scattering of storks. She wondered if she would care if it did happen. After the heat and hassle of the city, the angst of travelling and hotel life, she could see how a person might be seduced by the surrounding lushness and enervated by the green humidity.

Now and then they glimpsed houses with verandas and wooden balconies breasting the foliage, pot-bellied pigs, black with pink stockings, rooting in the dust, goats and chickens, buffaloes. As each house was swallowed up behind them, Allie thought, her heartbeat quickening, perhaps that's the one. Maybe that's where Eric Alabaster has gone to ground. And, with a pang, she wondered if that woman carrying a bundle of reeds on her head might be Eric's wife or if any of the schoolchildren in their bright blue uniforms and flip-flops could be his.

Eric Alabaster had published four novels between 1970 and
1985 and then he had disappeared. He had always been a reclusive
yet charismatic figure, a sun-bleached traveller, and when it
became apparent that he had gone missing several men claimed to
have been his closest friend and various women declared that he
had been in love with them. Alabaster had no family, except some
cousins in Australia with whom he hadn't kept in touch. For a
while it became common knowledge that Alabaster was an inter-
national arms dealer, a spy, a double agent working both for and
against the government. Rumours of murder or suicide and spec-
ulation as to his whereabouts died down as the years passed,
although his name still bobbed up like a cork from time to time in
conversation and literary criticism. It was not until one of her
authors had come forward with the idea of writing his biography
that Allie read Alabaster's books and determined to relaunch them
to coincide with the publication of the *Life*. Alicia Compton was
the editorial director of a small publishing house which had been
taken over by a large conglomerate and for the time being at least
it seemed that she had a free hand to develop her list. With apparent casualness she made enquiries among Eric Alabaster's former
associates which led her nowhere, and as far as his former publisher
was concerned, the trail had gone cold in India.

It had seemed to Allie as she read the novels that Alabaster
was speaking directly to her; she was his first reader, the one for
whom the books had been written. They were exactly the same
age. She had gazed at the pictures on his book jackets until his
lips almost moved in a smile, and then, as she planned her trip to
Delhi, it was as if a bottle had been washed ashore at her feet. A
bottle tossed into the Arabian Sea containing the message that
Eric Alabaster was waiting for her in Goa. It was the perfect place
to disappear, and who knew what masterwork might have been
penned beside that turquoise sea? With his white-blond hair and
light eyes he should not be hard to identify.

Allie became aware of Tasha's conversation with the taxi driver.

'Why are you coming here?' he was asking. 'You should go to north Goa where more tourists are going.'

'That's why we came here. We don't want to be tourists. Actually, we're sort of looking for somebody.'

'I think you're looking for me.'

'Take it easy, Tasha,' muttered Allie, regretting not for the first time that Tasha would be her companion in this earthly paradise; Tasha in India had proved quite a different person from the London Tasha, or perhaps, having cast off her metropolitan black, she was showing herself in her true colours. Allie's briefcase was full of the cards of publishers and academics, unsolicited manuscripts and those of the two writers she had signed up, while Tasha's wallet bulged with the scribbled names and addresses of boys in carpet shops and hotel waiters, the cards of jewellers and the man from whom she'd bought her pashmina shawl. It would serve Tasha right if that mahout she had got so friendly with in Delhi turned up on her door-step in Fulham with his elephant. Tasha Calloway was generally described as gamine; to Allie, her face was like a cat's, who rubs against your legs while knowing there is a dead bird behind the sofa.

Tasha had let her down badly in Delhi, taking off on a day's jaunt to the Taj Mahal, leaving Allie to cope alone with a portfolio of appointments. She had tossed Allie one of her postcards of the Taj, saying, 'You can send it to somebody and pretend you saw it yourself. After all, everybody knows what it looks like.' Now, through the taxi window, Allie could see coconut palms soaring against the hot blue sky. 'There will be plenty more pebbles on the beach,' she told Tasha, 'or fish in the sea.'

'Will you answer me something?' the driver asked. 'Why it is you people like to be naked on the beach?'

Before Tasha could reply, Allie said, 'No, you answer me something. How far is it to the Da Silva Guest House?'

'We are there, mamma.'

The Da Silva Guest House was composed of the original structure, where the family lived, and five built-on apartments which faced the sea. A shrine to the Virgin was set into the front wall of the house, and roses, hibiscus and jacaranda wreathed the veranda and wooden shutters. Each apartment was designed to take two people but although Allie, enchanted by the guest house's careless perfection, said that she was willing to share, she was relieved when Tasha insisted it would be better if they each had their own space. Allie was shown to Number Three, Tasha to Number Five. They saw a young couple disappearing into Number Four. 'Honeymooners,' Tasha mouthed, under the noise of the crows who strutted and flapped in the palm trees, cawing ceaselessly. As soon as they had dealt with the formalities, the women put on their swimming costumes under their clothes, slathered themselves in mosquito repellent and as low-protection sun-cream as they dared, and headed for the beach.

'Mad dogs and Englishwomen,' observed Tasha, as they walked the short distance.

They had seen several dogs already, pretty dogs with pricked ears, quite unlike the sad, scabby creatures that slunk about the city. Notices in their rooms had warned against wandering on deserted parts of the beach after sunset, particularly if they were scantily dressed, unless they were able to defend themselves.

'I've got a gecko in my cupboard,' said Tasha.

A gecko? It was a sign. *The Gecko* was Allie's favourite among Eric's books. Obviously they had been given the wrong rooms. Allie had found only a striped frog swimming round her lavatory bowl, and scooped it out with the red plastic jug which presumably had been supplied for the purpose.

'I'll swap rooms if you like,' she offered, pulling Tasha past the man who had stepped out from his shop, a structure hung with carpets and fabrics and fronted by a rail of sun-faded garments.

'But I really need a sarong,' Tasha protested, adding, 'no, it's okay, he's quite a sweet gecko. We've bonded.'

There were no pebbles on the beach, just shells and slivers and tiny glittering particles in the process of being ground into sifting sand. The fishing fleet floated along the horizon. Pineapple tops pecked by the crows and hollow coconuts were the only litter. Tasha picked up two coconut shells, doing a little dance and singing 'At the Copa, Copacabana'. Allie was reminded of the sinister, sinuous beach boys who writhed around Ava Gardner in *The Night of the Iguana*; Deborah Kerr arriving in her white dress at that ramshackle clifftop hotel and Richard Burton as Shannon, the whisky priest tied to his hammock like the poor tethered iguana.

'Look at this!' she exclaimed, running her fingers along the heavy, hewn flank of an upturned boat as they undressed in its shadow. 'Just think, Tasha – generations of fishermen have been putting out to sea in craft of this self-same design, if not in this very vessel, from time immemorial.' A lump came to her throat as she said, 'You know that poem by Flecker, "The Old Ships" . . .'

'Not that I recall,' said Tasha. 'Personally, I think dropping the poetry list was the best thing we ever did.'

They waded into the warm sea, which flounced around their legs. Tasha flung herself on to a wave. Unfortunately, this crazy granny spouting on about poetry was the price she had to pay for February in Goa. She was in no doubt that if they should happen on Allie's fugitive author, it would be her and not Allie that he would fall for. Anyway, old Alabaster would be a wizened wreck by now, out of his head on toddy, palm wine and drugs. Allie wasn't bad for her age though, she had to concede; tall, naturally thin and fair, divorced a hundred years ago. She never spoke about her private life and Tasha supposed she didn't have one, apart from her family, which didn't count. Tasha swam out a bit further and turned to wave. Allie stood gazing at the horizon, with the modest skirt of her swimming costume undulating gently on the surface like a jellyfish.

Allie was thinking about her grandchildren, little Alf and Rosy, setting them down with their buckets and spades in what shade the palm trees gave, anointing them with total sunblock, arranging the folds of candy-coloured Foreign Legion caps to protect their tender, hollowed necks, showing them the antennae waving from a spiral shell. She waved back to the bikini-ed philistine sporting on the crest of a wave and swam out to join her. It was absurd to be blubbering over her grandchildren when she was here, in a Shangri-La far too hot for them, on a quest that might crown her career.

Allie and Tasha were sitting under the woven palm-leaf roof of one of the restaurants strung along the sands, sipping pineapple lassi, with boldly patterned sarongs draped round their shoulders and two more in their beach bags. 'Might as well stick with the pineapple,' Allie had said. When they had emerged from the sea, six or seven hawkers were camped beside their clothes, one of them a young girl with a basket of fresh fruit on her head. Half-naked among the swelling crowd of brightly clothed, bejewelled traders and basted by the sun, they were a pair of pink sitting ducks. Sticky with pineapple juice and clutching their purchases, they had fled ignominiously at last from the wheedling, bullying voices.

'You must admit it has a mellow tone,' said Tasha, stroking a note from the drum on her knees. 'And your sandalwood beads do smell divine.'

'I'll probably give them to my daughter, Sal.'

Allie showed the boy who brought their drinks her copy of *The Gecko* with Eric's picture on its cover, but drew a blank.

'I had a word with Madame Da Silva. I've arranged for us to hire a couple of bikes tomorrow. We can make an early start into the interior,' she told Tasha.

'But I've rented a scooter from him. Mister Da Silva. I thought you could ride pillion.'

'Absolutely not. I've paid the deposit. Anyway, you don't have a licence.'

'You don't need one here. I paid a deposit too – anyway, I thought you'd be pleased that I'd used my initiative, like you're always telling me to.'

'We're not in the office now, Tasha. You'll just have to explain and get your money back.'

Tasha's straw siphoned up a piece of pineapple with a mutinous gurgle.

'I suppose you do realize,' she said, 'that there are probably dozens of ancient, white-haired, superannuated hippies in Goa. Perhaps that's your bloke walking along the beach, mahogany man there with the medallion and ponytail.'

We must remain friends at least for the duration, Allie thought. Then we shall see how warm that expensive pashmina keeps our young friend when she gets back to London and finds herself out on her ear, busking in the underground with her drum.

'Just think how all that pedalling will tone up our thighs. And walking on the sand and swimming, it'll do us more good than weeks at the gym,' she said.

Tasha stretched out a leg as if she could see no room for improvement in that taut calf.

They dined at another beach café on a table sunk in sand. The delicately spiced food was delicious. How pretty the blue fairy lights looping the fronded canopy were, like blue chillies hung out to dry in the warm wind, how clear the stars. How desolate Allie felt. Ghostly crabs scurried from the sea's lacy edge and disappeared in the darkness of the beach. If only it were Eric sitting here beside her, his hand over hers. Tasha was flirting with a dog.

What a waste, thought Tasha.

In a concerted effort at amusement they giggled at the dessert menu. Buddha's Belly. A Goanese speciality. They insisted they must try it. Slivers of striated cake decked with cream and star fruit.

'Strange but surprisingly good,' said Allie.

Tasha agreed. If Allie imagined she was going to spend every evening chortling over Buddha's Belly with her, she had another think coming. A couple strolled hand in hand along the beach. Allie became aware that she was humming 'Hello, Young Lovers' from *The King and I*. So it had come to this.

'It's been a long day. Shall we go back now?' she asked. At least Tasha wouldn't have recognized the song; everything before 1960 was pre-history as far as she was concerned.

'It's ten to nine.'

Allie sat it out for the duration of another drink before saying that she really had to get to bed.

'Okay,' said Tasha, but when they came to Fernandez Hideaway, the last bar on the beach before the track that led to Da Silva's, she sat down at a table, saying, 'You go ahead. I'll see you in the morning.'

'I can't leave you here by yourself. It's really dark.'

'Don't be ridiculous. I'm a big girl.'

'No, you're not.'

But she left her under the awning to the beat of a 1980s hit, and worried as she lay on her bed beneath the whirring ceiling fan, writing postcards, not tired in the least. She addressed the postcard of the Taj Mahal to her mother. Tasha captured by dacoits, Tasha wandering on the deserted beach, scantily dressed, Tasha the streetwise Londoner following some local Lothario into the darkness beyond the banyan trees to find herself lassoed by a liana and surrounded by jeering youths, unable to defend herself. Allie took her chair outside to watch the stars, and was disconcerted to see a security guard, a *chowkidar* in a quasi-military uniform patrolling the grounds with a rifle. She could hear the sea, and through the open windows of Number Four, the unmistakable sounds of the honeymooners making love. She went in again, locking her door and putting the key on her bedside table.

She was woken by a raucous massed choir of crows. Sunshine was streaming through her shutters. She showered, put on a white cotton dress, and went out on to her veranda.

'Morning!'

A middle-aged English couple in crisp shirts and shorts were eating Weetabix outside Number One.

'Your daughter beat you to it, then,' said the man.

'I'm sorry?'

'Off out on her scooter half an hour ago. What it is to be young, eh?'

All Allie could say was, 'Where did you get your coffee?'

'Kitchen,' said the woman. 'Why don't you trot along and get yours and join us for breakfast. You're welcome to some of our Weetabix – we always travel with a few boxes just in case, and Jonty won't set foot in Abroad without his Marmite.'

'Thanks,' said Allie faintly. She recognized them then as the popular thespians Jilly and Jonty Hazlecombe, stars of a dozen indistinguishable TV sitcoms. He played the irascible husband, she the long-suffering wife.

'Blasted milk's hot again,' said Jonty, peering into the aluminium jug. 'Can't these people ever get it right? Is the concept of cold milk quite beyond their powers of reasoning?'

'Give it to me, I'll take it back,' said Jilly patiently. 'I'll walk along with – sorry, what did you say your name was? We're Jonty and Jilly, by the way.'

'Alicia. I know you are – I mean, I recognized you of course.'

They left Jonty musing aloud, 'Alicia. We knew an Alicia once. Darlington rep, 1972, was it, darling?'

As Allie followed Jilly to the Da Silvas' kitchen, blinking away the tears caused by Tasha's latest betrayal, she reflected that, having recently read a magazine feature on the Hazlecombes, she knew rather more than she wished to about Jilly and Jonty's home life. The walls of their eighteenth-century coach house, with its superb view of the Thames, were crowded with the naïve Victorian portraits of pigs that they loved to pick up at antiques fairs or while pottering round junk shops. Jonty was partial to a particular black pudding that could be obtained only from a specialist butcher in Barnes; Sunday mornings often found Jonty in the couple's recently refurbished French farmhouse-style kitchen, enjoying 'cook's perks' of some fine château-bottled vintage as he experimented with the latest exotic recipe cajoled from a local chef while on a well-earned holiday off the beaten track. Jilly's tapestry chair backs, stitched during quiet moments between takes, were a byword among their host of theatrical friends. The Hazlecombe children, Ferdinand and Perdita, had followed their parents into the profession. Allie had seen them both recently, Ferdi and Perdi, now in their twenties, playing mildly mutinous teenagers in a middle-class drama she had been too lethargic to switch off.

Over coffee she found herself confiding her quest to the Hazlecombes and showing them Eric Alabaster's picture. Jonty prodded it with his finger.

'I'm pretty sure we spotted your chappie the other day. Along the coast at Benaulim. Hair down to his shoulders, wearing one of those thong thingies and nothing else. Haggling over a pineapple with half a dozen beach boys.'

'He was a German paedophile, darling!'

The Hazlecombes paused, as if listening for the canned laughter which did not follow their exchange.

'We're booked on the dolphin trip at nine. I'm sure they could squeeze another one in if you're up for it,' said Jilly.

'As the bishop said to the actress,' said Jonty.

'Maybe not this morning,' Allie said. 'I'd better wait for Tasha. We've rented a couple of pushbikes.'

When she saw dolphins it would not be courtesy of the Hazlecombes, jammed up against Jonty's hairless leg with its sea anemone of broken veins.

'Have fun then,' said Jonty, with a petulant quiver of his full lower lip.

Then he was on his feet, bending forward with one leg cocked behind him, left hand palm upwards on the base of his spine, right hand shielding his eyes as he scanned the horizon.

'"Has anybody seen our ship?"' he sang. '"The HMS—"'

'Dis-gusting,' supplied Jilly, breaking into a few steps of a sailor's hornpipe.

Allie remembered that they had returned to their first love, the stage, a few months ago to star as the Red Peppers in a brief season of Noël Coward's shorter works at a provincial theatre, for charity.

Eleven o'clock found Allie pedalling along with sea water spurting from her tyres, avoiding jellyfish and minute crabs that disappeared down tiny tunnels. She saw a sun-dried red chilli floating in a frill of foam. It was exhilarating, but she knew that at some point she must dismount and push the bike through the soft sand to the road and peer into people's yards and through their windows. How much easier it would be if Tasha were there. Allie had no doubt that Tasha had sped off to some assignation made last night under the coloured light bulbs of Fernandez Hideaway. In spite of herself, she smiled at the sandpipers running from her on their twinkling legs; she rested to watch them and a dozen men who were burned to the colour of the boat they were hauling ashore. Then at the approach of a group of women with bulging bags, each holding out a sarong to catch the breeze, gaudy billowing ships in full sail, Allie mounted her saddle and accelerated away.

On the road she encountered pairs of pink Brits on bicycles, local people going about their business, a herd of buffalo, huge velvet-winged butterflies that she tried to capture on her camera. A group of schoolgirls called out to her and Allie braked in the dust. They wanted pens, she realized too late. Had she known before she embarked on this trip how often she would meet this request she would have armed herself with a hundred plastic Bics. Ashamed of her penless state, but with her heart beating faster as she took her copy of Eric's *Angostura Bitters* from her bag, she searched each face for a trace of English paternity. The girls assumed the book was a gift, took it disdainfully, and walked on. At a roadside clothes stall Allie stopped again and pushed through the flap of carpet which draped its interior. Twenty minutes later she came out into the glare none the wiser about Eric but in possession of a grey embroidered skirt and blouse. Streaks of colour in the folds suggested they had once been blue. Sitting on an iron chair at a Coca-Cola stand, watching an ancient woman scratching red soil with a wooden rake, Allie was conscious of being thousands of miles from home and in someone else's country.

She cycled on until she came to a blindingly white church like an elaborate bridal cake with many coats of royal icing starting to melt in the sun. If anybody could tell her if Eric Alabaster was in this part of the country, it would be the parish priest. The church was empty. Bunches of flowers wilting on the ends of the pews were redolent of a recent wedding. Allie lit a candle, mumbling an embarrassed Anglican request to Saints Anthony and Jude to help her to find Eric, hoping that a fatherly old priest would emerge from one of the confessionals and perceive her as not just another vulgar tourist. She lingered in front of a painting of St Francis Xavier, with her new skirt draped over her head as a sign of respect, but no priest came.

'You might have waited!' Tasha was sprawled topless in a chair outside her apartment. 'Don't tell me you actually paid money for that faded ethnic tourist tat after all you've said! They must have seen you coming.'

'Cover yourself up! What would the Da Silvas think? Remember you're in a Catholic country.'

'That's okay, I'm a Catholic.'

Tasha's insolent breasts jeered at her, provoking her to say, 'Look, Tasha, let's not keep up the pretence that we're colleagues or even friends. As far as I'm concerned you're at perfect liberty to do anything you like. Go off with whom you like, get murdered by anyone you choose. It's fine by me.'

A sudden jagged pain seemed to split her skull, making her think of a tree struck by lightning. Holding her head in both hands she staggered into her room to lie down on the bed. Above her the ceiling fan whirled like a giant mosquito. She closed her eyes, realizing that she had stayed out too long in the sun.

Allie woke in darkness and was at once conscious of a raging thirst. The bottle of mineral water in her bathroom was empty. The frog was back, gazing at her from the closed lid of the lavatory. Tasha, she remembered, had bought several bottles of water from Madame Da Silva. The stars were low and bright as she walked the few steps to Tasha's room. When she pushed open the door she thought at first she had come into the honeymooners' apartment by mistake until she saw that it was Tasha sitting up in bed with the *chowkidar* she had seen last night. He was wearing his cap. His rifle lay across the sheet.

'Why are you always barging in where you're not wanted?' demanded Tasha.

'I'm sorry. I was only looking for some water.'

There was a tray on the floor, with dirty cereal bowls and a crushed plastic bottle. Beside it stood a large jar of Marmite.

'That's Jonty's Marmite! How could you, Tasha? And it's crawling with ants!'

Then she screamed. The gecko was cowering in a corner with a rope noose round its neck. It was much bigger than Allie had imagined, with its jaws open in a rictus of panic and spotted sides heaving. The gecko snarled at her, shooting out a forked tongue as she approached.

'Don't bite. I'm your friend. I've come to save you,' Allie whispered as she managed to grasp a frayed end of rope.

'Oi! Put that back, it's for our barbecue later!' Tasha shouted. 'Stop her, Xavier! Kill her!'

A shot whizzed past Allie's head as she dragged the gecko across the stone floor and into the night. She touched her hair and felt sticky blood as she ran.

The palm tree fans were opening and shutting in the wind, rattling their spines like porcupines' quills. Banyan trunks swayed and swerved, blocking the path as she lurched on in terror, clutching at her with fibrous tentacles. She could hear branches cracking underfoot as Tasha and Xavier pursued her, and screamed when a crow swooped into her face, battering her with black wings. A snake lashed at her from a liana; she saw that all the creepers were alive with snakes, coiled ready to spring and baring phosphorescent fangs. Now the gecko was hauling her into the undergrowth, bounding up the steps of a shuttered house and into a brightly lit room full of people. Safe. Thank God. She heard the rhythmic shuffle of maracas and her knees buckled as she saw Tasha gyrating topless to the beat of the drum that Xavier held between his knees. The claws of a crab waved from the muzzle of his rifle on the floor.

Jilly Hazlecombe seized her arm, saying, 'I thought you were never coming.'

'As the actress said to the bishop,' said Jonty. They were dressed in matching white sailor suits.

'Run along to make-up.' Jilly shook Allie hard, her eyes hard with contempt. 'You're on in five minutes. *Red Peppers* might be just a great big joke to you, but this is a charity performance and there's an audience out there entitled to a bit of professionalism.'

Before Allie could protest, the gecko pulled her over to the corner. Eric Alabaster lay in a low-slung hammock sipping liquor from a coconut, through a straw. A clerical collar hung crookedly round his neck.

'Eric! I've found you!' Allie felt tears running down her face. 'I've been looking everywhere for you! But I didn't know you were a priest! Why weren't you in the church?'

'I'm a whisky priest now. They locked me out of my church.'

He petted the head of the gecko, which was nuzzling up to him, planting huge front feet on his chest and licking his face. As Allie watched, its skin tone flushed through dingy brown to a vivid emerald green with purple spots.

'I never thought you of all people would be so cruel as to tie up a wild iguana, Alicia,' Eric said.

'But I didn't! I rescued him from Tasha and Xavier. They were going to barbecue him. I've come to save you too, Eric. I love you. I've come to take you back to London with me, where you belong. I didn't know it until recently but I've been missing you all my life. We'll always be together now, and I've got such plans for relaunching all your books – and you, my darling. Look, the iguana's changing colour like a chameleon. That shows he's happy now.'

Kneeling beside the hammock, she stroked Eric's bleached hair.

'Come to the beach with me. There's something I want to

show you,' said Eric, swinging his legs to the floor and cutting the rope from the iguana's neck.

He had his arm round her waist and as they walked Allie could feel her leg pressing against his. At the sea's edge he stooped and picked up a stick. ERIC ALABASTER, he wrote in large letters in the sand, and laughed as the sea obliterated his name.

'No!' cried Allie, grabbing at the stick.

Eric pushed her roughly to the sand, forcing the coconut shell of whisky to her mouth, scratching her face with its whiskery edges.

'Drink, damn you. You don't fool me, coming on like Deborah Kerr in your virginal white dress.'

When Tasha had knocked on Allie's door and got no reply she had assumed that she was asleep or sulking. Eventually, feeling hungry, she had taken the scooter and ridden a few miles inland to Rodriguez Bar and Restaurant, where she had enjoyed a drink earlier with one of the Da Silva sons. Before she could be joined by anybody more interesting, the Hazlecombes debouched from a taxi and invaded her table to regale her with an account of the dolphin trip. Nobody had drowned or been eaten by a shark; it seemed to Tasha very dull fare. To be stuck with the English abroad was her idea of hell; at least, unlike Allie, she had made an effort to get to know the locals.

'Have you ever thought of writing your memoirs?' she asked vengefully. 'You should have a word with Allie about it.'

When there was still no response from Allie the following morning, Tasha became alarmed and enlisted the help of Jilly and Jonty. They fetched Madame Da Silva with her key. Allie was in a sweaty heap on the bed, still in her cotton dress, all twisted in the sheet.

'She's burning up,' said Jonty. 'Get some water.'

Tasha brought a bottle from her apartment. Jilly held it to Allie's mouth, letting the water dribble down her chin on to her chest. Allie writhed, blindly pushing the bottle away, choking.

'Don't try to speak, lovey. Just drink. You've gone and got yourself all dehydrated.'

Allie sat up. Her head was throbbing and her skin felt tight and sore. Jilly's cool hand was stroking the wet hair back from her forehead, holding not a coconut shell but a bottle of mineral water to her lips. Tasha and Jonty were there and Madame Da Silva.

'Well, you gave us all a scare!' said Jonty.

'You certainly did. How could you be so stupid as to go racing around on a bike in the sun all day like that? I don't suppose it occurred to you that you'd ruin my holiday too if you made yourself really ill,' said Tasha.

'There, there,' said Jilly. 'Tasha's just having a reaction. It's the relief,' she explained to Allie. 'You're going to be fine. I've got some pills you can take.'

'No, thank you,' said Allie. 'Some people take a drink, others take a pill. I just take a few deep breaths. Or I would if I were Deborah Kerr in *The Night of the Iguana*. Which apparently I'm not.'

In a remnant of dream the green and purple spotted iguana deflated like a child's beach toy into a wrinkled balloon lifted by a wave.

'Stay in the shade for a day or two and you'll be as right as rain, eh, Madame?' Jonty advised. Madame Da Silva nodded.

'I'll bring you some tea,' she said.

Right as rain, thought Allie. I want rain. I want to go home. She saw the corner of a damp English park and a child on a swing soaring through an arc of grey air, her own arms extended to push it higher, over loamy mud silvered by racing clouds, a snatch of hazel catkins, a blur of pale sulphur pussy willow; her hands reaching out to catch the swing and bring it safely down.

'That's right, a nice cup of tea. You get some rest and then you can carry on with your quest for your writer chappie when you're feeling up to it,' said Jilly.

'No,' said Allie. 'Eric Alabaster doesn't want to be found. I realize that now.'

'Well,' Jilly said. 'We're off to the flea market at Anjuna but we'll pop back to check on you later. Jonty's got a proposition to put to you. In your professional capacity, of course.'

'As the bishop said to the actress,' said Jonty.

Electric-Blue Damsels

You see them in the underground with their schoolbooks and across the counters of shops and waiting on tables in restaurants, slinging burgers and pushing brooms; girls and boys in whom an exotic cocktail of genes has been shaken into a startling and ephemeral beauty: birds of paradise nesting in garbage, or captive tropical fish shimmering in the gloomy back rooms of dank pet shops.

At almost sixteen Fayette Gordon was not weaving blossoms in her hair, or diving for pearls in a green translucent ocean; she was a pupil at a comprehensive school, and in these summer evenings, which should have been heavy with the scents of frangipani and mimosa instead of those of melting tarmac and diesel fumes, she worked in a chip shop with the traffic's surf pounding on the pavement's crumbling shore. Her ancestry and origins were mysterious to everybody, except perhaps her grandmother with whom she lived, whose clenched teeth behind purple lips suggested the loss of a short-stemmed pipe. Fayette was breathtaking; at least her year-tutor Maurice Barlow always caught his rather pipe-smelling breath on catching sight of her unexpectedly in the corridor or on the tennis court. At once his teeth felt scummy and he put away the pipe, which convention, if increasingly begrudgingly, allowed him; a round red burn on his fuzzy thigh and a singed pocket testified to his haste on one occasion; her teeth, her blouse, her socks were so white.

It had been the worst sort of weather, as so often, for exams; the sort of weather which inspired unironic comments on 'flaming June', when swotting sweating adolescents in rolled-up shirtsleeves dreamed of sea and sand and returned from Sundays at the coast with the bruised purple fruit of love bites on their necks. Fayette's neck was unblemished and of course she did not sweat, except for a once-glimpsed row of tiny seed pearls beading her upper lip after a strenuous mixed doubles one lunch hour; her exam papers, although less than brilliant, would bear no unseemly smudges; she wore invisible white gloves. Maurice Barlow thought of white communion dresses, parasols and jalousies, iron-lace balconies, guavas and jacaranda. Thin silver bangles rolled up and down her cinnamon-coloured wrist as she wrote, and if he was invigilating he listened for the little clink of silver on wood and agonized if there was a long silence. Her hair, he had decided, was cinnamon too, the soft pale colour of the most delicious Edinburgh rock, that he would never taste.

As he sat at his kitchen table with the back door open, writing reports on school-leavers, the radio throbbed out 'Summer in the City'. He took a sheet of paper and attempted to compose a reference. *Fayette*, he wrote, is *Fayette Fayette Fayette Fayette*. He crumpled it and threw it in the bin and went out into the backyard. He pulled up a few tufts of groundsel that grew beside the gate and found himself ambling down the pavement. As he was out, he thought, he might as well buy himself some supper. The pockets of his creased Terylene trousers were weighed down with loose change, the key to the stock-room cupboard, a confiscated knife, a dried-out Tipp-Ex and other schoolmasterly impedimenta. The stain of a felt-tipped pen on the breast pocket of his shirt gave his heart a wounded look. She stood in front of the vats of boiling oil, leaning on the counter, brooding into the summer evening.

'Ah, Fayette. Business slack, I see.' Was in fact delighted to see.

'Be busy later when the pubs close.'

He loved it when his pupils greeted him by name in the pub, except that most of them, he knew, were under age. They bought his silence in halves of lager. Good old Maurice. Pupils came and went but Maurice was always one of the lads. He watched Fayette dunk a basket of raw chips into the oil and wished that they would take for ever to cook and suppressed a desire to lock the door so that he and she might stay pickled in time like those eggs in a jar on the counter. The oil sizzled and spat while the closing music of *EastEnders* was strained through the bead curtain behind which the proprietor and his family were watching television.

'Isn't that rather tactless?'

Maurice pointed to a tank of tropical fish, rosy and neon tetras brushing their fins against the plaster mermaid who reclined in the emerald green gravel combing her hair, in full view of their North Sea cousins dressed in overcoats of knobbly batter. Fayette did not answer.

'I wish you'd reconsider staying on for A levels.'

Fayette disturbed a flock of butterflies of coloured ribbon as she shook the last eleven years of her short life from her cinnamon-coloured hair.

'No way. I've had enough of school. I can't wait to leave.'

His eyes bulged cold and hard as the pickled eggs as she doused his chips in vinegar, smarting with salt at her dismissal of him and their years together.

'I think you're making a grave mistake, and one that, believe you me, you'll live to regret.'

He tapped the fish tank in emphasis.

'Believe you me,' mocked Fayette. 'Don't do that, it frightens the fish.'

'Fat lot you care.'

True to her word Fayette left school without an expression of regret. Maurice could remember the days when tearful girls had queued outside the staff-room door clutching damp autograph books and farewell gifts, but that had been before everything was so uncertain, before teachers were fallible and world leaders exposed as murderous liars and frauds; when girls like Fayette could step out into a secure and radiant future of physiotherapy and nursing, and teaching and secretarial posts, and then babies in coach-built prams. Fayette had announced her own plans to the careers master: she had decided to be rich and famous. Her education had ended in four minutes of ecstasy for Maurice at the leavers' disco.

'I never realized this record was so long,' she remarked as they danced.

He sat gloomily in the pub afterwards with a group of his colleagues, his Palm Beach party shirt exhibiting salty circles of drying sweat, nursing a tepid beer and dreaming of a Caribbean of the heart where he and Fayette could dance for ever, of a room with a frilly iron balcony looking out over the wide Sargasso Sea. Or Fayetteville, Arkansas.

'Cheer up, Maurice. School's out for summer. Made any plans for going away yet?'

'I was thinking of the Caribbean . . .'

'On your salary? A likely tale.'

'Room for a little one? Budge up, you guys.'

Sally Molloy swung her large tanned knees under the table, so that Maurice's and her thighs sighed against each other, nudging memories of gruelling sessions of dry-skiing in East Grinstead. He had conducted a desultory affair with her over the years; he supposed he ought to ask her to marry him, she wasn't getting any younger, but something always happened to prevent him from popping the question: one of them got hiccups or cramp or the toast caught fire. He feared now that she was about to suggest a take-away, so while Patsy Armstrong, who taught social studies, engaged her in a discussion of the relative merits of the graffiti in the girls' and the boys' loos, and they laid contingency plans for the next term's half-day strikes, he stepped over Sally's designer trainers, and slipped into the night, hardly able to believe that the summer stretched before him without a prospect in sight of a cycling holiday in Holland, pot-holing in the Peak District, or following in the footsteps of St Paul; three unappetizing carrots which had been dangled in front of him earlier in the year.

He had managed also to decline, by the inspired invention of a crop of verrucas, an invitation to stay with his married sister and her four small children and enjoy their new swimming pool. His refusal had been accepted with alacrity. Uncle Maurice was whistling, albeit a melancholy tune, as he set out early with his swimming trunks in a neat towelling Swiss roll under his arm for the local pool. The company of the school rat, who was with him for the holiday, was all that he desired or found congenial in his bereft state. Fayette had given up her job in the chippie on the day that she had left school. It was to buy food for this rat, whose name, coincidentally, was Maurice too, that he entered the pet shop with his hair still wet, cleaner and red-eyed from the chlorine. His heart stopped, and stumbled on its way again.

'So this is where the rich and famous hang out.'
'Hello, Maurice.'
'What are you doing here?'
'I work here, don't I?'
'Do you?'

She was all in white: a white t-shirt under white dungarees rolled to show the delicate bones of cinnamon ankles above white plimsolls, a smudge of sawdust delineating one cheek-bone, and a small net sticking out of her chest pocket. Fish tanks glimmered like televisions with the sound turned down in the gloom of the back room. A man in a brown overall was serving a customer with biltong, or knotted strips of hide for dogs to chew. Maurice went into the back room; Fayette followed.

'Small cod and chips, open, salt and vinegar, please,' he said, then stopped. It was like walking into a gallery and being stunned by wonderful paintings by an artist whose work he had never encountered before, or entering a cave of moving jewels, rubies, emeralds, topaz, diamonds and opals on black velvet; like looking into Chapman's Homer. He dismissed from his mind any comparisons between keeping birds in cages and fish in aquaria.

'What are those?'

'Electric-blue damsels.'

In a flash of sapphire Maurice saw how he could get his heart's desire. They were the deepest, glowing, electric blue; slender and swift in the water.

'*Abudefduf uniocellata*,' said Fayette.

'What?'

'Formerly known as *Pomacentrus caeruleus*.'

Was this the girl who couldn't tell hake from huss?

He stood entranced in front of a tank of sea-horses twining their prehensile tails around thin poles rising from coral fans; with their equine heads and long sensitive snouts they were as ancient and mysterious as fragments of sculpture found after centuries in the ocean among starfish and the waving fronds of anemones. The only sea-horses Maurice had seen hitherto had been dry and faded curiosities in the Shell Shop in Manette Street, across from Foyles. These were moist and living, magic and mythological, undulating and grazing the water.

'*Hippocampus kuda*. Did you know that they are unique in the animal kingdom in that the male becomes pregnant and bears the young?'

'No!' Maurice was enchanted at having become the pupil.

'He incubates the eggs placed there by the female for four to five weeks in a special pouch and hundreds of perfect tiny sea-horses hatch out. Can you imagine? I can't wait to see that!'

Her eyes were shining at the thought; an enthusiastic hand fluttered a moment on his sleeve. He caught sight of his reflection in the side of a tank of black mollies in viridian weed, an albino rat displaying long teeth in an ecstatic smile, and remembered the purpose of his visit.

'Are you an arachnophobe, Maurice?'

'I don't think so. Why?'

She directed his gaze to a tarantula, but the sight that stayed with him was a pretty speckled eel curvetting upwards through the rocky water to nibble from Fayette's fingers.

His brain turned to coral: emperor and clown, harlequins, rainbows, unicorns, angels and devils, queens, jewels, damsels, glow-lights, butterflies, cardinals, swordfish, surgeons, anemones, starfish, sea-horses, dancing shrimps, golden rams and silver sharks, flying foxes, albino tigers, lyre-tails, parrots and corals; freshwater and marine tropicals from the Indian Ocean and the Pacific swam through its branches. He took out a stack of library books. He joined the local Aquarist Society. He had to make frequent visits to the pet shop to be initiated into the mysteries of aeration and filtration, heating and lighting, salinity, and ultra-violet sterilization, ozonizing, feeding, bacteria and parasites. On one glorious evening Fayette allowed him to pick her up in his Morris Minor and drive her to an Aquarist meeting in the upper room of the library, but as there were no fish present she was bored and fidgeted and watched the clock, as in a dull lesson at school, eyed covertly by the flock of old goats who, until then, Maurice had considered a pleasant bunch of chaps.

The summer holiday was almost over. Maurice wondered how he would find the time to go back to school. He went into the pet shop intent on persuading Fayette to come with him to the aquarium at the zoo, and thereafter perhaps to Brighton, to all the aquariums in the country, in far-flung cities where they would have to spend the night.

'She's not here.'

'When will she be back?'

'She won't. She's gone.'

'Gone?'

He could have wrenched the tanks from the wall, screaming in splinters of glass and the gush of water and floundering fish, dying jewels drowning in air. But only for a second; he wouldn't hurt a fish.

'I only came in for some *Daphnia*.'

'Of course.'

He walked out of the shop, drowning in air.

One afternoon he encountered Fayette's grandmother in a tobacconist's but she did not remember him from the one parents' evening she had attended, in Fayette's first term, when she had been a shy and heartbreaking twelve-year-old, and he could not bring himself to enquire after his former pupil. He had had to tell his disappointed fellow Aquarists that Fayette would not be joining them again. It was after one of their meetings as he was walking home through an evening made unbearable by night-scented stocks and nicotiana mingling with the smell of diesel and chips that he saw a poster attached to the wall of a cellar wine bar, advertising live music by the Electric-Blue Damsels. He descended the steps and swam through the rocky interior where young people clung like limpets to the recesses in the walls. Now he did not want to be hailed by any pupils or ex-pupils; good old Maurice no more, he shunned the company of all but the rat, his fish and his fellow Aquarists.

The Electric-Blue Damsels were bad by any standards. The sound system was appalling. Dominating the all-female quintet was Fayette, now leaping to pound incompetently on a synthe-sizer, now screeching into a hand-held mike which splattered her voice on the damp cellar walls that threw it back in echoes through the cave. The audience loved them. Her cinnamon hair was a shock of electric blue and the long bare legs under the tiny vinyl skirt ended in blue shoes with spiked heels that could tear a man's heart out, sharp as the weapon of the surgeon-fish, that has a retractable scalpel at the base of its tail. As he stumbled out he remembered that electric-blue damsels are sometimes known as blue devils.

When he did not appear on the first day of term, Sally Molloy and Patsy Armstrong went to his house after school. There was no reply to their knocking so they went round to the back. A pond had been set into the yard, almost filling it; the tragic over-bred face of a bubble-eyed goldfish mouthed at the surface as they picked their way past the edge, making them gasp. The back door was open. They couldn't believe what they saw: the kitchen had liquefied. At first they thought it had flooded, then they saw that an enormous tank had been sunk into the floor. A Japanese bridge spanned its length, rising over the floating weeds and waterlilies, and at its centre stood Maurice scattering meal and watercress to a circle of the most enormous, most beautiful, metallic fish they had ever seen, phosphorescent gold and silver, monochromatic, pure white, black with reflections of scarlet or yellow, splashes of colour like ideographs and sunsets, a blazing red triangle on a snow-white head.

'Hi,' said Sally at last.

'Hi-utsuri,' Maurice replied.

'What?'

He blinked, staring at them, and did not explain. He wondered for a moment who they were.

'Did you want something? I'm very busy.'

'We just wondered if you were all right, as you didn't show up at school,' said Patsy. The woman who had once been his lover was speechless with affront, then she noticed something helping itself to what looked like a nut rissole on the bridge.

'That rat's school property, you know.'

'I wouldn't play Emil Jannings to her Marlene Dietrich.'

'What on earth are you on about?'

'*The Blue Angel.*'

They were none the wiser.

At the end of the bridge, in the front room, they could see the glitter of small fish in glass tanks.

'Did you get planning permission for this?'

He did not answer. The circle of koi fanned out and scattered like fragments in a giant kaleidoscope.

'Wouldn't they make wonderful dresses?' cried Sally. 'For *Come Dancing*. Did you sew on all the sequins yourself?'

He took a threatening step towards her as Patsy was adding, 'Or curtain fabric. Gorgeous!'

'There's only one new girl in your form,' said Sally as she retreated. 'Scarlett MacNamara.'

The combination of the exotic and the Celtic was suggestive of the name that caused him pain.

'What's she like?'

'Dark. Pretty. Very shy.'

He turned to watch his koi.

'I think I should tell you,' said Sally, 'that Patsy and I are leaving at the end of term. We're setting up an aromatherapy centre.'

'Good.'

They left Maurice standing on his Japanese bridge, staring out over the water like a man who was waiting for someone to come home.

Ennui

Domestic interior, Granby Street. Near number 247 Hampstead Road. Sometime in 1913 or 1914. A man is sitting at a circular table smoking a cigar. If he were to reach out, he could grasp the woman standing behind him by the waist or hip, and pull her on to his knee. But he's immobilized, and she has her back to him and is gazing in a reverie at the glass dome of stuffed birds on the chest of drawers.

What time of day is it? An hour when the corner of the heavy marble mantelpiece casts a deep shadow, motes of inertia settle like dust on the furniture, when ash crumbles at the tip of the cigar. The time of day when a man and a woman wonder why fate has cast them together in these lodgings, where the solidity of the rented objects augments their feelings of impermanence. Let us call them Hubert and Milly. Hubert is some years older than Milly, his thick hair silvered while hers is still dark.

Did she settle for him perhaps? *Faute de mieux*, after several disappointments, when the bloom of youth was fading? Maybe he saved her from some intolerable situation, from a brute of a man, or destitution. It might have even been true love. Traces of the charm that seduced many women linger in his features, coarsened by time and drink. In his brown suit, he looks the sort who'd be at home in a public house or on the racecourse. In fact, he has on occasion been mistaken for a publican. He has the air of a heavy loser, and his melancholy face suggests losses on the horses not yet admitted to her.

The tumbler on the table holds a clear liquid. Water, gin, a mixture of both. Or water with a splash of white rum, in memory of his days at sea. A Jack ashore, he calls himself, an adventurer who sailed under several flags, now washed up in London, marooned in Camden Town. With his luck it's probably water in the glass.

Milly wears a neat, short-sleeved blouse tucked into her long skirt, with a belt whose leather catches the light. Although the fabric's gone limp, a faint whiff of starch comes off her blouse, fresh in the mingling odours of old cigar and some other lodger's grilled mutton chops. Milly taps idly on the glass dome that holds the display of stuffed birds. Shimmering jewels, with eyes like jet beads. They've travelled with her from lodging to lodging, giving respectability and an illusion of home to dwellings shabbier than this, glowing in dusty corners when there was no fire in the grate. Emerald, jet, ruby and gold, they perch in eternity, with wings poised for flight.

The light quivers in the lustre of their feathers, making tiny pulses beat in glittering throats, their beaks about to open in liquid song. Sometimes, catching sight of them, startled by colour, her heart lifts and she wants to prise off the glass and stroke them with her fingertip. Today, they are dull-eyed, sad, dead little things who ought to be flying under sunny skies. Their dome is a cruel contrivance; she could carry them to the window and tip them into the sky, fling them on to the air, to go chirruping and fluting, into the skies of Camden Town, to soar over the buildings and tramlines to the trees of Regent's Park or Primrose Hill. But no doubt they'd be mobbed by the native birds.

It crosses her mind that among them there might be a bird of ill omen, a bird whose feathers you shouldn't bring into the house. Something had to account for her rotten luck. Some people say peacock feathers bring misfortune, even death. But maybe it's just the way their eyes watch you.

Milly's an expert in feathers and beads, working as she did in the back room of Madame Vertue, Milliner by Appointment. She was happy there, among the pretty silks and plumes. Shaping and stitching and gluing. Joking with the other girls. Until Hubert turned up drunk once too often and got her the sack. Cards. Dice. Feathers. Things that make your luck. Walking under ladders, a black cat, or a chimney sweep crossing your path. Hubert's employer, the artist, who keeps asking her to pose for him, he had peacock feathers in a copper vase in his studio last time she was there, doing a bit of cleaning. As well as great jugfuls of lilac and May, flowers she would never take indoors. Talk about provoking Providence. She's done it before, sat for an artist, never minded, but she doesn't fancy taking her clothes off now, for all the world to gawp at in some gallery. A friend of hers did it recently, only to have the critics condemn her as a 'hideous middle-aged woman in sordid surroundings'. She wouldn't have minded quite so much, only she wasn't even middle-aged, let alone hideous. But who ever cares about the feelings of the model? Well, not to mention the artist, however much of a gentleman he might be. Staring at you with his head on one side, screwing up his eyes. Measuring you with his brush at arm's length the way they do. Scrutinizing you while you sit there like a lemon, with all the life going on in the street outside, as it is now.

Milly shivers in the blouse she ironed last night while Hubert was out at the music hall. Down at the New Bedford, the Bedford Palace of Varieties, with the artist and his cronies. Sneaking out and shaming her in front of her mother, who'd come round for a bit of supper with them.

But her resolve would weaken, she could get talked round

again, desperate for a few shillings for the rent. The thin end of the wedge there. One minute you'd be sitting there respectably, dressed up as a coster girl, or something picturesque in a hat, and before you knew it you'd be sprawled naked on the bed with your throat cut. Posing as that poor girl in what the newspapers called the Camden Town Murder.

Hubert had sat for the artist several times in various costumes. But naturally he'd never been required to remove more than his jacket. Who'd want to buy a picture called *Nude with Bowler Hat and Cigar*?

She was a prostitute, the girl who died, but she wasn't expecting anybody that night. Her golden hair was done up in curling pins. It was said at the trial that her throat was cut as she slept. Milly hopes it was. The thought of those curling pins makes her feel sad. The girl was only twenty-two. They arrested a commercial artist for the murder, but the evidence didn't stand up in court. He was defended by the great Marshall Hall himself. Hubert's been behind bars and she suspects he keeps up with his criminal associates.

A painting of a woman hangs on the wall, against the mottled grey-green wallpaper. The woman, partly draped in puce material, lies on a couch, resting on her bare arms, leaning out of the picture and looking past the couple in the room. Her bright glance suggests that it is she who is alive, and they but components of a *nature morte: Still life with figures, stuffed birds, glass and box of matches*.

Nevertheless, Hubert's heart is thudding and his brain racing, but like a horse whose wind is broken it stumbles and stalls at every fence. He thinks he might take a ride on a tram to clear his head but he cannot move, and then there's the matter of the tram fare, and the price of a drink at the other end. He drums his finger on the table, notices the sound of Milly's fingers tap-tapping on the glass, and reaches for a match to relight his cigar. Coughs as the pungent smoke fills his mouth, and wipes his moustache. His stomach growls, complaining of too many oysters over the years, too much beer and champagne, eels and pies and liquor and mash and tobacco. He's pickled and smoked and kippered himself. He's a flitch of bacon. An old salt cod. If only Milly would go out of the room he could take a nip of what's left of the port in the decanter on the mantelpiece to settle his stomach. He wills her to move but she lounges there moping. If she put out her hand to ruffle his hair everything would be all right. If he could think of anything to say to put himself in a better light about last night. If he could put his hand in his pocket and pull out a handful of money. But he's done that, and knows his fingers will encounter nothing but fluff and shreds of tobacco, a shrimp's tail and a crumpled betting slip. He's done all the pockets in the house, furtively, and Milly's purse, and looked under the mattress in hope of a miracle. He's searched the tea caddy where she used to hide her savings. She's grown very sly. He sees her as she was when they first met, in her white dress. All in white but the boots, the boots were black. It's sad how women's true colours come out once they've got a ring on their finger. A noose round a fellow's neck.

He couldn't remember much of the day, before the evening. It was now a blur of plush and chandeliers, cupids and caryatids. But he recalled the old charlady, Milly's mother, sitting there in her plumed hat that Milly had given her before she'd lost her job at the milliners. The old girl had said nothing. In fact, she said, 'I'm saying nothing', but the feathers on her hat were positively trembling with disapproval. It wasn't his fault he had to go along to the Bedford with the artist, who wanted to sketch the boys in the gallery for a painting he'd been commissioned to do by one of his wealthy patronesses. Some people have all the luck. Take two innocent little lads in a school playground. Years down the road, one of them goes swanning off to Brighton and Paris and Dieppe at the drop of a hat, hob-nobbing in society, while the other ends up as his superannuated odd-job boy, in the soup and on his uppers.

Sunk in his thoughts, unaware of what he's doing, Hubert runs his finger down the side of his chair, between the wood and the upholstery. A jolt goes through him. An electric shock from hand to heart. His fingers close on paper and metal. The crinkle of notes and the hardness of coins. He exhales a silent prayer of thanks.

At last he turns, and pulls Milly on to his knees, where she sits, stiff as a statue, refusing to look at him, tossing her head when he tickles her under her chin.

'How do you fancy a night out?' he says. 'What say the first house at the Bedford and a slap-up supper?'

'Oh yeah, I fancy it all right,' she replies heavily, 'and then what shall we do for the rent?'

'Oh ye of little faith,' says Hubert, all a-twinkle now, 'trust your old Hubie, when has he ever let you down? How about a little kiss?'

The names of the man and woman could well be Hubert and Milly, or they might be Hubby, full name unknown, and Marie Hayes, who was possibly his wife. Hubby acted as a general fac-totum of the painter Walter Sickert and, singly and together, he and Marie were the models for many of his pictures. Hubby and Marie, in a painter's studio, posed in a tableau of their own life. Hubby was an old schoolfellow of Sickert's, who fell on hard times and was taken into the painter's household, and dismissed more than once for his drinking. At the outbreak of war, Hubby, deeming himself not too old to serve his king and country, set off for Aldershot to enlist. Perhaps he was grateful to the Kaiser for getting him out of his latest scrape.

It's thought that Marie stayed on in the painter's employ. This is the last we know of them, Hubby and Marie, who were immortalized on canvas as the embodiments of ennui. But they are all of us, any of a thousand couples trapped by time, in the hour when the shadow of the marble mantelpiece falls like the gnomon of a sundial.

Family Service

'I am going to remain very calm.' Then a scream like a demon came out of her mouth.

'Is nobody in this house but me capable of putting away a cereal packet? Look at this tablecloth! There's milk and sugar all over it. And the floor! I don't know why I bother – if I come into this kitchen one more time and find the sink full of dishes, I'll—'

Helen Brigstock clamped her hand over her mouth.

'Shut up, shut up, shut up,' she told herself. Her teeth fought against her fingers; she felt a painful bite as teeth met flesh. A cannonade of church bells exploded faintly beyond the steamed-up window.

Now, as when a child, Helen saw Sunday written in gold. But today how bleared and smeared and tarnished the letters. Her bulgy self, her unsatisfactory family. The sun, in a cone of dancing dust, struck grease and crumb, her distorted face reflected in the spotted kettle, highlighting every failure.

The day that had started so well had begun to go wrong when she made the mistake of stepping on to the bathroom scales as she dressed after breakfast. She would have to lose at least five pounds before Christmas and it was already the second Sunday in Advent. Scrambled egg and buttered toast weighed heavily on her as she finished dressing. If she didn't have any lunch ... or any roast potatoes at least ...

The potatoes had provoked her fury. She had come down to the kitchen to prepare them so that they, and the chicken, could cook while the family was at church and just because she had left the breakfast table first everybody had decamped, leaving the kitchen in a state of unbelievable squalor and the sink full of dishes that she would have to wash before she could peel the potatoes. She heaved a sodden saucepan from the washing-up bowl. Scummy scrambled egg wrecked her nail polish as she scrubbed. She would have no time to repair it. She almost told the church bells to shut up.

She turned the hot tap on hard to drown the image of her mother, her father and herself, arms linked, walking over a frosty field to church. Then there had been time to study the crystals on a leaf or frozen spider's web; once a fox had run past them, stopped, turned back and stared them full in the face.

At last, the faceted potatoes ranged whitely round the pink chicken in the oven, Helen ran upstairs to the bedroom.

'I don't believe it! I don't believe it!' A fat ladder had sprung up her new tights leaving her leg grinning through the rungs. She tore off the tights and started raking madly through a drawer, throwing things on the floor.

The piercing notes of a recorder transfixed her, stabbing tears from her eyes as she listened. Julian, her son, in his innocent way had reminded her of what Sunday was all about. Helen stood, with pastel underwear like sugared almonds round her feet. What did clothes matter? – as long as one had some on, of course. What did it matter if she was overweight? She had so much to be grateful for, her health and strength, one should just be glad that one had enough to eat. When one thought of the starving black millions ... Anyway, she could easily lose five pounds by Christmas.

Helen set off along the passage to Julian's room. She would sit on his bed and say, 'Julian, I want to thank you. With your music you have just taught Mummy a valuable lesson. Oh yes, you have, darling. I know you think Mummy knows everything, but sometimes it takes a little boy to ...'

She tapped on, and opened, his bedroom door.

'Darling – What on earth do you think you're doing, lying on your bed, not even dressed, playing that stupid thing? Have you any idea of the time?'

Her eye caught a toy snake at the foot of the bed.

'You little reptile,' she shouted. 'You've got no consideration – get dressed at once! Have you forgotten that you're supposed to be reading a prayer in church or does it mean nothing to you?'

Julian had been named, secretly, after the eldest boy in the Famous Five books, a tall, well-spoken boy. This Julian, at eleven, was small for his age, and whatever they taught them at Pembury Court, and sometimes Helen wondered what it was, it certainly wasn't how to speak properly.

'Besides,' she heard her own terrible voice go on, 'that tune you were playing – if you were to read your Bible, I think you'd find that not only did Jesus never say that He was Lord of the Dance, but also that there is no record of Him ever having danced ...'

Mother and son, he lying on his back in pyjama trousers, recorder dangling from his lip, stared at each other until Helen dropped her eyes and slammed out of the room to fling herself with a dry sob on to her own bed, biting the duvet.

'Pull yourself together, Brigstock!' she told herself sharply. 'This won't do!'

She found a pair of intact tights and pulled them on. They came up as far as her bra.

'It doesn't matter.' So what if they should roll down making an ugly ridge at the waistband of her skirt. 'You're going to church to worship God. It doesn't matter what you look like.' When the zip of her boot caught a mouthful of plump calf in its teeth, she didn't scream, so that she felt she had got the upper hand. Standing in the bedroom doorway, she shouted:

'Girls! Are you nearly ready? We've got to leave in eight minutes!'

'No answer came the stern reply,' she said aloud, wryly. Where on earth was Roger?'

'Roger?'

No answer from her husband. Oh, honestly!

'Roger!'

'I'm in the bathroom.'

'Well, could you please hurry up! There are other people in this house besides you. Jane! Hannah! Are you two ready?'

She stumped along to Jane's room, stooping angrily from time to time to pick up pieces of fluff, thread, hair, that glared up from the red carpet. When she flung open Jane's door it was with a great gobbet, like some disgusting domestic owl's pellet, in her hand.

Jane lay face downward on her bed reading, presenting an extremely irritating pair of jeans to her mother.

'Jane, what on earth do you think you're doing?'

'I'm just having my Quiet Time.'

'Your Quiet Time! I wish I had time to have a Quiet Time! If you really think you're virtuous lying there reading the Bible while your mother washes up and peels potatoes and picks up filth from the floor – you could at least read the proper version instead of that unpoignant rubbish with its silly drawings. Do you want to reduce The Greatest Story Ever Told to a strip cartoon? Well, do you? And if, if . . .'

Again Helen wished that someone would silence it, but the dreadful voice went on.

' ... if you've got any ideas about having "chosen the better part", forget them. I'd like to get hold of every single copy of that so-called "Good News Bible" and rip out the story of Martha and Mary. Talk about Unfair!'

Jane sat up, her fair hair falling back from her face.

'Sorry, Mum. Is there anything you'd like me to do?'

'Do? Do? Yes, you can get out the hoover and – oh, forget it – it's too late. Just get ready! And couldn't you put on a pretty dress for once instead of those awful jeans?'

Jane's voice was hurt.

'You said you liked them ...'

'I do – it's just – oh—'

Helen stood helplessly in the doorway, the wad of fluff greasy in her sweating hand, then crashed out of the room. She collided with Roger in the passage.

'Darling?'

She pulled past without answering. She locked herself in the bathroom and collapsed on the dirty-linen basket, head in hands, rocking backwards and forwards. 'Oh God, I don't want to be like this. Please help me.'

'Mummy?'

A loud knocking on the door.

'Go away. Just go away,' she muttered.

'Mummy, are you in there?'

Helen flung open the door.

Little Hannah stood, a dramatic figure in vest and knickers.

'Mummy, it's not fair. Jane's allowed to go to church in jeans, so why can't I?'

'Not fair? Not fair?' screamed her mother. 'Is it fair that there are splashes of toothpaste all over the bathroom floor and the dirty-linen basket is full of dirty clothes that no one but I will wash and that everyone else will expect to reappear miraculously clean and ironed? Is that fair?'

Hannah fled.

Helen heard Roger rattling the car keys.

'Oh, shut up!'

She stared at herself in the mirror – pale, red-eyed, her hair jumping at the comb in a mad electric mass. If only Father and Mother weren't watching . . .

At last they were all in the car and Roger switched on the ignition. Helen turned round, deliberately calm.

'Got your prayer, Ju?'

'Yeah, it's here.' He fluttered a grey piece of paper towards her.

'Good boy. Stop the car! Roger, stop!'

'What now? He's got his prayer.'

'His nails! Get out of the car, Julian! His nails are disgusting! He's not standing up in church reading a prayer with nails like that!'

'There isn't time. We'll never get a parking space if we don't leave now.' Roger pulled out.

'If anyone ever, except me, did anything, we wouldn't have this rush every Sunday.'

'I did stack the dishes for you,' came Roger's mild voice from his complacent baggy polo-neck sweater.

'For me? For me? You make it sound as if they were all my dishes—'

'Well, actually, darling, if you remember, your mother gave them to us on our—'

'Don't you drag my mother into this!'

'No one will see Julian's nails.' Jane attempted to arbitrate.

'God will.'

The church forecourt was jammed with the cars of the wise virgins. The Brigstocks were forced to park in a side street and arrived panting on the long path through the gravestones.

Roger put his hand on Helen's arm; she shook it off.

'Couldn't you have put on a tie? I don't subscribe to this

jeans and shirtsleeves religion. Now we'll never get a decent pew—'

'Calm down, darling.'

The peal of the bell had changed to a rapid commanding single note.

'It's the Hurry-Up Bell,' said Hannah hanging heavily on her mother's arm, who wouldn't look at her, as if it had not been she who had invented the term in the children's earliest years.

'We'll be stuck behind the choir stalls again. Julian, get off that grave, there are dead people in them, you know! Of course, if some people didn't spend three hours in the bathroom – that reminds me, I must put air freshener on my shopping list.'

'You know scrambled egg always upsets my stomach,' said Roger.

She saw that she had managed to wound him, too, at last.

'That's the thanks I get for preparing a nice family breakfast.'

'Hi.'

Sylvia, her friend, loomed up behind a mausoleum.

Helen cracked her dry face into a smile.

'Beautiful morning,' she said.

'Beautiful,' agreed Sylvia, 'if one happens to like paintings by Rowland Hilder,' and laughed as she overtook them.

Trust her. Why did she always have to try to say something clever? Helen wondered why they were friends. Anyway, surely Sylvia must have seen that Rowland Hilder snowscape with sheep a hundred times on the lounge wall? Then, suddenly cheered by the sight of her friend's immense bum swaying in peasant skirt above cowboy boots, she felt her own excess pounds fall from her, although her tights threatened to sag or bag. The frosty grass glittered, the path shone blue, the names of the dead were picked out in rhinestones and fool's gold.

She put an arm through Roger's and Julian's and pulled them to a halt.

'I'm sorry I was so ratty, darlings. It's just that—'

Hannah screamed.

On the path in front of them lay a dead blue tit. The family stood staring down at it. It lay, tiny, frozen; blue and saffron leaking into the melting path.

'Will you bury it, Daddy?'

'There isn't time, darling.'

'We could put it in that tomb over there, look there's a hole in the side,' suggested Julian.

'Don't be so ridiculous,' snapped his mother.

Julian shrugged.

'But, Daddy.' Hannah raised tearful eyes. 'Someone might not see it and – and – walk on it!'

'Daddy told you, there isn't time! Maybe on the way out.'

'Just because you don't care about a poor little dead bird. Well, I think God's cruel to let a poor little bird die in His own grave-yard!'

'It's all part of His plan, darling.' Roger attempted to lift his rigid daughter, whose shoes were glued to the path. 'We can't expect to understand. He sees the meanest sparrow . . . '

'It's a blue tit.'

'Oh, God.' Julian strode on ahead.

'I've told you not to say "God". Especially on a Sunday.'

Helen thumped her son between the shoulder blades of his school blazer, which had cost twenty-three pounds, although to look at the state of it you'd never guess. Behind her, she heard Roger's voice, infected by her, a hideous parody of her own.

'Will you stop snivelling, Hannah? Close your mouth! Did you clean your teeth this morning? They look like – like – mossy tombstones!'

'Well, I suppose everyone's forgotten that I'm supposed to be reading this bloody prayer,' said Julian as the Brigstocks entered the church and almost snatched their books from the smiling sidesman. They found a vacant pew near the back.

'Mummy, can I go and sit with—'

'Of course you can't! We'll all sit together!'

Then she realized that Jane had sloped off to sit with her friends . . .

She slumped heavily on to her seat.

'Of course, I'm parked behind a pillar!' thought Helen. She pretended not to notice that Roger was silently offering to change places and sank her knees on the cold stone floor, the clumsily broidered hassock swinging on its hook. She waited for the familiar peace to descend. Nothing happened. Her ruined hands writhed in her gloves. She became aware of Julian shoving up against her. She opened an eye to glare at him. An old lady was mopping and mowing, in a faint scent of lavender water and mothballs, her way into the pew. Why did old ladies insist on wearing musty velour jelly-moulds on their heads? Helen sat up. The choir was coming in.

'Let us sit, or kneel, to pray.'

Typical! Typical! She assumed that it was meant as a dispensation to the aged or handicapped; but half this casual congregation found sitting the best position in which to address its God. Well, she just jolly well hoped that God would prove as easy-going at the Judgement Day! Instead of closing her eyes, Helen stared at a window. The shadow of birds' wings flickered across the stained glass and fluttered on a pillar. A bowl of forced daffodils and honesty on the sill – the stained glass, the birds – sudden tears dissolved the lump in her heart making it warm and stringy like melted mozzarella.

'We have left undone those things which we ought to have done, and we have done those things which we ought not to have done—' said a voice in her head.

She had screamed at Julian's bare chest, which she so loved, with its pretty little bones, instead of offering him moral support when he was probably very nervous. She had shouted at him for not reading the Bible, and at Jane for reading the Bible, and at Hannah, and at Roger ...

Helen prayed that the prayers would go on until she was composed and had found a tissue.

'I'm sorry, Daddy,' she prayed.

The congregation came to itself. Helen concealed a sniff in the shifting of knees. She hoped that she would have a chance to repair, secretly, her face before she had to greet the vicar at the church door in the brutal Sunday sunshine.

At a given signal, Julian left her side and walked nonchalantly up the aisle. He stood at the front of the church, on the chancel steps.

'Dear God,' he began, as if reading a thank-you letter written to some obscure uncle. 'We thank you for our Homes and Families, our Mothers and Fathers.'

Helen heard no more; her eyes and ears were blocked with tears. Dimly she saw the sun streaming through stained glass tinting hair and ears ruby and emerald – Julian's ears, wonderful emerald transparent organs, his moist ruby mouth. Flesh; vulgar, beautiful – the choir sang an iridescent anthem.

The sermon came as an anticlimax. Advent. Helen tried to recapture her feelings, but they were gone, like the sun, which had disappeared, leaving the church dull and cold. Christmas – Helen heard only a panicky ripping of wrapping paper and the snickering sellotape.

'Stop sniffing,' she whispered savagely at Hannah and thrust her own wet tissue in a sodden ball into her lap.

Outside the church Helen felt pincers on her arm. She looked. The old lady who had pushed into their pew had laid a black glove on her coat sleeve.

'Such a nice little family,' she was saying. 'I see you every Sunday.'

Helen smiled. 'I do think it's important for a family to worship together,' she said.

The Brigstocks piled into the car and drove home to eat some pieces of a dead bird, which would have been browning nicely if Helen had switched on the oven.

Glass

The bus shelter was a skeleton. Her feet crunched its smashed glass, like coarse soda crystals under her shoes as she walked to the cash machine, and a glittering pyramid of uncut diamonds had been swept into the call box where an eviscerated telephone dangled. Someone had passed in the night who loved the sound of breaking glass. She had been thinking about the possibility of working in glass herself lately. She was an artist. Her cashpoint card bore the name Jessamy Jones; its number was a mnemonic of her children's birthdays. All grown up now, with children of their own. Jessamy had sketched their baby heads in tender pastels that stroked the curves of cheek and eye and ear and feathered hair; and a painting of them as children was sold as a postcard in the Tate. There was a wistful look about it, reminiscent of the nursery rhyme:

> Hark, hark, the dogs do bark,
> Beggars are coming to town.
> Some in rags and some in jags
> And one in a velvet gown.

Two people were waiting behind the man using the machine.

Judging from the time he was taking, he was negotiating a mortgage, buying a pension plan, and making his will. The woman on
his heels shifted her shopping bags and sighed; the boy lit a cigarette and looked murderous.

The autumn sunshine, gilding brick and berried trees, was
beneficent, like a matriarch bestowing gold and jewels on her
heirs, all their sins forgiven; the plane trees were dappled benign
giraffes. Jess stood a foot or so away to wait her turn, and looked
down, on to cubes of viscous glass. She hadn't noticed them for
years, but they must have been there all the time, those skylights
set into pavements, the little squares of thick opaque glass letting
out light from the cellars of shops, swimmy subaqueous light from
the dank green cottages and gloomy caves of public conven-
iences. There was something she should have been thinking
about, a decision to be made, but she stooped to study the tiles,
seeing them with a child's eye, as if for the first time, pinkish, yellowish, greyish, dirtily opalescent, the colours of fish. Children
are closer to the pavement, she was thinking, they know that the
striped awning that encloses the greengrocer's emerald slope can
suddenly snap in the wind and slap them in the face, that wooden
cellar doors could fold back like heavy wings and plummet them
into the underworld, that glass squares might hold more than
bears.

Crouching there at a child's level, she heard a mother's voice:
'Will you shut up, or I'll give you something to cry for!' A howling infant was dragged past her. Something to cry for. That
seemed doubly cruel, and unnecessary, as the child was already
smeared and incoherent with an abundance of grief.

'You have no heart,' Jess had been told last night. 'You
haven't got a heart.' Not true, not true. 'All you care about is
your work.' There was a pretty iron grille above the skylight.
'You've got to decide. Come with me to America, or it's over.'
Victorian, undoubtedly, the elaborate ironwork lattice. 'Crunch

time,' said the broken glass under people's feet. 'Make or break.'

Jessamy realized that she was squatting in the street and that she would be thought mad or drunk, if anyone noticed her at all; not that that bothered her, it was just that her knees were aching. She straightened up and looked into the shop window. From the back, in her huge sweater and jeans stiff with paint, she might have been a man, or girl, a woman or a boy; she was all of them, and none of them in particular when she worked. As she gazed, she realized the truth of the saying that charity begins at home; everything in this jumbled display had once been in somebody's home. An earlier proprietor's name was engraved in an ornamental strip across the top of the window: *Adèle. Coiffeuse and Wigmaker*: she must have been very sure of herself, to have her name incised in silvery Deco letters in the frosty glass. Where was Adèle now? The shop was closed and its interior dim; Jess saw her reflection doubled for an instant in the slightly distorted glass, as if another self had stepped sideways from her body and was looking at her. Beyond her selves, on a shelf, stood a light-fitting comprising three frilly-bottomed bells of crème brûlée, as brittle as the caramelized topping that you crackle with your spoon. Was it camp, covetable kitsch, that brass-stemmed cluster, or BHS circa 1990? It was hard to tell. Jessamy knew that she had only to flick a switch, pull a string, and her life would be bathed in sweet toffee-coloured light. What to do? But look! The twin of the lustrous pearly globe, flecked blue and orange like a party balloon, that had been suspended on three chains from her childhood ceiling. Every so often Mother had stood on a chair to unhook it and empty it of its prey; daddy-long-legs, flies, moths, all silhouetted against the glass, and once, most horribly, a red admiral.

Decide. Make a decision. Decide whether or not to pick up the phone when you get home. Decide whether to sit beside someone in a Virgin aircraft, holding hands over the Atlantic. She remembered holding up their entwined fingers, that seemed to float in the dusk above the bed, and saying 'our fingers make a candelabrum'. There, in the window, was a three-tiered cake stand, bordered in nasturtiums, with a tarnished fork, dating from the days when waitresses in white caps and aprons served cakes on decorous doilies, when the disseminated department store Bon Marché, down the road, had been the Harrods of South East London. She wondered if perhaps Adèle, looking down, ever paused in the Marcel waving of an angel's wing, and remembered. Over the noise of the traffic Jess could hear the boom and echoing crash of bottles being cast into the bottle bank, three council tumuli colour-coded Brown, White and Green.

Misbegotten garments, acrylic, fluorescent, trimmed with gilt and plastic, rubbed shoulders with the shrunken and drab in a brave, hopeless queue. A mildewed leather jacket brought a memory she would have preferred to forget, of a circle of Hell's Angels peeing on the brand-new leather jacket she had saved for months to buy, and on which she still owed money. That had been the initiation ceremony in which Jess was to be the official Old Lady of the leader of the pack. She had made her excuses and left. Well, fled in fact, pursued by burning brands and beer bottles. Her conversion to vegetarianism had come soon after, outside a butcher's shop. Tearing off the jacket, still smelly after repeated hosings and a trip to the dry cleaners, she had thrust it on a youth idling on a parked motorbike at the kerb.

'Here, take this jacket!' she had ordered, adding graciously, 'you can pee on it if you like.' He had vanished, *vroom vroom*, in a terrified trail of exhaust. She had gone home and applied to go to art school. The past, the past. What about the future? Was there a future in glass? Nobody was buying paintings; her last exhibition had been well received but not a single painting had sold. Out of embarrassment she had stuck red dots on a few

frames herself. Now she imagined herself in a booth at the end of
a pier, twirling glass like spun sugar in the flame of a blowtorch,
spinning the rigging of fragile ships, the legs of glass animals, fish
with fissile fins, bambis with glaucoma. How did one go about
getting such a job? Surely the position would be occupied by a
gentle, bearded young man? Off the edge of the pier with him! –
a faint hiss as a wave quenched and then closed over his Bunsen
burner.

'You've never loved anyone.' Not true. People from the past
stepped forward to prove it. Then she saw that they were reflections in the shop window; perhaps she had always been looking
in a mirror, watching others loving her? Damn. She had lost her
place in the queue. The light would be quite gone by the time she
got home. Two jacket potatoes would be splitting their sides in
the oven waiting for her; Jess took as her example Piero di
Cosimo, who had kept a bucket of boiled eggs beside him as he
painted, so that he need not break off work to eat. As she was
leaving the window, a flash of sapphire caught her eye, a shimmer
of turquoise and flamingo pink. A powder compact with a lid of
butterflies' wings under glass. There had been a shop window,
long ago, filled with those vibrant wings made into pictures of
silky tropical seas and black palm trees against savage sunsets; and
set in silver jewellery, vivid on black velvet. If you looked closely
you could see the veins in the wings.

Jessamy turned away angrily. Was this really what it was all
about? Are we so imprinted in childhood, like orphaned ducklings who bond with wellington boots, or cartoon chicks
squawking 'Mummy! That's my Mummy!' at exasperated wolves,
that we spend the rest of our lives in pursuit of long-dead butterflies, chasing babyhood bunnies in an endless circle round and
round the rim of a nursery bowl before sliding into the flames on
a sledge painted with a blistering rosebud? Look at the
Harlequins. What colours, she wondered, would activate her

children's nervous systems; some dress she herself had worn, a
necklace of glass beads? What English *madeleine* rolled in coconut
and topped with a glace cherry would dissolve into memory in
her lover's mouth? Then she speculated on whether we should
love one another if we were made of glass, with all the workings
visible, like transparent factories. We should have to; after all, we
found beauty in eyes, ears and noses which were nothing but util-
itarian. There was a boy going past, whose mouth was a more
blatant organ than most, with his big fragile upper teeth puck-
ering his lower lip like the skin of a deflating balloon. No heart?
She could feel it heavy in her chest. She was all heart, had been
from the start. Had she not been inconsolable when that pearly,
flecked balloon had burst? It had had a pair of cardboard feet, and
she had been left holding the disembodied feet in her hand. She
had kept them for weeks. Did not spring evening skies of Indian
ink drizzled over daffodil, or autumn sunsets like this one of apricot and sapphire, suffuse her with *tendresse*? She felt her eyes fill,
the aqueous humour, the vitreous humour, glazed with tears.
Decide if you want me in your life – a dear face fallen asleep over
a book, spectacles slipping down a familiar nose, discs of glass
magnifying closed eyelids veined like butterflies' wings.

At the bottle bank, a girl hesitated with a blue bottle in her
hand, unsure where to deposit it, and as she held it up, blue as
butterflies' wings from the Seychelles or the Philippines, Jess
made her decision.

'Green!' she called. 'No, brown!'

Too late. The girl dropped it into the white bin. Blue on white.
An arctic landscape. As Jess inserted her card, the cash dis-
penser's perspex eyelid closed in a slow malevolent wink as if to
say 'I'll give you something to cry for.'

The glass squares in the pavement glowed faintly phosphorescent now. She looked down at one of them; old, adamantine,
durable; it would take a pickaxe to break it.

Grasshopper Green

Agnes Cameron was one of the many exiles living in a university city on the south coast of England. She was sixty-two years old and in her address book the names of the dead outnumbered the living. Once her hair had been as bright as a red squirrel; now it was more like the grey-tawny pelt of an English squirrel, but it was always beautifully cut. Her small house was at the top of a hilly street and at night she could hear ships hooting in the docks and the putter of fireworks from celebrations on board the cruise liners, while yellow beams like searchlights criss-crossed the sky. During term time the desolate-sounding bellows of students out on the town reached her garden and sometimes she heard the cries of owls and foxes, the night people living their lives.

She had come here with her English husband and after their divorce she stayed on because she had an administrative job at the university. In every household there is one person who controls the weather and Michael had created storms and gloom. She had been a widow with two grown-up daughters when she met him and married him out of loneliness. Her girls and their families gave Agnes her greatest happiness but at the present time they were all living abroad. Some people take to gardening when they get older, others to charity work. Agnes had chosen birds.

After both her beloved cats died she had installed a metal pole like a double-headed shepherd's crook from which were suspended feeders of diverse nuts and seeds that attracted an enchanting variety of visitors.

It was Agnes's habit to open the back door last thing at night to let the ghosts of her two cats run inside and up the stairs to bed. One violet autumn evening as soft and moist as if a giant sponge had been squeezed out after a steamy bath, she was standing on her back porch in the moonlight, watching a procession of delicate slugs making its way up the wall of the house. The steps leading to the garden were studded with minute tender-shelled snails. Hearing the rustling noise of some animal under the hedge, she leaned too far forward, triggering the security light which extinguished the mystery of the garden. Highlighted in the yellow glare was the hooded figure of a young man on the balcony of one of the flats opposite. He was looking directly at her.

Agnes couldn't sleep. She had noticed him before several times, assumed he was a student, and felt nothing beyond a slight annoyance that he was always catching her staring through binoculars as if she hadn't anything better to do. Now she had an uneasy feeling that he had been spying on her.

She was dreading the morning because she had accepted an invitation to lunch-time drinks from a woman she disliked. She patted the bed where the cats lay. She switched on the radio. Music might prevent the grotesque cavalcade of a lifetime's blunders and regrets from trooping through her head, and divert her from imagining her parents' night-time loneliness and pain in old age. It was always Radio 3, because the World Service could be relied on to plant some atrocity in your head which would be with you for ever. Sometimes at night Agnes wondered if she was actually in a care home and everything else was fantasy. Perhaps she was really lying helpless at the mercy of a sadistic nurse, gazing through the window at the empty bird-feeder dangling from a tree, with the television out of reach and blaring out some sports programme. One of her grandsons was in the room. 'I never knew you were into rugby, Granny,' he said, and turned up the volume as he left.

A chance meeting had brought about the invitation to the drinks party. After being made redundant from the university two years ago, Agnes had the good fortune to get a job at Hazelwood Hardware in the row of high street shops which served the local residents when they didn't take the bus or drive to the malls and precincts of the city. She loved everything about it: the Hazelwood family who owned the shop, the rest of the staff, her green pinafore with the hazelnut logo on the pocket, the stock – from household utensils and mats and cleaning products, to nails, screws, light bulbs, spring and autumn bulbs, garden tools, candles, doilies, Christmas fancy goods – it was often remarked that you would always find what you wanted in Hazelwood's. Agnes bought her bird food there in bulk, at a discount, and one of the Hazelwood boys dropped it off in his van. Then last week, out of the blue, Old Mr Hazelwood, now retired, had gathered the staff together to tell them that Hazelwood's was closing down. Everybody, including Agnes, had cried.

A couple of days later Agnes was taking her lunch-break, feeling desolate at the prospect of the coming closure, filling the time by drifting in and out of the charity shops. 'Sixty-two years old and still nobody to play with at dinner time,' she thought, remembering how interminable an hour seemed in a school playground. Things improved when her little sister Jeannie started school; at least they had each other at playtime.

She bumped into Vee Saunders, whom she knew from the university, in the Salvation Army shop. Vee was a folklorist whose profession, Agnes thought, lent respectability to a relish for cruelty. She was also a specialist in children's literature and was of the mistaken opinion that all children delight in the gruesome and yukky. Always in a hurry, she would gallop into Agnes's office to use the photocopier, like a superannuated Rapunzel with a flying plait of grey hair which hung to her waist.

Vee was examining a fringed and tasselled brown-and-mauve-patchwork suede tunic.

'Oh hello,' she said. 'I was just looking for something a bit glitzy to wear on Sunday. We're having people for lunch-time drinks.'

Agnes spotted a silver-grey jacket with mother-of-pearl buttons, which she herself had donated, and held it up.

'This would suit you. Oh – sorry, it's a ten.'

'No, it's a tad on the dreary side. I think I'll settle for the suede.'

'Isn't it more folklorey than glitzy – borderline woodcutter?' Agnes was tempted to say.

Vee grasped her arm, 'I say, how awful of me! You wouldn't like to join us on Sunday, would you? Do say yes! I haven't seen you for ages, except in Hazelwood's of course, and it would be lovely!'

Agnes was up while it was still dark, before the birds were awake, to blitz the house in case anybody offered her a lift home and accepted her invitation to come in. When you live alone vigilance must be your watchword. Nobody thinks anything of scattered newspapers and coffee cups and dented cushions in a family house, and the lingering smells of last night's garlic, candles and wine only add to its homeliness, but the singleton's residence must be beyond reproach even if no visitors are expected. A Jehovah's Witness might catch you napping, or Kim and Aggie from the TV show *How Clean is Your House?* spring out from your bathroom cabinet in their white lab coats, snapping on their marabou-trimmed Marigolds. At the back of her mind hung a faded sampler whose cross-stitched legend read: *Thou God See-est Me*. She knew from her parents' declining years that there was a slippery slope ending in ketchup and Pepto-Bismol bottles rubbing shoulders on the dining table, corn plasters in the fruit bowl, crepe bandages uncurling into the tub of margarine smirched with crumbs and jam, and pills and tubes of unspeakable remedies muddled up with piles of junk mail. She spent hours shredding her identity from her own post. And as you get older there's always the danger of leaving the house with a fleck of toothpaste mocking the brooch on your lapel, or a dribble of soup down your blouse from a treacherous spoon, because even your old faithful possessions turn against you.

At eight o'clock she ran her bath. Then she saw it. How could it be? How, today of all days, could there be a grasshopper on the bathroom ceiling? It was out of season as well as in an impossible place. It should have departed with the summer, to wherever grasshoppers go but, verdant and sappy, it made its plight hers. Despite last night's mugginess, there was a definite chill in the air this morning, and bad things happen to grasshoppers in the winter. They have to go begging for a grain of corn to the industrious ants, who will turn them away saying, 'You sang all summer long, now you can dance!'

Oh, why had she looked up at the ceiling? Why was it always her fate to be the one to notice the injured bird, the trapped butterfly twirling in a spider's web, the ladybird toiling up the window of the bus, climbing and falling, climbing and falling? As a child she had ruined many a family outing by sobbing over some poor dead creature, behaving like 'a big wet lettuce' or 'a dying duck in a thunderstorm'.

If she managed to catch the grasshopper, using an inverted glass and sheet of paper, without breaking off one of its legs, and put it outside, a bird might snap it up. If she didn't, it could unfold those tensile legs and spring into her bath and drown. Or frazzle in one of the halogen ceiling lights. Or be discovered at some later date, dead or alive, in her make-up bag. She turned off the lights and opened the window, hoping the grasshopper would have the sense to leap through it, and went to make some toast. Maybe she could use it as an excuse to get out of the party, saying that an unexpected visitor had turned up.

'Oh, do bring her along,' Vee would cry. 'The more the merrier! Or is your visitor a he, perchance?'

'I'm not really sure.'

'Intriguing! You *are* a dark horse, Agnes!'

And then she would pitch up with the grasshopper in her handbag, and Vee would start banging on about Aesop and La Fontaine.

Agnes always ate her breakfast standing over the sink, with binoculars at hand so that she could watch the birds. She spotted a nuthatch walking backwards down the metal pole of the bird-feeder and raised the binoculars. A flash of sunshine caught the window and the lenses of the binoculars, signalling to the youth she suddenly saw on his balcony. She dropped the binoculars and her toast fell into the washing-up bowl. She hadn't seen him come out for his morning cigarette, wearing his usual hoodie, boxers and flip-flops. Then he turned and appeared to be fixing something to the wall.

The telephone rang. It was her sister Jeannie in Elgin.

'I found a grasshopper in the house this morning,' Agnes told her.

'"Grasshopper Green is a comical chap—"' Jeannie began.

'Not when he's on your bathroom ceiling, he isn't,' Agnes interrupted. 'Listen, pet, can I call you later? I've got to get ready for a lunch-time drinks party.'

'Get you,' said Jeannie. 'I'm impressed.'

When Agnes went back into the bathroom the grasshopper was

perched on the rim of the bath. Agnes succeeded in catching it, and put it outside the back door. The garden glittered with spiders' webs.

The Saunders home proved to be an Arts and Crafts house hung with scarlet Virginia creeper, and self-righteous solar panels ruining the roof. The front room was already crowded when Agnes arrived. She recognized several people but knew none of them well. The handsome Saunders children were handing round cocktail sausages on silver foil platters, £4.99 a pack in Hazelwood's. Vee had let down her Rapunzel hair and was wearing the suede tunic over ribbed grey leggings and fringed pixie boots. She gave Agnes a quizzical look, as though she was about to comment on her unremarkable dress and thought better of it.

'This is my old colleague Agnes Cameron, Drew,' she said to her husband, a short man with an arched nose which he wrinkled to expose tufts of hair. Agnes knew that he was some kind of scientist. He stared at her.

'I've seen you in Hazelwood's, where I'm working now,' Agnes told him.

'Let me find you a glass of wine,' he said.

The wine went straight to her head and she remembered she had had no breakfast. Drew's nose hairs glittered humorously at her.

'So, Agnes Cameron, from the land of the deep-fried Mars Bar, where do you stand on this Scottish Independence lark? Looks a bit inevitable now, don't you think?

I don't know, she thought irritably. *I can remember my granny calling it a piece of nonsense years and years ago.*

She heard herself saying, 'When anybody asks me that, for some reason I think of a board game my sister and I used to have, called *Touring Britain*, or something like that. You had to throw a dice and move little cars about on a yellow map of the British Isles to get home to Ullapool or wherever, and when people talk about devolution I'm always reminded of that game and it's as if a little saw, a jigsaw, is cutting through the border, widening a blue gap, until Scotland floats away like an island ... I expect you're sorry you asked.'

'So. Hazelwood's, eh? I always say you can get anything you want there.'

'Actually, Hazelwood Hardware is going into receivership.'

'That's a pity,' he twinkled, as if she hadn't just informed him of the death sentence on a family firm passed down through three generations. 'I was about to invite you to give a paper on fork handles to my students.'

'I was never an academic,' she informed him. 'Incidentally, I've often wondered what exactly goes on in the Life Sciences Building?'

'Ha ha ha,' he answered.

'So you are about to doff the green tabard,' said Vee, who had joined them. 'What will you do now?'

'I've decided to move to Edinburgh, and edit a small philosophy journal with learned contributors, and collect the works of the Scottish Colourists.'

'We'll miss you,' Drew said, refilling his own glass. 'I suppose we could always look you up when we come to the Festival. We'll crash on your floor, as the kids would say.'

'How marvellous, Agnes. The life of the mind is paramount. That's what you must aspire to,' Vee told her. 'By the way, will Hazelwood's be having a closing-down sale?'

Yes, the life of the mind has its attractions, thought Agnes. She had seen them demonstrated by more than one former professor. She could grow a beard and load up a back-pack with books from charity shops and ride around on the buses all day reading them, not noticing that nobody ever sat beside her, because her mind would be on higher things.

Of course no one offered her a lift home. She stood at the

kitchen window watching the birds darting and swooping on to the feeders. She had absolutely no idea what she would do when Hazelwood's closed down. Blue tit, great tit, coal tit, long-tailed tit, woodpecker, jay. Thank goodness that horrible student wasn't on his balcony. Then she saw what he had been fixing to the wall. A camera.

She stared at it, too shocked for thought, then pulled down the blind and sank into a chair, clutching her head. *Ugh!* There was something sticky in her hair. Her fingers were all enmeshed in a spider's web clotted with tiny flies. She must have brushed against it when she put the grasshopper out. Vee and Drew had let her stand there at the party in a dreadful cobweb hairnet. Like the heroine of some grim fairy story Vee had dredged up – *The Tale of Little Cap O'Flies*. No wonder people were looking so oddly at her. She was sure that some of them had been sniggering.

What to do, what to do? That terrible camera. It was like a CCTV camera. This must be the student's revenge. He had thought she was spying on him and he was getting his own back. She went icy cold, then burned with shame, as a dreadful certainty possessed her. The boy was taking pictures of her to post on YouTube. The invisible woman exposed to the herd of students who had trampled her on the pavement the other day and galloped on regardless. *Old Bat in Dressing Gown Dropping Toast into Washing-up Bowl* had probably gone viral by now. How many hits would *Woman With a Grasshopper Crashing into a Spider's Web* score? Could the camera penetrate her bathroom window? Her grandchildren would witness her global humiliation. She must hide. Flee. But where? It could only be to Scotland. Maybe Scotland would welcome her home with outstretched arms, like a kind granny framed in her doorway saying, 'Come away in!'

Agnes went through to the front room to telephone Jeannie. If she hadn't kept the blind down for the rest of the day she might have seen the student come on to the balcony and unhook the trainers he had hung out to air. Close-up they looked nothing like a camera. Then, lighting a cigarette, he pulled his phone from his pocket.

Heron Cottage

The sisters really had no business to be in Heron Cottage that afternoon. They spoke in whispers at first, half expecting to hear the sharp crack of a stair and Miss Martin's voice demanding what on earth they thought they were doing in her kitchen, although they knew that she was lying in the secret, unthinkable chamber at the back of T. H. Lovelock and Sons, Undertakers and Funeral Directors. Yet they felt a camaraderie, as if they were engaged on some prank that the fifteen years between their ages had denied them until now. Miss Martin's string shopping bag, with a wisp of dried onion skin caught in its mesh, hung from a hook on the door, and a red vinyl cook's apron garnished with tomatoes. A present, Rosamund supposed; she had never seen Miss Martin cooking anything. But not so incongruous after all perhaps, for the apron advertised Heinz tomato soup, and presumably Miss Martin dined on the few vegetables she grew.

Rosamund, the elder of the trespassers, Esmée Martin's nearest neighbour, had been entrusted years ago with a key for use in an emergency. This was the second time she had used it. The first had been the horrible afternoon when, realizing she had not seen Miss Martin about for some time, she had found her in bed, delirious and dehydrated, and had had to call an ambulance.

The funeral was to be held the day after the sisters let themselves in, and such family as Miss Martin had were arriving in the evening to spend the night at Heron Cottage. Rosamund had suggested, and would have been dissuaded easily had Lucy not agreed with such alacrity, that they should pop round and tidy up a bit for the bereaved, if distantly related, family. Rosamund wondered how much her impulse owed to guilt and neighbourliness, and how much to a wish to entertain Lucy who was on a visit from London.

'There may be things going bad in the fridge,' she had said. 'And the beds should be aired.' Her voice had sounded too hearty to her, brazen and tactless, as if she had spoken of decomposition and the sheets of a deathbed and the waiting bed of cold clay in the spring rain, but Lucy had been excited at the prospect of entering Miss Martin's house. She had only glimpsed her in the garden and, reading the obituaries, had been surprised to learn that the old thing had been quite a well-known poet in her day. She regretted now not having pursued the acquaintance. Ros might have asked her to tea or drinks, she thought, sure that Miss Martin would have warmed to her. The faded deckchair, the ancient panama at dusk, night-scented stocks, assumed in memory the poignancy of a thousand lost summer evenings.

Rosamund and Lucy had driven into Sevenoaks early to buy food suitable for Miss Martin's Londoners at the deli. It had been Lucy's idea to leave them the makings of an evening meal and breakfast.

'Shouldn't we get some baked meat?' she had asked, noticing a glistening purple knob of bone protruding from a yellow-crumbed ham. 'Isn't that what you're supposed to have at funerals?'

Rosamund, catching sight of herself in the glass above the counter – so much older and stockier and wiser and wearier than her sister – rolled her eyes heavenwards and told Lucy, 'They're not having anybody back to the cottage afterwards. Just everybody going to the pub.' It seemed bleak and unsatisfactory, and she feared it would all peter out in embarrassment.

Now, in Miss Martin's kitchen with its scrubbed wooden draining-board and stone sink, the aconites outside shivering in the sun, she set the trendy old-fashioned brown paper carrier bag from the deli on the table and opened the little fridge. Apart from a carton of milk, which vindicated her, and an unopened packet of butter, it was quite empty.

'It's colder inside than out,' said Lucy. 'Aren't those celandines pretty? *She* would have loved them . . .'

'They're aconites. She did.'

Pneumonia aggravated by malnutrition. It was all so hideous. And unnecessary. How could she not feel silently accused? But it really hadn't been her fault. Everybody knew Esmée Martin was practically a recluse and fiercely independent. And she'd been as fit as a fiddle the last time Rosamund had seen her. Nobody could have seen how thin she was under that great duffel coat, and she wasn't even particularly old. You didn't expect someone of sixty-odd to pop off like some hypothermic pensioner.

Rosamund, in an old navy-blue jersey discarded by one of her sons, quilted waistcoat and jeans, sat down on a wooden chair at the scrubbed table and swept the fallen pollen from the dead catkins in the yellow jug into a neat heap. Rosamund had never been in Miss Martin's house without admiring some seasonal twigs, leaves, flowers or berries, old roses in an old Sheffield bowl, red poppies in a green jug, ox-eye daisies in white, cornflowers in blue glass, a crazed pink vase of spindleberries. Lucy, who was closing a drawer of calm bleached tea towels, had affected, for her stay in the country, a style not unlike Miss Martin's own; she wore an oatmeal sweater over two print frocks, one half-buttoned, and a pair of flat-heeled boots. Now she was pulling open the doors of a wooden cupboard. She jumped back as something crashed down and rolled across the floor.

'Lucy!'

'Well, well, well! Take a look at this!' Lucy retrieved, and held up a jar of peaches in brandy while the sun streamed through its glass and spilled golden juice on to the floor.

The shelves of the cupboard were stocked, stacked, brimming, with exotica: Rose Pouchong and Earl Grey and Lapsang Souchong tea, chocolate Bath Olivers, *langues de chat*, angels' trumpets, brandy snaps, marzipan and glacé fruits, coffee beans and chocolate coffee beans, little plum puddings, Turkish cigarettes. Bottles glittered in the darkness of the shallow cellar.

'Well! The stingy old . . .' Rosamund struggled to articulate the scraggy, scrawny, *old-fashioned* thing that was in her mind '. . . boiling fowl! When I think of all those Tetley teabags! One was lucky to be offered a Happy Shopper bourbon! You would imagine, looking at this lot, that every day had been Christmas in Heron Cottage.'

'You don't suppose,' said Lucy, 'that it was for someone special? No, perhaps not . . .' As the sisters dismissed the possibility of any romantic explanation for the hoard, Lucy had a regretful glimpse of herself seated at the kitchen table, nibbling an exotic biscuit and nodding sagely at some confidence. She followed Rosamund into the front room and found her kneeling in front of the big ugly old radiogram, opening the doors of its cabinet.

Rosamund lifted out friable black records in brittle brown sleeves and laid them on the carpet. 'I'd never have taken her for a jazz fan,' she said. 'These must be worth a bob or two.'

'Curiouser and curiouser,' Lucy said. 'Do we really ever know anybody else? If they were digitally remastered . . .'

Rosamund pictured Esmée sitting on her stoop with a blue-black voice and a trumpet wailing 'I hate to see that evenin' sun go down' over the darkening garden, and sitting on, damp with dew until her white head was a reflection of the white moon. And yet she had never heard that music pouring from the cottage or seen Esmée sitting so.

'At a pang of, could it be, jealousy,' she said, suddenly peevish, 'Well, we might have saved ourselves the trouble. There's enough food here to feed six times the number of people who'll be coming tomorrow. Even if they couldn't be bothered with the old girl when she was alive.' She returned to the kitchen and picked up their carrier bag, and added defiantly one or two items from Esmée's store.

'Just like Miss Haversham ...' Lucy was murmuring to the stopped clock.

'Havisham. I'm surprised at you, Lucy!' She locked the door behind them and they stepped out into Miss Martin's garden where Miss Martin's spring cabbages grew. Lucy pulled open the door of the little shed, and a small wicker hamper tumbled out at her feet. The shed was stacked with empty Christmas hampers. They stared. Then Rosamund, outfaced by the baskets, touched the fallen one with her toe. 'This might come in handy. Bring it, Lucy, it won't be missed. What do you want to do about lunch?'

'"How about a pigfoot and a bottle of beer,"' Lucy suggested, recalling one of Miss Martin's records.

'Pub all right then?' Although they'd be there again tomorrow. The funeral baked meats they had bought in the deli would come in handy for supper. Suddenly Rosamund stopped on the path that led through the field to her house. 'What's that you've got there? What are you hiding under your jersey? Show me at once!'

Lucy, blushing as deep a pink as the blighted, half-opened rose that had hung on the hedge all winter, drew out a bundle of letters and postcards, secured by a thick rubber band.

'How *could* you? How could you be so – shabby? If that's what living in London's made of you . . .'

A dozen secret urban shames stained Lucy darker red.

'It's people like you, your rotten Thames Water Board taking our water that nearly killed our river for ever!' Rosamund was going on, slightly incoherent with anger, as Lucy shouted,

'I'm going to put them back! I just thought they might give a clue! You can take them back yourself when you go to air the beds, which you seem to have forgotten was the main purpose of our visit!'

A gurgling to their left proved that the spring rains had saved the river but Rosamund was too enraged to hear it. Lucy broke away and ran to the house, and up the stairs to her bedroom, and stood panting against the white-painted latched door. She heard Rosamund come into the kitchen, and start banging about in the larder. Lucy lay face downwards on the faded patchwork quilt on her bed and eased the rubber band from the letters. She pulled out a postcard of Masaccio's *La cacciata dal Paradiso Terrestre*, Adam and Eve in agony, and turned it over, looking first at the signature. *Edward.*

What do the dead feel when they watch the living pawing through their precious possessions, the fleshy curious fingers' invisible acid etching the papers that testify to the dead one's tenancy in this world? Should Esmée Martin have been observing this young woman sprawled on her sister's spare bed, an impulse towards an impossible, incorporeal lunge and snatch might have stirred the air; or perhaps Esmée watched Lucy as dispassionately as did the cross-stitched sampler on the wall above her. After all, Esmée might have thought, with now-lofty detachment, that thin bundle of cards and letters seemed too slight to bear the suspended weight of half a lifetime's longing.

'This can't be it. This can't be all there is.' Lucy stared at a card with 1967 postmarked across a Helvetian stamp. *'I wish you could see it – beautiful wild flowers and wonderful cakes . . .'*

'Wonderful cakes?' Was this a message from a man sick with love among the gentians and edelweiss of the Alps? Patently not: why then had Esmée preserved it, with not so much as a bleached petal to speak of passion? Lucy hated him, this heartless eater of cakes. He had not loved Esmée Martin at all.

Esmée had read it as 'cakes' too, once, and wept. Much later, she had seen that the word, in his careless scrawl, was 'lakes', but by then she had realized that his feelings for her were nothing like hers for him, and her mind's eye retained a picture of Edward sitting on a chalet balcony jutting into a postcard-blue sky, with a froth of *café au lait* on his moustache and a big Swiss gâteau in his hand. He wore *lederhosen*, whose braces were appliqued with hearts and flowers, and his bare knees touched the walking-skirt of a laughing woman seated at his table; sunshine, glittering off white peaks, gilded two alpenstocks lolling together against the carved wooden railing, making twin dazzling suns of their encircled spikes. 'Cuckoo cuckoo cuckoo,' mocked the little bird in the clock on Esmée's kitchen wall, although technically she could not be cuckolded, and the man was married to someone else.

Lucy extracted the very first letter, sent from Cadogan Square:

My dear Miss Martin

I know I have no right to write to you in this way, but since we met last night at the Ansteys', I have not been able to put you out of my mind. I shall be at the National Gallery tomorrow at three, in front of Watteau's La Gamme d'Amour. I shall wait for one hour. If you do not wish to meet me, I would ask your forgiveness of my presumption in hoping that you felt as I did.

Edward Leyland

'*My dear love,*' the second letter read, '*you have made me happier than any man deserves or dreams to be ...*' There was an antique valentine embossed with twin doves in beribboned paper lace, which Lucy pressed to her own lips with a sigh, and thereafter a bunch of cards with brief messages – '*usual place at seven*' – '*Tomorrow*' – '*Tuesday*' ... and then a sad handful of apologies for meetings missed, cancelled outings, plans gone awry. Lucy sensed the death of love as she read them.

Folded and refolded very small, creased as if it had been crumpled in despair and then straightened again, and its ink blotched and blurred, a last letter fell on to the bed. Lucy deciphered its closing words through a mist of her own tears – '*... until then. One day, when you have forgotten all about me, you will see a tall man walking up your cottage path with his arms full of flowers, and you will wonder who this stranger can be, but just for a moment, until he sees your face at the window and breaks into a run, and drops his silly flowers as he opens his arms to hold you in them once more ...*'

Lucy cried, because he had never come up the path of Heron Cottage with his flowers, and for herself because there had been nothing in her own life to match Esmée Martin's love or tragedy, and she felt an emptiness and tawdriness and dissatisfaction with all her unromantic lovers. She wanted Esmée Martin's past, the lonely longing, the dashed hopes of the woman who had half-starved herself and saved up for Christmas hampers so that she might produce a feast at a moment's notice, sustaining her thin body on rich products past their sell-by dates, who had risen early each morning to keep her house spotless and tend her garden in case he should appear, who had played her sad records as the moon rose, and faced her chaste bed at the death of another day with a prayer that the dawn would bring a stranger who was not a stranger.

Lucy put on her coat and slipped the correspondence into her

pocket. Rosamund was in the kitchen, loading some dull hus-
bandly garments into the washing machine. Lucy suddenly felt
sorry for her.

'We'd better get going, if we're having lunch at the pub,' said
Rosamund.

'I'm just going to put those things back,' said Lucy. 'I didn't
read them, by the way.'

Rosamund smiled. 'I'm glad,' she said.

Lucy glanced up through Esmée Martin's window and saw a tall
man walking up the path, a sheaf of lilies in his arms, white and
gold against his black coat. She opened the front door and the
stranger took off his hat, revealing thick silver hair.

'Good afternoon,' he said. 'I was so sorry to hear the news. Are
you one of the family?'

Lucy shook her head.

'I wonder if I might come in?' he asked.

Lucy saw that he was a straight-backed, vigorous-looking man.
She stepped back, holding the door for him.

'I'm – was – a very close friend of Esmée,' she told him.

'So was I. There are some things of mine, some letters, I
believe, that she would have wished me to have. Of sentimental
value only – of no interest to anyone else.'

An authorized biography of Esmée Martin materialized in the
air between them, and vanished.

'I understand,' she said. 'Those lovely lilies should be put in
water at once. For tomorrow. Shall we have a drink while I find
your – letters? Esmée prided herself on keeping a nice little
cellar . . .'

'Really?' He looked surprised. 'I'm Edward Leyland, by the way.
I'm afraid I shan't be able to stay for the funeral.'

'Lucy Pierce.' She held out her hand, which he pressed while
smiling into her eyes.

Lucy smiled back, letting her hand linger in his. 'I'm staying with my sister,' she said. 'Rosamund ...' – who would have to wait because Lucy had not decided yet whether she should have some of the romance that had been Esmée's, or if Edward Leyland was to be made to atone for the waste of a life.

The Last Sand Dance

After the taxi dropped him off, Alfred rode on beside her in a dark shape of Eau Sauvage and cigar smoke. Zinnia was driven south, with her eyes shut to retain his presence and her fingers closed on the note he had folded into her gloved palm to pay the cab, unsettled by his scent, once familiar and now exotic, and the impression of his heavy coat that she still held in her arms. The nylon spiracles of Zinnia's wide fur collar, electrified by the long-ago lovers' brief parting embrace, made an aureole round her small head like that of a red squirrel's tail against the light, and stirred her own hair into the tiny scarlet-tipped feathers of an African Grey parrot. It was late March, Passover and Easter just round the corner, and the clear moonlit night was cold enough to encourage a thin frost. She was on her way home from the theatre. When Alfred had telephoned to ask her to a play he had agreed to review for a quirky literary periodical, although his field was really Byzantine art, Zinnia had thought it might be a lark, especially as they had not seen each other since the funeral of a reprobate dramatist six months ago. The play, *Istambull*, had attracted rave notices at last year's Edinburgh Festival and won a Fringe First award.

Zinnia Herbert was an actor, with an unreconstructedly actressy

West End glamour about her, even though she had not appeared on a stage north of Wimbledon for several years; Zinnia was one of those stalwarts who never quite become a star, whose kindness to their fellow thespians and the humblest ASM are legendary in the profession, whose obituaries will make even those readers who had assumed they had died long ago sigh at their youthful beauty and long to go backstage to express their belated appreciation. Zinnia had been born into show business, to a variety act called The Two Herberts who, while not entirely responsible for the death of music hall, were certainly in at its demise. Zinnia herself had made her début at the age of three, at the Hackney Empire, singing 'I've Never Seen A Straight Banana'. In fact, as it was wartime, she had never seen a banana at all.

She might have guessed, she thought in the taxi, that any production staged at a venue with such an unpleasant name, recalling ancient cruelties, would be dire. The Pillory Theatre was the converted billiard room of an old gin palace, and specialized in previously unperformed, and often never seen again, works by young playwrights. Zinnia and Alfred had perched uncomfortably on the edge of the avant-garde, on an itchy banquette which was a superannuated bus seat blobbed with polished strings of chewing gum, and scarred by cigarette burns that sighed puffs of dust at every shift of haunch and hip. A fellow critic acknowledged Zinnia and Alfred with a languid wave, another rolled his eyes towards the kippered ceiling, and one or two people stared as if they thought they ought to recognize them, for Alfred, with his beard, green silk scarf, fedora and unlit cigar, cut as theatrical a figure as Zinnia in her russet fur, sniffing a scented handkerchief as if it were an orange stuffed with cloves or a nosegay wafted by a disdainful spectator at a historical scene of public humiliation. The rank air was noisy with the ripping of ringpulls and the crackle of discarded plastic cups that had held wine. Zinnia looked at the programme of *Istambull* and groaned.

'You didn't remind me. I can't stand two-handers. I'm always hoping for a knock on the door or for somebody to come jaunting in through the french windows.'

No scenery and not a french window in sight, not even a telephone to relieve the tedium; it was quite obviously not going to be her sort of play, and then a cat-o'-nine-tails of blond braids whipped her face and red wine splashed over her ankles as latecomers barged past with a surly demand of 'Scuse me'.

I'm afraid I can't. You are inexcusable,' Zinnia told them, adding to Alfred, 'do you remember the days when people said, "Excuse me, *please*"?'

'You are at your most *grande dame* tonight. I love it. Marry me,' he whispered into her hair.

'Well, they might at least do the perpetrators of this sorry entertainment the courtesy of arriving on time, particularly as it started twenty-two minutes late. Besides, I'm married.'

Afterwards, outside on the pavement, wrinkling her nose at her coat sleeve, Zinnia said, 'I feel as if I've spent the evening in an old chip pan, or in the dustbag of a Hoover that hasn't been emptied for years. And I'm sure several vertebrae have fused.'

'You might have woken me,' Alfred complained. 'You know I always sleep through the first act, and as there was no interval ... presumably to prevent any escape at half time. I give the director credit for that at least. Did you manage to get your head down at all?'

'Only forty winks right at the end. Why can't young people speak any more? That dreary sub-dialect they all use – I mean *yews*. They're all at it – actors, weather girls, broadcasters. And have shampoos and dry cleaners gone out of fashion?'

'Yoo hoo, Dolly!'

A middle-aged woman was waving at them from across the street, calling the name of a character Zinnia had played in a recent television sitcom, one of the dotty next-door-neighbour parts which casting directors had made rather her forte.

'Yoo hoo, yourself!' Zinnia responded, waggling a zany little wave, with a daffy smile, through a gap in the traffic.

'Let's get out of here,' she said. 'Where would you like to eat? I'm taking *you*, as you treated me to that delightful show. Such a glamorous life you lead, my dear.'

'Don't be silly, *I* invited *you*. What do you feel like eating? I don't know about you, but I'd just like a bowl of noodles.'

Zinnia slipped her arm through his, remembering with affection how this big, powerful, rich man had always sought comfort from food served in round, peasant or nursery shapes – a plate of pasta, a bowl of soup, a pot of tea, a dish of lentils – and how he was not above tucking a napkin under his chin on occasion, and how his chopsticks would glean the last grains of rice from a succession of ceramic lotus leaves; and a whiff of his *eau de toilette* brought a pang of regret.

'Let's find you some noodles, then. How about the Golden Dragon over there?'

'Or you could just come home with me, and I'll bring you something delicious on a tray.'

It was as much the impossibility of superimposing her present-day self on Alfred's memory of her as the thought of her husband Norman at home that made Zinnia pull Alfred briskly to the restaurant. They both had children older than most of the Pillory audience: she a daughter by her first marriage and two grand-daughters, Alfred two sons and three grandchildren, and Norman's son's girlfriend was expecting a baby. Zinnia was more excited than Norman by the news; she adored babies and shopping for them. Norman was grumpy about becoming a grandfather, although he was well of an age for such an event. Zinnia felt a frisson of desire, a flattered flutter, at Alfred's suggestion. But at her age. And she had spent so many years atoning for her own successes and polishing Norman's fallen star that she had lost all sense of herself as desirable. Norman Bannerman had been a big name in television drama in the seventies and now, when there was such a dearth of new plays on the small screen, he was all but forgotten.

'I wonder if old Norm's plays have stood the test of time?' mused Alfred, painting a little pancake with plum jam. 'Do you think they'd hold water now?'

'Of course they would! They're plays, not sponges or colanders! If you take that away from Norman, you leave him with nothing. As a matter of fact, he's working on a stage play now, and I'm sure it's going to be wonderful. You have a noodle in your beard.' Zinnia took a sip of jasmine tea from a tiny cup of scalding porcelain emblazoned with a dragon.

'I don't know – I'm afraid they might have dated badly. Poor Norman,' Alfred persisted.

'Noodle. Remove it, please.' Zinnia was starting to feel a remembered irritation.

'You'll have to fill me in on tonight's debacle,' Alfred went on. 'I don't suppose you thought to make any notes, did you?'

Habit made her apologize.

'Come home with me. You can fax Norm to say you won't be back.' He flipped the last pancake on to her plate.

'Just along there on the right, please,' Zinnia told the taxi driver. 'Past the big tree.'

Ingram Road was a curve of white stuccoed terrace houses, like a thousand London streets, with nothing taller than a slender eucalypt, a magnolia or an occasional misshapen pollarded lime in its walled front gardens, but there was one Olympic plane tree growing out of the pavement, whose shadows dappled the houses on either side and across the road with light and shade like the patches on its great trunk. The plane's bare branches hung with shrivelled fruits splashed moonlight over Zinnia as she stepped out and the taxi's running motor set off a scolding car alarm. She hurried into the house before an irate neighbour could identify her as the culprit, without asking for the receipt which Norman would demand in the morning. A paper lantern shone in the front room of the new young couple next door. It was not Joel and Maxine's fault that they knew nothing of the history of Ingram Road, or that to the older residents Number Eighteen, where they had moved so cheerfully and noisily with a hired van and a gang of friends helping, would always be the house where widowed Jim Bacon had been barbecued on his late wife's electric blanket. Joel and Maxine had a little silver cat called Mignonette, who wore a pearlized flea collar that was reflective in the dark.

Upstairs Norman switched off his bedside lamp and lay resenting the discreet clatter of Zinnia washing up his supper things. At last he heard the stairs creak, then the sound of the bathroom shower and the whine of the hair dryer. She came soundlessly into the bedroom on velvet mules, bathed the dressing table in a kindly apricot glow and sat down to brush her hair. He thought she looked like a B-movie actress playing a film star. There ought to be lightbulbs round the mirror reflecting that slithery kimono slipping off one shoulder, he decided, the sleeve falling back up her arm as her hair leaped to the bristles of her silver brush. A ritual hundred strokes for the head that had long ago lost its golden lustre. Norman blacked out several of his imaginary lightbulbs, swept aside the pots of theatrical unguents and goo to make room for a bottle of gin, and tacked a broken star to her dressing-room door. This was a dame on the skids. Box-office poison. Then, in embittered inspiration, he had her peel off her eyelashes and pull off her wig to reveal the bald, clichéd head of a drag queen.

'Well, well, well, if it isn't Mrs Norman Maine! Tell me, my dear, how went the show tonight?'

Zinnia's gasp at his voice, and the clashing of glass bottles on the glass-topped dressing table as she dropped her brush, gave Norman a visceral wriggle of pleasure.

'Darling! I hope I didn't wake you. I was trying to be so quiet.'

'I heard you taking a no doubt much-needed shower.'

'You're not kidding! I felt absolutely soiled – contaminated.'

Embarrassment as fine as a cloud of powder from a powderpuff drifted across the room as Zinnia, realizing the implications of this exchange, unscrewed a jar of face cream. Norman was at his most dangerous in his *A Star is Born* mode. If only his parents hadn't called him Norman he might not identify so with the leading man of the film whose own star fell as his wife's rose.

'So, apart from that, how did you enjoy the play, Mrs Lincoln?'

'It was filthy. The theatre was filthy, and the play was filthy. Self-indulgent, illiterate, pathetically boorish. So depressing, it's as if Shakespeare, Chekhov, Ibsen, Beckett, you of course, or any of the great dramatists had never lived ...'

Zinnia worried that she should have placed Norman higher in this pantheon, perhaps between Shakespeare and Chekhov, but all he needed to know was the play had been rubbish, and, relieved, he said, 'Sorry you had a rotten evening, but I did warn you, didn't I?'

'You did,' she said ruefully and gratefully. 'I should have listened. I thought it might be a lark, but it turned out to be' – she thought of the Chinese restaurant – 'a dead duck.'

The smell of the cream which Zinnia was smoothing into her arched throat brought Norman a memory of lying in his mother's bed, a sick child propped up on her pillows, watching her rubbing in Pond's Vanishing Cream. It had never worked though, he reflected. Mother was with them still. He decided to visit her the following afternoon. It would beat another long day in the garden chewing the lonely cud of nonentity, while Zinnia was off recording voice-overs for washing-up liquid commercials, and then watching television with his unfinished play dozing fretfully like an untended baby on his desk.

Zinnia got into bed and reached for his hand beneath the covers. Deliberately mistaking her intention, for neither could remember the last time anything more than a homely hug had passed between them, Norman said, a dog with the bone of jealousy clamped in his teeth, 'Do you mind awfully, old girl? Sorry to let you down, but I'm feeling somewhat queasy. That casserole you left me must have been a bit off. Been in the freezer too long, I guess. Nothing to worry about, I'm sure – I hardly touched it. Chucked it in the bin as soon as I realized. Blimey, Zin, you've been on the garlic, haven't you? Hope your chum was too, for his sake. Or should I say saké? I've seen that gin bottle in your dressing room. You'd better get a grip on yourself, people are starting to talk.'

Bewildered and hurt, flushing in her smooth nightdress that suddenly irritated her skin, Zinnia asked, 'What on earth do you mean?' But Norman had rolled over into contented sleep. She wished with all her heart, with her clenched fists and tears leaking into her lavender-scented pillow, that she was in Alfred's kelim-covered bed in his dark, frankincense-and-myrrh-fragrant mansion flat. Alfred's antecedents had sailed from Smyrna. His grandfather had opened the family carpet business in the Burlington Arcade and his uncles and brothers were importers of dried fruits and nuts, and dealers in works of art and sweet heavy wines, otto of roses, orris root and amber. Zinnia pictured heaps of dates and figs, salted almonds, cashews, pistachios, halva, Turkish delight sleeted with soft sugar, frosted glacé bonbons, glowing embroideries and sheer bolts of silken colour. While Alfred lay in damask sheets beneath exiled textiles, the personification of the romantic Levant, Norman the Nebbish snored

softly beside her in striped pyjamas buttoned to the neck with his
breath giving little snickers, as if he were making jokes at somebody's expense in his dreams. If only she had married Alfred
when they had first met, but she hadn't, and they had both married, and divorced, other people. Then, when she was single
again, and her beloved daughter Nerissa away at university, she
had fallen for Norman's lanky, vulnerable charm. Zinnia had forgiven and forgiven Norman for his cruelty, because she knew it
stemmed from his own pain, but she felt unable to bear much
more of his malice. Yet, even now, if bitter, going-to-seed
Norman were to turn to her, she would take him in her arms.

In the morning, Norman found himself alone in bed, vaguely
aware of a breakfast tray on his bedside table, of gilded strands in
the marmalade and rainbows playing about the facets of the crystal jar, and lay half-dozing. His thoughts were tender, vulnerable
things, green walnuts, soft-shell crabs on a damp seashore, a
violet snail reflected in a pavement after rain, unfledged birds in
pink and mauve, the fuzzy green almond buds of the magnolia,
little boys. Norman wrestled languorously with his conscience,
hardly breaking sweat, knowing he could lick it with one hand
tied behind his back; he overpowered it and flung it into a
pathetic whimpering heap beside the bed. He reached for the forbidden bookshelf in his memory and took down a faded volume
with a picture of schoolboys on its torn cover, riffling through the
specked pages until he found his place. What Norman liked best
was the beating of boys, preferably in some raffish educational
establishment on the south coast, but what he could never deter-
mine was whether he wanted to be Old Seedy, the gowned and
mortar-boarded avenger, or one of Seedy's devil-may-care but
ultimately chastised and chastened young tormenters. The swells
and eddies of desire, the sucking surf, the quivering rod, the
crashing waves outside the mullioned windows, the breakfast tray

flying, caught by a guilty elbow as his wife, with misplaced levity, popped her turbanned head round the door to enquire brightly, 'Shall I do you now, sir?'

In a second she was on her knees, scrabbling among the spilled breakfast things, apologizing,

'I'm so sorry, I thought you'd have finished by now. I'll get you some fresh tea and toast as soon as I've mopped this lot up. Entirely my fault.'

'For God's sake, woman. You're not in *ITMA* now. You always have to be on, don't you?'

'What do you mean, *on*? And you know I'm not old enough to have been in *ITMA*. It was supposed to be a joke.'

She sat back on her heels to face him.

'*On*. You of all people should know what *on* means. On stage. On camera. Performing. Playing to the gallery. You can't even do a bit of housework without getting yourself up like Mrs Miniver in a pinny or Lucille Ball prancing around with a feather duster, can you?'

Zinnia's hand flew to her scarf-wrapped head, she glanced down at her striped matelot top, toreador pants and ballet slippers, and a blush crept up her neck and burned her face.

'I just bunged on the first things that came to hand, to do a few chores.'

'Forget the breakfast, I don't feel up to it anyway. Just get me some Pepto-Bismol and a glass of water. You'll be pleased to know that by barging in like that you've completely broken my train of thought and probably destroyed my play. I hope you're satisfied.'

Zinnia stared at him in horror, a person from Porlock who had pranced roughshod in ballet shoes through her husband's dreams, opening her mouth to beg forgiveness for something that could never be put right, but before she could speak Norman went on, 'Isn't it time you were off to do your washing-up commercial? Don't let me keep you. Your public awaits, and you're dressed for the part. "Da da the dreams of an everyday housewife ..."' he sang.

At the sneer in his voice, Zinnia, her lip quivering, said, 'Funnily enough, when I was putting out the rubbish I didn't see any sign of that casserole you said you threw away. *You* used to do that once, remember? Put the garbage out on dustbin day.'

'Perhaps it wasn't food poisoning after all. Could be a recurrence of my old complaint, chronic Zinniaphobia. Anyhow, don't bother about leaving me lunch, I'm going out, as I expect you've forgotten, but I can't expect a star of stage, screen and the kitchen sink to remember the mechanics of my dull life, can I?'

'I hadn't forgotten, as you didn't tell me. Look, Norman, I had hoped that we could make a fresh start this morning, but I see I was wrong. I'm sorry I went to the theatre with Alfred last night. It was a mistake. But it was all perfectly innocent, I assure you. Don't humiliate me by pretending to think otherwise. That's what all this is about, isn't it? You're jealous because I saw Alfred.'

'You flatter yourself, duckie.'

When Norman stumped off to the bathroom, Zinnia caught sight of herself in the mirror and saw that she looked very silly indeed. She wanted to telephone Nerissa, but it had never been her way to whinge. She blew her nose and was wiping her eyes when Norman came back into the bedroom with his bare chest looking its age in the morning sunshine. The ache of affection she felt then was obliterated when he said, 'Chin up, Mrs Miniver. Smile though your heart is breaking, laugh, clown, laugh, and all that crap. Even when the darkest cloud is in the sky, you mustn't sigh and you mustn't – attagirl, big blow now, troupe away, my brave little trouper, the show must go on.'

Zinnia screamed at him, 'This is not a movie – it's our lives! You're not Norman Maine! At least Norman Maine had the decency to walk out to sea and look like James Mason! You know who you are? Norma Desmond! That's who you are, Norma Desmond!'

'That makes you a dead monkey then. And at least Judy Garland had the grace to overdose.'

Ingram Road was where the boys of St Joseph's School came to smoke and eat takeaways in their breaks, and the residents often slipped on greasy chicken bones. As he left the house, Norman came upon old Father Coyle, a shrunken praying mantis who occupied a grace-and-favour apartment in the attic of the Palladian school building, prodding with his stick a vinegary chip paper that had adhered to the trunk of the plane tree. Father Coyle, in his little black suit and biretta that was too large for his head, often took his constitutional along Ingram Road, hoping to catch out truanting pupils, even though he was too frail now to do more than shake his stick at them.

'Not long till Easter now, Father,' Norman remarked encouragingly.

'Is that so, so?' replied Father Coyle.

Norman went on his way, in real life, in a blue morning pouring through the spreading, arching, gracefully trailing twigs of the tree, where Old Seedy's gown was a grubby rag stuffed away somewhere and forgotten, and a pair of passing schoolboys in their untucked shirts and black blazers attracted neither a thought nor a glance. The daytime Norman, who would sicken at the notion of striking a child, set off on his journey to visit his mother.

Maria Bannerman lived in sheltered accommodation in West Kensington. She had had to sell Norman's birthright, the family home, to afford her self-contained flatlet in Glebe Park, a purpose-built block with a resident warden on the premises in case of emergencies. Norman's father, who had died at ninety in full possession of his faculties, had owned a small engineering works which had specialized in making tin openers. The recession had almost put him out of business and the ring-pull revolution, particularly in the pet food industry, would have bankrupted him had he not had the vision to diversify into shackles, leg-irons and handcuffs for home use and export to select regimes abroad, and electric prods that were licensed to teach cattle a lesson but destined to burn smoother flesh as well. The company, Bannerman Aluminium & Steel (GB) had been sold, at a loss, on Norman's father's death so, as Zinnia had remarked, Norman was spared making any major Shavian or Ibsonian decisions about his inheritance. He was glad to be shot of the firm and his father's disappointment that it was never Bannerman & Son. He had hated working there in the holidays, fearing the sharp, ribald apprentices and the cynical, laconic foreman, but what a success his first television play *Pigs and Spigots* had been, set on the shop floor, with cradles and ladles of molten steel and dialogue that had jammed the switchboard with protests.

His mother was ninety-two and fit as a flea, although, with her bright eyes magnified by the spectacles clamped to her beak and fuzz of white hair, she looked, to Norman, like a fledgling in a flowered overall. He found her pegging washing on to the communal lines in the garden behind the flats. Her next-door neighbour Jack Bedwell, whose television could be heard shouting a racing commentary through his closed window, was holding a basket of wet clothes, which contained, to Norman's distaste, several items of his mother's underwear.

'Norman! What a lovely surprise! I hope this doesn't mean you won't be coming at Easter?' she added anxiously.

'No, Mother. I just felt like coming to see you. We'll all be there at Easter, three-line whip, eh?'

He knew that it was vital to the residents' prestige to have the family visit on the prescribed occasions.

'Zinnia's not with you today then, son?'

Maria looked hopefully down the path, through borders of forsythia at its yellow apotheosis, with the green about to take over.

'Sorry. I did ask her, but you know how it is with these famous actresses ...'

'We was just talking about you,' put in Jack, passing Maria a pair of bloomers. 'I was only saying to your mum, when's your Norman going to get the old BBC to put on some of his plays again? With all the old rubbish and repeats they have on nowadays, they can't be any worse than them, can they? You want to have a word. It's all cops and crime and hospitals, where's the entertainment in that? Get enough of that as it is, thank you very much. Old Elsie had 'er pension snatched last week, only a young kid, he was. I'd chop off their hands if it was up to me. I'd do it myself.'

'Shall we go in, Mother, if you've finished?' Norman took the plastic basket from the old man.

'Used to be a really pleasant area round here in the old days,' Jack went on. 'Now it's liquorice allsorts. Remember, Maria, when we had the old muffin man come round, and the milkman with his horse and cart and the cats' meat man ...'

'The cats' meat man!' exclaimed Maria, and the two old people stared mistily into the distance, as if the cats' meat man would descend from the clouds to save them all.

In his mother's flat Norman drank tea from a cup that tasted of bleach. The muffin man, he thought, that's pushing it a bit, and pictured a nursery-rhyme figure in striped stockings, with a bell and a tray round his neck, but he had to sympathize just a little with the old people, who felt like aliens in their childhood landscape, which had changed out of all recognition.

'When you live on your own,' his mother explained, not for the first time, when he complained of the taste of bleach in his cup, you can't afford to let things slide, you've got to keep everything up to scratch. Of course, Shirley, my home help, comes in, as you know, but she's from the criminal classes, bless her. One of those big families of the criminal aristocracy. I suppose, being brought up to prison and hospitals from an early age, it was natural that she should be drawn to disinfectant, even if she isn't as thorough as I'd like. She doesn't need to work, you know, her husband's got a shop off the market, specializes in reproduction antiques and chandeliers, all the genuine article. Shirley was a nursing auxiliary for a while and then she cleaned the police canteen, but that didn't suit her either. Her home's a little palace from what she tells me, a regular Aladdin's cave. More tea, son? A piece of cream cake? It's only just past its sell-by, Shirley got it for me.'

As Norman sipped and nodded, his alter ego, Larry Parnes blacked up for *The Jolson Story*, detached itself from his body and fell to its knees, clasping Maria round the waist in its white-gloved hands and burying its face in her flowered lap. Don't you know me, Mammy? I'm your little baby!

Norman departed uncomforted, leaving his mother in her few square feet of life, scouring the stainless-steel sink, keeping things up to scratch. Exhausted and irritable after the long journey home by tube and bus in the rush hour, he breathed the air of Ingram Road with relief, noting the song of a blackbird on a satellite dish and daffodils in the gardens. Maxine from next door was coaxing the little cat Mignonette down from the lowest branch of the plane tree.

'Beautiful evening,' said Norman. 'There's a real hint of spring in the air at last.'

'Yeah, I know. Everything coming into bud, and the blossom out.' Maxine patted the tree trunk, with the cat over her shoulder in its collar silvered with the glimmering early evening light.

'Dear old tree,' she said. 'I'm going to miss it.'

'What do you mean, miss it? You're not moving again already, are you?'

She was a pretty girl, her arms poignant in the sleeves of her boyfriend's pink polo shirt.

'Oh no. It's just our insurance company. They say it's got to come down. I'm really, really sad, because I'm very much a tree person, very into trees, but they won't insure us unless it comes down, because of the roots. In case they cause problems in the future. Ouch, Mignonette, you're scratching me. I'd better go in.'

She backed away, clutching the struggling cat.

'No, wait! You can't just land a bombshell like that and walk away!'

Norman grabbed her arm, the cat leaped away, and Joel appeared, with a can of Coke in his hand, saying, 'Everything all right, Maxie? Take your hand off her arm. What do you think you're doing? I'll have you for assault if you don't watch out.'

'Is it true, what she just said, about the tree?'

' 'Fraid so, mate. Shame, but there you go.'

'But you can't just do that! You can't just move in like vandals and chop down mature trees to suit yourselves. There are laws about that sort of thing. It's ridiculous. We'll see what the Council has to say about it. I'll get a preservation order if necessary.'

'Too late, mate. The Council has given its consent. It can't afford to take on the insurance company in the courts, so it's caved in under the threat of litigation. What's called market forces, old chap.'

'No, it isn't, it's called hooliganism!' said Norman. 'I don't believe I'm hearing this. Tell me I'm dreaming, somebody. Are you two aware that the paid thugs of cable television have destroyed the roots of thousands of trees all over London so that their pornography can be piped into the homes of people like you? Are you?'

'Let's go in, Joel,' said Maxine.

'Hang on.' Joel shrugged her off. 'Nobody talks to me like that. I've a good mind to kick his head in.'

'Just try it, punk.' Norman thrust a clenched fist under Joel's chin. 'Come on, I dare you.'

'Oh, leave him, Joel, he's not worth it. He's just a twisted old loony.'

'Old loony, am I?' Norman swung a punch, which Joel side-stepped.

'Zinnia!' Norman yelled, with tears of rage in his eyes, 'Zinnia! Where are you, you stupid cow? Come and give me a bit of support for once in your life, damn you!'

He turned back to Maxine and Joel.

'I thought you young people were all about saving the planet? What about the environment you're all so keen on? What about the Newbury bypass protesters, then? Young people, and old, risking life and limb to try to save those trees, living in tunnels, yes, and the opponents of the export of live veal calves who have laid down their very lives for their principles, and you stand there calmly telling me that you have arranged the murder of the oldest, noblest, most majestic tree in this street. Old Jim and Edith Bacon must be turning in their graves! You ought to be ashamed of yourselves. Is this the sort of world you want for your children? Don't you walk away from me! Come back here!'

Norman kicked their gate, hurting his foot on wrought iron.

'Goths and Visigoths! Barbarians! Veal-eating, Coke-swilling pigs, I hope you die of mad cow disease!' he shouted at their slammed front door.

Where the hell was Zinnia when he needed her? There was no note, no sign of any supper. Not knowing what to do with himself, Norman poured a glass of whisky and went into his study. He saw at once that the pages of his play had been disturbed, but he was in such turbulence himself, agitating his drink into a

whirlpool that spiralled out of the glass and splashed everything
in its radius, that the violation of his work scarcely registered. As
the confrontation replayed in his mind, he became aware of faces
watching it from neighbouring windows. He put down his glass
and went out again, to ring the doorbell of the Patels who lived
opposite.

After Norman had left the house that morning, Zinnia had not
known what to do with herself. She had worked hard all her life,
she had paid her dues. Surely she was entitled to enjoy what success she had without Norman spoiling everything and making a
nonsense of her life? Yes, she was a trouper. Was that something
to be mocked and sneered at? Why could he not just let her be,
without judging her every action like some sarcastic schoolmaster or a vicious director humiliating her in front of the rest of the
cast and making her forget her lines? She had a recurrent nightmare now, of being late for the theatre and running and running
along endless backstage corridors, through doors which opened
into surreal dressing rooms, until at last she stood on the stage in
tears, trying to force her voice through locked lips above the
babel of the audience. But no sound would come, and when she
looked down at herself, she was naked or dressed in a clown's costume. She remembered how Norman, on his way out, had asked,
'Anything in the post?'
    'Nothing to write home about,' she had replied, concealing the
letter inviting her to open the fête at their local hospice.
    At a loss, in the kitchen, she stared at the vermicelli of a
hydroponic hyacinth on the window-sill and saw that overnight
two strawberries left on a plate had bloated and their seeds turned
black like the bristles in a drunk's bruised red face. She drifted
into Norman's study with the feather duster still in her hand. The
heart of the Evil Empire, she thought. She was forbidden to touch
Norman's desk, but this morning, with the sun casting a tracery

of plane tree twigs and bobbles over the word processor, the
papers, books and writer's paraphernalia and toys, and glinting on
the gold pen Norman's dad had left him, the pen that Norman
had to use for all his 'real', his creative, work, Zinnia picked up
the manuscript of Norman's unfinished play, *The Last Sand Dance*.

Act I, Scene i. A seedy theatre somewhere in the provinces.
The stage is lightly sprinkled with sand. Enter stage left shuffling, two sad old vaudevilleans, male and female, in striped
blazers and flannels, bent stiffly at the waist and waving straw
boaters and clutching canes. Turning to the sparse audience of
comatose pensioners, *he* sings in a cracked cockney voice,
  '*When you wore a turnip,*
  A big yellow turnip,
  And I wore a big red nose . . .'
while *she* executes a grim little dance. Onstage costume
change . . .

Zinnia sank back into Norman's chair. Her legs were weak and
tingling, the little hairs on the back of her neck and arms standing on end. 'You bastard! How could you do this to us?' He had
dug up her dead parents and was killing them again with his pen.
She read on, clammy in her matelot top, the horripilant pages
trembling in her hand.

Onstage costume change. The straw boaters are sent whizzing
into the wings, and Egyptian robes and red fezes with black
tassels thrown unceremoniously on. The aged pair catch
them clumsily and struggle into them over their blazers, etc.
They break into a grotesque sand dance, à la Wilson, Keppel
(Kepple?) and Betty. Tot runs on, stage left, tripping cutely
over her too-long Egyptian robe, holding her fez on with one
hand and staggering under the weight of a giant papier-

mâché banana. Sings, 'I've Never Seen a Straight Banana' . . .

'Wakey, Wa-key!! Hey, you down there with the banana!'

At the disembodied voice of Billy Cotton, the trio cower and crouch like victims of an air raid as an enormous balloon with the spectacled features of the great bandleader floats down from the gods, and his signature tune blares out, Dah, dada dah dah dah, Somebody Stole My Gal . . .

Zinnia was shaking, and nauseous at the knowledge of her own innocent collaboration in this parading of her family to public scorn. It was she who had told Norman how the Two Herberts had been turned away from their audition for the *Billy Cotton Band Show* on the wireless and how it had broken The Two Herberts' hearts. 'Boater? What boater?' she heard her father's voice in memory, 'I thought you said put on your bloater!' He had a large fish on his head.

Her eye caught the glitter of Norman's fountain pen. The murder weapon. Although she could hardly bear to touch it, she picked it up, feeling the weight of its machine-turned gold in her hand. A pen bought with the proceeds from manufacturing instruments of torture. So that is what they mean by the banality of evil, she thought. Its agents are the jovial grandpa finding a sixpence behind a grandchild's ear, the benevolent boss with a pen clipped to his clean overall pocket as he jokes with his employees on the shop floor, the Rotarian adding an afterthought to his speech at the charity dinner.

'Your play stinks, Norman,' she said aloud. 'It stinks to high heaven. The only place bad enough to stage it is the Pillory Theatre.'

Zinnia threw the pen to the floor and stamped on it, but it would not break. It rolled from her ballet pump, hard and inviolate. She tried to grind it into the carpet The cap came off, but still the pen was unharmed. She tried once more and failed, and then she picked up the shiny barrel. It was bleeding a little blue ink from the nib and had caught a piece of fluff, like a feather in a crossed beak. Zinnia opened the window and flung the pen and its cap as hard as she could. She heard them bounce off next door's dustbin. Then she telephoned her daughter.

'Nerissa, I have nourished a viper in my bosom.'

Much later that night the telephone rang again in Nerissa's house. Nerissa's husband picked it up.

'Stephen?' said Norman's voice. 'I don't suppose you have any idea of where my wife might be? She seems to have disappeared and I'm getting a bit worried. It isn't like her.'

'She's here, if it's any of your concern,' said Norman's step-son-in-law, and put down the phone.

A fortnight or so after Easter, Zinnia's taxi driver stopped his cab at the corner of Ingram Road.

'I can't get through. Seems to be some sort of disturbance going on down there, or an accident. Looks like they've got the emergency services out.'

'Oh, I do hope it isn't anything dreadful. Can you wait for me here then? I'll be as quick as I can, I've just got to pick up a few things. Oh dear, there seem to be lots of people and the police!'

It flashed through her mind that Norman had killed himself, but reassuring herself that he was not Norman Maine, she hurried on. She could see spinning blue lights, flashing amber, yellow machinery, a heavy digger slewed across the road, a television camera crew, a banner strung across the street, a crowd holding hands around the trunk of the plane tree. They spilled over the pavement and into the road, shouting and singing 'We shall not be moved'. Zinnia stopped and looked up into the branches of the tree. There were huge black and white birds, vultures, huddled there, and she realized that they were boys from St Joseph's. At the top of the plane tree, as high as he could climb, stood Norman, arms outstretched, straddling two boughs.

His face, patterned by sun and shadows, was radiant, as if he was in his element, the air, at last, or he was an ancient tree deity returned to redeem the world of men. Below him, his people waved broken branches and twigs and sang hosannas. Tears were streaming down Zinnia's face. Everybody was there, all the neighbours, the Patels, the Smiths, the Peacocks, the Patterson-Dixes who spoke only Esperanto, Joel scuffling with somebody, that family of Exclusive Brethren who never spoke to anybody, and now, unbelievably, the boys were hauling old Father Coyle up in a hoist, with his skinny black silk ankles poking out like sticks and everybody cheering him.

A television reporter had made it almost up to Norman, who shouted down into the furry boom they called a dead rat, 'We are the people of Ingram Road, and we had not spoken yet, until today! But now we have found our voice, and we are saying, for all the world to hear, "Hands off our tree!" This is the will of the people and the people will be heard! The plane tree shall not fall!'

The wind ruffled his hair and billowed his white shirt, cleansing him of old familial shame and failure and recent guilts. He could hear, lower down, the buzzing of a saw, a policeman shouting, and he was aware of the boys scrambling and swinging from the branches like monkeys in their black blazers. As he heard the quavering benediction of Father Coyle through the swaying bunches of twigs, withered fruits and new baby growth, it came to him that all he had needed, all along, was an audience to make him whole again. Far beneath his triumphant feet, Old Seedy was cut to pieces by the teeth of the saw and sent flying in fragments of dry dead wood.

The crowd was swelling with the red-blazered girls of the comprehensive and latterday punks and hippies and eco-warriors with their dogs. Norman heard faint chimes of an ice-cream van over the din, and he almost lost his grip and his footing as he thought he saw Zinnia's distinctive tiny scarlet-tipped head above her foreshortened daffodil-yellow jacket, ducking into a black cab parked at the corner. It happened so quickly, and she was lost to sight so fast, in the blink of an eye, in the whisk of the tail of a rat leaping aboard a ship bound for the Gulf of Izmir before the tide turned.

The Late Wasp

'Well, we've got a super day for it, Darren.'

'Yes, sir,' replied Cheeseman miserably.

They set off across the asphalt to run the gauntlet of the classroom windows. Mr Glenn with his rucksack, a huge orange edifice bristling with buckles and straps, inherited from his father, bouncing on his back, and Cheeseman with a Tesco carrier bag trying to hide itself against his leg.

As they passed the sixth form common-room a girl, lying languorously half out of the window, called to someone inside.

'Glenda's wearing shorts.'

Her friend appeared beside her to watch Mr Glenn stride past on white legs that might have survived a fusillade of paprika, his peppery beard at a defiant angle.

'The saddest story ever told.'

She drew deeply on a sweet cigarette and passed across a crumpled paper bag of rhubarb and custards, striped pink and yellow lozenges, provoking memories of school puddings of yesteryear before the canteen was turned into a cafeteria. The girls were due to leave school in a few days and, overcome by nostalgia for their youth, were feeding it on childish sweets and reducing the insides of their mouths to exquisitely agonizing sponges with bittersweet crystals and shards of sugar. Such was their hyperaesthesia that a shoe bag on a peg or a first-year child with name-tapes on the outsides of its socks could reduce them to tears despite, or because of, the poignant knowledge that soon all this would mean nothing to them. The common-room ashtrays were spangled heaps of glossy wrappers, lollipop sticks, spent cartridges of sherbet fountains.

'Where are they going?'

'Why are we here? Where do we come from? Where are we going?' replied her friend closing the window.

Mr Glenn and Darren Cheeseman were setting off on a Ramble on the Downs. As they crossed the tennis courts a low volley – 'Cheesey's wearing a Harrington' – smacked into the back of Darren's head.

'He can't be' – struck his ear as he turned.

'Why not?' – thud.

'Nobody wears Harringtons any more' – caught him full in the face.

Mr Glenn seemed unaware of this rally which had left dull red marks on Darren's face under his glasses, or of the rude sign which he made behind his back. He was staring, as Darren was now, at the glittering coaches, parked at the gates, into which Mrs Nihill, French, was counting with a clipboard the rest of the second year, girls in short vivid skirts, boys and girls with hair spiked into crests and cockades with school soap, like an officious florist bundling heaps of dahlias into a refrigerated vehicle, for export to Boulogne. On the steps of the second coach Bob Drumbell, PE, rested for a moment, his brutish hand on the sparkling Bermudas of Hannah Guilfoyle, History, as she climbed aboard.

'It's not fair,' thought Cheeseman.

'It's not fair,' thought Mr Glenn.

If it was anybody's fault that they were standing, in silence, together at the bus stop that was the starting point of their outing, it was Cheeseman's. A form had been issued to each child in the second year proposing a day of Educational Visits and giving a choice of four: Boulogne, Brighton, Bodiam Castle at varying prices, and a Ramble on the Downs, free. Everybody except Darren Cheeseman, a new boy who had failed to settle, had signed up for the trip to Boulogne.

'It's quite encouraging, isn't it, that little Cheeseman has opted for the ramble?' Mr Glenn, Geography, a new boy himself, had said in the staff-room. 'Perhaps at last we've hit on something that interests him.'

Mrs Nihill snorted. She prided herself on her work on the pastoral side.

'I very much doubt if that's the case. Lives in two rooms with his dad on the Belmont Estate – Mum's done a bunk, Dad's out of work ...' she boasted, giving a Gallic shrug and brushing a crumb of Ryvita from her Crimplene knee. *Quelle* know-all. No doubt already in her imagination she was heaving her haunches round the *hypermarché* behind a heaped trolley. At her accusation of greenness Mr Glenn felt his face turn red and buried it in his World Wildlife Fund mug. When he raised it he realized that he had been elected in a silent ballot to accompany Cheeseman to the Downs. Hannah Guilfoyle, far from showing disappointment that he would not be going to Boulogne, had laughed at his plight. In fact, it was probably she who had proposed him.

Cheeseman, alone in the library at lunchtime, spotted his approach from the window.

'Darren, if it's a question of money ... I'm sure something could be arranged – the school has a fund ...'

'What money? Look, sir,' he pointed to a picture in the book he was reading. 'Did you know that the chalk blue butterfly is occasionally found in albino form? Do you think we'll see one on our ramble?'

As the library door closed behind Mr Glenn, Cheeseman

pulled out a comic from beneath the book and resumed reading: 'Dear Cathy and Claire, Please help me. Although I am only thirteen my . . .'

'Here comes the bus,' Mr Glenn was able to say at last. He paid the fares and followed Darren to the back seat. At each stop ancients mounted slowly with their shopping bags. If buses travelled by bus, Mr Glenn reflected, this one would take ten minutes to heave its wheels up the steps, turn to greet its cronies, have a joke with the driver, then fumble in a pocket somewhere in its metal side for its senior citizens' bus pass. Mr Glenn glanced round; apart from Darren he was the youngest passenger by some forty years. So old and yet they all seemed to have so much still to say. He wondered why the driver did not turn round and roar, 'Silence!' and was disturbed by an image of a playground full of grey- and white-haired children leap-frogging and kicking footballs and turning skipping ropes.

He was shamed into moving his rucksack from the luggage space to make room for two shopping trolleys, beldams in faded tartan, which lurched together as the bus, meeting another in the narrow lane, had to reverse with a great scraping of twigs on the windows; and the two green gaffers hooted at each other as they passed.

It was as he was sitting down again that he saw someone enter the bus without paying his fare; elegant, narrow-waisted in black and yellow stripes. He came in by the window, and it might cost him his life. He sat unnoticed on the glass. Mr Glenn squirmed. He saw himself rise and lunge down the aisle on his freckled legs, scoop up the wasp in his handkerchief and flap it out of the window. His face grew red, his bare skin sweated on the prickly seat, as he braced himself for ridicule.

'Wasps are early this year,' he heard.

'I had two in my kitchen yesterday.'

The wasp moved tantalizingly to the rim of the window. 'Now,' said Mr Glenn to himself. 'Quickly. Don't be such a great wet, Glenn, just get up and do it. You know you should.' He willed it to crawl over the edge into the air. It sat and he sat. Beside him Cheeseman was rustling about in his carrier bag. He pulled out a can and ripped it open; a few sticky drops fell on to Mr Glenn's thigh.

'Want a drink, sir?'

'No,' said Mr Glenn sharply. 'Put it away.'

The wasp zoomed down the zone of the scent. A flat cap snatched from a head whipped it to the floor, a blunt toe squelched it. The early wasp was the late wasp. Mr Glenn stared out of the window trying to think that it did not matter that something beautiful was broken; that something which should have been alive was dead.

The bus rumbled on like an old tuneless Wurlitzer while the driver gave a virtuoso demonstration of its revs and groans and wheezes at every bend and hill. So that when Mr Glenn and Cheeseman at last disengaged themselves and the rucksack, they stood on the grass verge with slight headaches, stunned by silence as the bus's green backside wobbled away in a cloud of heat haze and exhaust.

'This way, I think. Over the level crossing and up that field and then on to the hills.'

Mr Glenn looked up at the exposed surface of chalk. He saw it as a bride and the path that led up to it as her glittering train. He didn't offer this conceit to Cheeseman as he followed him on to the level crossing. On either side of them the flashing rails raced away into the past or future. Glenn stood with a sense of being no one and nowhere, stranded in eternity on the wooden island.

'Come on, sir!'

'Yes, yes. Thank you, Darren.' He stumbled gratefully on to the path where thistle-heads flared among the glittering dust and stones.

'You feeling okay?'

'Yes, I'm fine, thanks. I just felt a bit funny there for a moment – I didn't have time for any breakfast – I was a bit late getting up.'

He felt his rucksack, which contained his lunch and a copy of *Cities of The Plain*, Part I, pat him encouragingly on the back for almost achieving a conversation. He looked round for something to say to consolidate his success.

'Look,' he cried, pointing into the blue. 'That bird – isn't it a kawk or a hestrel – oh, dear, you've missed it.'

'Which do you think it was, sir?'

'I'm not sure. Definitely some sort of bird of prey. I expect you'd have been able to identify it.'

Darren didn't respond to the flattery; he pulled a long piece of grass and stuck it in his mouth, chewed irritably, wrenched it out, threw it away and pulled another.

'Do you smoke, sir?' he spat.

'No, I don't. Why? And there's no need to call me "sir" today; after all we're here to enjoy ourselves.'

'Oh, really?'

Mr Glenn hoped he had misheard, but unease started to churn away again. They were now on a track evidently used by cows, balancing on the edges of deep ruts whose thick clods of dried mud crumbled like stale gingerbread under Mr Glenn's boots and pierced the soles and sides of Darren's plimsolls. Mr Glenn cleared his throat.

'Why don't you put your bag in my rucksack, then you'll have your hands free?'

'Sokay.'

'No, go on.'

Mr Glenn crouched down on the mud offering his buckles.

He squatted there until his knees cracked and sweat dripped into his eyes, feeling like a foolish frog on a dried-up river bed, fearing that Darren had sneaked away, or was going to kick him.

'Darren?'

At last he felt the straps being lifted and the carrier bag falling into the rucksack.

'Mind my thermos!'

As he straightened up he fell forward on his hands and knees. He brushed a bead of blood from his knee, which was jolly painful, a bit of grit must have got embedded, and looked at Darren for some concerned query. He saw him wipe a smirk from his mouth with the back of his hand. As schoolmaster he should have felt gratified to see a pupil taking literally that often-repeated command – 'and you can wipe that silly grin off your face!' As it was he decided to risk septicaemia rather than take out his first-aid kit.

Darren seemed inclined to lounge and flop on every fence post and tree stump.

'Is it much further, sir?'

'Is what much further?'

'This place where we're going to.'

'We're not going anywhere in particular. This is supposed to be a Ramble. We just ramble around and observe the wild life and flora . . .'

'Who's she?'

Mr Glenn, heaving a pedagogic sigh, exhaled panic and the knowledge that he would disappoint as he bowed his head to enter a green tunnel which led uphill through a little wood.

'A green thought in a green shade . . .' he said.

'No answer came the loud reply,' he added silently, holding a bramble to stop it from whipping across Darren's face, and having done this once, felt obliged to hold back every branch, bramble, briar, nettle that he encountered. Unspoken words jumbled about in his head like plastic fragments in a broken kaleidoscope. From time to time he cleared his throat. Suddenly Darren had to stop short to avoid falling over Mr Glenn's haunches, as he sank to his knees and seemed to be adoring something.

'Fly agaric,' he breathed, turning a face flushed with pleasure to the boy's.

Darren looked. A sort of half-eaten toadstool, curled up at the edges, red with white blotches.

'Is it poison?'

'Yes, it is. Very.'

'Deadly poison?'

'It could be. Don't kick it.'

'It was mouldy anyway. Do you think we'll find any Death Caps?'

'No.'

After a few more minutes' silent trudging Mr Glenn pointed to swags and garlands of green berries tinged with yellow looping the trees.

'Just imagine what it will be like in the autumn, the whole wood decked with necklaces of scarlet beads. This is white bryony, isn't it? I think it's black bryony that has the heart-shaped leaves ...'

'Are they poison?'

'Really Darren, anyone would think you intended to poison the whole school!'

He laughed uneasily when Darren did not reply and added quickly, 'Those black berries are dogwood. They used to make arrows from it in the olden days.'

'How could they make arrows from berries, sir?'

Mr Glenn sneaked a look at his watch. He reckoned lunch could be spun out for three-quarters of an hour, if he ate very slowly.

'Do you like them old-fashioned watches, sir? I've got a digital watch at home.'

'Really. What's that you've found? Something interesting?' he said eagerly.

'Looks like an old pair of tights. Wonder how they got there?'

'I haven't the faintest idea,' he blushed.

Darren was waving them about on the end of a stick.

'Funny place to leave a pair of tights.'

'Do throw them away and come along!'

Mr Glenn was anxious lest Darren root up something worse. Darren flung the tights into the air; they caught on a branch where they hung dangling – obscene and sinister empty legs.

'There's a little plateau just ahead where we can stop to have our lunch. I don't know about you, but I'm starving.'

'I found a corset in a car park once, in Croydon.'

'I say, a Roman snail!' Mr Glenn bent gratefully over this piece of wild life which sat obligingly in their path.

'Revolting.'

'Oh, I think he's rather magnificent.'

They stared at the moist granular body under the creamy swirls of shell, the glistening knobs on the ends of the horns, a tiny green leaf disappearing into its mouth.

'Revolting eating snails, I mean, I couldn't, could you, sir? I bet that's what they're doing now – eating snails and frogs' legs, and getting drunk, I bet, knocking back the old vino.'

Jealous venom frothed like garlic butter through Darren's teeth. He leaped at a liana hanging from an ancient honey-suckle.

'I bet Miss Guilfoyle enjoys a drink, don't you, sir? And Mr Dumbrell.'

He swung gibbering four inches from the ground, his glasses lewd blank discs of malice.

Mr Glenn's shorts crushed out a sharp scent of thyme as he sat down, the warm grass tickled his legs pleasantly. Behind them rose the chalk face, now more like a wedding cake with green icing than a bride and below them the valley: river, church spire, village and fields and beyond them the town.

'Magnificent view.'

'It's a bit, well, rural, innit?' said Darren critically.

'For goodness sake, Cheeseman. Mind where you put your feet – you're treading on a harebell. You wanted to come on this flaming ramble.'

He reached for his rucksack, his hands shaking with anger.

'Did I?'

When Darren had realized that no one else had signed on for the ramble, pride had not allowed him to admit that he did not want to go, or to apply to the school for financial help towards the trip to Boulogne on which he wanted passionately to go; it would have been pointless to ask his father for the money. He had intended not to turn up at school that morning and spend the day wandering round the town, eat his lunch in the rec, perhaps do a little shoplifting; but as ill-luck would have it, his father, on his way to buy cigarettes, had walked him to the bus stop and several of his classmates had been on the bus. So here he was stuck halfway up a hill with this berk in shorts bleating about harebells.

'I don't believe it. I do not believe it.' Mr Glenn was scrabbling in his rucksack; out came Proust, out came a thermos flask, out came a first-aid kit, out came Darren's carrier bag.

'I seem to have forgotten my lunch,' he had to admit at last, handing Darren his.

A forlorn tableau of bran rolls bulging with salad, yogurt, two apples, one red, one green, and a bar of chocolate floated before his eyes. He licked his chops as he watched Darren bite into an oblong of white bread. He unscrewed his thermos, and poured a stream of clear hot water into the cup; he had forgotten to put in the tea. After a few minutes he moved closer to Darren.

'That looks tasty.'

Darren pushed the bag towards him.

'May I? That's awfully kind. What's in them?'

'Those are ketchup, and those are ketchup and salad cream.'

'Super,' said Mr Glenn faintly. As he sank his teeth into the flaccid, oozing bread, he noticed a little blue dot of mould on the crust.

'Can I offer you a little hot water in exchange?' he asked hoping for another sandwich.

'S'all right, thanks, I've got some shandy,' said Darren and drank it. Mr Glenn watched him pour the last few drops on to the grass as he sipped his water.

Darren stood up. 'See you in a minute,' he said.

'Right. Don't get lost.'

Mr Glenn went in the opposite direction. When he returned Darren was not back. He stole a sandwich and lay back luxuriating in Darren's absence and watched a bee rummaging in a knapweed's rough purple wheel and took up his book to avoid the memory of a wasp.

The shadow of a cloud fell on his page; he looked up expecting to see white sails on the sea at Balbec and was surprised to find himself on grass not sand, and realized that Darren had not returned and jumped up and pushed his way through the wayfaring trees into which the boy had disappeared. Little tracks ran in all directions. He whirled like a demented humming top, seeing Darren lying at the bottom of a crevasse, then launched himself forward, fighting twigs and brambles. Suddenly he heard very faint music ahead and burst through the bushes, half expecting to come upon Pan or some satyr or faun piping in the glade.

Darren lay stretched at ease, his head against a white rock, his eyes closed, a corkscrew of smoke spiralling into the blue from a cigarette between the fingers of one languid hand, while the other beat time to the music of a tiny radio. Mr Glenn, calcified with rage, the frustrations of the morning whirling like furies in his brain, stood and stared. Then he tiptoed towards the erstwhile faun.

'I say!'

As he turned at the shout something heavy hurled itself at his shins and he felt a sharp pain in the seat of his shorts; he howled and danced clutching his torn shorts and rubbing his bruised, perhaps broken, legs. Two golden retrievers leaped round him barking, clawing his chest and arms, thrusting hard yellow heads into his face, while he flailed feebly at them and Darren sat laughing.

'Cindy! Bella! Down!'

With a last snap they writhed in a yellow heap at his feet. Two navy-blue figures in denim skirts and t-shirts were sliding down the chalk towards them.

'Do you know this man?' one demanded of Darren, who was fondling a dog.

'Madam, do you take me for a denizen of Gomorrah?' said Mr Glenn.

'I beg your pardon?' She bristled at a suspected insult.

'Do you know this man?' repeated her friend.

Mr Glenn waited for Darren to say, 'I've never seen him before in my life.'

'Tell her, Darren.'

At last Cheeseman looked up from tying the dog's ears in a bow on top of its head.

'He's my teacher,' he said. 'Mr Glenn. Whitcombe School.'

'Well, if you're sure ...'

'Funny sort of teacher, encouraging a child to smoke ...'

'Oh, that's the sort of thing they teach them at school these days, didn't you know? They're all Marxists and sociologists ...'

'We're on a nature ramble,' said Mr Glenn with dignity, backing away with his hand on his shorts. 'Come along, Darren. We're going to look for fossils.'

Darren was reluctant to leave the dogs.

'Who's a good boy then? Good dog! Aren't they nice dogs, sir?'

'Bitches,' corrected his teacher loudly.

'We had a dog once,' began Darren conversationally, 'but he had to . . .'

'Shut up, you little creep, and walk in front of me.'

'This looks a likely place,' he said stopping at the foot of a glossy glacier of chalk. 'Let's have a nose round here.' The chalk felt dry and silky under their feet. 'Don't go too high.'

'Found one!' shouted Darren at once.

'Let's have a look. No, I'm afraid not,' he had to add, reluctant to disappoint.

'What about this one then?' holding up an equally undistinguished lump of chalk.

'I don't think so. Have another look.'

Darren hurled his stone at the cliff face causing a small avalanche. Mr Glenn grubbed silently. Black clouds smudged the sun.

'I say, Darren! I think I've— Yes, it is – it's part of an ammonite!' He looked round. Some thirty feet above him, clinging to the stump of a scrubby bush, was Darren.

'Come down at once,' he croaked.

Darren turned and waved, then gripped again the bending stem; a stream of stones trickled from each foot. He scrabbled up a little higher resting one foot against the bush.

'Darren! Come down. It's dangerous! If you don't come down at once I'm putting you in Detention!'

Darren inched upwards.

'Right! You're in Detention!' His voice rose to a squeak. He felt his own feet tingle, his knees wobbled and he felt the ground sway as he looked upwards. He shook his head hard and the landscape righted itself. Darren had not moved. There was nothing above him to grasp.

'Are you stuck?'

Darren, crouched on the chalk face, was paralysed and dumb.

Glenn looked round wildly – the navy-blue ladies – anybody; only a useless black crow flapping wildly into a black bush high above.

'Hold on. I'm coming up—' he had to shout. Despite his stout socks and boots Mr Glenn suffered acutely if he had to stand on a chair to change a light bulb ... He set off on all fours up the scree, keeping his eyes fixed on white stones, with plants too shallow-rooted to grasp, his shirt stuck to his back, slowly, slowly, toe-holds crumbling under his boots. A fine drizzle glazed the chalk, little lumps slipped under his fingers.

'It's all a question of momentum,' he muttered. 'Just keep going forward, don't stop, don't look down.'

A little rock hit him on the forehead and then Darren hurtled past screaming. Glenn snatched at him and caught his sleeve; his fingers tightened on the bone in the skinny arm; he took his whole weight in one hand and pulled him up beside him, to hold him in so close an embrace that he saw a smudge of dried salad cream fringing his lip. Instinctively, he put up his hand to wipe his own mouth, lost his grip on the chalk and started to slide. Darren tried to pull him back but was dragged down himself. The radio fell from Darren's pocket and bounced down the stones. Teacher and pupil, a tangle of arms and legs, slithered, a grotesque terrified spider, after it. Glenn, catching a tuft of tough grass, dared look down; they were only ten feet from the ground. He guided Darren's fingers to a tiny ledge and placed his foot in a hollow. So they continued their unheroic descent.

At the foot Glenn sat down heavily on a heap of stones, his arms round his shuddering legs. Between his boots he saw the cracked blue case of Darren's radio; he picked it up; a battery rolled away.

'I'm afraid it's broken.'

Darren snatched it, then threw it down and stamped on it, grinding the plastic and blue and orange wires into the chalk.

'Don't matter,' he said. 'It's only a cheap old thing. I've gotta Walkman at home.'

'Like your digital watch,' thought Mr Glenn.

As they sat on the bus Mr Glenn, his knees still shaking, gloomily composed tomorrow's essay: 'A Ramble on the Downs', Darren Cheeseman, 2G.

'The best bit about the ramble was when I found a pair of old tights. Mr Glenn got bit on the bum by a dog, then I got stuck up a cliff and my radio got smashed. Then we went home. Tired but happy at the end of a perfect day.'

They stood on the drizzly pavement looking at each other, the two wets, chalk-stained, damp, grazed, bleeding in their ruined clothes.

'There's no point in going back to school now,' said Mr Glenn. 'We can make our separate ways home from here.'

Darren stared past him through his rainy glasses; Mr Glenn followed his gaze to the hill far away, a white cake iced in vicious green; bland, treacherous, impossibly high, but conquered. Suddenly Darren shot out an awkward fist and punched Mr Glenn lightly on the arm.

'See ya then, Glenda.'

Mr Glenn punched clumsily back.

'See ya, Cheesey.'

The Laughing Academy

After he had closed the door of his mother's flat for the last time McCloud took a taxi to Glasgow Airport to catch the shuttle back to London. The driver turned his head and said through the metal grille, 'I know you. You used to be that, ehh . . . ' he broke off, not just because he couldn't remember the name but because the burly blond man in the back had his head in his hands and was greeting like a wean, or a boxer who has just lost a fight and knows it was his last. He concentrated on getting through the rush-hour traffic but when a hold-up forced them to a crawl, a glance in the mirror showed that the blond curls were tarnished and the cashmere coat had seen better days. As the smell of whisky filtered through, he recognized his passenger as Vincent McCloud the singer.

Looks like the end of the road for you, pal, he thought. The end of the pier. Re-runs of ancient *Celebrity Squares*, and guesting on some fellow fallen star's *This Is Your Life*; he could see it all, the blazers and slacks and brave Dentu-Creme smiles and jokes about Bernard Delfont and the golf course, that only the old cronies in their ill-fitting toupees would get. Like veterans at the Cenotaph they were, their ranks a little thinner every year. That mandatory bit of business they all did, the bear-hugging, back-slapping, look-at-you-you-old-rascal, isn't-he-wonderful-ladies-and-gentlemen finger-pointing routine – as if the milked applause could drown the tinkle of coloured light bulbs popping one by one against the darkness and the desolate swishing of the sea. As the taxi driver pondered the intrinsic sadness of English showbiz, he thought he remembered that McCloud had been in some bother. Fiddling the taxman, if he minded right. They were all at it.

McCloud was trying not to remember. He'd stood at his mother's bed in the ward, slapping the long thick envelope whose contents brought information about a *Reader's Digest* Grand Prize Draw that her eyes were too dim to read.

'Made it, Ma! Top of the world! This is it, the big yin! A recording contract and an American tour!'

He didn't want to recall all those black and white movies they'd watched together on the television, the smiles and tears of two-bit hoofers and over-the-hill vaudevillians and burlesque queens who were told, 'You'll never play the Palace,' and did. His mother had thought he'd be another Kenneth McKellar.

'That's you, Jimmy.'

McCloud realized that the cab was standing at the airport and the driver was waiting to be paid. Old habits die hard, and McCloud was grateful that the man had failed to recognize him and had not proved to be of a philosophical bent. He gave him a handsome tip.

'Enjoy your flight!' the cabbie called out after him as McCloud went through the door carrying a heavy suitcase of his mother's things.

On his way to the plane McCloud bought a newspaper, a box of Edinburgh rock and a tartan tin of Soor Plooms, acidic boiled sweets which he used to buy in a paper poke when he was a boy. He felt like a tourist. There was nobody left in Scotland for him now.

'Do you mind?' said an indignant English voice.

It seemed he had barged into someone. He glowered. In his

heart he had been swinging his fist into the treacherous features of his former manager, Delves Winthrop, that nose divided into two fat garlic cloves at the tip and the chin with the dark dimple that the razor couldn't penetrate.

'Don't be bitter, Vinny,' Delves had counselled him on the telephone after the trial. 'That's showbiz – you win some, you lose some. Swings and roundabouts. And you know what they say, no publicity is bad publicity . . .'

In that, as in his management of McCloud's career, Delves had been wrong. The Sunday paper which had expressed interest in McCloud's story had gone cold on the idea, and his appearance on *Wogan* had been cancelled at the last minute. Box Office Poison. McCloud, branded more fool than knave, had narrowly escaped prison and bankruptcy, and had – the taxi driver's surmise had been correct – a guest appearance on a forgotten comedian's *This Is Your Life* to look forward to, and a one-night stand at the De La Warr Pavilion, Bexhill-on-Sea. The small amount of money he'd managed to hold on to was diminishing at a frightening rate.

While McCloud was homing through the gloaming to a flat with rusting green aluminium windows in a vast block in Streatham, Delves was soaking up the sun on the Costa del Crime with some bikinied floozie. McCloud hoped it would snow on them. Bitter? You bet Vinny was bitter. He sat on the plane contemplating the English seaside in February, his heart a rotting oyster marinated in brackish sea-water. Wormwood and gall, sloes, aloes, lemons were not as bitter. His teeth were set on edge as if by sour green plums. It came to him that Delves Winthrop owned a house on the south coast, not a million miles away from Bexhill.

At Heathrow he lit a cigarette, great for a singer's throat, and telephoned his former wife, Roberta. She was friendly enough at first, and then he lost it.

'Is either of the weans with you? I'd like a word.'

'The weans? What is this? Sorting out your mother's things, the perfect excuse to get legless and sentimental, eh, Vinny? I might have known you'd come back lapsing into the Doric. I'm glad *we* flew straight back after the funeral.'

'Is Catriona there, or Craig? Put them on, I've a right to speak to them. I'm their father, as far as I know.'

'Ach, away'n bile yer heid, Tammy Troot!' Roberta put the phone down.

Tongue like a rusty razor blade, she'd always had it, since they'd met when he'd been a Redcoat at Butlins in Ayr, and she a holiday-maker hanging round the shows, Frank Codona's fun fair it was, thinking herself in love with the greasy boy who worked the waltzer. The Billy Bigelow of Barassie. Well, at least he hadn't gone round to her house, as he'd half intended, the emissary from the Land O' Cakes standing on the door-step in a tartan scarf to match his breath, with sweeties for his twenty-seven- and twenty-eight-year-olds, the door opened by Roberta's husband. Of course he knew they'd left home years ago. He'd rung on the off-chance that one of them might be there. They'd always been closer to their mother.

McCloud let himself into his stale and dusty fourth-floor flat and found two messages waiting on his machine, the first from his daughter Catriona sending love, the second from Stacey, a young dancer he'd been seeing for the past six months.

'Hiya, darling, guess what? I got the job!!! Knew you'd be proud of me. Listen, babes, we leave on Wednesday so I've got masses to get ready. Oh, hope everything went okay and you're not feeling blue. You know I'd be with you if I could. Call you later. Love you.'

'Dazzle Them at Sea' the ad in the *Stage* had read. Royal Caribbean Cruises. He'd spoken to Stacey yesterday on the phone, just catching her before she trotted off to the audition at the Pineapple Studios in Covent Garden. He could tell from her voice, which sounded as if it were transmitted over miles of ocean by a ship's telephone, that in her heart she was already hoofing under sequinned tropical stars.

Her neon-red words hung in the air, then faded as grey silence drifted and extinguished them.

McCloud stowed the bag of his mother's things on top of the wardrobe, feeling guilty at leaving them there but knowing it would be some time before he could bear to look at them. There were objects in that bag he had known all his life, pieces that were older then he was. Desolation suffused him as he stood on the strip of rented carpet. With Mother gone, nobody would know who he really was ever again.

He found the copy of the *Stage* and read the ad again. Stacey had joined the company of Strong Female Dancers who Sing Well. McCloud could testify to her strength, he thought, but reserved judgement on the singing.

He sat in the living room with framed and unframed posters and playbills stacked against the wall, a glass of whisky in his hand, studying the Directory, the gallery of eccentrics like himself who lived on hope and disappointment: 'Look at me!' they begged. 'Let me entertain you!' Clowns, acrobats, stilt-wakers, magicians, belly-dancers, once-famous pop groups, one-hit wonders, reincarnated George Formbys still cleaning windows, fire-eaters, Hilarious Hypnotists, Glenn Millers swinging yet and the Dagenham Girl Pipers defying time. Then there were the Look-alikes, fated to impersonate the famous, and those whose tragedy lay in a true or imagined resemblance to somebody so faded or obscure that it was inconceivable that the most desperate supermarket manager or stag-night would dream of hiring them. McCloud read on, keeping at bay with little sips of whisky the thought that his own face would soon be grinning desperately there, until he came to the Apartments column.

'Sunny room in friendly Hastings house. Long or short stay. Full English breakfast, evening meal available. Owner in the profession.'

A sunny room in February? McCloud was tempted, although there were three weeks to go before his Bexhill booking. The lime-green fluorescent flyers piled on the table filled him with fear every time they caught his eye, and he worried that his accompanist was going to let him down. The last time he'd seen Joe Ogilvy in the Pizza Express in Dean Street, the boiled blue yolks of his eyes and red-threaded filaments in the whites had not inspired confidence. He could go down and case the joint, get a bit of sea air. He put the thought of Sherry Winthrop, Delves's crazy wife, out of his mind, and dialled the number.

However, as he drove down the following morning, crawling along in the old red Cavalier with a windscreen starred by sleet, and Melody Radio, the taxi-drivers' friend, buzzing through the faulty speaker, he imagined Delves's house, to which he had never been invited. Neither had anybody else as far as he knew. It was common knowledge, among those who knew Delves had a wife, that Sherry had been in the bin and she was never allowed to come to London or to be seen in public. She had been Delves's PA, but now he was ashamed of her. She was younger than Delves, of course, and had been quite lively once. In McCloud's mind's eye the Sussex house was tile-hung, its old bricks mellowed with lichen and moss, standing in a sheltered walled garden with a prospect of the sea, and grey-green branches of the southernwood which gave it its name half-hiding the stone toadstools either side of its five-barred gate.

If you listened to Melody Radio, you'd think that love were all, that the world was full of people falling in love and the sky raining cupid's little arrows. And McCloud liked gutsy songs sung from the heart by people who'd been through the mill, that made

you feel life was worth living despite everything. Take the rhine-
stone cowboy singing now, for example, he hadn't a hope in hell
of riding a horse in that star-spangled rodeo, but there he was
with his subway token and dollar in his shoe, bloody but
unbowed. Tragic if you thought about his future, but it cheered
you up, the song. It was not in McCloud's repertoire, he was
expected to wester home via the low road to Mairi's wedding and
his ain folk, but he sang along lustily.

His spirits lifted as he left London's suburbs behind. 'Seagull
House, Rock-A-Nore Road, Hastings'; the address had a carefree,
striped-candy, rock-a-bye, holiday look about it, and he felt almost
as if he were going on holiday with a painted tin spade and pail.
The memory of his mother, holding her dress bunched above her
bare knees, laughing and running back from the frill of foam at the
tide's edge, pulling him with her, was more bittersweet than
painful, and he resolved to remember only happy times. That was
the best he could do for her now. She had told him a poem about
fairies who 'live on crispy pancakes of yellow tide-foam', and he'd
tried to remember it for his own children, Catriona and Craig,
with their little legs, paddling in their wee stripy pants. Catriona
worked in a building society now, and had assured him that it had
been for the best, really, that she'd had to leave the Arts
Educational Trust when he couldn't find the fees. Craig hadn't
found his niche yet and was employed on a casual basis behind the
scenes at the National. Great kids, the pair of them. McCloud was
not ready yet to admit that whatever he had done as a father was
done for good or ill and he was now peripheral to their lives, and
the thought of his little girl out in the dark in a dangerous city was
too painful to dwell on. He was eager to hit the coast, and so
hungry that he could have eaten a pile of those crispy pancakes.

Sherry Winthrop stood at the lounge window of the 1930s bungalow, 'Southernwood'. Flanked by two tall dogs, in her

pale-green fluted nightdress with her short auburn hair, she might have been a figurine of the period. She was watching the sails of the model windmill on the lawn whirling and whirling in the icy wind, and old gnomes skulking under the shivering bushes. Beyond the front garden's high chain-link fence was a tangle of sloes and briars on a stretch of frostbitten cliff top, narrower every year as boulders of chalk broke off and fell, and beyond that, the sea. A hand on each Dobermann's head, she stood, her mind whirring as purposely as the windmill's sails in the crashing sound of the waves. At length, knowing that she must get dressed and take Duke and Prince for a run, she went to make a cup of coffee. The kitchen, modernized by previous owners and untouched since, was decorated and furnished in late-fifties Contemporary style. Sherry would have preferred to go back to bed and lose herself in the murder mystery she was reading but she felt guilty about the dogs' dull lives with her and would force herself for their sakes. Was she not afraid, living alone as she did, to read, late into the night, those gruesome accounts of the fates of solitary women? The dogs were her guards, although sometimes she imagined they might tire of their hostage and kill her, and sometimes she felt it would be almost a relief when the actual murderer turned up at last. There was never one around when you needed him, she had learned. Like plumbers. She just hoped that when he did show up he'd only drug the dogs, not hurt them, and it would be quick and the contents of her stomach not too embarrassing at the autopsy. Had Sherry cared to watch them, her husband's stack of videos would have shown her deeds done to women and children beyond her worst nightmares.

She was conscious of the thin skin of her ankles and her bare feet as she unlocked the back door and let the dogs into the garden. There was a freezer packed with shins and shanks and plastic bags of meat in the garage. Crime novels apart, Sherry was quite partial to stories about nobby people who were always cutting up the dogs' meat and visiting rectors with worn carpets in their studies, and American fiction where they drank orange juice and black coffee in kitchens with very white surfaces.

The time she had needed a murderer most was after she'd lost the baby in an early miscarriage. Delves hadn't wanted children anyway, so he didn't care, and she'd ended up in the bin. It had taken her years to get off the tranquillizers but she was all right now, just half-dead. Sometimes, for no reason, she'd get a peculiar smell in her nose, a sort of stale amyl-nitratey whiff, a sniff of sad, sour institutional air or a thick meaty odour that frightened her. She had woken with it this morning, a taint in the air that made her afraid to open her wardrobe lest she find it full of stained dressing gowns.

She would have done something about her life ages ago, if it hadn't been for the dogs. When Delves had brought them home as svelte one-year-olds, they had spied on her and reported her every movement to Delves on portable telephones hidden in their leather muzzles, but Delves had lost all interest in her long since and her relationship with Duke and Prince was much better. It was just that it would be impossible to leave with two great Dobermanns in tow, or towing her. Delves had no wish to remarry – why should he when there was always some girl stupid enough to give him what he wanted – and he said it was cheaper to keep her than divorce her.

There was nothing of the thirties figurine about her when, in boots and padded jacket, she crunched the gravel path past 'Spindrift', 'South Wind', 'Trade Winds', 'Kittiwakes' and 'Miramar', with Duke and Prince setting off the dogs in each bungalow in turn.

It was three o'clock when McCloud, having found a parking space, walked up the steep path, through wintry plants on either side and past a rockery where snowdrops bloomed among flints and shells, and rang the bell of Seagull House. It was tall, painted grey with white windows, a deeper grey door, bare wistaria stems, and a gull shrieking from one of the chimneys. He felt some trepidation now, wishing he'd checked into an anonymous B and B or a sleazy hotel with a scumbag who didn't know him from Adam behind the desk. His fears proved groundless. The ageing Phil Everly look-alike who opened the door showed no sign of recognition. Later, McCloud would learn that he was the remaining half of an Everly Brothers duo whose partner had died recently from AIDS, but for the present Phil simply showed him to a pleasant attic room and asked if he would be in for the evening meal. McCloud decided that he might as well. Left alone, looking out over the jumbled slate and tiled roofs, a few lighted windows and roosting gulls, he wondered what he was doing here. Then he unpacked and walked down to the front and ate a bag of chips in the cold wind among the fishing debris that littered the ground around the old, tall tarred net shops along the Stade. Not very far away, Sherry Winthrop was drifting round Superdrug with an empty basket to the muzak of 'The Girl From Ipanema', avoiding her reflection in the mirror behind the display of sunglasses.

The following day McCloud drove over to Bexhill. Bexhill Bexhill, so good they named it twice. McCloud sat nursing a cup of bitter tea in the cafeteria of the De La Warr Pavilion. He had opened the doors of the theatre and taken a quick look, at the rows of seats and the wooden stage, and his throat had constricted, his heart flung itself around in his tight chest and his skin crawled with fear. He had closed the doors quickly on the scene, shabby and terrifying in the February daylight. Then, like the fool he was, clammily he'd asked the woman in the box office how the tickets for the Vincent McCloud show were going.

'Oh, well it's early days yet. Everything's slow just now. Mind you, we were turning people away for Norman Wisdom, but that's different. Anyhow, we can usually rely on a few regulars who'll turn out for anything. Did you want to book some seats?' she concluded hopefully.

McCloud sat among the scattering of elderly tea-drinkers, his prospective audience if he were lucky, with 'Let's Call The Whole Thing Off' going through his head. The woman in the box office must have taken him for a loony. Maybe he was. Maybe that's where he was headed, the Funny Farm. He saw the inmates racing round a farmyard in big papier-mâché animal heads, butting each other mirthlessly and falling over waving their legs in the air. Or the Laughing Academy. He'd heard the bin called that too, a grander establishment obviously, and then he remembered reading of someone setting up a school for clowns. He pictured the Laughing Academy as a white classical building with columns, and saw its pupils sitting at rows of desks in a classroom with their red noses, all going 'Ha ha ha ha, ho ho ho' like those sinister mechanical clowns at fun fairs. He cursed Delves Winthrop for all the bookings not made, the poor publicity, the wasted opportunities, the wonky contracts, the criminally negligent financial management, and he cursed himself for not having broken away while his voice and his hair were still golden.

He thought about Norman Wisdom who travelled with his entourage in a forty-seater luxury coach, with a cardboard cutout of himself propped up in one of them, and he remembered the child, a mini-Norman look-alike in a 'gump suit' who followed Norman round the country with his parents, and speculated on their weird family life; father driving, mother stitching a new urchin cap for the boy's expanding head and the kid in the back working on his dimples, mentally rehearsing a comic pratfall; a star waiting to be born. The hell with it. He was down, but not out yet. McCloud finished his tea, stubbed out his cigarette and went out into the sea fog which had swirled up suddenly, and found a ticket on his windscreen. He had forgotten to pay and display.

When he had arrived he had been momentarily cheered by the De La Warr Pavilion, that Modernist gem rising above the shingle with its splendour damaged but not entirely gone, the white colonnade and the odd houses with their little domes and minarets and gardens and white painted wooden steps, but now he saw that Bexhill-on-Sea was a town without pity. He bought a bottle of whisky and drove back to Hastings.

Phil was in the hall of Seagull House talking to a woman with a little dog.

'Let me introduce you,' he said. 'Mr McCloud – Miss Bowser, and her schnauzer Towser. Miss Bowser has the flatlet on the first floor.'

Beatrix Bowser, a gaunt grizzled girl in her sixties with hair like a wind-bitten coastal shrub, wearing a skirt and jersey, held out a rough, shy hand.

'I did so enjoy hearing you sing that lovely old Tom Moore song on *Desert Island Discs* recently, Mr McCloud,' she said gruffly, and fled upstairs with the little grinning brindled chap at her heels.

'Is she in the profession?' asked McCloud, imagining a novelty act with Towser wearing a paper ruff and pierrot cap whizzing round the stage accompanied by Miss Bowser on the accordion.

'Retired schoolmistress. Classics. Beatrix is one of the old school. I'm sorry, should I have recognized you?'

'No,' McCloud said. 'I'm out for dinner, by the way.'

On the way to his room he took a glass from the bathroom, and he poured himself a shot and lay on his bed thinking about the grip of Stacey's strong dancer's legs.

*

The sea fog seeped through Southernwood's windows and the dogs were restless in the dank, chilly air, making Sherry uneasy with their pacing, clicking claws on the lino as she lay in bed reading.

'Settle down, you two!' she commanded. 'Come on, up on the bed with Mummy!' She patted the old peach-coloured eider-down. As she did, the dogs hurled themselves towards the front door barking dementedly. Sherry froze in terror. The door bell rang. The dogs were going mad, leaping and battering the door. The murderer had come and she didn't want him. The bell sent another charge through her rigid body. Unable to move, to creep to the telephone, she sat upright, praying that the dogs would frighten him off.

A man's voice came through the door, distorted by the bark-ing. Sherry looked round wildly for a weapon, her mind lurching towards the back door, the garden fence and the flight through darkness to 'Spindrift', seeing herself beating on its door while its inhabitants, as she had done, cowered in fear, refusing to open. Feeling the hands round her throat.

'Vincent McCloud—' The voice was snapped off by the letter box and dogs' teeth.

Half-aware of feeling like someone in a film, Sherry slid her legs to the floor, and slipped on her dressing gown. The front door was unlocked and opened a crack. McCloud saw a bit of her face, a brass poker, two thrusting muzzles with the upper lip lifted over snarling teeth.

'I'm terribly sorry to disturb you. Can I come in a minute?'

'Friend!' said Sherry, keeping the dogs, who had no conception of the word, at bay with the poker. 'Lie down!'

Slavering, they sank growling to the floor.

'Delves isn't here,' Sherry said. 'In fact he's hardly ever here. What do you want?'

'Oh – I was just passing.' McCloud attempted a disarming grin.

'Pull the other one,' said Sherry, tightening the belt of her dressing gown. 'If you're hoping to get at Delves by doing anything to me, forget it. I'm his least valued possession.'

'I wasn't, I swear. Look, the truth is, I had to be in Bexhill and I thought I'd look you up. And take a look at the Winthrop lifestyle, I must admit.'

'Well, now you've seen it. Bit different from what you expected, eh? The heart of the evil empire. You might have telephoned first.'

'And you'd have told me not to come. Look, here's my bona fides.' He took a lime-green flyer announcing his concert from his pocket.

Sherry studied it and handed it back without comment. She was beginning to experience an odd, long-forgotten sense of having the upper hand, and enjoying it.

'Do you want a drink?' she asked. 'Before you go. Another drink, perhaps I should say.'

They were sitting in the front room, Sherry with her feet tucked up under her on the sofa, and McCloud in a chair. A bottle of Cloudy Bay stood opened on the table, a rectangular slice of onyx on curlicued gilt legs. McCloud put out a tentative hand to Prince, who didn't bite it off.

'This is Delves's wine,' Sherry said. 'I don't often touch his precious cellar. It's too dangerous, living on your own. And it's horrible replacing it. I feel so guilty that I'm sure they think I'm an alkie, and if they think you really need the stuff, they just fling it at you without even a bit of coloured tissue round it. That blue tissue always makes me think of fireworks – light the blue touch paper and retire. Sorry, I'm rabbiting on. I'm not used to having anyone to talk to and I got a bit carried away.'

'It's nice to hear you talk. We never got a chance to get to know each other, did we?'

'No. But I never get the chance to know anybody. People round here keep themselves to themselves, well, I suppose I do too. I've sort of lost touch with my family. After I was ill, you know, after I – my baby – well, I think they were embarrassed, didn't know what to say to me. And they never liked Delves. Or vice versa.'

As Vincent clicked the table-lighter, an onyx ball, at a cigarette, Sherry was thinking that she might get in touch now. Suddenly she missed them dreadfully. McCloud was thinking how pretty she looked, now that the wine and the gas fire had flushed her pale face. He was thinking too that, if he drank any more, he wouldn't be able to drive. He'd had a good snort or two before setting out, as Sherry had noticed.

'May I?' He refilled their glasses.

'Do you want some stale nuts or crisps?'

'That would be nice. I am a bit hungry.'

'I could make you a sandwich. It will have to be Marmite.'

'My favourite,' said McCloud.

'Vincent,' she said, as he ate his sandwiches, 'are you on your own? I mean, is there anybody in your, you know, life?'

He shook his head. 'There was, a girl, a dancer. She was young enough to be my daughter. I don't know what she saw in me. Well, not much, evidently.'

Sherry's dislike of the glamorous nubile cavorter was appeased when Vincent added, 'A two-bit hoofer who'll never play the Palace.'

He found himself telling Sherry about his mother, and how he had deceived her about the recording contract.

'I wanted to make her happy. Or proud of me. I don't really know for whose sake I did it. Anyway, either she can see me and know the truth, or she can't.'

'She would just want you to be happy. And I bet she *was* proud of you.'

Vincent saw his young self against a painted backdrop of loch and mountains. 'Och, aye,' he said flatly. 'Look, Sherry, I ought to be going. After all, I got you out of bed.'

A deep blush overtook the rosy flush on her face. Motes of embarrassment swarmed in the air around them, settling on her dressing gown.

'You shouldn't really be driving. You must be over the limit.'

'Probably.'

'There is a spare room. Only we'd have to air some sheets. Everything gets really damp here. I think it's the sea. Everything rusts.' Including me, she thought, not knowing if she wanted him to make a move towards her. She knew she was lousy in bed. Delves had told her.

'May I really stay? Thank you. Please don't worry about the sheets, I'm sure I've slept in worse.'

'I could give you a hot-water bottle.'

'Real men don't use hot-water bottles. Have you got any music? The night's still young.'

He flicked through the few albums. Tape and CD had not arrived at Southernwood. He held out his arms. They danced awkwardly, to 'La Vie En Rose', watched by the dogs with Duke howling along to the song.

'They think we've gone mad,' said Sherry, invoking a memory of the bin, and remembering her own inadequacy. She broke away from Vincent and sat down abruptly.

'Look, Sherry, I don't know what upset you but I'm sorry.' He was disturbed by the feel of her body through the dressing gown and nightdress. She shivered at the loss of his body close to her.

'If you think I was trying to use you to get back at Delves, you're quite, quite wrong. This is nothing whatsoever to do with him.' He knelt beside her and took her hand. 'We'll leave it for tonight. Maybe we can go out somewhere tomorrow. Would you like that?'

Sherry nodded. Then remembered that she had started out calling the shots and said, 'We'll take the dogs to Camber and give them a good run over the sands. Okay?' she added a little uncertainly.

'Fine. And I'll take you out to lunch.'

He dismissed the thought of his dwindling bank balance, and realized he should call Seagull House, to let them know he hadn't done a runner or gone over a cliff.

Sometime later, lying wakefully with his cold hot-water bottle in sheets that smelled faintly mildewed, having refused a pair of Delves's damp pyjamas and wearing the tartan boxer shorts Stacey had given him – 'Tartan breath' was one of her names for him – he sensed his door opening slowly. Sherry. Two shapes leapt through the gloom and landed on the bed and made themselves comfortable either side of him.

'Thanks, boys. You're pals.'

He eased himself out and padded to Sherry's room. 'The dogs have taken over my bed,' he said, shutting the door behind him.

She was soft and warm as he took her in his arms, and inert. He kissed her gently and then harder when a fluttering response came from her lips.

'I don't do this . . .' she struggled to say.

'No. Only with me.'

'I've forgotten how. Rusty . . .' she was saying into his mouth, feeling herself to be as attractive as an old gate. She was warm and soft. His lips grazed breasts like little seashells just visible in the darkness. They made love gently. It was nothing like being in bed with Stacey, he thought, which sometimes felt more like an aerobics session than passion.

'I thought you'd forgotten how,' he teased her, and said, 'You are quite wonderful, and beautiful.'

After a late breakfast of toast and Marmite they drove to Camber. A pair of firecrests flashed past them, bright against dun tangles, as they climbed the path between prickly bushes to the dunes.

'Oh look, aren't they pretty!' said Sherry. Then she screamed. She saw a dead bird impaled on the thorns, and then another and another. All around them hundreds of little birds were stuck on the thorns, netted in the wire diamonds of a broken fence; grey-brown sodden masses of feathers glued and pinned to every bush.

'What's the matter?'

She was paralysed with horror. 'We've got to go back!'

'Why?'

'Can't you see them? Look! Everywhere. Songbirds. Trapped. Pierced with thorns. Please, please, we've got to get out of here!' She was crying, tugging his arm violently.

As he saw them it flashed through Vincent's mind that this was some horrible local custom perpetrated by the people who owned the closed pub they had passed and he felt that they were in an evil, barren place. Then he looked harder as the dogs came bounding back to find them.

'They're not birds, darling! Look! They're some sort of, of natural, vegetable phenomenon. Cast up by the sea perhaps, just bits of – matter, dead foliage or something.'

Sherry was not convinced. The shape and colour of them were so dead-birdlike. Vincent pulled one off a bush.

'See?'

It lay, disgusting, in his hand. She did see now that the matted hanks had never been birds, but still the place seemed the scene of a thousand crucifixions. She was trembling with the thorny impact of it. Vincent wrapped the two sides of his coat round her, pulling her tightly to his chest.

'"Come, rest in this bosom, my own stricken deer, Though the herd have fled from thee, thy home is still here."' Then he said, 'You're frozen. Come back to Seagull House with me. There are some kind people there, and then we can decide what we're going to do next.'

And there's a little dog, he realized, but decided to worry about that when they got there. They walked back past the shuttered chalets and beach shops to the car, Vincent trying not to think about the De La Warr Pavilion, shuddering at the image of himself on the stage, hanging on to the mike for support, belting out 'My Way'. '"Regrets, I've had a few …"' and a heckling voice shouting 'More than a few, mate!'

Maybe he would give the rest of the whisky to Phil or Miss Bowser. Sherry was suddenly reminded of an afternoon near Christmas some years ago when she had delivered presents to her sister's house. The three children had been sitting in a row on the sofa with a big bowl on the low table in front of them, threading popcorn on strings for the birds. Like children in a story book, except they were watching television. The picture of them made her happy.

A Mine of Serpents

Gerald found two burnt-out rockets in the front garden when he went to check that the dustmen had replaced the lids properly. Bonfire night went on for weeks nowadays, it seemed, with bangs like gunshots ricocheting off the pavements and fracturing the sky. Some of them probably were gunshots. Two of his tenants, Kathy and her little boy Stefan, came down the steps, going to school.

'Got all your fireworks for tonight, then?' Gerald accosted the boy, 'All your bangers and rockets, eh?'

'No, they're too dangerous. We're going to the organized display at Crystal Palace.'

'Too dangerous?! Organized display?! We used to *burn down* Crystal Palace every Guy Fawkes when *I* was a nipper!' Gerald was gratified by the kid's doubtful look at his mother.

'No, of course not,' she snapped. 'Mr Creedy was teasing you.'

'Why?' he heard as Stefan trotted along, skinny as a sparkler with his little plastic lunchbox, the wind billowing out his pink and green jacket like a spinnaker, or an air balloon that might take flight and drift over the rooftops. No such luck.

'Catherine wheels,' he shouted after them. 'Named for your mum. Saint Catherine!'

Kathy, with a K, hunched her shoulders in her thin jacket. Pleased with the history lessons he had given the child, Gerald disinfected the bins. His description of his young self as a nipper was apt: he and his twin Harold had been nippy as corgis, in their hand-knit cardigans; biting the legs of other children, up to sly dodges, smirking, ears pricked, Brylcreemed quiffs a-quiver as the cane swished innocent flinching flesh. The Creedy twins were not popular but their dyadic aspect gave them status; two-faced, double-dealing, duplicitous, two peas in a pod, they needed no one else. Maggoty peas, some said.

Now Gerald uprooted a painful thought of Harold, with a green weed that had dared to survive the first frost and flaunt itself from the drain. Harold, estranged and sulking, six doors away. No weeds were permitted on board *Bromley Villa*; Gerald ran a tight ship; if he didn't care for the cut of your jib . . . similarly, all was shipshape and Bristol fashion at *Bickley*, Harold's trim craft – the nautical analogies stop here; the twins had been drummed out of the Second South Norwood Sea Scouts, dismissed the Service with dishonour after several ship-mates had walked the plank off the coast of Bognor. Gerald's inquiry of little Stefan about fireworks had been routine malice; not so much as a damp squib would be allowed to violate the back lawn of *Bromley*, or, God forbid, fire to flicker anywhere near the garden shed.

On his way upstairs, Gerald passed the half-open door of Madame Alphonsine and glimpsed her laying out the Tarot. She waved a card in greeting; the Hanged Man as usual, he supposed. What a disaster her tenancy was, and yet he had been powerless to prevent it, putty, or molten wax, in her pudgy, baubled hand. One day a leaflet had come through his door, advising of her psychic expertise in palmistry and with the crystal ball. It gave, unaccountably, his address. The next day she had materialized and somehow become ensconced, with her scented candles and other noxious paraphernalia, in the vacant room which he had not yet advertised, and since then loonies had trooped in to have their gullible palms read and cross hers with silver, in addition to the folding money she charged for solving Problems of Love, Health and Finance, and casting out Evil Spirits. One confused supplicant had brought a sickly potted palm.

Gerald had sought the help of the Church to cast Madame Alphonsine out. Father O'Flynn, sitting in the Presbytery sucking broth through a straw, for a parishioner had socked him in the jaw, shook his head sadly. The Reverend Olwyn of Belvedere Road Reformed played him a tape of Doris Day singing 'Qué Será Será'.

'Ours is a Broad Church, Duckie . . .' she told him, striking a match on her cassock.

'Necessarily,' he replied, squeezing past her.

Tony, from Some Saints, popped round at Gerald's request and got a promise from Alphonsine to drop in at next Sunday's Wine and Bread Do, and some items for the Operation Steeple-chaser Car Boot, most of them highly unsuitable; and Mr Dearborn of The True Light of Beulah embraced her with a hearty 'Praise the Lord! Sister Alphonsine! Long time no see!'

'Yo, Reverend,' said Madame Alphonsine.

Gerald had given up.

Madame Alphonsine heard his master-key in the locks of the tenants who were out, and his footsteps going downstairs. She had heard, too, his conversation with Stefan. From her window she watched old Miseryguts pottering about in the garden shaking his fist at a mocking splash of pink stars against the cold blue sky; set off, no doubt, by some kiddies truanting from school, bless them. He had been like a bear with a sore head since his quarrel with his brother. The needle in the wax noddle was working nicely. She saw him unlock his precious shed and disappear inside.

Harold would not be the only absentee tonight; Gerald's two friends would be otherwise engaged. They missed the fireworks every year. By November the fifth they were right down at the bottom of their box, as still and cold to the touch as two abandoned ostrich eggs in a nest of straw. Percy and Bysshe were tortoises. As if they had copies of the Church's Calendar in their shells, they would rise again at Easter, symbolizing stones rolled away from the tomb, their dusty carapaces patterned like chocolate Easter eggs.

'Why do you call them Percy and Bysshe?' Gerald lived in hope of being asked.

'Because they're Shelley,' he would reply. The old jokes were the best. His had amused Harold for thirty years. To think they had fallen out at their time of life, and over their birthday cake. Each had accused the other of eating a crystallized violet before the candles had been lit. In fact, Gerald had eaten it, but he was damned if he was going to back down now. And neither, of course, would Harold. Well, let him eat cake until it came out of his silly, pointed ears. No, the ears weren't silly; Gerald rubbed his own; rather unusual design, that was all. Distinguished. Having checked that the tortoises' hibernating box was undisturbed, he locked the shed. A piercing pain shot down his leg. He cried out as something sharp stabbed the other leg. It was as if his trousers were peppered with burning shot. He danced from foot to foot, slapping and rubbing at himself. The pains vanished as suddenly as they had attacked, and he was left feeling shaken and foolish, incredulous that his skin was not pitted with tiny wounds.

He sat down in the kitchen, grateful that he *could* sit down; with a cup of tea and a bag of marshmallows. As he dunked, a little smile played over his lips while the faint pins-and-needles in his legs evoked happier Bonfire Nights of long ago: the time he and Harold had filled that girl's gumboots with Jumping Jacks, and didn't *she* jump, with her wellygogs going off like firecrackers. Actually, they hadn't – that had been a cherished fantasy – even the Creedy twins had not been so stupid and cruel, but he recalled the exhilarating smell of gunpowder in the air; waiting for Dad to come home to light the bonfire, rockets in milk bottles, Catherine wheels nailed to the fence, chucking bangers into the fire, cocoa and burning black and cindery roasted spuds, melting marshmallows on sticks, whose bubbles blistered your mouth; the clanging of ambulance bells and fire engines racing along the streets. Oh, the glamour of those firework names: Bengal matches, Roman candles, Mount Vesuvius, Silver Rain; the weeks of eyeing them in the corner shop, planning what to get; the thrill of pinching them from under old blind Mrs Hennessey's nose, (the shame of being frogmarched to the police station). But the most prized, the most wonderful of all, had been the Mine of Serpents. Magic and evil, the fat midnight-blue cylinder printed with red and yellow waited magnificently until last to explode its writhing gold and crimson snakes into the black sky.

Everything had changed, and for the worse. Homogenized and bland. Only yesterday, in the supermarket, he had seen hot towels like the kind you got in Indian restaurants; to be microwaved for use at garden barbecues. Lost in reverie, he consumed the pink and white pillows: Light the blue touchpaper and retire. Do not hold in the hand. Do not return to a firework once lit; every year somebody had returned to school scarred; one boy had never returned. Gerald ate until he felt like a bloated cushion, overstuffed with pallid foam rubber. The thought of the glorious time a spark from the Creedys' bonfire had ignited next-door's Giant Selection box failed to revive him, and he went to lie down. The pains in his legs started up, his head ached, he had cramps in his arms. If they didn't wear off, he'd have to go to the doctor. If Harold were here, he'd know what to do. He thought about Madame Alphonsine; she had brought trouble on his house. Why had she been guided to Bromley Villa by her crystal ball? He consoled himself with Percy and Bysshe, safe from frost, fire, thieves and predators, snug as two bugs. He wondered miserably if Harold would be eating hot dogs and candy-floss at Crystal Palace, or watching pyrotechnics on the Thames on his black and white telly to the sound of Handel's Firework Music, while Gerald lay dying.

At five o'clock he limped out to the surgery, passing Madame Alphonsine and a client in the hall.

'. . . a long robe?' the client was saying. 'Okay, and what did you say he'd be carrying? A scythe? Right, I'll watch out for him. Thanks, see you, then.'

Green vapour trailed in the sky, a crimson chrysanthemum showered its petals as he hobbled against the tide of people heading for Crystal Palace.

'Ten pence for the Guy?' two children begged him.

'Call that a Guy? You ought to be ashamed of yourselves!' Gerald kicked the black plastic sack that formed its body, bursting the balloon that was an apology for a head, and yelled as a burning needle skewered his foot.

He sat in the waiting room reading a poster: *Follow the Firework Code. Keep Pets Indoors.* His were. The doctor could find nothing wrong with him.

Gerald was feeling much better when he arrived home. The back door was wide open; he couldn't believe it. There was a fire in the middle of the lawn, Stefan was capering round it with a sparkler, like a demented elf with a fizzing wand; they were all out there, all the tenants. Madame Alphonsine was handing round cocoa. But most terrible, terrible, the shed door was swinging open on its hinges. He rushed out. His darlings were gone! Their box was gone. He ran to the fire, to tear it apart with his bare hands.

'Where are they, where are they, what have you done? Murderers! Murderers!' His voice rose in a harsh scream as they held him back.

'Where are who?'

'My tortoises! My boys ...'

'But you took them yourself! I saw you!' Kathy was shouting. 'In a wheelbarrow!'

Then he saw it all. Only one person would be spiteful enough to take the tortoises. Dear old Harold. With the spare key entrusted to him. The tortoises were safe. He looked across the back gardens. Puffs of smoke were coming from the garden of Bickley. Harold sending smoke signals. Signalling triumph. Ignoring the grinning Guy burning in a suit exactly like his best, Gerald grabbed the heavy blue and red and yellow shawl from Madame Alphonsine's head and flapped it above the flames; signalling a truce under the shooting stars and sea anemones and serpents that floated in the sky.

The New Year Boy

Every New Year's morning, when they were children, Monica and her brothers woke to find a present under their pillows, some pretty sweeties or a tiny toy or book. The New Year Boy had visited them in the night while they slept. Monica had believed that the New Year Boy, like Father Christmas, came to everybody's house, and it was not until later that she had realized that he had been conjured up by her Scottish grandmother. She saw him as a cherub or cupid or *putto*, the depiction of the baby New Year in a Victorian illustration or scrapbook; magical and rather mischievous, with his beribboned basket of gifts.

There was nothing from the New Year Boy now, of course – it would have been alarming if there had been – but when Monica woke on New Year's Day and groped for her glasses on the bedside table, she encountered her new diary. She held it in her hand, knowing it to be a jaunty little fellow in a red jacket, with a pencil at the ready like a neatly furled umbrella, or perhaps a sharp, slim, cheerful chap in a flat cap. She smelled the newness of the pristine white pages sandwiched between red covers. As she lay in her large bed, under the billowing quilt and embroidered throws, a big woman in red satin pyjamas, she was at the heart of a kaleidoscope; before she put on her glasses the room was a shifting jumble of colours; a glitter and clutter, dull gold of icons and gilded *putti* and baby angels who flew about the walls playing musical instruments. Rich dyes and designs of fabric and tapestry glowed in dark jewelled tones.

Sometimes at night, when the old house shifted, a string of a mandolin twanged, a balalaika throbbed a deep note in the darkness, a zither sighed, or the piano started from a doze with a loud crack of contracting wood. Monica taught the piano and the guitar, but she retained her childhood love for the harmonica. It had been love at first sight; the moment she had set eyes on that mouth organ in the music shop window, grinning through wooden teeth set in red tin lips, she had known it was her instrument, for it had her name on it – Harmonica. It could be cheery, it could be melancholy; its merriest jig had undertones of the blues. She could never pass an indigent old busker wheezing out 'Scotland The Brave' without flinging a coin into his cap. Every conceivable joke about her name had been made long ago.

When she opened the heavy curtains the moon still hung like a mistletoe berry in the grey hungover sky; to the east clouds were cold dirty cinders with flashes of unburnt silver foil and orange peel. She turned on the radio and came in on a dirgey Stabat Mater droning echoes of chilly stone in clouds of powdery incense. She switched it off, snatched up a harmonica and treated the people in the upstairs flat to a brisk rendition of 'A Guid New Year Tae Yin An' A' ', and tidied up the kitchen while her bath was running.

The New Year had been seen in with a few friends; Monica had served ginger wine and black bun sent from Scotland, cherry brandy and slivovitz in gold-rimmed glasses painted with fruit. On the last stroke of midnight a first-footer had lurched over the threshold. He was asleep on the sofa now. Monica had forgotten all about him, and the mouth organ and the clatter of dishes had failed to wake him. A first-footer should be dark, and this one had a mat, almost a mattress, of grey-white beard and hair, both wiry and soft like hanks of sheeps' wool caught on a fence. Paperchains susurrated gently in the snores that were drowned by the running of the bath taps, broke from their moorings of Sellotape on the ceiling and covered him in pastel coils. Peter, twice divorced, a piano shifter by trade, slept on, sprawled across the inadequate sofa, a huge man in a soft shirt like a Russian peasant's blouse and trousers still tucked into boots. His subconscious was telling him that it was safer to stay asleep because he would not remember if he had carried out his intention to propose to Monica.

Monica, who had been a widow for fifteen years, stood spoiled for choice in a bathroom full of scented soaps, talcs and bubbles. She had no children of her own. She was an Aunt. An Aunt decreed by her nephews and nieces and her pupils, she thought, to be the cleanest aunt in Christendom. Old students sent her photographs of their children, and sometimes the children themselves to teach. Several of her pupils had done well: 'taught by Monica Baker' did not have quite the cachet of 'studied with Nadia Boulanger', but there was her name in the potted biographies in the programme notes, and that gave her great pleasure. She had come upon one ex-student twanging out 'The Streets Of London' in the underground at Piccadilly Circus.

'You can do better than that, Michael,' she had said, and fined him ten pence, as was her custom, for sloppy practice. Monica adored her brother's children, loved introducing them, saying 'This is my nephew,' or 'These are my nieces,' presenting them like a bouquet of spring flowers. Her favourite niece had given her the diary and Monica thought of her now, as she stepped into fragrant bubbles, her dark hair that smelled so fresh, of sun and wind and faintly of the sea. She wondered if her own hair had had that perfume, when she was young, with her young husband. This morning she would walk in the park, as she did every New Year's Day, and remember him. He had died on the first day of the year, when the scent of hyacinths, so blue and pure and piercing, had filled this flat.

As she padded back to the bedroom in her robe to dress, she noticed for the first time how stale and nicotine-smelling was the air. She must open all the windows, especially in the sitting room, and fumigate the place before she went out. She had an engagement that afternoon, playing the piano at a New Year party at a nearby retirement home, although it was a mystery to her why previously sane people should exhibit, as a symptom of geriatric decline, a sudden desire to play bingo and sing songs from the Boer War. She would take along a harmonica and try them with a few riffs of Dylan and Donovan. There would be cake and paper cups of sherry. Last year, when pressed to imbibe the dark sweet liquid she had conceded with, 'Oh, just a thimbleful, thank you, I insist . . .'

The young Filipina nurse had looked bemused and disappeared, returning ten minutes later with a battered silver thimble, into which she solemnly dribbled three drops of sherry. This year Monica resolved to accept her paper cup with good grace and leave it undrunk on the top of the tone-deaf piano.

Dressed in magenta and mazarine blue, Monica strode in her green boots into the sitting room, and screamed. Peter jumped to his feet, smacked in the eye by a walking hangover. A black cigarette fell from his lips to the carpet. He ground it out with his boot. Monica stamped her foot in its green boot. He watched with dull interest; he had never seen anybody stamp her foot in rage before. Had he or hadn't he asked her to be his wife? He thought she might be a bit – colourful – to face first thing every morning. Her eyes were framed in harlequin rims.

'You're looking very – bright,' he said. 'Oh, I almost forgot, I brought you something last night. A New Year present, but I didn't get round to giving it to you.'

He fished in the pocket of his army-surplus greatcoat which was slumped in a corner, and pulled out an empty vodka bottle. He dropped it and it rolled away, a glass cossack hopelessly drunk on parade. He drew something from another pocket.

'Happy New Year.'

It was a broken blue hyacinth in a pot.

Monica snatched it, rushed over to the window, and flung it out. 'I'm going for a walk!'

Pausing only to slash a scarlet lipstick across her mouth, throw on a necklace of heavy amber and a viridian poncho, she dashed out of the front door. Peter lumbered after her, struggling into his coat.

'Something I said?' he panted. 'The hyacinth? I'll get you another . . .'

A drizzling rain was making the park very green. Monica stalked in tears past the bench in the bare pergola where she had intended to sit holding the hand of her husband's ghost. Peter pounded along beside her.

'Monica, wait! About last night, did I . . .?'

'Go away. Please. I need to be alone with my thoughts, I – I've got a professional engagement this afternoon.'

'A gig?'

'An engagement. I don't play gigs. I'm an artiste.'

Thirty years ago she had played a summer season at the Gaiety Theatre, Ayr, billed as the Nairn Nightingale, accompanying herself on the concertina, with the Jinty McShane Dancers, game old birds in tartan tutus, pirouetting behind her.

A squirrel watched them from a branch now.

'I'm sorry, I've nothing for you,' said Monica.

She remembered the warm gingerbread boys with melting icing buttons that she made for her pupils. As she spoke, an old black bicycle wobbled round the corner, a small boy at the pedals, and a panting father clutching the saddle from behind to steady him. They careered to an ungainly halt.

'Excuse me,' Peter said. He unwound the long scarf from the astonished and perspiring, but too puffed-out to resist, father's neck and looped it round the boy's waist, putting the two ends in the father's hands.

'Try it like this,' he said. 'It never fails.' They got the bike upright and Peter muttered in the father's ear, 'The trick is knowing when to let go.'

As father, bicycle and boy riding high and confident disappeared into a green blur, Monica had to wipe her glasses, both sides of the lenses, and as she replaced them she saw Peter's terrible mat of hair and beard spangled with silver drizzle, and perceived him in that second as a viable proposition. Perhaps ... she visualized a pair of shears – there was enough of it to stuff a cushion – and remembered an electric razor of her husband's that she had kept, an obsolete old Remington with twin heads of meshed steel. Peter, meanwhile, had found an irritating bit of walnut shell stuck in a tooth, and recalled that her books were double-parked on her shelves. There would be no room for his own.

'Peter ...'

He looked at her; a tough nut to crack, an obdurate Brazil, a tightly closed pistachio. He had had a narrow escape. 'I'll leave you to your thoughts,' he said, and left her on the path.

Later, at home that evening, regretting the cup of sherry to which she had succumbed at the elderly residents' party, Monica thought about the electric razor. Suppose she had taken it from its case and blown away a speck of hair, a tiny particle of him which she had; lost for ever. The old-fashioned radiator rumbled, the wind whimpered in the chimney, and a drift of soot pattered

on to the paper fan in the fireplace. She settled comfortably, a
magpie in a big glittery nest, with room to stretch her wings. She
reached for her diary and began entering her name and address
with faint anticipation. All those white pages, waiting to be
filled.

Pigs in Blankets

The Old Post Office Restaurant was usually closed on Mondays but today because Zac, its proprietor, had learned that 24 April was National Pigs in a Blanket Day, he had decided to open for a special dinner. His former partner in Lampreys, the gastropub they used to run in London, had sent him a hilarious e-card that morning. 'Oink oink,' it said.

'Look at this, Fee,' he said to his wife Fiona. 'We've got to celebrate!'

'But it's an American thing,' she objected. 'We're supposed to be traditionally English.'

'We can set new traditions. That's what it's all about,' he told her.

Zac, who was tall and broad-faced, with his belly beginning to overhang the belt of his jeans, and grey-blond curls peeking from his chef's coat and tumbling over his forehead, considered himself as English as roast beef, whereas Fee was a delicate hedgerow rose. Mabel, their youngest child, petal-skinned, with pollen-coloured curls and egg yolk plastering her face, sat on her mother's knee grabbing at the remains of breakfast on the table. The old adage, 'new house, new baby', had proved true in their case. Mabel had been born exactly nine months after they moved

into the Old Post Office. They had worried about their two
teenagers, Lola and Alfie, settling in, but they had palled up with
a group of local Goths whom they had met in the graveyard and
had adjusted remarkably quickly. They were at school in the
neighbouring town, dropped off by the mother who was doing the
school run that week. There was such a great sense of community
in the village, Zac and Fee found.

It was a customer at Lampreys, who had a holiday cottage in
the village, who alerted Zac to the post office's imminent closure,
and Zac and Fee had been first in the queue. They had not regretted for one moment leaving the frantic hubbub of Lampreys – the
chewing-gummed, vomity, urine-stained pavement outside, nor
the cigarette butts floating in rainwater in the ashtrays on the
patio. They had found a paradise of wild-river lampreys, elvers
and crayfish, and watercress floating on the fast-running water
above the bright gravel of the stream at the foot of the garden.

'I have never touched a leaf of watercress since we did the life
cycle of the liver fluke in biology at school,' said Fee. But she was
learning, and loved to tend her *potager* and gather flower petals
to sprinkle on salads and puddings, to crystallize in sugar or fry in
a delicate batter, and she hoped eventually to publish her most
successful recipes as *The Old Post Office Cookbook*. She wouldn't
be including the monk's hood sorbet – that had been a mistake,
although it was such a pretty colour. She hadn't actually known
that it was monk's hood until she had consulted Merry and
Pippin who ran The Old Pharmacy and Herbarium about the
lethargy and sickness which had overtaken her and the rash on
her hands. 'You have been very lucky that you only had a tiny
taste and that nobody ordered it,' they told her. 'That's monk's
hood, or wolf's bane and a most virulent poison.' They prescribed
a posset of frumenty, and in a few days she was as right as rain.

That was one of the good things about the village. Almost anything you might need was right on your door-step. Unlike some

commuter communities, this was a working village: there were kindly, weather-beaten Merry and Pippin, Jim and Jane making their stunning pottery at The Old Forge, which had supplied the restaurant, the Hendersons at The Old Village Stores and Deli, Timbo at The Old Smokehouse, Bill Wills-Tillet, purveyor of fine game, Barnaby at The Old Brewery – not to mention the outlying organic growers and breeders. And there was the Tesco Superstore less than an hour's drive away for everything else.

Zac propped the blackboard announcing the evening's Pigs in a Blanket celebration on the cobbles outside the restaurant. On either side of the door a bay-tree shaped like a peacock stood on its single leg in a square lead tub. There was nobody about, until a cat galloped up the middle of the road with something in its mouth. Zac hoped it was one of the gang of thrushes that had made off with the native *escargots* he had nurtured so carefully, to go with the new season's garlic. There were no reservations, it being a Monday, but Fee had rung a few chums, and besides, most people would pass the blackboard during the day. Some might even recognize the blackboard, because it had been salvaged from the village school before it had been converted into holiday apartments, although it was unlikely that any of them would come to the Old Post Office tonight. Merry and Pippin from The Old Pharmacy and Herbarium were off the guest list too. They were, as one would expect, tiresomely vegetarian, and besides, Zac didn't care for silver-haired women with wrinkled arms in matching polo shirts.

The opposition to the restaurant had faded away now; when they first opened there had been a few die-hards who stomped through the dining tables waving obsolete pension books and demanding postage stamps but their protest was short-lived and Zac wouldn't have known them now if they passed him in the street.

*

Fee was in the back garden, picking early elderflowers while Mabel played at the edge of a flower-bed. The baby toddled towards her holding something in her creamy fist.

'Yuk! Nasty! Not in your mouth, poppet! Give it to Mummy!'

She retrieved a skewer piercing the bodies of several slugs. It was one of Zac's 'slug kebabs' – a useful tip he'd heard on *Gardeners' Question Time*. Much greener than using pellets, and more fun to sneak out at night with a hot skewer.

It was bliss in the garden, all green and white, in the bittersweet scent of hawthorn and elderflower, with a bee creaking in the freckled bell of a foxglove. Beyond the garden, even more green and white, a sharp slice of acid yellow and the distant glitter of polythene on the horizon. Fee still marvelled at the peace sometimes. It was even quieter now than when they had first moved in; the ghastly church bells, which deafened them twice on Sundays and also on Thursday nights when the bell-ringers practised, had fallen silent, and the evil roosters next door, who once woke them at dawn, had gone the way of all fowl. When the cocks had started fighting, old Mr Dainty sold them to Zac, who dispatched them with vengeful glee. How piquant their coral combs had tasted, stuffed with minced chicken and saffron. Old Dainty had gone too now and his house was on the market. Fee picked up her trug of elderflowers, and Mabel, and went inside to wait for the delivery of Gloucester Old Spot chipolatas from Aunt Pettitoes Organic Piggery – 'Historic Breeds A Speciality'.

Later, when Lola and Alfie were back from school and had eaten their tea, the family were sitting at the zinc counter in the kitchen, swaddling baby sausages in blankets of streaky bacon. Mabel was in her high chair playing with a lump of dough; Fee had decided to enrobe some of the piggies in pastry.

'Look, Lola, aren't they cute? Just like babies in shawls. A row of little newborns in the maternity ward,' she said, holding out a baking tray to show her daughter, who growled.

Ella and Kellyanne, two of the part-time girls who helped in the kitchen and waited on the tables, were chopping, respectively, potatoes and feathery dill. Their long white aprons reached their ankles in the front, and at the back, exposed Kellyanne's long legs in denim shorts over black tights, and Ella's miniskirt and stumpy bare legs and Ugg-type boots. The bills of their white baseball caps rasped together as they leaned in to share a whispered joke. Alfie watched them hungrily through a curtain of dyed black hair. The girls lived in a row of what had once been tied cottages a mile or so outside the village and they cycled to and from the restaurant.

Normally, Zac would have served pigs in blankets with a special roast and devils on horseback, as he had at Christmas, but tonight, because he wanted the menu to be light and spring-like, a bit impromptu and insouciant, like himself, and because the pigs were to be the main event, he had decided on a Jersey potato salad as an accompaniment, with a frisson of wild garlic leaves, washed down with a splendid wheat beer provided by Barnaby at The Old Brewery. There would be a choice of puddings – elderflower parfait and a crème brûlée made with the pink tender stalks of new rhubarb. He was on his second tankard of wheat beer and his bonhomie glistened in his curly hair, rouged the cupid's bow of his lips and collected in the deep cleft of his chin. Outside, the birds sang in the April evening and Zac felt a rush of happiness. Here he was, surrounded by his family and loyal staff, and soon to be entertaining a bunch of convivial friends. This is the life, he thought. I'm like a pig in clover.

'"Fingers in Band-Aids", some folk call the ones in pastry,' he said. 'And in Germany they call them "pigs in nightgowns". Only in German of course.'

'Daddy's been silver-surfing again,' sneered Lola.

Zac reached across the counter to give his daughter a hug, and knocked her white baseball cap, which had been perched pointlessly on the back of her Goth hair, to the floor.

'Gerroff me! And you lot can shut up sniggering!' She glared at Alfie and Kellyanne and Ella.

Fee sighed. 'I'm off to give Mabel her bath. And I expect a better atmosphere in this kitchen when I come back.'

She took a swig from Zac's tankard as she passed. 'Mmm, this isn't bad. Pour us one, will you, love. I'll take it up with me.'

They opened at seven, and at eight o'clock the restaurant was still empty. There was a bell above the door, left over from the post office days, and it had not sounded once. Ella and Kellyanne had changed into their uniforms of black jeans and t-shirts and short white aprons, and were lounging about in the steamy kitchen, snacking on sizzling pigs in blankets. Zac went through the restaurant and into the street. He looked at the blackboard propped up on the cobbles. It was blank. It had been wiped clean. He couldn't believe it. He dragged the board between the tables waiting in their white cloths, sparkling with expectant glasses and silverware, into the kitchen and dumped it on the floor.

'Where are Lola and Alfie?' he demanded.

'Graveyard, I expect,' giggled Ella, through a mouthful of sausage and bacon.

'I expect a little respect from you, young lady! And you, Missy! Stuffing your faces like a couple of chavs!'

His face, crimson and beaded with sweat, loomed at them. They gaped in shock at this transformation. Then the restaurant bell clanged.

Zac blundered through, to find Merry and Pippin seating themselves at the best table.

'Hello, Zac', they said. 'We thought we'd treat ourselves tonight. What's the vegetarian option?'

Wordlessly, he backed away. It crossed his mind to serve them with some of the superfluous pigs in blankets and say that they were made from soya, but he returned, to plonk down a large dish of potato salad in front of them and a platter of assorted leaves.

'Enjoy your meal, ladies!'

'Yum yum,' said Pippin.

'Rather!' said Merry.

Back in the kitchen, Zac was ashamed of his outburst. He tried to explain to the girls that he'd shouted at them out of disappointment that nobody had come, after all their hard work, and that he felt hurt and let down by his friends. He was appalled that anybody would be so malevolent as to wipe his blackboard. Unspoken was his horrible idea that he knew who the culprits might be.

'Please don't go,' he pleaded. 'You know you're welcome to eat anything you like!'

'I've never been called a "chav" in my life', said Kellyanne, untying her apron. 'Come on, Ella. He can stuff his pigs in blankets.'

'Hope they choke him,' said Ella.

They heard Fee's footsteps on the stairs. She came into the kitchen holding her empty tankard, to hear Zac calling 'Mi casa es su casa' at the girls' departing bicycles.

'Did I miss something?' she asked warily, for she, unlike the girls, had seen the other side of Zac before.

She took in the trays of wizening sausages.

'Well,' she said brightly. 'I know what's for lunch tomorrow. And the day after . . .'

Pink Cigarettes

As the cab dawdled down Pimlico Road Simon slithered and fretted on the polished seat. The shops, which had so recently enchanted him with glimpses of turquoise and mother-of-pearl and chandeliers spouting jets of crystal lustres against dark glass, now threatened him with a recurrence of his old complaint, boredom. He looked neither to the left nor the right lest he see again a certain limbless torso, a gilded dodo or a headless stone lion holding out a truncated paw. Surely it would be kinder to put it out of its misery? He saw himself administering the *coup de grâce* with a mallet and sighed, and closed his eyes, but was too late to escape the sight of two Chelsea Pensioners lurking like windbitten unseasonal tulips among the grey graves of the Royal Hospital. He pulled off his red tie and stuffed it into his pocket. His misery was complete as they crossed the King's Road and he turned from the fortunates on the pavement in their pretty clothes to his own reflection in a small mirror; nobody, he feared, could call him yesterday's gardenia, more like yesterday's beefburger in a school blazer. He had been forced to leave the house in his uniform, and he had a cold. He had poisoned his ear with a cheap ear-ring and it throbbed with the taxi's motor.

He thought that this was the most unpleasant cab in which he

had ever ridden – a regular little home-from-home with a strip of
freshly hoovered carpet on the floor, a photograph, dangling from
the driver's mirror, of two cute kids daring him to violate the
Thank you for not smoking sign, and a nosegay of plastic flowers in
a little chrome vase exuding wafts of Harpic. He remembered
with envy a taxi ride he had once taken with his mother; she had
had no time to look out of the window or be bored. She had
replenished lipstick and mascara and combed her hair and then
she had taken from her bag a bottle of pungent pink liquid and
a tissue and rubbed the varnish from her nails, decided against
repainting them, and lit a cigarette, and when she had stubbed it
out on the discarded tissue, the ashtray had gone up in flames. It
had been lovely.

He was thrown forward when the cab braked suddenly as the
car in front pulled into a parking space.

'Woman driver!' said the cab driver.

'Or a transvestite,' said Simon.

The driver did not reply, but added ten pence to the clock after
he had stopped. Simon ran down the steps, hoping to avoid being
spotted by the housekeeper, who had taken an unaccountable dislike to the slender, blond amanuensis of the tenant of the
basement flat.

'Don't kiss me, I've got a cold,' he greeted the old poet who
opened the door. The cocktail cabinet was closed; that was
always a bad sign. He wondered if he dared risk opening it while
the old man was pottering about in the kitchen, dunking a sachet
of peppermint tea in a cup of boiling water.

'Simon?'

He lounged in the doorway wasting a winning smile on his
host.

'Would you like a tisane?'

'Wouldn't mind something a bit stronger . . .'

'There's some Earl Grey in that tin,' said the cruel old buzzard who was dressed today in shades of cream, with a natty pair of sugared almonds on his feet and a dandified swirl of clotted cream loosely knotted at his throat, and a circlet of gold-rimmed glass pinned with a milky ribbon to his wide lapel. Simon became conscious again of his own drab garb.

'Sorry about the clothes,' he said sulkily, 'my mother was around when I left so I . . .'

'I've told you before, dear boy, it doesn't matter in the least what you wear.'

Simon was not mollified. He watched him lower his accipitrine head appreciatively into the efflorescence from his cup, complacently ignoring as usual the risks Simon took on his behalf, and risks for what? He stared out of the window at a few thin early snowflakes melting on the black railings.

'Snow in the suburbs,' he said.

'I should hardly call this the suburbs.'

'It was a literary allusion.'

'Not a very apt one, as anyway it has stopped snowing. Now, are you going to have some tea, or shall we get straight down to work? We've got a lot to get through today.'

'*We*,' echoed Simon bitterly and sneezed.

'I expect that lake of yours is frozen this morning?' added the poet.

'Not quite.' Simon proffered a stained shoe.

'I've got an old pair of skates somewhere. I must disinter them for you.'

Simon, who thought that they were already on thin ice, drummed his nails on the windowpane. The scent that had intrigued him early in their acquaintance he knew now to be mothballs and it was coming strongly off the white suit.

'You're very edgy this morning. For goodness sake stop fidgeting and pour yourself some absinthe, as you insist on calling it.'

With three boyish bounds Simon was at the cocktail cabinet

smiling at himself in its mirrored back as he poured Pernod into a green glass. It was amazing how good he looked, when he had felt so ugly before. Was he really beautiful or was there a distortion in the glass, or did the poet's thinking him beautiful make him so? He could have stood for an indefinite length of time reflecting, sipping his drink, a cocktail Sobranie completing the picture, but the old man came into the room casting his image over the boy's. Simon turned gracefully from the waist.

'Got any pistachios, Vivian?'

'No.'

'You always used to buy me pistachios,' he whined.

'It would take my entire annual income, which, as you know, is not inexhaustible, to keep you in pistachio nuts, my dear. Now, to work.'

Simon gazed in despair at the round table under the window spilling the memorabilia of more than eighty years: diaries, khaki and sepia photographs, yellow reviews that broke at a touch, letters from hands all dead, all dead, with here and there a flattened spider or a fly's wing between the brittle pages, or the ghost of a flower staining the spectral ink, into boxes and files and pools of paper on the floor. Simon shuddered. His task was to help to put them into chronological order so that the poet might complete his memoirs, while the little gold clock that struck each quarter made it ever more unlikely that he would. He plunged his hand into a box and pulled out a photograph of a baby in a white frock riding on a crumpled knee, which, if it could be identified, would no doubt belong to someone very famous. He tried to smooth it with his hand.

'Do be careful, Simon! These things are very precious!'

'It's not my fault!' Simon burst out. 'I don't really know what I'm supposed to be looking for, and when I do manage to put anything in order, you snatch it away from me and mess it all up again!'

'What? Listen, Simon, I want to read something to you. Go and sit down. Have a cigarette. Are you old enough to smoke, by the way? There are some by your chair. Light one for me.'

Simon gloomed over the cigarettes, like pretty gold-tipped pastels in their black box, not knowing which to choose. He had expected tea at the Ritz and hock and seltzer at the Cadogan Hotel, and here he was day after day grubbing through musty old papers for a book that would never be finished, that no one would publish if it was finished, and that no one would read if it was published ...

'Of course, it never occurs to some people that some other people are going to fail all their O Levels,' he muttered.

'No, we didn't have O Levels when I was at school,' agreed Vivian. 'Listen, Simon, this will interest you ...' The words spilled like mothballs from his mouth and rolled around the room, '"and so I set foot for the first time on Andalusian soil, a song in my heart, a change of clothing in my knapsack, a few pesetas in my pocket, travelling light, for the youthful hopes and ideals that made up the rest of my baggage weighed but little" – you might at least pretend to be awake ...'

'I am. Please go on, that last bit was really poignant.'

'Oh, do you think so, Simon? I'm so glad. I rather hoped it was.

Simon selected a pink cigarette and, wondering if it was possible to pretend to be awake, fell fast asleep. He woke with a little cry as the cigarette blistered his fingers.

'I thought that would startle you,' chuckled the poet, 'you didn't expect that of me, did you?'

'I don't know ...'

What deed it had been, of valour or romance, he would never know, but his reply pleased the old man.

'Come on, I'll take you out for a drink, and then we'll have some lunch.'

*

Simon attracted some attention in his school blazer in the Coleherne.

'This is a really nice pub,' he told Vivian. 'Do you know, three people offered to buy me a drink while you were in the Gents?'

The poet stalked out, the black wings of his cloak flapping and smiting people, and Simon had to scramble up from the dark corner where he had been seated and follow him.

Much later, as he ran across the concourse at Victoria and lunged at the barrier, he collided with a friend of his mother, on her way to her husband's firm's annual dinner dance in a long dress and fur coat, a dab of Home Counties mud on her heels.

There was nobody in. That is to say, his parents were out. Simon made himself a sandwich and took it upstairs. His room was as he had left it: the exploded crisp bags, the used mugs and glasses, the empty can of Evo-Stik, the clothes and comics, records and cassettes on the floor untouched by human foot, for no one entered it but he. He looked out of the window, and the pond in the garden below, glittering dully in the light from the kitchen, provoked an image of himself curvetting round its brackish eight-een-inch perimeter on a pair of archaic silver skates. He shivered and pulled the curtain, vowing feebly once again to extricate himself as he flopped down on the bed. When he had met the poet, not expecting the acquaintance to last more than an after-noon, he had constructed grandiose lies about his antecedents and house and garden, and had sunk a lake in its rolling lawns. He became aware of the sound of lapping wavelets; somebody next door was taking a bath, and he felt loneliness and boredom wash over him.

It was boredom that had led to his first timid ring on the poet's bell. One afternoon, in Latin, deserting from the Gallic Wars and tired of the view from the window, the distant waterworks like a grey fairground where seagulls queued for rides on its melancholy roundabouts, he had taken from his desk a book; an anthology whose faded violet covers opened on names as mysterious as dried flowers pressed by an unknown hand. Walter Savage Landor, Thomas Lovell Beddoes and Lascelles Abercrombie, whom some wit, in memory or anticipation of school dinner, had altered to Brussels Applecrumble. Vivian Violett – Simon selected him as the purplest, and turned the pages to his poem.

'What's that you're reading, Simon?'

'It's only an old book I found in the lost property cupboard.' Simon lifted tear-drenched eyes to the spectacles of the master who had oozed silently to his side.

'Let me see. My goodness, Vivian Violett! That takes me back ...'

'Is he good, sir?'

'I think that this is, er, what's known as a good bad poem ...'

He wove mistily away, adjusting his headlights, shaking his head as if to dislodge the voices of nightingales from his ears.

'Is he dead, sir?' Simon called after him.

'Oh, undoubtedly, undoubtedly. Isn't everyone? You could check in Who's Who, I suppose.'

'You are a creep, Si,' whispered the girl sitting next to him, 'I got a detention for reading in class.'

'Of course,' said Simon.

'Poseur,' she hissed.

'Moi?'

Simon, for whom the word decadence was rivalled in beauty only by fin-de-siècle, found that, at the last count, Vivian Violett was alive and living in London.

The next day he climbed the steps of an immense baroque biscuit hung with perilous balconies and blobs of crumbling icing, to present himself in the role of young admirer. His disappointment at being redirected to the basement by a large weevil or house-keeper in an overall was tempered when Vivian Violett opened his door, an eminently poetic Kashmir shawl slung round his velvet shoulders, and scrutinized him through a gold-rimmed monocle clamped to the side of his beak and a cloud of smoke and some other exotic perfume. The poet was charmed by his guest.

'I do enjoy the company of young people,' he sighed, 'especially when they're as pretty as you ...'

Simon reclined on faded silk, fêted with goodies, not yet knowing that he was not only the only *young* person, but almost the *only* person to have crossed the threshold for many years.

'You must tell me all about yourself,' Vivian said, at once swooping and darting into his own past to peck out tarnished triumphs and ancient insults, shuffling names like dusty playing cards; a mechanical bird whose rusty key had been turned and who could not stop singing. From time to time he cocked his head politely at Simon's poor attempts, over a rising mound of pistachio shells, to attribute a little grandeur to himself before flying again at the bookcase to pull down some fluttering album of photographs or inscribed volume of verse to lay them at Simon's feet. It was then that the idea of Simon helping with the memoirs was born. A faint murmur about having to go to school was brushed aside like a moth.

'Nonsense, dear boy. You will learn so much more with me than those dullards could ever teach you. Besides, I have so little time ...'

Simon was struck with sadness; the figure dwindling to a skeleton in its embroidered shawl had been, by its own account, the prettiest boy in London. Already he had noticed in himself a tendency to grow a little older each year.

'You will come and see me again soon, won't you?' the poet pleaded.

'Very soon,' promised Simon over the ruins of a walnut cake.

'Such a pity one can't get Fuller's walnut cake any more,' mourned Vivian for the third time.

'Mmm,' agreed Simon again, without knowing in the least what he was talking about.

'I hope you don't find this too cloying, Simon,' resorting to a tiny ivory toothpick, a splinter of some long-departed elephant.

Simon was dribbling the last drops from his glass on to some crumbs on his plate and licking them off his finger; the effect was agreeable, like trifle,

'Do you know that poem of mine "Sops in Wine"? Of course you must, it's in the *Collected Works*,' – a volume which Simon had claimed to possess and which he had glimpsed only on a shelf of one of the tottering bookcases which lined the room – 'I'll say it to you.' And he laid back his lips like an old albino mule and brayed out the verse, sing-song in a spray of crumbs.

Simon reached for the decanter of madeira as if it might drown the sound of the last plausible train pulling out of Victoria, for he had not told his parents of his proposed visit. He need not have worried because when he telephoned home they had gone out.

That had been the first of his visits, and as he lay, weeks later, on his bed wondering how he could make the next one the last, toying with the idea of a severe illness, the telephone rang. He had difficulty at first in recognizing the voice of his best friend.

'Do you want to come round to my place?' he was asking.

'Okay, I'll be round in ten minutes.'

But as he was leaving the house the phone rang again.

'Oh Simon, I've just had such an unpleasant encounter with the housekeeper, complaints of playing my radio too loudly, accusations of blocking the drains with bubbles, I mean to say, have you ever heard of anything so ridiculous ... all lies of course, you know she wants to get me out, it's all a conspiracy with the landlord so that he can re-let at a grossly inflated price. Bubbles! What would you do with such people, Simon? I know what I'd do, you must come and see me tomorrow, Simon, I'm so upset and lonely and blue ...'

'I really can't. I've really got to go to school.'

'Well, have dinner with me then at least.'

'I haven't got the fare,' said Simon weakly, 'my building society account's all ...'

'Of course I shall give you some more money tomorrow, you should have reminded me.'

'I've got to go. The phone's ringing. I mean, there's someone at the door!'

On his way to school the following morning Simon was overtaken by his friend Paul.

'What happened to you last night? I thought you were coming round?'

'I was, only I got depressed ...'

'Old Leatherbarrow's been asking about you, you know. Why haven't you been at school? Are you ill or something? You don't look too good.'

Suddenly school was an impossible prospect.

'I don't think I'll come in today after all.'

'Well, what shall I tell him? He keeps on at me! He'll be phoning your parents soon!' Paul's voice rose among the traffic.

'That's all right, they're never in. Tell him I'm suffering from suspected hyperaesthesia. I'm waiting the results of tests. Don't worry, I'll sort it out.'

He turned and left Paul standing on the pavement exhaling clouds of worried steam.

'Simon, it was sweet of you to come!'

Simon was shocked to see him still in his dressing gown, albeit one of mauve silk with a dragon writhing up its back, and a pair of unglamorous old men's pyjamas. The flat smelled stale, like a hothouse where the orchids have rotted.

'Aren't you going to get dressed?' he asked disapprovingly, being young enough to think that if a person was old or ill it was because he wanted to be so.

'I will, now that you're here,' said Vivian meekly. 'I wasn't feeling very bright this morning.' His hand shook and a purple drop spilled to the carpet as he handed Simon a conical glass of *parfait amour*.

'Ah, meths,' said Simon, 'my favourite.'

'What are you grinning at?'

'Old Leatherbarrow. The St Lawrence Seaway ...' replied Simon enigmatically. The forced daffodils which he had brought on an earlier visit hung in dirty yellow tags of crêpe paper against a small grisaille.

'Why have you been so ratty lately?'

Have I? I'm so sorry, Simon, if I should have appeared to be ratty towards you, of all people, the person in the world to whom I should least like to be ratty when I am so grateful to have your friendship and your help. I suppose I have been worried. A thousand small unpleasantnesses with the housekeeper, and most of all about this ...' he waved a hand at the tower of papers on the table. '"Time's winged chariot ..." and Christmas ...'

'Christmas?' said Simon. 'Christmas is okay—' and stopped.

'I shall go and dress now. Can you amuse yourself for a few minutes? Then perhaps we could do a little work on the memoirs. Where did we leave them?'

'You had just enlisted in the 'nth Dragoons,' he said as Vivian disappeared into the bedroom. Simon entered with a drink as he was impaling a cravat with a nacreous pin.

'Ah, my little Ganymede,' said the poet, smiling palely, 'what should I do without you?'

*

It was raining when they set out that evening for the Indian restaurant round the corner.

'Oh dear, oh dear, where's my umbrella? Simon, haven't you got a hat?'

'Of course not.'

'We don't want you to catch another cold. You'd better wear this.' He placed a large soft fedora on Simon's head. 'Yes, it suits you very well.'

Simon smiled at himself in the glass. He wondered if Vivian minded that the hat looked so much better on him.

A fake blue Christmas tree had been set in the restaurant window and cast a bluish light on the heavy white tablecloth and imparted a spurious holiness to the bowls of spoons and the candle holder by staining them the rich deep blue of church glass. Two pink cigarettes were smoking themselves in the ash-tray. In an upstairs room across the street, behind a sheet looped across the window, an ayatollah or mullah was leading a congregation of men in prayer; their heads rose and fell. Simon felt suddenly the sharp happiness of knowing that, for a moment, he was perfectly happy. He smiled over his wine at Vivian. The old man gripped the handles of his blue spoon and fork.

'I don't think I can bear,' he said, 'to spend another Christmas alone in that flat.'

'But it's a lovely flat,' answered Simon inadequately, and then there was silence while the waiter brought the food.

'I can't face any more unpleasantness. Days and days of not seeing you ...'

'Mushroom bhaji?'

'No. No. You help yourself.'

Simon looked with embarrassment at his own heaped plate but was too hungry not to spear a surreptitious forkful and tried not to look as if he was chewing. He crumbled a poppadum while he tried to think of something to say.

'Do you know what I have been thinking?'

The poppadum turned to ashes in Simon's mouth.

'Why don't I spend Christmas with you?'

Simon choked on unimaginable horrors: carols round the telly, stockings suspended from a storage heater, a mournful quartet in paper hats silently pulling crackers, Vivian crushed like a leaf between his parents in bulky, quilted body-warmers, asking for *parfait amour* at the bar of the local; their sheer incomprehension . . .

'What do you think, Simon?'

When he could speak he muttered desperately, 'I'm not sure that you'd get on with my parents.'

'We have one thing in common anyway, so that's a good start.'

'They're really boring. We never do anything much. You'd be bored out of your mind.'

'I'm never bored when we're together. Besides a quiet family Christmas is just what I need, what I've missed all these years. We could do some work on the memoirs. I'm sure your parents would be interested. We could go for long walks, that would be very good for me, and you could introduce me to your friends. What do you say?'

'I—'

'It's a large house, as you've told me, so I shouldn't be in the way.'

Simon had to stop him before he actually begged. Maybe his train would crash tonight, maybe his parents would have run away . . .

'I think it's a great idea,' he said, raising his glass, 'I'll tell them tomorrow.'

Vivian had to apply his napkin to his eye. He reached for Simon's hand and pressed it, then fell with a sudden appetite on the cold food in the silvery blue dishes.

'I wonder where those skates have got to?' he mused. 'Must be in a box somewhere, on top of a bookcase or under the bed. Ring me tomorrow when you've spoken to your parents, won't you?'

He put Simon in a taxi, and he was driven away with a despairing flourish of the black fedora through the window.

Simon could not ring him the next day, which was Saturday, because of course he had not spoken to his parents. On Sunday he woke late from a nightmare of Pickwickian revelry on the garden pond to the realization that he had left the hat on the train. He went downstairs to find a message in his mother's hand on the pad by the telephone: 'Violet Somebody rang. Can you call her back?'

'They're delighted,' he told Vivian on the telephone, tenderly fingering the lump on his head where he had banged it on the wall. 'I can't talk now, but I'll come to see you tomorrow.'

He arrived hatless, sick with guilt, a dozen excuses fighting in his brain, clutching a paper cone of freezing violets, at Vivian's house. Before he could descend the steps the housekeeper flung open the front door.

'If you want to see Mr Violett, you're too late. They've taken him away.'

'What?'

'Last night. It seems he was climbing up on some steps to get something off the bookcase. Pulled the whole lot down on top of himself. There was an almighty crash, I dashed downstairs with my pass-key, in my nightie, but there was nothing I could do. It seems the actual cause of death was a blow to the head from an ice skate.'

A stout woman, wearing if not actual, then spiritual jodphurs, appeared on the step beside her. 'This is Mr Violett's great-niece. She's taken charge of everything.'

As Simon turned and ran he thought he heard the great-niece boom, 'Of course he was always a third-rater,' and the house-keeper reply, 'Oh, quite.'

He hailed a passing cab, and as he sat, still holding his violets, he saw that the windscreen carried the Christmas lights of Sloane Square in a little coloured wreath all the way to Eaton Square. 'There must be a good bad poem somewhere in that,' he said to himself.

'The headmaster would like to interview you, Simon, about your frequent absences.'

Simon knocked dully on the door, stuffing his handkerchief into his trouser pocket, his heart and thoughts miles away.

'Don't kiss me, I've got a cold,' he said, then saw in the mirror behind the astonished pedagogue the reflection of a red-eyed schoolboy in a blazer, whose crying had brought out spots on his nose, and as he pulled out his handkerchief again, saw a broken pink cigarette fall to the floor, and an irrecoverable past diminishing in the glass, when he had been Ganymede for a little while.

Pumpkin Soup

At four o'clock in the afternoon of Halloween Violet was sent to tie an enormous bunch of black and orange balloons to the gate.

'Make sure you tie them securely or they'll blow away!' said her stepmother, with a look which suggested she wished that the wind would lift the balloons and carry Violet, still clutching their strings, over the hills and far away. 'And don't trip over. I told you not to get dressed up so early. The party doesn't start till six.'

Suki watched Violet set off up the long drive, a small black figure in a witch's hat, dwarfed by the bobbing balloons. She went into the kitchen and began opening packets of chocolate cobweb cup-cakes and putting them on plates, and tipping orange skull-shaped snacks into bowls. Through the window she could see her husband Dan and their own two sturdy toddlers having fun on the Haunted House bouncy castle which had been delivered that morning. It quivered on the grass like an evil black jelly, battle-ments and turrets rippling in the wind that flung their shrieks of laughter, and the cawing of the rooks, into the ragged inky clouds.

Suki had not wanted Violet to come this weekend but Dan had insisted. It was his turn to have her, and Violet's mother, his first wife, had made other plans. Violet was an unrewarding child, pale with mauve shadows under her eyes. After Dan's divorce came through Suki had tried to bond with her, taking her shopping, giving her a makeover, teasing her about boys – but Violet, at ten years old, preferred to skulk in her room with her nose in some childish book of fairy tales or legends. On Violet's previous visit, Suki had given her a handful of party invitations to deliver in the village to which the family had moved recently.

'Walk past the first house you come to,' Suki had warned. 'It's called Woodbine Cottage. On no account put one through that door.'

'Woodbine Cottage?' said Violet.

'I know!' said Suki. 'How sad is that, calling your house after some olden-days cigarettes that my grandfather used to smoke?'

'It's another name for honeysuckle,' said Violet.

'Just go.'

'I'm on it,' said Violet.

Woodbine Cottage was where a Miss Greenwood lived. A mad old biddy, thought Suki, who had never actually spoken to the tall, elderly woman whom she had seen in her front garden with a cat, and waiting at the bus stop in the rain, as she drove past. Woodbine Cottage was picturesque enough, she had to admit, and especially in autumn with its berried honeysuckle and Virginia creeper flaming up the walls, but the garden was a riot of thorns, seed heads, pods and fungi. There were even those red toadstools with white spots that you only see in picture books.

Now, on Halloween, everything was under control, thought Suki. The house was decked with plastic phantasmagoria, broomsticks, bats, cobwebs and spiders, the fridge was stocked with black and orange vodka-laced jellies, all the other food was defrosting, the barbecue was set to go, the candles in the ceramic pumpkin lanterns were waiting to be lit, the fireworks were in place, and the boys' skeleton costumes and masks, and Dan's ghost outfit were laid out on their beds. The thought of her own silky plunge-neckline black dress, fish-net tights, red glittery shoes and Wicked Witch of the West's hat gave her a little thrill as she imagined slipping into them. The church clock struck the half-hour. There was time for a fragrant dip before she got changed. No thought of the end of summer, the division of darkness and light, or of Celtic or Christian festival, or of her stepdaughter Violet, troubled her as she sank into the bubbles with a glass of wine balanced on the edge of the bath.

The church clock was striking seven when Suki stood at the front door with Dan, sheeted like a ghost, and the two plump little skeletons who were her sons, welcoming their guests. Cars parked, music pounded, trees bowed in the wind.

'Where's Violet?' said Dan.

As he spoke, Suki's heart stopped.

A giant pumpkin was staggering up the path. She saw Violet's arms clutched round it, her skinny legs below, and above it, her face split in a jack o' lantern grin. Behind the pumpkin came a witch carrying a steaming cauldron, and stalking in the rear, a coal-black cat.

The points of their witch's hats clashed as Miss Greenwood, setting down the cauldron in the kitchen, said, 'I've brought a contribution – some of my special Halloween pumpkin soup.'

When Miss Greenwood lifted the lid and poured the aromatic liquid into the pumpkin shell, Suki saw it all. The duplicitous Violet had put an invitation through the door of Woodbine Cottage. And had been hob-nobbing with the old crone and her cat.

Yet there was something seductive about the soup. She couldn't resist a taste, a spoonful . . .

The next thing Suki knew was waking in darkness. She was somewhere cold and slippery, clinging to the floor of – a bouncy castle. It broke free from its moorings as she screamed. She slid from wall to wall, and then, suddenly in equilibrium, she peered out of a battlemented window. Above her shone the crescent moon; below, fields, rivers, houses, spires, minarets, mosques, lurched towards her and then retreated as the wind bore the castle up again. There were splinters of barbecued flesh between her teeth and a burnt-out sparkler in her hand. Slowly, slowly the castle drifted over little human habitations and began its descent.

Violet was the first to wake in the morning. She pulled back her curtains. The bouncy castle splodged like a melted jelly on the grass. Sticking out from it, were two bent, red pointy shoes. Then, first the toe of one shoe, then the other, tentatively uncurled. Violet hurtled down the stairs and over the grass, running towards the ruby slippers.

Radio Gannet

There were two sisters, Norma and Dolly, christened Dorothy, who lived in a seaside town. Norma and her husband, Eric, resided in a large detached house in Cliftonville Crescent, while Dolly's caravan was berthed at the Ocean View Mobile Home Park, on the wrong side of the tracks of the miniature steam railway. Norma and Dolly's elder brother, Walter, was the curator of the small Sponge Museum founded by their grandfather.

Eastcliff-on-Sea was a town divided. The prize-winning municipal gardens overlooked Sandy Bay where all the beach huts had been bought up by Londoners wanting traditional bucket-and-spade holidays, and as their offspring watched the Punch and Judy show while eating their organic ice cream, or played a sedate game of crazy golf, they could see the lights of the fun fair winking across the tracks, and hear the shouts of less privileged children on the rides and smell their burgers, doughnuts and candy-floss drifting on the breeze from the ramshackle plaza that was Ocean View.

Norma had five children and fourteen grandchildren, thus ensuring that she had somebody to worry about at any given moment. One particularly hot summer night, she lay awake fretting at the news that a giant asteroid was on course to hit the earth sometime in the future. She groped for her bedside radio and switched it on low so as not to disturb Eric. Her finger slipped on the dial and out of the radio came the squawk of a gull, followed by a voice singing 'All you hear is Radio Gannet, Radio gaga, Radio Gannet. Greetings, all you night owls, this is Radio Gannet taking you through the wee small hours with Joanne and The Streamliners and their ever-lovin' "Frankfurter Sandwiches".'

At the female DJ's voice, Norma sat bolt upright, hyperventilating. Over the music came the spluttering of fat in a pan, and a muffled expletive. It was the indisputable sound of her sister Dolly having a fry-up. 'Whatever happened to the good old British banger?' grumbled Dolly. 'Answers on a postcard, please.'

Norma sat transfixed, picturing Dolly at the Baby Belling with her tail of grey-blonde hair hanging over her dressing gown, slipshod in downtrodden espadrilles, in that terrible caravan with its tangle of dead plants in rotting macramé pot holders, Peruvian dream-catchers, etiolated things growing out of old margarine tubs, the encrusted saucers left out for hedgehogs by the door, the plastic gnomes bleached white by time. The budgie. The cat. The slugs.

She hadn't seen her sister since their father's funeral, when Dolly had grabbed the microphone from the vicar and launched into 'Wind Beneath My Wings'. Dolly was dressed in frayed denim, cowgirl boots and a kiss-me-quick cow-girl hat.

In the morning Norma dismissed the radio programme as a bad dream. She was taking a brace of grandchildren to buy their new school shoes for the autumn term. It was one of those days when people tell each other that 'it's not the heat, it's the *humidity*'. In the shoe-shop they were served by an apathetic girl with a film of sweat on her upper lip who showed little enthusiasm for measuring the children's feet, gazing ahead as if watching a procession of Odor-Eaters marching into eternity. Music played in the background; a common family was creating havoc with the Barbie and Star Wars trainers. Norma looked fondly at her grandchildren.

Their legs were the colour of downy, sun-kissed apricots in the sensible shoes she was insisting on. Suddenly, there it was again, the squawking gull, that idiotic jingle.

'This is Radio Gannet coming to you on – some kilohertz or other, I can never remember. Kilohertz – what's that in old money, anyway? I blame the boffins in Brussels, myself. This one's specially for you, all you metric martyrs out there: "Pennies From Heaven" – hang on, a road traffic report's just coming in. It's Mr Wilf Arnold ringing from the call box on the corner of Martello Street where a wheelie bin has overturned, shedding its load . . . '

As soon as she had paid for the shoes Norma hurried the children round to the Sponge Museum to consult her brother. Walter's nose had grown porous with the passing years; it was an occupational hazard.

'Great Uncle Walter, have you ever thought of making the museum a bit more interactive? You need a hands-on approach if you're going to compete in the modern world,' said Matilda.

'Yeah, like Sea World. With octopuses and killer whales and sharks. Everything in here's dead,' agreed Sam.

'There's far too much of this touchy-feely nonsense nowadays in my opinion,' said Walter. Norma nodded agreement, imagining herself in the wet embrace of an octopus.

'Go and improve your minds,' Walter told them. 'And if you behave yourselves, you can choose a souvenir from the shop. How about a nice packet of Grow-Your-Own Loofah seeds?'

When they had slouched away, sniggering, Norma told Walter what she'd heard, recounting how Dolly had signed off, saying, 'Keep those calls and e-mails coming, and as always, my thanks to Mr Tibbs, my producer.'

'Mr Tibbs? Isn't that her cat?' said Walter.

'Exactly. She's totally bonkers – remember the spectacle she made of herself at the funeral? *I* wouldn't have said that Daddy was the wind beneath Dolly's wings, would you, Walter?'

He considered. 'Well, he did sponsor her for that bungee jump off the pier, *and* he made her that fairy dress with glittery wings for her birthday.'

'It was *my* birthday,' said Norma.

'Yes, I'm afraid our father always indulged Dolly,' admitted Walter.

'Well, look where it's got him. I hardly think even Daddy would approve of her latest venture. We can only trust that nobody we know will tune into Radio Gannet.'

Walter's Rotarian connections and Norma's aspiration to serve as Eastcliff's Lady Mayoress hung unspoken between them.

'Radio Gannet, eh? How appropriate.'

Walter remembered a plump little fairy flitting about the table at a children's party, touching cakes and jellies with the silver star at the tip of her magic wand. Norma thought about her sister's three helpings of tiramisu at her youngest son's wedding. She'd turned that into a karaoke too. Then the sound that she and Walter had been half-listening out for, that of a display cabinet toppling, recalled them to the present.

'Where is this so-called radio station to be found?' asked Walter.

'Oh, at the wrong end of the dial. Where you get all those foreign and religious programmes.'

'But is she legal? I mean, do you think she's got a licence to broadcast? It could well be that our dear sister is a pirate, in which case something can be done to put a stop to her little game. Leave Dolly Daydream to me, Norma.'

It was time for a weather check at Radio Gannet. 'Let's see what Joey the weather girl has in store for us this afternoon. Over to you at the Weather Centre, Joey.'

The Weather Centre was the budgerigar's cage which hung in the open doorway with strips of seaweed trailing from its bars. Dry seaweed denoted a fine spell, while when it turned plump and moist, rain was in the offing.

'Pretty boy, pretty boy,' said Joey.

'Pretty dry – good news for all you holiday-makers, then. Uh oh,' Dolly stretched out to touch a ribbon of kelp and found it dripping. The caravan park was shrouded in grey drizzle. 'Joey says better pop the brolly in the old beach bag, just in case.'

Joey was popular with the listeners. A recent beak problem had brought sackloads of cuttle-fish and millet from well-wishers, many of them students. 'I'm only sending this ironically,' one of them had written. Dolly was flattered; she knew that students do everything ironically nowadays: watch kids' TV, eat Pot Noodles; they even iron their jeans ironically. She placed her 78 of 'Any Umberellas' on the turntable, put her feet up and reached for the biscuit barrel.

Dolly was truly happy, having found her niche at last in public service broadcasting. Her *Send a Pet to Lourdes* campaign was coming along nicely and the coffers were swelling with milk-bottle tops and unused Green Shield stamps; the jigsaw swapshop was up and running, and the day-care centre had asked her to put out an announcement that they had exceeded their quota of mul-ticoloured blankets. That *Unravel Your Unwanted Woollies and Make Something Useful* wheeze had been a triumph; the charity shops were full of its results. But fame, Dolly knew, came with a price. Like every celebrity, she had attracted a stalker. Hers had staring yellow eyes and a maniacal laugh. He tracked her through the plaza on pink webbed feet, he snatched ice lollies from her hand in the street, and chips from her polystyrene tray, tossing them aside if she hadn't put on enough vinegar. He brought a whole new meaning to 'take-away' food.

Radio Gannet went off the airwaves altogether when Dolly had to go down the shops; at other times listeners heard only the gentle snoring of the presenter and her producer Mr Tibbs.

*

'Coming up – six things to do on a rainy day in Eastcliff, but now it's paper and pencils at the ready, for *Dolly's Dish of the Day*. And it's a scrummy Jammie Dodger coffee cheesecake recipe sent in by Mrs Elsie Majors of Spindrift, Ocean View Plaza. For this, you'll need four tablespoons of Camp Coffee, a large tin of condensed milk, a handful of peanuts for the garnish, and a packet of Jammie Dodgers, crushed. And here's a Dolly Tip for crushing the biscuits: place them in a plastic bag, tie securely, and bash them with a rolling pin. If you haven't got a plastic bag handy, the foot cut off an old pair of tights will do just as well ...

'Thanking you kindly, Elsie,' she concluded. 'Your pipkin of Radio Gannet hedgerow jam is winging its way to you even as we speak.'

Or will be, as soon as Dolly has soaked the label off that jar of Spar Mixed Berry and replaced the lid with one of her crochet covers.

In Cliftonville Crescent Norma and Eric were listening in horror as the programme continued.

'This one's for all you asylum seekers out there – "They're Coming To Take Me Away Ha Ha". That ought to get the politically correct brigade's knickers in a twist. Which reminds me, don't forget to text your entries for the Radio Gannet Political Correctness Gone Mad competition. "Fly's in the sugar bowl, shoo fly shoo," she sang. '"Hey hey, skip to my loo ..."' and Radio Gannet went temporarily off the air.

'Dolly inhabits a parallel universe,' said Norma, scarlet with shame.

How it rained. Pennies from heaven. Stair rods. Cats and dogs. In the museum the sponges trembled and swelled in their glass cases, great sensitive blooms and castles and honeycombs saturated with the moisture in the air. Walter listened glumly to

'Seasons In The Sun' on Radio Gannet. He'd been in touch with the authorities. Yet, like the man in the song, the stars that he'd reached were just starfish on the beach. His only visitors had been a couple of Canadian tourists on the Heritage Trail. Apparently they'd been misled by something they'd picked up on their hotel radio and were expecting an exhibition of sponge cakes through the ages. From King Alfred to Mr Kipling.

Dolly's voice broke into his thoughts.

'Joey at the Weather Centre has handed me a severe weather warning. "How high's the water, Mamma? Six feet high and risin' . . ."'

Walter rushed out to check his sandbags.

That night a tremendous crash brought Norma and Eric leaping from their bed to the window. Norma had lain awake worrying about an asteroid hitting the earth. Now she was about to experience the collision of two worlds. Cresting a tsunami was her sister's caravan and then the whole parallel universe was deposited in Cliftonville Crescent. It was like a scene from a Stanley Spencer Resurrection: the entire population of Ocean View Mobile Home Park were struggling out of their caravans in their night clothes, clutching plastic bags doubtless filled with old Green Shield stamps and unwashed milk-bottle tops, and there was Dolly splashing through the debris with her producer Mr Tibbs, Joey the Weather Girl, and a herring gull perched on her head.

The Running of the Deer

As the pair of shire horses, harnessed together, dragged a tree trunk across the horizon, in the lull following the morning rush hour of commuter traffic, bicycles and school-run vehicles, Richmond Park settled back into its ancient aspect. Some of the oak trees, grown from medieval acorns, had been standing here long before the land was walled and made into a royal hunting park. The horses, silhouetted against a gauzy November sky which leached the colour from the trees and the birds and the airy globes of mistletoe in their branches, passed from sight and the landscape momentarily belonged to itself and its innumerable non-human population. That is, until the palest smudge of sun burned through the grey and, just as if a wet brush had touched the page of a child's magic painting book, faint tints appeared and deepened. At that moment, a lanky figure in a flapping black coat entered the park through the Richmond Gate and strode up Queens Road which stretched empty in front of him.

On either side of the road groups of fallow deer and red deer grazed in the bleached tussocks or lay in the bracken among fallen branches scattered like discarded antlers which, twisted, polished, bleached, decaying, provided homes and sustenance for their thousands of tiny residents. Ever alert, the deer raised their heads as the man passed but no sentinel gave the signal to run as he loped on, apparently not noticing them or the shrill squadron of ring-necked parakeets, flashing sudden vermilion and crimson and scarlet above his head, or the lumbering green kite which fell from the windless sky, almost garrotting him. He was grasping a heavy shopping bag, and from time to time he groaned aloud and swung the bag backwards, smiting himself across the shoulders. Either he was unaware of his bizarre behaviour, or he thought he was quite alone. But somebody was watching him, concealed in the wooded slope on his right-hand side.

There goes The Poet, she thought, flagellating himself like some medieval penitent. With a supermarket carrier bag. What could The Poet have done, she wondered, to deserve such self-punishment? Had he committed a horrible crime, leaving behind the body of some poor woman, was he just atoning for a night of dissipation, or was his anguish simply the outward expression of an internal artistic turmoil? Clare Carnevale, who was a freelance photographer working on a project of her own in the park – a pictorial diary of a year in its life – had observed this man several times and, struck by his dark and somewhat haggard looks, had decided that he must be a poet. Despite her practical appearance, professional waistcoat bristling with pockets, binoculars and cameras, Clare was of a romantic and archaic turn of mind, and now she pictured The Poet fleeing from a tableau which might have come from a Victorian painting, wherein an abandoned wife, or mistress, stood distraught in a tumble-down cottage, with wide-eyed hungry children clinging to her skirts.

Clare, a small, brown woman in her late thirties, lived alone by choice in a bijou residence near the river. The cottage had come down through the family from her great-grandmother, a doughty widow with seventeen children, who earned her living as a rat-catcher. It was damp and cluttered with her photographic

paraphernalia and books, the walls a jumble of sepia family portraits and her own work. She was happy there, occasionally
entertaining family and friends, turning a blind eye, out of ances-
tral guilt, to any rodents she came across indoors or in her little
garden. The things which gave her most pleasure in life were all
visual: she loved the dappled coats of the deer and the way they
fold and unfold their legs, the parakeets, and tiny brown birds
with dabs of red lacquer and slicks of yellow paint on crests and
wings, and the staccato gait of crows; she loved convoluted and
tortuous roots and branches which swept down to the ground in
sheltering needle-strewn caves, tree stumps vivid with emerald-
green starry moss, russet and tawny colours, and her heart beat
faster at the sight of scarlet berries, flaming leaves reflected in the
dark brimming water of the ponds, fly agarics, and the little jellified toadstools like sea anemones which she had found this
morning – and cherry blossom and cold spring flowers such as
primroses, wood anemones, violets and sheets of bluebells, and
cow parsley – each season took her by surprise yearly, as forgotten plants emerged again – and sometimes it was all too much
and she felt as if her heart would burst.

As she went about her business, though, she 'collected'
interesting-looking strangers, in the street and the supermarket
and the park, unknown to themselves, and gave them names, and
so she peopled her life with acquaintances, such as Mr Bojangles
the busker, the Mouse and his Child, a sad-faced father and his
little boy, Blanche Dubois, Reynard the fox, Woody woodpecker,
Whitey the albino blackbird, the Monarch of the Glen, a particularly magnificent stag with a chandelier of antlers – and more.
Clare loved them all at a distance and was always secretly
cheered by seeing them, but today, watching The Poet, she felt
uneasy. What was in that heavy shopping bag he was hitting himself with? Maybe he had weighted it, and filled his pockets, with
stones and was making his way to one of the ponds in the Isabella

Plantation to end it all. Perhaps he was heading, appropriately, for Gallows Pond.

Clare followed him at a distance, unsure of what she would do if he were to wade into the pond. Was it deep enough to drown a man? She imagined his heavy black coat absorbing the water and pulling him under; coots, moorhens, ducks and geese shrieking as she plunged in, mud gripping her legs and sucking her down, slimy roots lassoing her feet, the two of them splashing and wrestling in a desperate, ungainly, doomed struggle. If he *had* done some dark deed, might it not be kinder to let him make an end of it, or would that be robbing his victim and family of justice?

She was distracted from these thoughts by a creature, seemingly half tree, half man, who emerged from a thicket, his bulky dun-coloured clothes and hair and beard matted with burrs and curly fronds and twigs. This person was one of Clare's collection and she longed to photograph him, thinking that perhaps he was some elemental spirit or even the *genius loci* of the park, but she was daunted by his baleful glare. She called him Tammylan, after a character in the Enid Blyton books *The Children of Cherry Tree Farm* and *Willow Farm*. Not meeting his eyes, she hurried on, following The Poet's rakish progress. It occurred to her that Enid Blyton was perhaps more scholarly than she was given credit for, and had based Tammylan's name on that of the legendary Tam Lin who was captured by the Queen of Elfland. Tammylan was a wild man of the woods, who befriended four London children who had come to live on a farm. He was good and kindly, nut-brown and blue-eyed, a woodcarver and naturalist who knew all there was to know about the birds and animals who loved and trusted him. How many parents nowadays, though, would be happy to let their children roam the countryside with a man who lived in a cave with a curtain of bracken and heather across its entrance?

Clare had seen her Tammylan talking to the shire horses over the fence of their pasture, reaching up to offer first one of them and then the other something from one of the many bags which hung about him. The horses bowed their great heads over the fence and graciously accepted his gift. Clare, who had been told this fact by the Park Manager whom she had met when she was photographing some of the children's activities at the Holly Lodge Centre, knew that the horses were called Jed and Forté. Formerly dray horses, they had been retired from their work at the Bass and Burton's and Young's Breweries and had exchanged the traffic of the streets for the park, where they were now employed on forestry work. Clare loved Jed and Forté more than almost anybody here, or anywhere else. It was not just their size which made them seem noble; anachronistic in both equine and human terms, powerless over their own lives and yet symbolic of the dignity of labour down the ages, Jed and Forté stood four-square and totemic on their great hooves, stirring an inexplicable sense of loss in those who saw them.

More people were about now: joggers, the confederacy of dog walkers who met up every day, in their striped hats and scarves, as disparate in breed as their pets; a mother with a buggy talking on her mobile while ambling in the wake of a toddler, who was crouched down examining something he, or she – the child was so muffled up it was impossible to tell – had found on the path. Such a pity, Clare thought, that we have to lose that ability to live in each moment, our infant curiosity and wonder at the world; as a photographer, she had retained it to some extent, after all, her *raison d'être* was to capture and fix a unique minute, but she was always conscious of the passing of time.

Never more so than now, as she almost lost her target, who had struck out across the rusty bracken. Avoiding ant hills and a group of deer startled by a lone dog, she passed a pair of youngsters, heads linked by earpieces, whose school uniforms betrayed their truancy. Clare was, of course, on account of her age, invisible to them, and they almost bumped into her. One of the dog walkers – she recognized his red woolly hat – had left his dog with the group and was hurrying towards the dog-free zone. She realized that The Poet too was making for Pembroke Lodge, the magnificent Georgian mansion overlooking the Thames. Clare slackened her pace, feeling slightly foolish and also a little disappointed that there was to be no watery drama after all.

She could have a cup of coffee at the cafeteria and then head for home. Or she might wander on up to Poet's Corner, in the hope of seeing again a flock of waxwings marauding the beautiful spindle tree growing beside the Rustic Panel commemorating the eighteenth-century poet James Thomson, who was known as 'the poet of *The Seasons*'. Most of his work was forgotten now, except for *Rule Britannia*, whose words he was assumed to have written. Thomson was born in Scotland but came to live in Richmond, and was buried in the churchyard nearby.

Clare decided to climb King Henry's Mound, the highest point in the park, from where, on a clearer day than this, you could look across London to St Paul's Cathedral, and westwards to Windsor Castle. There was still a chance that she might encounter The Poet, although it seemed rather pointless now. He probably wasn't a poet at all, but the sort of person who looked at the deer and thought, 'Yum yum, venison!'

The sun had withdrawn, defeated. Clare was cold and her mood had soured. How she hated Henry VIII, and how typical of him to have a mound on top of a prehistoric burial ground. It had been said that he stood there to see a rocket fired from the Tower of London, to signify the execution of Anne Boleyn, but it was also claimed that he had been in Wiltshire at the time. A feeble alibi, if ever there was one. Clare walked round the perimeter of Pembroke Lodge behind a mother and daughter, arm-in-arm, who were casing the joint, picking their way over faded confetti mixed with leafy detritus, discussing whether it would be the right venue for a wedding reception two years hence.

'You have to picture it in summer,' said the mother, consulting a booklet, 'the laburnum walk and all the lovely irises – you could have your napkins themed to fit in with the flowers. Champagne on the terrace with superb views over Kingston and Ham!'

'A view of ham?' said the daughter, dully.

'Oh, how fascinating,' her mother went on, 'apparently the lodge used to be an old mole-catcher's cottage in the olden days, before it had a makeover. And Bertrand Russell lived here as an orphan.'

'Who?' said the daughter. 'I thought it was supposed to be the Countess of Pembroke? And what do you mean, "mole-*catcher*"? Don't you have to have them removed?'

'And turkeys nested in these very trees!' offered the mother, as if she were playing her trump card.

'Well, *that's* not very appropriate for a summer wedding – turkeys – is it?'

The mother sighed heavily, and they moved out of earshot.

Clare walked towards the Ian Dury Bench, placed there in memory of the musician, who had loved the park. She thought she would sit for a moment, despite the cold. This interactive bench was solar-powered and you could plug in your own headphones and listen to some of Ian Dury's songs and his appearance on *Desert Island Discs*. But as Clare approached, she saw that it was occupied by a woman sobbing under the plaque which read *Reasons To Be Cheerful*. She hovered awkwardly, but before she could speak, the woolly-hatted dog walker brushed past her and sat down. Clare, unnoticed, stepped aside.

She learned, through the broken words and the low hum of condolences, that the woman had been bereaved recently, that her dog Dylan had died, that she had made the decision to end his life, and that she could not be consoled.

'Jenny,' said the man, putting his arm round the weeping woman, 'you mustn't grieve so. Dylan will be waiting for you at Rainbow Bridge.'

'Rainbow Bridge?' said Jenny, lifting a face all swollen and smeared with anguish. 'What do you mean?'

Clare listened as he described gently the iridescent bridge twixt earth and the animal heaven where our departed pets live in happiness and harmony. 'There is just one thing missing, though, from their blissful afterlife – us!! But when we cross over Rainbow Bridge, up go the ears, the tails wag nineteen to the dozen, our beloveds leap into our arms, and we are reunited once more.'

Clare dissolved in tears. Why had nobody ever told her about Rainbow Bridge? There were pets who had been waiting decades for her to arrive. Would they all come running to greet her? What about the goldfish? And Great Grandmother Carnevale? Would she have been transmogrified into a pied piper in a bombazine dress, leading a troupe of smiling rats in haloes?

There were no waxwings in the spindle tree but its fruits trembled on their delicate stems in the wind which had sprung up, displaying their orange seeds in lobes of glowing pinkish red and lifting her spirits. She was standing by the Rustic Panel, which was shaped rather like a church lych-gate, reading the verse by John Heneage Jesse:

> Ye who from London's smoke and turmoil fly,
> To seek a purer air and brighter sky,
> Think of the Bard who dwelt in yonder dell
> Who sang so sweetly what he knew so well . . .

'Yes, but the poor old bard only lived to forty-eight!' said a voice behind her. 'Caught a fatal chill on a boating expedition.'

Clare turned. Standing there was The Poet – and Tammylan – both holding take-away cups of coffee.

'I think you know us both by sight,' The Poet said, holding out his hand. 'James Thomson, by coincidence. Fellow Scot and poet, by coincidence too. But no relation. And this is – oh well ...'

Tammylan was shuffling away.

The black coat was cashmere, she saw, and didn't, as she'd imagined, smell of mould. Nor was there a taint of stale wine on his breath. He was smiling. She was aware that her own face was pinched and puckered by the cold.

'Clare Carnevale.'

'I know – I've seen you. And your work. There's something I've been wanting to ask you ...'

'And I you! If you don't mind ... Why were you groaning and beating yourself with your shopping bag this morning? Have you— I mean, is something terribly wrong?'

'Was I?' He sounded surprised, glancing down at his bag. 'No idea – just the usual morning failure and remorse, I suppose. Or worrying about school fees – I've got a boy at White Lodge, the Royal Ballet School.'

'Oh.'

'Maybe I was thinking about work – that's what I want to talk to you about. You see, I've got this idea, to do a kind of *Seasons*, like my namesake – though I suppose his *Castle of Indolence* is more appropriate in my case – sort of documenting a year in the park, the management, the flora and fauna, symbiosis, all that stuff – and I thought some illustrations might help. I wondered if you'd be interested in collaborating. Me doing the words, you the pictures ...'

'Me doing the pictures, you the words,' she almost echoed him. 'I—'

She broke off as a frantic yelping, coming their way, made them both whirl round. A small white dog, all tangled up in a green box kite which dragged behind it, was lolloping along on three legs, now running in circles, biting at the ever-tightening string which tied its fourth leg, now trying to escape from the bouncing kite. A sudden gust of wind filled the kite, lifting it and the dog from the ground. Clare screamed, breaking into a run. But James Thomson was there first, and stretching out a long black arm, hooked the dog from the air. He set it down at her feet. Clare looked at him.

'Okay,' she said. 'I'll do it.'

Shinty

In the autumn the little girls of the Vineyard school would build fragile mansions from the fallen leaves in the shrubbery. The houses had no roofs except the laurels, rhododendrons and firs above but the grandest of them boasted walls three or four feet high and many rooms. The groundplans were scratched with sticks on the sandy soil and marked out with foundations gathered from the deciduous drifts of oak, sweet chestnut leaves, acorns, beech mast and pine needles. Wind, rain or spiteful shoes could demolish in seconds the work of many playtimes. The Vineyard was an ordinary primary school in a Kent town but it was privileged in its building, a Georgian house, and took only girls.

The smell of damp sand and cold leaves came back to Margaret so vividly as she read the advertisement in the paper that forty years dissolved and she might have been in 'the shrubs' with her greatest treasure, an ostrich egg, crushed to chips of yellowish white shell in her hands. Chestnut cases pricked her fingers, the bitter taste of flat pale unripened fruit was in her mouth, and she remembered a girl called Jean Widdoes, who had scraped together a hovel in the dankest corner of the shrubs, where she dwelt alone in the long dinner hour.

Ronnie Sharples Reads From Her
Latest Best Seller
Flowers of Evil
At Dorothy's Bookshop, Flitcroft Court,
Charing Cross Road
Thursday 23 September 7.00
Ring to Reserve Signed Copies
Glass Of Wine Or Ale
Women Only

Veronica Sharples, her old classmate, whose books automatically shot straight into the number one slot of the Alternative Best Sellers.

Margaret rang Suzy at once, at work. They had been best friends at seven and were best friends still. Suzy, who had always ended up with at least ten extra stitches on her knitting, now had her own computer graphics company. When the class had started their tea cosies, Veronica, given first choice, had picked 'Camel and salmon, please Mrs Lambie.' The colours had stayed with Margaret all these years. All that remained when it came to Margaret's turn was dull orange and bottle green; the crimson lake and sea-green knitted fluted jelly that she had envisaged for as long as it took to distribute the wool, that would transform their broken-spouted teapot, was not to be; in fact it turned into a kettle-holder full of holes. She could hear Mrs Lambie's voice now, striking terror along the desks in needlework:

'Unpick it!' 'Unpick it!' 'Unpick it!' 'That's a lovely little run-and-fell seam, Veronica. You're developing into quite a nice little needlewoman.' No terror in adult life would match that of double needlework with Mrs Lambie.

'Are you sure we're ready for this?' Suzy asked. 'I mean, Veronica Sharples ... will we have to have our bodies pierced to pass ourselves off as fans? There's no way I'm paying out good money to feed her monstrous ego and you know her books are quite unreadable. Dennis Wheatley and *The Girls of the Chalet School* meet the *Clan of the Cave Bear* at *The Well of Loneliness* – no thanks. What would be the point of going? She'd only think we were impressed.'

'This is the point,' said Margaret, 'we'll go in disguise. Surely you don't imagine she'd remember us anyway? Be in the Beaujolais at six on Thursday, and we can fortify ourselves for the fray. Bring your shinty stick.'

She put the phone down without hearing Suzy's whine of 'It'll be just like school, everybody standing round watching Veronica showing off,' but realized she was humming 'The Deadwood Stage' and was transported back to the wash-basins, as the lavatories at the Vineyard were known, where Veronica leaped on to a toilet seat, breaking it, in her imitation of Calamity Jane. Whip crack away, whip crack away, whip crack away! 'Do the "Dying swan", Veronica,' someone begged, and Veronica closed her eyes, assumed a doleful expression, clasped her hands in a coronet above her head, and died on the tiled floor, as a coterie of clumsy cygnets waited in the wings for tuition in the art of the arabesque.

Veronica was the arbiter of fashion and her dress code was as immutable as her social strictures. Jean 'Fish-Face' Widdoes, whose mother by cruel chance was a widow, who worked in a chip shop, had once turned up, horror of horrors, in a knitted pixie-hood, and on another occasion in pink ankle socks edged with a blue stripe. 'Baby's socks, 1/11 in Woolworths,' pronounced Veronica, who had spotted them at once. 'Oh, look, your legs are going all blotchy to match your socks.' It was extremely bad form, and dangerous, to admit to any home life – especially if, like Linda Wells, you had a brother who was mental. To bring to the classroom a faint reminder of the previous night's fried food was a serious offence, and one which did not endear Jean to the teachers either, although they did not grasp their noses at her approach, as the girls did. The Dolphin Fish Bar in Arbutus Road was a hundred yards downhill from the swimming baths, and on Saturdays, when Jean helped in the shop, there was always the threat that Veronica and her pals would appear in the queue, blue-lipped and red-eyed, reeking of chlorine, sleek-haired mobsters in cotton frocks and cardigans. Jean paid protection in extra chips and free pickled eggs. Once, when Margaret was in the Dolphin with her own mother, she heard Jean's mother suggesting that Jean might like to go swimming with her friends sometimes instead of serving in the shop. Jean shook her head so vehemently that the big white turban she wore slipped right down over her face. 'Oh, go on, Jeannie, plee-ease, be a sport, we'll call for you tomorrow,' pleaded Veronica, so eloquently that Jean was persuaded that she would not be *the* sport. Foolish little Fish-Face, forgetting about the diving board as she trotted along with her costume rolled in her towel. 'It looks like a fish, it smells like a fish, but it sure don't swim like a fish,' Veronica summed it up.

'Why don't you like Jean?' somebody challenged Veronica one day.

'Because she's got a big conk and she's smelly.'

When Margaret told Suzy to arm herself with her shinty stick for the reading, she was making a reference to the half-moon-shaped scar above Suzy's ankle, the memory of a wound inflicted when Veronica had tripped her up, making her fall on the sharp-edged tin that held the shinty balls. For reasons best known to Miss Short who taught Hygiene and PT, and presumably with the headmistress Miss Barnard's approval, the Vineyard girls played shinty rather than hockey. Perhaps the smaller sticks made the playing field look larger. There was no gymnasium, and wet games and PT lessons took place in the cloakrooms. Miss Short was particularly fond of an activity called 'duckwalking' wherein the girls had to crook their arms into wings and waddle at speed round the narrow benches and pegs hung with coats and shoebags. Quacking was forbidden. If there had been a Junior Olympic Duckwalking event, Veronica would have walked it, with her bony wings pumping from her blinding white vest – somebody's mum always used Persil – and jaunty little navy-blue bottom jerking from side to side over speedy plimsolls as she lapped the field. Veronica was Miss Short's pet duckling and Miss Short turned a blind eye to a wing winding a rival, as she did to wet netballs smacking an opponent's face or knees grazing asphalt in a heavy fall; but it was at shinty that Veronica really shone, her own sharp shins, the blade bone of her nose, honed to a finer point than Jean's despised conk, cutting a swathe through the opposing team, although she was never a team player.

After speaking to Suzy, Margaret decided that the years that had passed since Veronica had seen her old schoolmates would provide sufficient disguise, and besides, Veronica had not watched them, as they had watched her, on the television, strutting her stuff on o1 For London. As is customary on that programme, the interview took place in a restaurant of the guest's choice, and Veronica had opted for Bob's Eel and Pie House, an establishment in Smithfield which had repulsed trendiness, where, elbows on the Formica table top, mouth full of jelly, she had chomped on working-class solidarity while charting her progress from the rural and cultural poverty of her childhood to her present cult status. All had gone swimmingly until the interviewer had asked, in his affable Scottish way, 'Are ye no slumming it a wee bit the night though, Ronnie? I mean to say, rumour has it that you have your own special table in the Groucho, where you're to be found most evenings?'

The camera lingered on him as eels, mash, liquor and peas slid down his face from the plate upturned on his head, and then tracked Veronica as she wrenched open the door of the Ronnie-mobile parked outside and was chauffeused away at speed.

Margaret was no longer the plump child she had been when 'Twice round the gasworks, once round the Maggot' had been Veronica's estimation of her size, but as she got ready for the evening's entertainment, her dress felt a little tight. How typical of Veronica to make her put on weight today. 'Pooh! can anybody smell gas?' Veronica would taunt when Margaret was out of favour. Home was Number 5 Gasworks Cottages. Suzy lived in a tiny village, just a street with a shop, a pub and a church, a farm, a scattering of villas and cottages and a crescent of new council houses. She came to school on the bus.

When Margaret, dressed as herself, Margaret Jones, who had recently celebrated her silver wedding, mother of four grown-up children, regional director of a large housing association, arrived at the Beaujolais, she saw a black fedora waving at her through the smoke of the crowded room. Suzy had got herself up as a gangster in a wasp-waisted pinstripe suit, and as Margaret squeezed on to the chair she had managed to reserve, she flashed open her jacket to show the butt of a gun poking from her inside pocket.

'I was going to get a violin case but I thought it would be a bit obvious,' she said.

'Mmm. That's *so* much more subtle. Sorry I'm late, there's been a bomb scare at Charing Cross and half the Strand's closed off. Bloody security alerts, it's probably just some jerk of a commuter who left his briefcase on the concourse.' She poured herself a glass of wine from the bottle on the table. 'Sweet of you to save some for me. Cheers. That thing in your pocket is a toy, I hope?'

'Realistic, though, eh? What happened to your disguise, and where's your shinty stick?'

'Funnily enough, I couldn't find it – possibly because Veronica Sharples was the only girl who had her own shinty stick – and unbeknownst to you, there is a liberty bodice with rubber buttons concealed beneath this workaday print. I've come as Jean Widdoes.' She had just remembered how Jean Widdoes had been the only girl in the school, perhaps the last girl in the world, to wear one of those obsolete padded vests.

'Jean Widdoes is dead,' said Suzy.

'What? I don't believe you. When? Why didn't you tell me?'

'Sorry. It was while you were in France in the spring. My mother sent me a cutting from the local paper. Her car was hit by a train on a level crossing. It was an open verdict. I didn't send it on to you because you had enough troubles of your own, and then I suppose I just blocked it out. Couldn't bear to think about it.'

'It doesn't bear thinking about.'

She wished she had not brought up the liberty bodice. PT lessons had been made hell on its account until Jean learned to take it off beforehand and hide it in her shoebag.

'Remember that awful time her mother dragged her screaming into assembly and she was clinging to her in hysterics, and Miss Barnard said, "I still have my cane, Jean"?'

'Yes – they knew how to cure school phobia in them days – I wish we weren't doing this,' Margaret said. 'Shall we just go and have something to eat instead? It doesn't seem so amusing now, and you could do with some blotting paper.'

'What, and waste this suit?'

Margaret wished herself miles away from bodies and braying laughter, and fumes of wine, smoke and charcuterie, in the heart of the Kent they had shared, a tumble-down place of old yellow-lichened red brick, sagging garden walls held up by old man's beard, old rabbit hutches and chicken runs, Virginia creeper and apples and rosehips against blue autumn sky, dark lacy cabbages, quinces and wasps, the bittersweet smell of hops.

But there was Legs Diamond waving two tickets at her and

saying, 'I made a special trip at lunch-time to get them. There are bound to be coach-loads of Ronnie's little fans.'

She took her ticket, drained her glass, stubbed out her cigarette and squeezed herself out of her chair to follow her friend.

'There she is!' Suzy clutched Margaret's arm outside the shop, whose window was dominated by a blown-up photograph of Ronnie surrounded by pyramids of her books. 'No it isn't, it's a clone. My God, there are hundreds of them. Surrounded by Ronnie Sharples Wannabes, what a terrifying prospect. Do you think we'll be all right?'

'No,' said Margaret.

'It was your idea, remember. Another nice mess you've got me into ...'

As that could not be denied there was nothing to say. Miss Barnard's voice came faintly through the ether, 'Margaret Adams, you are a bad influence and you, Susan Smithers, are weak and easily led. Together you make a deplorable pair. I am separating you for the rest of the term.'

Apart from the chums, as Margaret christened herself and Suzy grimly, the audience was composed of young women and girls with short hair gelled back from their foreheads, dressed in polo shirts tucked into knee-length khaki shorts fastened with snake belts.

'*Gott im Himmel!* The Hitler Youth!' whispered Suzy.

'They've all copied exactly what she was wearing on *01 For London*! What must it be like to have a following like that? The Michael Jackson of literature,' Margaret whispered back, thinking that they looked like a troop of Boy Scouts that Baden-Powell wouldn't have touched with a tent-pole. Camp as a row of tents. Then she recalled Veronica, sleek-haired after the swimming baths, except that she had worn a cotton frock in those days. Each of the clones carried a copy of Ronnie's latest book, *Flowers of Evil*, and some of them carried six-packs of Thackray's Old Peculiar Ale.

'Original title . . .' Margaret commented, of the book.

A shop assistant was trying to hold the door open just wide enough for several of the scouts to evict an old wino woman who had managed to infiltrate, while repelling latecomers at the same time.

'So much for sisterhood,' as Suzy remarked.

Dorothy, the bookshop's owner, was looking worriedly at her watch. Ronnie Sharples had a reputation for unpredictability.

'She'll be here,' Dorothy's friend and business partner was re-assuring her. 'Her girlfriend was on the phone again only an hour ago to confirm we'd got the right ale in.'

'Did you reassure her that the dumb cluck who shelved *Wicca and Willow* with the Craft Books was sacked on the spot as soon as she confessed?'

If only Ronnie's sidekick hadn't spotted it when she was in checking the window display. The event had almost been cancelled.

A small table held a jug of water, a bottle of red wine, half-empty, a similar bottle of white, some plastic cups, and a crate of Thackray's Old Peculiar, the extra-strong Northern ale which was all that Ronnie, despising the Kentish hopfields of her youth, would drink. More cans were stacked below.

'Our Ronnie was always heavily into uniforms, wasn't she?' said Suzy, as she paid for two cups of wine. Margaret felt a pang of shame remembering how she had cajoled her parents into buying a new blazer that they could ill afford. There was a Vineyard uni-form of blue blazer, gym-slip, white blouse and blue and white striped tie, but it was optional; a few girls, like Margaret whose was second-hand, wore blazers but that was as far as it went. Until the arrival of Veronica in the middle of the third year, in the full rig or fig. She even sported a blue pancake, with a badge. The force of Veronica's personality was such that Easterfield's the High Street Outfitters enjoyed an unprecedented boom, and the more berets there were on heads meant, to Veronica and the gang she had formed at once, the more berets to toss into trees and pull down over people's eyes. Strange though that she, the proponent of the Windsor knot in the school tie that was such a useful garrotte, should have made Miss Harvey, who wore a collar and necktie with her tailored coat and skirt, the target of her scorn.

'Old Ma Harvey looks a right twerp in that tie,' Veronica decreed, and it was so. Margaret, who loved Miss Harvey and yearned for a tweed or tartan tie, cried for Miss Harvey secretly in the wash-basins. Her heart bled for Miss Harvey, knotting her tie in the mirror in the morning, sitting on her desk, swinging her legs as she read them *The Kon-Tiki Expedition*, unaware that she had been diminished by Veronica calling her a right twerp. Veronica put up her hand.

'How did they go to the toilet, Miss Harvey?'

The class was shocked at the rudeness and audacity of Veronica's question, but Miss Harvey laughed like the good sport she was. Margaret longed for brogues like Miss Harvey's too, shiny brown and punched with interesting patterns of holes. 'Old Ma Harvey', indeed. Veronica and her gang knew nothing of the real Miss Harvey.

'I bet she wears trousers at home,' Margaret told Suzy. 'She only has to wear a skirt at school because it's the law.' Suzy agreed. They had lurked outside Miss Harvey's house one afternoon in the holidays in the hope of seeing her but a cross old lady in gardening trousers had advanced on them with a trowel as they passed the gate of Heronsmere Cottage for the tenth time, and they had run away. Cycling home from Miss Harvey's village, they wondered how someone as nice as Miss Harvey could have such a grumpy old mother.

'Remember how Veronica got the Grammar uniform before we'd even sat the scholarship?' Margaret asked, as they waited for her to appear.

'And wore it on Saturdays!'

'If only she hadn't passed . . .'

'Jean Widdoes passed too, didn't she? But she didn't go, for some reason.'

'Do you think I should tell them that Ronnie didn't turn up as guest speaker at the Sevenoaks Soroptimists?' Suzy was saying as the audience grew restive on its seats, when the heavy glass door crashed open, flattening the assistant against a bookcase.

Twin Tontons Macoutes with mirror sunglasses swung inside, followed by Ronnie, elfin in white t-shirt and black jeans. Scattered applause, whistles and disappointed sighs came from her fans, in their shorts and polo shirts. Sidling behind as the door banged shut came a tall, drooping young woman in limp viscose, with long pale hair pushed behind her ears. Mog, Ronnie's latest partner and general factotum. Rumour had it that she had been bought as a slave in Camden Market. The crocodile Kelly bag that Mog carried suggested that Ronnie had tried to make something of her, but Quality Seconds had prevailed. A plaster was coming unstuck from one of her heels where her sandals had rubbed blisters.

'It's guts for garters time if we get clamped again,' were the first words the faithful heard from their idol, and Mog's muttered reference to a disabled sticker was lost as she ripped the tab from the can of Thackray's handed to her by the genuflecting Dorothy, and gave it to Ronnie.

'I think we should make a start as soon as you're ready,' Dorothy suggested timidly. 'We are running a tad late . . . if you don't mind. I'll just give brief introduction . . .'

'A tad late?' Ronnie interrupted her. 'Half of bloody London's closed off. Think yourself lucky we're here at all.'

'Oh, we do, Ronnie. We do.'

'Ronnie needs no introduction,' put in Mog in a monotone as flat as her face.

'Shut up, Mog, or I'll cancel the cheque for your assertiveness class.'

Ronnie gave Mog an affectionate nudge which sprayed Old Peculiar over her frock. Mog gazed down on her adoringly and gratefully at this public display of intimacy. Margaret whispered into Suzy's ear a poem they had learned in school:

> Rufty and Tufty were two little elves
> They lived in a hollow tree . . .
> Rufty was clever and kept the accounts
> While Tufty preferred to do cooking.
> He could bake a cake without a mistake,
> And eat it when no one was looking!

'It's like the black hole of Calcutta in here. Haven't you got any air conditioning?' Ronnie demanded and at once a Tonton Macoute switched on the electric fan that stood by the till sending a whirlwind of leaflets into the front row of the audience, as the police and ambulance sirens drowned Dorothy's apologies while she scrambled after the papers. Mog, flanked by the bodyguards, was seated in the front row, after reassurances that a thorough search of the premises for incendiary devices had been made, as ordered, earlier. Ronnie suspected that she was a prime target.

'It would be like the IRA's biggest coup ever if they got Ronnie,' Mog explained. 'We have to be like constantly vigilant. Security's a real hassle.'

Dorothy, stained with shyness at the ordeal of public speaking, was motioning for silence in the ranks.

'Okay, okay, let's 'ave a bit of 'ush. Right, well, we're really honoured to have with us tonight someone who needs no introduction from me. Dorothy's is proud and privileged to welcome the writer who has been called variously "the lodestar of lesbian literature" and the "Anne Hathaway *de nos jours*". So please put your hands together in a great big Dorothy's welcome for your own, your very own, RONNIE SHARPLES!!'

Suzy gave Margaret a questioning nudge under cover of the catcalls and whistles that broke out, as Dorothy sat down heavily after her lapse into the persona she had assumed for her role as mistress of ceremony at the ill-starred Old Tyme Varieties at the Drill Hall one Christmas.

'Don't tell me you haven't read *Dyke Lady of The Sonnets*, or *Second Best Bard*, which proves Anne Hathaway wrote the plays,' Margaret replied.

'Hi gang.' Ronnie waited for silence to follow the return of her greeting, then snatched up the copy of *Flowers of Evil* that lay, bristling with bookmarks, in Mog's ample lap. She opened the book, and took a swig from her can.

'Hope you've all bought a copy, or three . . .'

Only two pairs of hands were still as a flock of books rose and flapped their pages in the air.

'Right then, we can all go home . . .'

Through the laughter came the sound of the door rattling and the Tonton Macoute posted there shouting, 'Can't you read, dickhead? It says Wimmin Only!' She held the bulging door, calling over her shoulder, 'Boss, some wanker says he's your dad!'

'Oh, for fuck's sake! Deal with it, Mog. Get rid of him. Take the bloody diary and see if I've got a window after Christmas. Just do it, you great waste of space!' Ronnie's lips were thin bloodless scars of fury in her livid face. The front row squirmed in their seats. Before Mog made it to the door the gatecrasher disappeared and a megaphone was thrust in, and the bouncer stepped back to admit a uniformed policeman.

'Nobody is to leave the building until the police give clearance that it is safe to do so,' he said, and backed out, pulling the door closed behind him. Yellow official tape sealed them in. Ronnie ran to the door, dragging it open. 'What is this, a police state, now?'

She was thrust courteously but ignominiously back inside as an explosion down the road erupted ale from cans and hurled books to the floor.

'Bye bye, Daddy. It was nice knowing you,' Ronnie attempted to retrieve lost face. 'Where d'you think you're going, madam?' She grabbed Mog by the hair.

'People may be hurt, Ronnie. I've got my first-aid badge, I must go.'

'They need paramedics not bloody Brownies, you dipstick!' But Mog twisted free, leaving a hank of pale hair wound round Ronnie's fingers, and escaped.

'You're fired! And I want that bloody ring back!'

A cluster of clones surrounded Ronnie, comforting, placating, tacitly offering themselves as replacements. She pushed them aside. 'Where's the loo in this dump? I need some space.'

'This way Ronnie, I'll show you,' Dorothy was saying sooth-ingly, but Ronnie shoved past her and strode to the back of the shop and wrenched open a door. When it proved to be a cup-board holding cleaning materials, she shut herself in anyway, defying anybody to recognize a cliché of farce, sharing her space with a Vileda mop and bucket.

Margaret turned to Suzy, and saw that she was crying.

'Her father was such a nice man,' she sobbed. 'He was really good fun. Remember when he bought us all icecream after the pageant, the one when Ronnie was Elizabeth the First, and we were scullions?' She scrubbed at her eyes with a tissue. 'Only that pathetic Mog had the guts to do anything.'

'Look, the explosion was miles away, probably right down in Trafalgar Square. It sounded pretty feeble anyway, a small incen-diary device. There's no way Mr Sharples could have been in it.'

Her own feelings of guilt at not having done as Mog had done, and uselessness, made her voice impatient. Instinct told her that people were not bleeding and dying yards away, but how could she be sure?

The cupboard door opened and Ronnie emerged, clinging to the mop handle looking ill.

'It's Mrs Mop, the Cockney Treasure,' said Margaret, trying to make Suzy laugh.

'What's *your* problem?' said a voice behind her.

Margaret turned, her smile withered by the hate on the face that was saying, 'Sitting there sniggering in your Laura Ashley frigging frock. I suppose it offends your middle-class mores that someone like Ronnie should be a working-class gay icon. Some people just can't stand to see anybody from the wrong background succeed. Why don't you piss off back to Hampstead, Lipstick Lesbian, and take your fashion-victim girlfriend with you?'

'It isn't Laura Ashley,' was all that Margaret could say. She was frightened, expecting a fist in her face. She turned round again, trembling, but Suzy had slewed round indignantly.

'Working class? You've got to be joking. If you believe that you'll believe any of Ronnie's hype and lies. Veronica Sharples was the first girl in our class to have a patio, *and* the first to have a car, one of those green half-timbered jobs, *and, and* she went on holiday to the Costa del Sol before it was even invented, so don't give me that underprivileged crap. *And* you should have seen her lunch – a big Oxo tin crammed with sandwiches, and that was just for playtime.'

'Leave it, Suze,' said Margaret.

'Leave it, Suze,' her accuser imitated her.

'*And* your working-class icon went to Cambridge.'

'So what?'

'So nothing, except Veronica Sharples is a fraud as well as a lousy writer. *And* they had their own chalet at Camber Sands!'

Margaret heard Veronica's childish voice pipe, 'Anyway, *we've* got a vestibule!' and her own defiant retort 'Well my dad's getting us one tomorrow, so there!'

She pulled Suzy to her feet. 'Come on, we might as well get a drink, as we seem to be stuck here for the duration. Everybody else is helping herself.'

A can of Thackray's was preferable to a necktie party, she decided, noting the mirror shades of a Macoute reflecting the argument, even though Old Peculiar might not mix with the wine Suzy had drunk earlier.

'I suddenly realized I – I mean, all of us – might have been killed,' they heard Ronnie say. 'Somebody better deal with that bucket in there.'

As they stood apart in a corner, drinking their ale, Margaret thought about her ostrich egg. When her father had brought it home from a Toc H jumble sale, she had begged to be allowed to take it to school. Her mother had relented at last, against her better judgement. Margaret had been standing in the playground, the centre of an admiring circle, holding the big, frail, miraculous thing, when Veronica had come up behind her and grabbed Margaret's hands and clapped them together shattering the shell,

'Now look what you've been and gone and done! Oh' – Veronica crowed – 'dear what a pity never mind. What will Mummy say now? Boo hoo.'

That was what she always said when she made somebody cry: Oh dear what a pity never mind. But why had she wanted to make other children cry? Was it in rehearsal for her life as a writer, a testing of her power to move to tears? If so, art had failed to imitate life. Perhaps, then, Veronica had no choice, her character as predetermined as the blade of her nose. Margaret pictured a phrenologist's porcelain head with bulging prominences marked Spite, Ambition, Envy, and a tiny section just big enough to contain the blurred word Talent.

'There's something I never told you,' Suzy said.

'Let me guess, you kissed Veronica in the bike shed?'

'I was her best friend for a day.'

'What? You traitor! How could you?' Her childhood was cracking like eggshell.

'No, she made me, it was awful. It was a Sunday and she just suddenly appeared at the top of our lane, and I was playing with that little girl Doreen, she was only about four, with her doll's pram, and I was wearing my mum's white peep-toes and one of her old dance frocks. Veronica said she'd tell everybody at school that I played with dollies if I wouldn't be her best friend. And the worst thing was, Keith Maxfield shouted out "Oo's that queer gink?" as she came down the lane, no, the worst thing was, my mother, mistaking her for a nice little school friend, invited her to tea. She pushed my baby sister down the stairs, accidentally on purpose. When I was walking her back to the bus stop the cows came down the lane and Veronica said, "I do pity you, Suzy, living in all this cows' muck."'

'Oh dear what a pity never mind.'

'And she tried to hang my teddy from the apple tree with elastic . . .'

'This catalogue of crimes only makes your perfidy more indefensible. Why didn't you tell me?'

'I was going to – you must remember how scary she was – and anyway, on the Monday, that new girl Madeleine came, and Veronica forgot all about me. Natch. I was only ten, Margaret . . .'

'Only obeying orders, you mean.'

A crash of glass might have been a damaged window of an adjacent shop leaving its moorings, or the sound of someone in a glass house throwing stones. As people converged on Dorothy's window to see what was happening in the street, her own little jagged lump of guilt began to cut. There was a girl named Angela Billings who had a slight speech impediment. One playtime stumbling over her words, Margaret had produced an accidental approximation to Angela's diction.

'Hey, listen, Margaret's super at taking-off Angela Billings! Go on, Margaret, do it again!' called Ronnie.

Shamefaced after feeble protestations, Margaret had. And again, enjoying the brief warmth of Veronica's friends' laughter, Veronica's arm round her shoulder.

'She got bitten by a horse fly,' Suzy was saying, 'and she said it would be my fault if it went septic and she had to have her leg off. I was sick with fear.'

Time passed. Dorothy looked increasingly desperate as people milled aimlessly around her. Ronnie looked at her watch, as if she had another appointment.

'This is getting ridiculous. Get Scotland Yard or the Bomb Squad on the phone,' she commanded. 'They've no right to keep us cooped up in here like a load of bloody Bosnians under fire. Where's that Little Hitler with the loud hailer?'

'History was always Veronica's strong point,' said Suzy, loud enough for Ronnie to whirl round and demand, 'Do I know you?'

'Torture, wasn't it, that really turned you on? Medieval punishments? An early interest that was to bear fruit in your mature work. No, you don't know me. But I wonder if you'd do me the honour of signing this book for me?' She pulled a book off a shelf. Ronnie struck it away contemptuously.

'Are you out of your trees? Why should I sign somebody else's book? I don't even *read* other people's books!'

'Is it? Oh dear what a pity never mind, an easy mistake ...'

'The Old Bill wasn't very helpful, Boss,' reported a twin.

'Look, Ronnie, in the circumstances, I'm prepared to double your fee – if you'll just give us a short reading ... we're running

out of booze . . . ' Dorothy pleaded, as fans, following Suzy's lead,
surrounded Ronnie waving books and pens.

As Margaret, her second can of Thackray's half-drunk,
watched them, the scene dissolved into the wash-basins where a
little girl executed an arabesque against the snowlight of a winter
afternoon. She was just a child, she thought, we were all only
children. A muzzy mellow maternal benevolence suffused her,
absolving her of her betrayal of Angela Billings; far away, made
tiny by the perspective of the years, Ronnie danced, as fragile and
guiltless as a ballerina pirouetting atop a musical jewel casket to
a tinkling tune. Margaret turned to Suzy, her eyes bright with
unshed tears.

'School,' she told her, 'is a place for learning—'

'No! You don't say! I'd never have known.'

'No, I mean – lessons in life. About ourselves, our limits and
weaknesses, and how to overcome them . . .'

'No wonder they call this stuff Old Peculiar. And I thought
you flunked that Open University Philosophy course . . .'

Margaret had to swallow her tears, just as if someone had given
her the good playground pinch she had been tempted to inflict
on her friend.

'What I'm trying to say is – Veronica can't be held responsible
for Jean's suicide.'

'Nobody suggested she could, just because she ruined the childhood of a short and presumably unhappy life. "Every child has the
right to be happy," that's what you've told me often enough, isn't
it? Mummy?'

Margaret plonked down her drink, and made towards Ronnie,
bursting with something, she didn't know what, that she had to
say to her.

Ronnie was berating an abject Dorothy:

'Look, there's no way I'm giving a reading of any kind whatsoever at this shambles. The whole thing's a monumental cockup.

You can give me a cheque for three, no make it four, times what we agreed, to compensate for my time and mental trauma and' – she looked round for something to add to the bill – 'and the break-up of my relationship!'

'You aren't too complimentary about her thighs here,' Suzy's voice was loud in the respectful silence cast by the reference to the departed Mog. She had got hold of a copy of *Flowers of Evil* and was stabbing her finger at the opening line.

Ronnie's face was white, the bone in her nose razor sharp, and two crimson patches blazed on her cheeks. Margaret knew that look, that dangerous painted doll face: something was about to get broken; a house of leaves kicked to pieces.

'Veronica,' she said; as Ronnie ripped the cloth from the table and empties, the bottles and plastic cups and a jug of water crashed to the floor.

'How dare you make remarks about my lover's thighs!' she shouted at Suzy. 'I do know you – you were at school with me! I know who you are, bitch, you're that Fish-Face creature aren't you? Who the hell let you in here to wreck my reading? My God, you've got a nerve! Get her out of here!'

The Tontons Macoutes were moving towards Suzy as Ronnie yelled, 'Still stink of chips do you, Fish-Face? Go on, give us a pickled egg!' The macoutes closed in on Suzy. One of them twisted her arm behind her back.

'*And* there was something fishy about your mother! Wasn't she the local tart or something?'

Margaret grabbed at the other bodyguard's arm, her fingers slipping in slick sweat, and was shrugged contemptuously off, bounced against a bookshelf.

'Freeze! Hold it right there!' Suzy had scrabbled the gun from her pocket with her free hand and had it trained on Ronnie's head. Her attacker dropped her arm and stepped away.

'It's only a gun, you wimps!' Ronnie shrieked, 'Get it off her!'

The entire audience, but for Margaret and the bodyguards, oozed backwards against the windows and the sealed door.

'Do something! Kill her, put her in hospital! You're all pathetic, you're all fired, the lot of you! I forbid you to so much as open one of my books as long as you live! Give them all back!'

'Cool it, Veronica,' said Suzy. 'You know what this reminds me of? A wet PT lesson in the cloakroom. Shame we can't get out on the shinty field and hack each other's shins, isn't it? Still, never mind. Forgotten your plimsolls again, have you, or perhaps the truth is that you don't in fact possess any plimsolls? Take a pair out of the school box then, quick sharp – those khaki ones with no laces. Vests and knickers, everybody, and you can take off that ridiculous liberty bodice, Jean Widdoes, I don't care if your mother does say you've got a weak chest, it's your weak brain that concerns me. Buck up, you're like a lot of old ladies!'

A sycophantic titter came from the back. Suzy crossed the room and pressed the gun behind Ronnie's ear. She addressed the paralysed fans.

'Right, form two teams, Reds and Greens, quick sharp! Margaret, give out the bands!'

Margaret almost stepped forward to distribute the rough red and green hessian bands but realized she was in a bookshop where Suzy, with a gun, was imitating Miss Short. However, the fans and Tontons were scrambling into two untidy lines, fighting not to be at the front. A couple of cravens had stripped to vests and knickers.

'Dorothy, you're Green Captain. You, Veronica, can be Captain of the Reds. Where's my whistle?'

'Here, miss, you can use mine.'

A silver whistle was pulled from a polo-shirt pocket and an eager figure darted out, and dashed back to her place.

'Thank you, dear, you can take a House Point.'

Ronnie was marched at gunpoint to the head of one line. Half Dorothy's team defected at once.

'Back in your own line, you Greens, quick sharp! Right, everybody squat down, hands on hips, elbows out. On the whistle, go! Duckwalk once right round the room, back to the end of the line, then bunnyhop a complete circuit again, and then, Captains only, duckwalk once round again. Got that? First team all home in a nice straight line is the winner!'

'I don't believe this,' Ronnie was protesting when the gun forced her to her haunches. Suzy's finger tightened on the trigger. She blew the whistle and jabbed Ronnie behind the ear.

'Okay, Sharples. Duckwalk till you drop.'

Ten minutes later, the shop door opened and a policeman announced, 'All clear, ladies. You can come out now.'

But nobody heard him through the clamour and shouts of 'Greens! Greens!' 'Reds! Reds! Reds!' and 'Cheat! Cheat!' as the two big ducklings slugged it out, scarlet-faced and panting, wings pumping, as they waddled for dear life over the chaos of torn books, spilled beer and crackling plastic cups.

Shooting Stars

The smell of hot pasties on the November air – flaky pastry oozing mingled scents of sweet spices and savoury juices – brought tears to Phoebe's eyes as she walked past the shop. The lighted interior in the gathering dusk, the sound of cheerful voices within, pierced her with such a sense of desolation that she stopped and let the aroma drift around her.

Phoebe, however, was not some starving Victorian waif lingering outside a pastry cook's or pie shop to fill her empty belly with the vapours of the food she had no pennies to purchase. Her hunger was of quite a different kind. She was standing outside the Student Union shop on a university campus, blocking the path of students coming and going at the end of the academic day. Although her age and her charity-shop clothes were similar to theirs, the buggy whose handle she was grasping with fingers turning red in the cold wind set Phoebe apart from the students milling around her. She had stepped out of their world and become invisible – her contemporaries simply did not see her as they buffeted past with files and bicycles and backpacks.

The new term had started a few weeks ago and it seemed to Phoebe that she was the only person on her own. Everybody else was either in a couple or a noisy group; even the foreign students far from home could not be as lonely as she was. But, she reminded herself, of course she was not alone, and the reason for that was Oscar, who lay back in his buggy listening to the taped music spilling out of the shop, taking in the scene with a solemn gaze. Phoebe should have been one of them, the students with their new stationery and t-shirts and hoodies with the university logo, but this tiny person wearing a multi-coloured stripy hat and mittens had put paid to her dreams and ambitions.

Phoebe had won a place to read Chemistry, but in the interim she had mistaken a gap-year romance for true love, and when the bitter truth that she was pregnant dawned, Josh, Oscar's father, had disappeared. Her letters, e-mails and phone calls went unanswered.

They would have been able to make it work between them, Phoebe had thought, sharing the child-care, taking turns to study. As things were, with no family to support her, Phoebe had bundled her few possessions and Oscar in his second-hand buggy on to a train and come to the university city anyway. The short-cut from Oscar's nursery ran through the campus, so she was reminded every day of what she had thrown away. She could have tracked Josh down but pride and a broken heart forbade it. She could never, never forgive him for abandoning his child. Her own father had taken off soon after she was born and, having provided the young Phoebe with several 'stepfathers', her mother had finally married a man of gross appetites whose dislike of Phoebe was reciprocated. Now, a single mother trailing home from a dead-end job, Phoebe supposed she was repeating the pattern and wondered bleakly what the prospects were for Oscar.

As she pushed him along, Phoebe was dimly aware of fireworks going off somewhere. The last time she had watched fireworks was with Josh, kissing while a magical garden bloomed in the sky. This year she hadn't bought even a packet of sparklers to amuse Oscar. The immediate prospect for him was tea, and then a bath in the old-fashioned tub in her landlady's draughty bathroom. Phoebe had been lucky to find the two rooms she rented from Dorcas, an elderly Quaker, because most of the houses nearby were divided into student lets and had overflowing wheelie bins and loud music pounding through the night. Often, when she lay awake under the patchwork quilt made by Dorcas, Phoebe heard the laughter of students coming home from clubs and pubs and, sick at heart, told herself how lucky she was.

Dorcas was a retired professor, of something – Phoebe hadn't really been listening. She was a bit of an old busy-body, offering to babysit – as if Phoebe had anywhere to go. She reminded Phoebe of her chemistry teacher, whom she had let down so badly. By day, Dorcas wore her white hair piled on her head, and at night, while she made cocoa in the kitchen, it hung in a plait down her back.

Dorcas was always busy: gardening, going to meetings, baking, doing Quakerish things. It made Phoebe feel guilty, when all she wanted to do in the evening was slump in front of the telly. Dorcas had bullied her into joining the library but she had lost her appetite for reading. For everything except Oscar. Even so, she felt herself to be dull and mechanical in her play with him. And he watched her warily, as if he feared she might resent him.

Phoebe approached the house by the alley which led to the back gate. A fireburst halted her. The indigo sky was full of shooting stars.

'Look, Oscar! Pretty!'

But he was already leaning forward, his face alight with joy, reaching out to try to catch the falling stars.

In the afterglow, Phoebe pushed the buggy up the garden path. A first frost had blackened many stalks but left untouched an enormous pumpkin near the door.

The curtains of Dorcas's sitting room were undrawn; lamps cast a soft glow over book-lined walls and pictures, logs burned in the grate. Phoebe stood still, as if seeing the room for the first time. The books on the shelves were illumined, they seemed almost to dance out to her in the flickering fire-light. The door opened, framing Dorcas with her white coronet of hair, waving something incandescent. She held aloft the fizzing wand of a sparkler, showering the orange pumpkin with gold and silver stars. Phoebe unbuckled Oscar and clasped her radiant child tight as she went forward to meet her.

A Silly Gigolo

Miss Fentiman's memorial service marked the turning point of Susan Simmons's life but in later years all that Susan could recall of the event was a pair of nylon stockings and the shame of wearing them, and the hideous harness of the belt with its dangling suspenders which held them up. She was sure that everybody was laughing at her wrinkled ankles and the twisting seams bisecting the backs of her legs, which felt oddly naked, as well as itchy. Susan, aged fourteen and the smallest girl in her class, felt a new sympathy for the hobbled horse in the scrubby paddock beyond her bedroom window.

You won't have heard of Susan Simmons – this particular one anyway – though the name of The Suzanne Simone Touring Company might ring a faint bell. Suzanne, the *doyenne* of the company, first trod the boards in the chorus line of an amateur production of *Fings Ain't Wot They Used To Be* at the dawn of the 1960s, not long after the termination of her undistinguished career as Susan Simmons at the grammar school where Miss Fentiman had once been the headmistress.

Miss Fentiman's photograph was displayed on a corridor wall, among those of other luminaries in caps and gowns, and smiling sports teams clutching silver cups, archaic lacrosse sticks, hockey sticks, netballs, racquets and oars. There they hung disregarded, these Suffragettes and pioneers of education in their long dark skirts and high-necked blouses embellished with a pin or cameo brooch, who had grasped the baton from Miss Beale and Miss Buss and who stood on the shoulders of bluestockings, so to speak, gazing through wire-rimmed spectacles and *pince-nez* into the future they had created – a jostling line of girls in green knickers and white Aertex blouses queuing up outside the gym.

When Miss Fentiman died in a nursing home at a great age, the current headmistress, Miss Vine, announced that all the senior girls would attend her memorial service at the Parish Church. Susan's life was uneventful and at first she felt mild excitement at missing a morning's lessons and experienced a moment's self-importance at being one of those who would represent the school, tempered by awe at the thought of entering the big grey church with its spire and stained-glass windows. These feelings transmuted instantly to horror at Miss Vine's next pronouncement. To ensure that the girls brought credit to the school, there would be a uniform inspection before they set out to walk in an orderly crocodile to the service, and all girls were required to wear nylon stockings rather than socks.

Susan did not possess a pair of nylons. Nor could she borrow any. Susan lived with her widowed adoptive mother on a smallholding on the edge of the town, in a ramshackle, semi-rural settlement of which most of her classmates were unaware. Her mother, gaunt, weather-beaten and older than the other girls' parents, went bare-legged throughout the seasons, shod alternately in plimsolls and wellingtons. Her parsimony – a word Susan came to associate with the parsnips which formed a large part of their diet – was such that Susan earned her dinner money by doing chores. There was no possibility of asking her mother for the two and eleven pence or so that a pair of stockings would cost. Nor was there any point in trying to feign illness. And once she was on the bus to school there was nowhere to hide – these were the days when members of the public believed it their duty to report to the authorities any youngster on the loose during school hours.

The alternatives were to kill herself or to paint her legs with cocoa or gravy browning as they did in the war. Otherwise, she could steal a pair of stockings. Mum's larder didn't run to such luxuries as cocoa or gravy, so Woolworths was her best bet – once, in the toilets, she had overheard a girl boasting about shoplifting a bottle of perfume from Woolies. Susan had been deeply shocked. But now she reflected that Woolworths owed her something in recompense for the disaster of the grey socks.

There was a craze at school then for patterned knee socks, even among the rebels who hitched up their skirts over the waistband and loosened their ties as soon as they were out of sight of the school, in case they encountered any boys, even though they risked detention if spotted by a member of staff. Susan, who wore her dead father's socks with her toes in the heels and the surplus folded under her feet so that they looked like ankle socks, had longed for a pair of these grey, patterned, knee socks. She liked the look of them on girls like Clare Alabaster with long slender legs, and she wanted so much to be like everybody else. If only she had those socks, girls and staff alike would see that she belonged. At last she had managed to save enough money to buy a pair in Woolworths. She couldn't wait to get home and try them on. But when she did, one sock stretched perfectly to her knee-cap, while the other stopped midway up her calf. Was it her – had she never noticed that one of her legs was much shorter and fatter than the other? She swapped the socks over. Same result. She pulled and stretched but nothing made any difference. With bitter tears she acknowledged that they were mismatched socks. How could this have happened? How could Woolworths have done this to her? Why was she such a fool as to have chosen this particular pair?

Nothing in Susan's upbringing had informed her of the possibility of taking things back to a shop, and besides, it was an ordeal for her to speak to a shop assistant in the first place – the Woolworths ladies were so grand that she was shrunken and humbled by their condescending to serve her at all. So Susan was condemned to wear the odd socks to school, hoping that nobody would notice. But of course they did. Everything was noticed.

After Susan had endured several tormented nights followed by fearful mornings when she departed for school unable to eat any breakfast, her mother asked her, one day when she came home grey-faced with no appetite, if there was anything wrong. It was tea-time and the memorial service was due to take place on the following morning. Between sobs, and without hope, Susan told her about the nylons.

'Finish your greens,' said Mum. 'It's not the end of the world.'

'It probably is,' said Susan.

When she had washed up their plates, Mum took Susan up to her bedroom.

Susan sat on the edge of the bed with its lumpy spinach-coloured quilt. Then she couldn't resist lying down on it; she had a strong feeling, almost like a memory, of wanting to burrow underneath it.

Mum was pulling out a drawer from her chest of drawers and rummaging in it. She tossed things backward on to the bed where Susan was lying. More of her dad's socks, a scentless lavender bag faded from purple to white, vests and a box of scented soaps in the shape of pine cones.

'You might as well have these,' she said, holding in her calloused hand a cellophane packet printed with a picture of a pair of elegant nylon-encased legs in high-heeled shoes and a jaunty teddy bear, with a pale blue bow round his neck, doffing a top hat. Bear Brand Fully Fashioned Stockings.

Susan took it, feeling a sudden sadness at Mum's earth-rimmed fingernails on the never-worn stockings.

'They look too – glamorous,' she said.

'You'd better have this too.'

Mum flung Susan a pinkish-grey suspender belt, with perished elastic and four dangling straps.

'I expect it's much too big but you can put a safety pin in the back,' she said. 'One of the buttons is broken but you can use a sixpence instead.'

'But—' Susan started to say.

'Oh, don't worry, I'll lend you the sixpence! Don't go frittering it on the way home though, or it'll come out of your dinner money.'

She stumped out of the bedroom, leaving Susan to follow, with all the questions the Bear Brand stockings had raised unasked.

As Mum had predicted, the suspender belt was far too big, and Susan was in an agony of fear that the safety pin would spring open during the service, piercing her back and letting suspender belt and stockings tumble in dingy shame to the church floor. The uniform inspection had passed better than she had hoped for, though, with her form mistress, Miss Lodge, shaking her head silently at her battered hat and threadbare second-hand blazer, and passing on to the next girl, Clare Alabaster, with a smile.

'Well done, 4A!' she said. 'Some of you have made a real effort.'

It was later, when they were back at school, taking off their hats and blazers in the cloakroom, that Clare Alabaster, lounging against one of the wash-basins, spoke the words which would change Susan's life for ever.

'Shocking how many people turned up in seamed stockings! I mean – talk about old-fashioned!'

She twisted her leg to admire her own perfect calf, sheathed in pale nylon and all of a piece, unsullied by any unsightly seam.

'Of course,' said Clare, looking at Susan, 'I don't blame some people, but honestly! Haven't they ever heard of seamless nylons?'

Seamless nylons! All at once, Susan wished she had had the gumption – Miss Lodge's favourite word – to steal a pair of seamless stockings from Woolworths, felt a pang of pity for her mother, and resolved that never again would Susan Simmons be numbered among the ignorant, the unfashionable, the pitied. Then, in a vision, a line of teddy bears, sporting pale-blue bow ties and spangled top hats, high-kicked their rhinestone-studded legs across a stage and vanished in a burst of stardust.

Susan rushed into a lavatory cubicle and tore off the suspender belt and the stockings, and replaced them with her mismatched grey knee-socks, which now seemed like dear old friends. The sixpence Mum had lent her to replace the broken button rolled under the door but she managed to retrieve it when she emerged. Then she went out of the school's front door and stalked down the road, although it was only lunch-time. The smell of stew from the canteen followed her but nobody noticed her departure.

Susan did not get off the bus at her usual stop but stayed on until the bus station. She wandered through the heart of the town until she came to the White Hart Hotel. There was a little garden there, fronting the high street, behind a chain-link fence. Susan sat down on a rustic bench.

She felt the bench sag as somebody joined her.

'Waiting for somebody?' he said.

'Yes,' said Susan, after a moment's thought. 'Are you?'

'Stood you up, has he, your boyfriend?'

'No.'

'Well, I've been stood up, good and proper. I had an appointment with a lady at this hotel but she's obviously changed her mind. She lured me down here and now she's left me in the lurch – and out of pocket.'

They sat in silence, he with a hat which had seen better days resting on his knee and Susan with her dented school hat in her lap.

Then the man asked, 'I don't suppose you could stand me a cup of tea – or something stronger? Keep me going till I get back to London.'

'You can have this sixpence,' said Susan, getting up and handing him the coin.

As she walked away, he called after her, 'Did you know you've got odd socks on?'

Years later, Suzanne Simone, as she was then, realized that the man who had been stood up at the White Hart Hotel was probably a failed gigolo, but she didn't give him much thought. She had encountered his type many times in the theatre, and one day she came upon his likeness in an art gallery. It was a self-portrait painted by Sickert in middle-age, with the ironic title *The Juvenile Lead*. The gallery was in Southampton where the Suzanne Simone Touring Company was enjoying a short run at the Nuffield Theatre of *Anything Goes*, the musical which states that most guys today that women prize today are just silly gigolos. Suzanne, of course, had the starring role, while Mum, persuaded into tights in her old age, had found her niche backstage, where she kept the company's accounts and took a grim delight in docking the players' wages for any suspected misdemeanours.

A Silver Summer

In the summer of 1962, a girl sits at the edge of the lunch-time pastoral in Lincoln's Inn Fields. Although she is alone among the flowers and bees mumbling in old, sun-warmed stone, she is not a wallflower herself, merely waiting to be asked to join the dance. Meanwhile she observes the quadrangle quadrilles, the furtive two-steps, a fandango of fan-tails in the blue air above white discarded shirts and white legs in rolled-down stockings. Barristers stroll across the daisied grass, swinging the big blue bags that contain their official robes, and if any whiff of corruption escapes those tasselled drawstrings, Tessa, daydreaming in the scent of roses, cannot smell it and is reminded of shoe-bags on the pegs at the school she left three months ago, and thinks how far away it seems. Her glossy hair, cut in a fringe above green eyes, is iridescent like starlings' feathers in the sun. She has just made an appointment at a Hebe Hair Salon, which will rather spoil it.

Her lunch-hour over, Tessa returns to Sheldon's Silver & Antiques in Chancery Lane. Mrs Sheldon has an aura of Chanel and Lalique, *poudre de riz* and Biarritz. She flies to the Riviera every January with her sister and has photographs of the two of them on the Promenade des Anglais at Nice, with a famous band-leader of the thirties. Mrs Sheldon smokes Black Cat in an amber cigarette holder, and her cough, like her rage, is formidable. Tessa worships her and thinks she has a heart of gold. Well, silver gilt, perhaps. Pinchbeck anyway. Tessa is learning fast; she studies the little book of silver hallmarks on the train on her way home each evening.

'I've been rushed off my feet, Tessa!' Mrs Sheldon accuses. 'Get me a cup of tea, there's a good girl, and then we'll need some boxes from over the road.'

The first order is fine, because Tessa likes going to the Italian café next door and saying, 'Tea for the lady, please,' as she's been instructed, so that Alf will make it precisely to Mrs Sheldon's requirements. The café is always steamy, busy and noisy, with Ilda, Alf's sister, shouting, 'Chump chop and chips twice, right away!' to the cook.

The second command fills her with dread. Going across to Dodd and Dodsworth's, the Legal Stationers, to ask for spare boxes is the only aspect of her job which she hates.

'The boy will take you down to the cellar for a look,' says courteous, obliging, old Mr Dodsworth.

'For a feel, don't you mean?' mouths the Dodd and Dodsworth boy, through wet, slack lips, and then says loudly, 'Follow me, Modom, *if* you please!'

Paunchy at nineteen, in a shiny blue suit, with a complexion suggestive of solitary pleasures, the Dodd and Dodsworth boy leads the way. As soon as they are in the cellar, he switches off the light and pushes her against a stack of stationery. Today, Tessa escapes with a grazed lip and faint bruises on the arms that clutch a pair of cardboard boxes.

'Don't lounge there with your hands in your pockets, boy. Smarten yourself up,' Tessa hears old Mr Dodsworth say as he holds open the door for her.

'Yes, sir,' says the Dodd and Dodsworth boy.

Mrs Sheldon is fuming, about to lose a sale.

Business is good. The tourists, Swedish and American, are buying silver; Nigerian law students in bright patterned cotton are buying gold; freemasons are buying seals and fobs and gold balls that open to reveal secret symbols for their watch chains; nurses are buying filigree silver belt-buckles; judges are buying Spy cartoons to hang in their Chambers. Mrs Sheldon's great-niece Natalie comes in to help sometimes, freeing Tessa to take and collect repairs from the bead-stringers in Hatton Garden and the engravers and silversmiths in Clerkenwell. She loves walking through Leather Lane market and climbing dark, splintery staircases in ancient buildings, trusted with precious things. And yet sometimes, in the hot, glittery streets and the gardens of Lincoln's Inn, she feels a little lonely.

A dealer, one of those mysterious men who pull diamonds and bits of jewellery in twists of tissue paper from hidden pockets, asks her for a date. He is at least forty and Tessa is glad when Mrs Sheldon refuses on her behalf. A young barrister takes her to lunch at a Chinese restaurant, where the waiter scorns her for being vegetarian, and a clerk begins to wait for her at the top of the escalator each morning. Mrs Sheldon is so pleased with Tessa's work that she gives her an old paste ring with a stone like a cabochon ruby. Tessa buys her mother a little gold brooch with MIZPAH on it.

'Wasn't there one that said "Daphne"?' her mother asks, but she wears the brooch every day, round the house. She tells Tessa not to worry, the right boy will come along some day.

It is a sultry afternoon, just before closing time, when a woman buys the Capodimonte figures of the Four Seasons. Tessa is told to run across the road for a stout box.

'Please be quick, I'm in a hurry!' she pleads with the Dodd and Dodsworth boy, staying safely halfway down the cellar stairs.

'I'll bet you are!'

He drags her off the step into darkness as he flicks off the light, crushing her against him, pressing her closed fist on his swollen trousers, as they struggle, trying to get his hand up her skirt.

'Begging for it, aren't you?' he pants. 'I've been watching you! I bet you've had it off with half the blokes down Leather Lane.'

Tessa wrenches a hand free and hits him hard across the face. She gropes for the light switch and grabs a box. As she backs up the stairs, fearful of a hand shooting out to grasp her ankle, she sees, horrified, a pigeon's egg ruby of blood welling from the corner of his lip, where her ring had caught it.

'Shouldn't have done that,' he says. A fat tongue flips the ruby into his mouth.

Cars brake and hoot as Tessa runs through the traffic, and trips over the kerb.

'Hey, are you okay?'

She sees a blur of olive skin, blond curls, blue denim, and feels a hand on her arm, helping her up.

'Yes, yes, I'm fine, thanks.'

She rushes inside. Her face is on fire, and her hands feel filthy as she swaddles the porcelain babies in newspaper and tissue and tucks them into a bed of wood-wool. Too humiliated to speak of the incident ever, to anybody, she plans desperate stratagems for getting out of going to Dodd and Dodsworth's again, and scrubs her hands sore at the sink, dragging the cabochon ruby from her finger.

She is on her way to the tube, passing the Silver Vaults, when a boy falls into step beside her, making her jump. He pulls her back from the gutter on to the pavement.

'Is this your day for getting run over? I'm sorry – I didn't mean to startle you. I was hoping you'd come this way. Just tell me to get lost if I'm bothering you. I'm Tyler,' he adds hopefully.

Tessa realizes that she is with the most beautiful boy she has ever seen.

'No, it's all right. I was just on my way home. I'm Tessa.'

'Well, Tessa, could I buy you a cup of coffee or something?' A shiny blue suit pushes past them, unnoticed.

'You're American, aren't you?' says Tessa as they walk on.

'From New York. On vacation. I'm just here in London for another few days before joining up with friends in Paris. Doesn't seem like such a hot idea now.'

'What doesn't?'

'Paris. Now that I've met you.'

Tessa phones her mother to say she will be late. They walk, and talk, until they come upon a little restaurant called San Marino. Although it is still early, the waiter sets a candle in a chianti bottle on their table, and sings 'O Sole Mio' as he waltzes around with the cutlery, under the plastic vine leaves hung with coloured fairy lights. They can't get over how much they have in common – music, films, books – and the most amazing thing is, apart from the fact they might never have met, that Tyler's mother used to sell jewellery in Bloomingdale's. Later, on the Embankment, they kiss under a green sky with faint hazy stars, while the tide tries to race away with the reflections of the shimmering glass globes that loop the river.

Alf is in a bad mood the next morning when Tessa goes in for Mrs Sheldon's tea and a cup for herself.

'That's the one for the *lady* ...' he says, as if she didn't know by now.

And Ilda is moaning about the veal or salami or something.

'Easy meat!' she mutters fiercely.

Tessa is too excited to pay them much attention. Tyler is meeting her for lunch.

Mrs Sheldon is in a foul temper too. Perhaps it's the weather; the sky is oppressive with heavy clouds like Old Sheffield plate with the copper wearing through. Business is slow. Mrs Sheldon abruptly tells Tessa to get on with cleaning some silver. She strides up and down the shop with a long ash on her cigarette. Silver shivers on the glass shelves at every sharp turn of her high heels, porcelain tinkles in fear. You could cut the air with the verdigrised knife Tessa is dunking into the malodorous Silver Dip. A fine powder drifts over her hair and dress, into her nose, as she brushes polish from grooves and interstices. By mid-morning her hands are grey. She sits like Cinderella, wondering what she has done wrong, while Mrs Sheldon serves the customers.

At a quarter to one, she glances out of the window.

Shock sucks the breath and colour from her as if with a straw, and blows it back again, flooding her face with icy red. Tyler is across the street, talking to the Dodd and Dodsworth boy.

'Nn-oh!' Tessa screams, jumping up, upsetting the Silver Dip, tangling with a long-coated *schnorrer* in the doorway, deaf to his curse. Tyler starts running.

'Tyler! Wait! Oh, please wait. Tyler!'

She chases him to the tube, glimpsing his blond head, his long denim legs through gaps in the crowded pavement. She almost has him, and grasps air with her grey hands. Then she knows she has lost him.

Ilda's words 'Easy meat' slap her face, like a raw, dirty slice of veal, as she understands their meaning. The fat worm of lust and malice that lurks in those blue trousers has impelled the Dodd and Dodsworth boy up and down the Lane to do its spiteful work. She turns back towards the shop, where everything is tarnished now. The loss of Tyler and the disgrace are too much to bear. She finds herself in Lincoln's Inn Fields, sobbing into the grass.

Eventually she sits up, wiping the falling tears with the backs of her hands, leaving great smears. 'I *will* find him again, whatever it takes. I'll go to, to Bloomingdale's, to the Ivy League, whatever that is, they'll be able to help me trace him and tell him the truth.'

Tessa walks back slowly, as the sky, like a battered old salver, starts oozing drops of Silver Dip. People would say, 'There's no smoke without fire.' Throw a bit of mud, and some of it sticks, she knows. Well, sticks and stones might break her bones, but names would never hurt her! She is a drowned grey rat, but determined, by the time she reaches the shop; full of plans for making smoke and fire in a certain cellar, for which somebody else would be blamed, and for throwing mud and making it stick.

Slaves to the Mushroom

'Overalls, ladies!'

That was the signal for the work force to peel off its rubber gloves, remove its protective clothing and down tools and hurry across to the new canteen, where the wearing of overalls was forbidden.

'And gentleman,' added the supervisor, catching the offended eye of Robbo, the only male worker who wore one of the firm's issue green-and-white gingham, nylon smocks, his crinkly hair tied back in a matching checked bandeau.

The morning break lasted ten minutes and workers were faced with a choice of visiting the cloakroom or the canteen; the buildings were several hundred yards apart and although there might just be time to queue for a cup of tea, after a visit to the toilet there would not be time to drink it. Robbo and his friend Billy headed for the cloakroom, jumping over the trough of disinfectant that everybody was supposed to walk through on leaving the shed.

Some people had been working all night and were due to knock off for the day. Others had started their shifts at seven or eight o'clock, and the canteen served a good breakfast menu:

toast, eggs, bacon, sausages, tinned tomatoes, fruit juice, tea and coffee. The workers sat at yellow Formica-topped tables and flicked their cigarette ash into silver-foil ashtrays. Although the food was cheap, some workers, those Asian women for example who did not prefer to huddle in the cloakroom, brought their own food and thermos flasks.

Sylvia carried her tray over to the nearest table where a group of people who had just started that week sat together and, finding herself opposite a black man with an artificial hand, saw an opportunity to tell the story of how, when hunting as a girl, a hound had bitten off her nipple. He was unimpressed, stirring his tea arrogantly with the spoon held in a sort of pincer.

'They're called dogs,' he said.

'Well, this was definitely a hound,' replied Sylvia huffily. 'I should know.'

The canteen was clean and warm; outside the aluminium-framed windows sleet was whipped about a dirty-looking sky. Spanish words and laughter from a table of black-haired women chalked up the most decibels and was rivalled by Urdu or some such from the large sari-ed contingent, who were bussed in by their own coach. Sylvia decided to forgive the man, and give him and his fellow newcomers a friendly word of warning. She lowered her voice.

'You have to watch those Asians,' she said. 'They take your mushrooms if you don't keep an eye on them. Lean right across the beds and grab all the best ones. Work in gangs, they do, go up and down cutting the big ones. No wonder they always get such big bonuses. We don't stand a chance. You've got to watch them.'

'How long have you been working here?' a girl asked.

'Fortnight pay day.'

The supervisors whistled up their teams and tea break was over. A drift of icing sugar lay over the leaves and a flash of February sun gilded the icy puddles in the gravel as they crunched

back in their wellies to the sheds, throwing half-smoked cigarettes into the bin of sand outside the door.

Green Star Mushrooms Limited was a member of a large group of
companies and supplied chains of pizza restaurants, shops and super-
markets as well as having numerous smaller outlets for its white
cultured fungi. It consisted of an administration block, a building
that housed generators and machinery, storage and packaging
depots and six vast windowless sheds like aircraft hangars where the
mushrooms grew. Each shed was divided into four sections, and
each section housed four long bays, each in four tiers, like aluminium bunk-beds packed with compost. To pick from the lowest
bed, workers had to crouch on the floor; aluminium step-ladders
were used to reach the second and third levels, and the top bed was
attained by a central flight of steps, and when all the pickers were
installed up there, a section of the walkway was slid over the
entrance and nobody could come down again until it was removed.
A long polythene wind tunnel was suspended just above their
heads. Swinging about like monkeys was frowned on. The sheds
seemed dark until you became accustomed to the electric light.

'Right. Everybody into number thirteen,' Shirley the supervisor called.

'Lucky for some,' said Robbo.

Sylvia stuck her number on the boxes and baskets she had
picked, and unhooked her ladder and tray and bucket and made
for the door. She was dismayed to see the heaps and piles of boxes
and baskets the Asians were staggering along with. That pretty
little girl who had started on the same day as she, smiled at her
as she put down her pyramid. They had been friends for a morning until she had been enveloped in the silken cluster of her own
kind, and now unless she smiled Sylvia could not recognize her.
They all looked alike, with their long black plaits down their
backs, except those whose plaits were grey.

'Hello, Sheila,' said Sylvia, thinking again that it was a sensible English-sounding name.

'Hi, Sylvia,' said Shreela. 'How many pounds have you picked this morning?'

'Enough,' said Sylvia, standing on tiptoe to hoist her heavy bucket of stalks and broken mushrooms and compost and empty it into the huge polythene sack on a frame provided for waste. She could see who was going to get a bonus and who wasn't. Shirley and an assistant stood at the door weighing them and noting down each person's pickings.

No mushrooms were allowed to be taken from one room to another; neither was any equipment without first being sterilized. Step-ladders had to be dunked into a vat of disinfectant, first one way up, and then the other, likewise trays and knives. The floor was awash with suds and stalks and bits of mushrooms; there were men whose job it was to keep the floors clean, and to empty the rubbish sacks. Sylvia wondered what became of the stalks, wondered if they were utilized in some way. It seemed such a waste; surely they could be used to make packet soup or something; great vats of grey soup ladled out to the homeless and hungry. She had decided not to ask, since her enquiry as to what the compost consisted of was met with the short answer 'shit'. It was better not to think about that; the crumbly dark compost smelled of mildew and nothing worse, but she imagined it was shovelled out from battery houses where chickens were kept in cruel and grotesque captivity; she had seen one once on a visit to a farm and the smell had been overpoweringly disgusting. The battery was not unlike this place, she thought.

'At least we've got room to turn around and flap our wings,' she remarked to the women waiting to dunk their ladders.

'Pardon?'

'Sylvia, you're dreaming again. Get on with it.' Shirley had

materialized in her white official wellies. Sylvia's knife slipped
from her fingers and fell to the bottom of the vat. She had to
roll up her sleeve and plunge her arm in, but she couldn't reach
the bottom. She panicked, flapping her wet arms about. This
was total disaster. She didn't know whether to run away, out of
the shed into the bleak countryside never to return, or to try to
manage without her knife, but there was no way she could break
the stalks off as neatly as she could cut them. She was elbowed
out of the way and was making desperate bids to reach the
knife, leaning right over the murky water until she almost fell
in, her face scraping the surface. Someone grasped her ankles.
Sylvia screamed, flailing about, certain that she was to be
drowned. Then she felt the ground beneath her feet and turned
to scream at her attacker. It was Dexter towering over her, grinning.

'Looking for something?'

She would have given him a piece of her mind but she saw
Shirley approaching.

'My knife,' she gasped. 'I dropped it.'

Dexter reached down and effortlessly brought out the knife, his
brown arm dripping dirty pearls. Sylvia could have kissed it. She
scuttled off to number thirteen, her ladder with her rack hooked
over it and a pile of boxes and baskets clanking behind her. She
had been late clocking on, having to change into her wellies, and
the only ladder left had been this rusty job with one wheel.
Funny how she always got lumbered with the leftovers. As now,
when she arrived in the shed, everybody else had nabbed the best
places. She was confronted with a sparse sprinkling of tiny mushrooms in the only vacant bed.

'What are we picking?' she asked the woman next to her, who
with her friend formed a deadly team. They had been there only
as long as Sylvia but had already chalked up fat bonuses and were
due to be promoted to Valerie's team of skilled pickers. Sylvia

would have to wait the statutory six weeks before promotion and the rate she was going, might not achieve it even then.

'Down to five pence,' said the woman. Sylvia received the news glumly. It took her for ever to fill a box with these hateful buttons. The closed mushrooms were categorized according to size – five pence, ten pence and fifty pence, large and extra large. 'If we got five pence for each mushroom we picked, that would work out at more than two pounds thirty an hour, wouldn't it?'

Nobody answered.

'Fives into two pounds thirty goes – forty-six. So that's forty-six mushrooms per hour, I mean pence per mushroom we ought to get, isn't it, Marie?'

Again Marie didn't bother to answer Batty Sylvia, who went on happily with her calculations while her basket remained empty.

'Fifty pence per mushroom, now that would be, um, two pounds thirty divided by fifty equals, knock off the noughts and that's four and three fifths per mushroom, we ought to get ... '

'Something a bit wrong with your calculations, gel.'

It was that Dexter strutting along in his tight jeans like a cockerel in a yard of hens.

'Don't you gel me,' said Sylvia crossly, then she remembered he had retrieved her knife.

'Dexter! Sylvia! Get on with your work.'

Someone made a ribald noise.

Sylvia blushed. Having her name shouted out like that as if she was a naughty little girl in school, by a chit of a girl half her age. She bowed her head over the bed and started cutting mushrooms, but her heart was thudding as she saw Shirley approach.

'I dread it when I see those white wellies coming,' muttered Robbo who was working the opposite side of her bed, where she could see great clusters of fifty-pence mushrooms disappearing under his knife. Sylvia liked best the open mushrooms, big as saucers, big as elephant's ears: half a dozen of them filled a basket; they were more like the mushrooms she had found in the fields as a girl in the early morning or the evening with the rough grass silvered and wet with dew.

'What are these?' Shirley was shaking the box.

'My buttons,' said Sylvia.

'Why are they in a box? You know buttons go in a basket. Where are your ten pences?'

'Here,' Sylvia held out a green plastic box. A few mushrooms rolled about on the bottom.

'You've got your open and your closed mixed up. And they're supposed to be of uniform size. Get them sorted out, and get your act together.'

Act? Sylvia's back felt as if it were breaking, her knees creaked as she crouched. She lapsed on to her knees, feeling wet mud seep through her trousers. She picked until she had exhausted that bed and then unhooked her rack from the side of the bed, folded up her ladder and carried them, with her boxes and baskets, to another bed. She had forgotten her numbers, a roll of sticky labels that had to be stuck on every box and basket that she picked, so that her quota could be assessed. She found them lying in a muddy pool. Everything was so mucky, the fingers of her rubber gloves were engrained with sticky black mould, her sleeve stinking of disinfectant, her wellies bleared, her overall had a wet dirty patch right across the stomach and there was a smear of compost on her cheek. Some people managed to look quite neat and composed at the end of the day; not Sylvia. She was wrecked by dinner-time. If you didn't wear your rubber gloves your fingers were stained and your nails packed with black mould that a scrubbing brush could not remove. Like the supermarket trolley which inevitably Sylvia got, the one with the squeak and the wheels that went in the wrong direction, her ladder was unstable and her rack hung at a perilous angle,

endangering her mushrooms. Pull, slice off the stalk, mushroom
in box or basket, stalk in bucket, stoop, bend, up the ladder,
stretch, pull, cut, down the ladder, empty bucket. Nobody was
talking much today, except the Asian women who talked inces-
santly. It was amazing that anybody could have so much to say.
To Sylvia's eye they moved like a flock of brightly coloured
locusts leaving the beds bare behind them.

'It's not fair,' she complained to Shirley. 'They're picking all
the mushrooms.'

'That's what they're paid to do.'

Talk about inverted prejudice.

Later, however, she was pleased to hear Shirley telling them off
for indiscriminate picking, dropping everything into their baskets
regardless of size, and appointing two of their number to sort
them out. Downright cheating.

Getting her act together: Sylvia saw all the mushroom pickers in a Busby Berkeley-style sequence, turning their buckets
upside down and beating them like drums, swarming up the aluminium supports like sailors in the rigging, kicking out their
arms and legs starwise, their green-and-white gingham overalls
twirling as they tap-danced in their wellies, juggling mushrooms
and flashing knives spreading out the pink palms of their rubber
gloves as they fell on one knee behind Shirley, the star in her
white wellies.

'Where's your radio, Sharon?' she called.

'Pardon?'

'I said, where's your wireless today?'

'I left it in the toilet.'

'Go and get it then.'

'I can't.'

'Go on.'

'You go and get it if you're so keen.'

Sylvia knew there was no way she could leave the shed. On

her first morning she had heard someone who asked to go to the toilet told that she should have gone at tea break.

"'Radio Mercury, the heart of the South,'" she sang in compensation, and then,

'You and me, we sweat and strain
Bodies all achin', racked with pain
Tote dat barge, lift dat bale—
Get a little drunk and you lands in jai-ail.'

Robbo joined in in a surprising bass voice, given the overall and bandeau, and then he and Billy dissolved into cackles. It wasn't that funny, thought Sylvia, but she was glad she had made them laugh. Sometimes this place was like a morgue with everyone silently picking, lost in their own thoughts and in the smell of mildew. Then Shirley came along and detailed Sylvia and a silent lad named Gary to clear one of the beds that had been picked. People were supposed to clear the beds as they went along, but this one was full of a debris of broken stalks and deformed mushrooms and frail thin toadstools, illegal immigrants who had sneaked in somehow. Gary didn't mind, he mooned through the day, pale as a mushroom, just achieving his quota and never thinking of a bonus, but Sylvia was seething on the top step of her rickety ladder as she grubbed out the left-overs, losing valuable picking time while others filled their baskets with mushrooms that should have been hers.

'What's for dinner, Stewart?' called Marie.

Stewart couldn't read or write but he always knew the menu off by heart.

'Sausage, beans and chips. Quiche and salad. Macaroni cheese. Fruit slice and custard or ice cream.' He spoke thickly as though his mouth was already crammed with bangers and beans.

Sylvia looked at her watch. It had drowned in the disinfectant and presented a bloated, dead face.

'Right, bring your mushrooms to be checked and go to dinner.'

The newcomers who had not yet been issued with gloves had to scrub their hands in the trough in the passage. Sylvia hurried past them, through the foot-bath and into the fresh freezing air, narrowly missing a fork-lift truck, and lighting a cigarette as she went and joined the queue in the canteen. Maintenance men and the other workers were already seated at some of the tables. She carried her tray over to an empty table where she was joined by Marie and her mate, Dexter, Stewart and Sharon.

'Ooooh, my back. It's killing me. When I took this job I'd no idea there'd be so much heavy lifting.'

'And carrying. And climbing.'

'What did you do before?' Marie asked Sylvia.

'Oh, all sorts of things. Shop work, bar work, kennel maid ...'

'I'm surprised you wanted to work with dogs, after what that hound did to you.'

'Oh well, it didn't mean any harm. Just got over-excited.'

A guffaw of crude laughter greeted this. Sylvia concentrated on threading a piece of macaroni on each of the tines of her fork. She hated vulgarity, and besides the incident had not happened to her but to somebody else she had heard of.

'I was working in a Christmas-cracker factory up until a few weeks ago.'

'Why d'you give it up?'

'Oh, the novelty wore off.'

She might have added that she had a job in a balloon factory, but she blew it, and that she used to work in a pub until she was barred, she had been a postwoman but she got the sack, and that she had worked on a newspaper but it folded. That hadn't been her fault; she was just the tea lady. She had to work, Jack couldn't and she had to support them both. She didn't like leaving him alone all day, but it couldn't be helped.

'I picked fifty-eight pounds this morning,' she heard someone say. 'What did you do?'

'Fifty-three.'

You could buy mushrooms cheap if you wanted, on Friday afternoons, but to do that would have meant Sylvia's missing the firm's minibus which dropped her at the top of her road. Anyway she hadn't felt like eating a mushroom since she started this job; even a mug of mushroom soup brought on a bout of nausea. She had had a narrow escape on her first morning. Shirley had come up to her and said, 'You're not eating mushrooms are you?'

'No, I'm chewing gum.'

'Well, you're not really supposed to eat in here at all.'

'Sorry.'

Phew. A few minutes before, she had been eating mushrooms, popping the little white buttons into her mouth as she worked, just as one eats strawberries when strawberry picking. Now the nasty monopods clodhopped through her dreams, and the smell of the compost was enough to turn her up. One old bloke, with one eye, did eat the mushrooms, but he was the only one, and she was sure Shirley turned a blind eye.

Just before the half hour was up, Sylvia made a dash for the cloak-room. She didn't bother with make-up any more, or to comb her hair. Every pair of trousers she possessed was stained at the knees with brown marks that wouldn't wash out, and she was too tired to care. After her first day her arms had been so stiff that she could hardly move them, her back felt as if it was broken and her legs felt as heavy as trees. She was getting used to it now, and managing quite well with just the fractured spine. As she emerged from the ladies' cloakroom she encountered Robbo and Billy coming giggling out of the gents'.

'What have you two been up to?' she asked in a friendly fashion, but they didn't answer. Nevertheless she was pleased to follow them because she had forgotten which shed they were in, and they all looked alike to her. There had been the awful time she had left her numbers in the canteen and had to gallop back to get them, only to find they had been put in the dinner waste, and she had had to rake through a refuse sack of banana skins and cigarette butts and slimy yoghurt cartons and half-eaten sandwiches to find them, and then she had run back to the wrong shed and wandered for what seemed hours like a lost soul through all the wrong sheds opening doors on silent beds of ghostly mushrooms, and throbbing machinery and men hosing down the floors. She was crying when she finally found her team. She was supposed to be working on the top stage and the trap door had been shut, and people had had to move all their ladders and boxes to let her in, and of course all those people who worked in gangs and pairs had grabbed all the best places.

Halfway through the afternoon they had to change sheds again, so racks were unhooked, ladders folded and perilous pyramids of boxes and baskets carried to be weighed. Sylvia had done a bit better since lunch and was feeling quite pleased with herself as she dunked her step-ladder in the disinfectant, first this way, then that. Sharon had brought her radio and the afternoon was passing quite pleasantly until Billy started teasing Stewart about living in a hostel.

'What sort of a hostel is it then?' he kept saying.

'It's for the handicapped,' Stewart said.

'Why d'you live there then, Stewart?'

'Leave him alone,' someone shouted.

'Pick on someone your own size,' suggested somebody else and everybody laughed. Billy was a slender five feet two, and Stewart was a lumbering six feet, bursting out of his cardigan. Then Billy started jostling Stewart and knocked a basket of his mushrooms to the floor. Stewart gave a howl as they rolled away in the mess of muddy compost and stalks and lunged at Billy with his knife. The man with the artificial arm leaped forward and seized the knife in a lightning pincer grasp. Stewart fell to his knees snuffling as he gathered up his dirty mushrooms, like precious jewels, and replaced them in his basket.

'It'd serve you right if I had an epileptic fit,' he told Billy.

'Robbo. Billy. Outside.' Shirley's white wellies had sped silently down the aisle. Robbo and Billy followed them out to the tune of 'Rat In The Kitchen' from Sharon's radio.

'They're for the chop,' said Dexter. 'Tippling on the job again.'

In the administrative block Robbo and Billy faced the boss in her white cap with the Green Star insignia. Robbo had removed his bandeau and his hair spread out on the shoulders of his green and white overall.

'By the way,' he said, 'remember when I cut myself with my knife?'

'You'd had your tetanus jabs,' interrupted Shirley.

'It bled quite a lot if you remember, all over the place ... all over my mushrooms.'

'Well?'

'Well, I just wondered if I should have mentioned that I was HIV positive ...?'

He and Billy departed laughing to pick up their cards, leaving the two women to ponder the credibility and implications of his statement.

'Five o'clock people, pack up your things.'

As she carried her things to the door Sylvia saw little Sheila's silky trousers coming down the steps from the top bed. That was all she could see of her, so hung about with brimming baskets and piled with full green boxes was she. It was unbelievable. Sylvia had worked really hard, and Sheila's efforts made it look as though she hadn't tried at all.

'You've done well, Sheila,' said Sylvia. 'Let me give you a hand with some of those.'

She put down her own poor pickings and took some of Shreela's from her.

'Oh, thank you, Sylvia. If you just take these for me I'll go and get the rest.' The rest. Sylvia knelt quickly and peeled off Shreela's numbers from four of the boxes and stuck on her own. Then she piled them on top of her boxes and carried them to be weighed. She could see that Shirley was impressed as she wrote down the amount. Then she went back to help Shreela with the rest of her load. She joined the queue to wash the step-ladder, wash the rack, stack them up, then dashed to the cloakroom for her coat. No time to change out of her wellies. The minibus was waiting. If Fred was driving, you were allowed to smoke; if the other Fred was driving, you weren't.

As the Green Star minibus snouted out into the lane Sylvia reflected that she would have lots to tell Jack when she got home – Billy and Robbo getting the chop, Dexter rescuing her knife, her bumper crop; and he would tell her all about his day, the tussle with a spray of millet, hard pecking on the cuttlefish, conversations with himself in the mirror. She wondered what to have for tea; whatever it was, it wouldn't be mushrooms on toast. Behind them in the sheds, thousands of tiny white nodules no bigger than pins' heads starring the black compost were starting to swell.

Soft Volcano

'There is nothing like the sound of children singing hymns for deceiving us into thinking that there is some hope for mankind.'

So thought Rose Rossi as emanations of goodness came from the grey and green pullovers of the children on the Virginia-creeper-wreathed, hop-entwined stage. Shrill recorders pierced the wooden rafters and played havoc with strained parents' voices and left them straying somewhere round the children's heads. The Harvest bread began to wobble and red apples were swelling and doubling their number.

Richard Garlick heard a raindrop fall on the mimeographed songsheet of the woman next to him. He looked at the window; it was closed. So far, aware of Janet on his left, he had sensed the woman on his right only as a brown velvet sleeve, a ringed hand, a shiny brown shoe, vague red clouds of hair. He turned his head slightly and saw the words on her paper all blurred and starting to run. She must have known what to expect, yet she had come unarmed with handkerchief or tissue. Women's tears usually irritated him, but these which rolled down steadily and motivelessly set up an answering prickle in his own eyes. Janet nudged him and thrust a couple of tissues into his hand. He placed them on the brown velvet knee.

'You know who that was?' Janet whispered in the playground as parents and children massed and blocked the narrow iron gate.

'Duncan Rossi's ex-wife – remember she bought the Mill House last year? You know, the racing driver!'

The divorcée passed them, pale and with pink-rimmed eyes, holding by the hand a red-haired boy. Then Gary and Mark hurled themselves on them and had to be zipped into anoraks and the family went home to the house beside the general store and sub-post office which Richard had inherited from his father.

There was the usual nine-fifteen rush in the shop the next morning, of mothers who had delivered their children to school. Mrs Rossi drifted in on the tail-end, in a fur coat and muddy jeans; her dog, tied to the hook outside, howled loudly and tried to spring through the door every time a customer entered or left the shop. She asked Richard to cash a cheque and ordered a lot of groceries to be delivered to the Mill House. She gave no sign of recognition and Richard said nothing.

The sale of the Mill House had been negotiated the previous January, just before her divorce. The car had squelched up the path through the little wood. Duncan at the wheel with a hang-over, herself sulking beside him and James in the back with a cold. She had looked at the grey house, the stone heron over-looking the millpond full of yellow leaves, hanks of dun grass, thin blackening nettles, rasping teazels, tangled English melan-choly, and thought, 'This will do very well.'

Since then she and the boy had been abroad and it was just a few days since they had taken up residence there, and been surprised by the reddening leaves of the sumach trees in front of the house. All else that remained of cultivation were the Michaelmas daisies and papery disks of honesty. Half a mile up the river that fed their sluggish pond, among brambles' barbed arches and hollow hemlock stems and dried seed heads rattling in the wind, stood a hexagonal concrete pillbox, relic of the war, of which there were many on the North Downs. James had discovered it and intended to occupy it, taking with him matches and food. The entrance turned at a tangent into black-ness. The smell drove him back. For a few minutes he stood outside, despising himself, then suddenly turned and fled home, as if a dead Nazi soldier had risen with a rusty bullet hole in his rotted uniform and was pursuing him stiffly and bloodlessly through the wood.

The scarlet sumachs were blazing like sunset at the top of the path. Richard had left the new Cortina Estate at the foot to save the tyres from the sharp stones embedded in deep leaf-falls, and was carrying a heavy box of groceries. As he walked two bottles clinked together and the gold and colourless liquid slopped in their necks. He thought he heard voices ahead of him and an animal tearing through the undergrowth: Mrs Rossi's bloodhound bitch who left a lemon tang in the misty air. As he followed the citronella trail of anti-mate through the little wood he heard Mrs Rossi's voice clearly,

'Yes, darling, they are beautiful, but poisonous.' As he passed through their gate he saw a rope of red and green bryony berries looped over the hedge. The boy had disappeared when Richard arrived at the back door.

'Oh, it's you, Mr Garlick, stalking us through the woods. I was quite sure it was a murderer. It's so quiet here in the after-noons.'

'I don't think you'll find many murderers in these parts, Mrs Rossi,' he said, putting down the box on the kitchen table. There were a couple of chairs, several tea chests.

'Settling in now, are you?'

'Not really,' she said, and made no mention of payment, and Richard, wispy-haired with glasses, known in secret moments to his wife as Bunny, didn't like to.

'Thank you very much, Mr Garlick.'

'Right then, I'll be off.'

'By the way, I should thank you for the tissues yesterday. It was nice of you.'

'It was nothing.'

Neither seemed capable of dislodging him. At last the bloodhound came to their rescue, rushing in and propelling him with huge fore-paws through the open door.

'Richard! That's the third time Gary's asked you to help him with his model!'

'What? Oh. Right, son, let's be having you!' He rubbed his hands together in simulated eagerness and advanced towards the little pieces of grey plastic.

Because he was in the shop most of the day, Richard was in the position, if he so wanted, of sociologist or chronicler of local mores. He had noticed, over the last year or so, that the topic of property values and house prices, the plight of young couples, discussed in unctuous tones by those who had achieved their mortgage, had given way to the subject of extensions. Janet, behind the little post office grille, among the stamps and leaflets, had been fired by all the talk, and now nothing would do but the loft must be converted into a den for the boys. Richard was sent up a ladder to clear it of junk in readiness for the men who were coming to give an estimate of cost. What Janet termed 'junk' were the dear furnishings of his boyhood, among them glass jars powdered with sherbet crystals and sweet splinters, a cabinet of glass-fronted doors, and a long, bevelled mirror with dark-green glass corners and 'Fry's Cocoa' in chocolate-coloured letters across its face.

They were eased downstairs and placed, with a pang, outside the shop to await the dustmen. Richard saw his father's watery eye glinting in the mirror and longed for the evidence of his betrayal to be gone. He had hardly spoken to Janet during breakfast.

The dust-cart's dusty buzz was growing louder. Richard sat at the check-out and watched rain accessorize after the fact by blurring the glass and spotting the wood. The shop door crashed open and Mrs Rossi stood there, soaked, bare-headed, accusing.

'You're not consigning those beautiful things to the dustmen!' she stated. 'How much do you want for them?'

'You can have them,' he said surprised.

'Don't be silly. Any antique dealer would snap them up.'

Janet, who had emerged from behind her bars, was beaten back by a rush for Family Allowances and could manage only a twisting scornful finger at her temple over her customers' heads.

'They're yours if you take them away.'

'Right,' she said, 'I will.'

She went out into the rain and attempted to lift a corner of the cabinet but was forced to straighten up, red-faced and defeated. She pulled the mirror away from the wall it leant on and was almost knocked backwards by its weight.

'I'll hire a van,' she said.

The dust-cart was drawing up.

'I'll bring them up this afternoon,' he heard himself say. 'I can borrow a van.'

His reward was the first real smile he had had from her. They went inside.

'Can I talk to you?' she suddenly said quickly. 'I've no friends here. I sensed, I hope I'm right, that you are not badly disposed towards me.'

The shop door jarred, a woman came in, took a wire basket, and after making some decisions, was caught agonizingly between the choice of tomato or fruity sauce. Mrs Rossi hovered at the cheese display.

'Let me persuade you,' said Richard at last, rising and plucking a bottle of ketchup from the shelf and depositing it in the woman's basket, her mouth opened at his unwonted masterfulness.

'I'll have the other,' she said, replacing his bottle. Two more people came in while she was at the check-out.

'I'll see you later,' said Mrs Rossi, giving up hope and leaving. The bell clanged behind her.

'That's him,' said Mrs Rossi. They were in the sitting room, where the Fry's Cocoa mirror had been propped against the wall. It was carpeted with a green carpet but otherwise was not much more settled than the kitchen, where the glass cabinet and glass sweet jars had been put, and James could be heard clashing a long spoon about in the jars scraping up the sweet sediment. She held out a framed photograph to Richard, of a black curly-haired man in oily overalls, grinning in a crooked laurel-wreath. Richard recognized the face from newspaper and television.

'He's always been a heavy drinker, but he could always get in shape in time for a big race. Lately he's been getting worse and worse. You know he hasn't won anything since the American Grand Prix. He has terrible rages. He's an ice-cream Italian Scot,' she added by way of explanation.

'If ever I told James off, he'd say "Mummy doesn't love you, only Daddy does". Can you imagine? Now I keep having the feeling that he's somewhere around. That he's watching us. He wanted James at the time, you know. He's often threatened to kill me.'

She was walking round the room, ran her finger along the window-sill, seemed defeated by dust, and sat down.

'I'm not dependent on him for money,' she said, 'I've got some of my own.'

Richard tried to keep his mind on her problem while watching her mouth move and wondering how it would feel to kiss it.

'Perhaps if you were to take a job?' he ventured. 'Something part-time, so you wouldn't have so much time to brood.'

'Are you offering me a job?' she laughed. 'In the shop? Would you give me a pale-blue nylon overall?'

'My wife doesn't object to wearing one.' Even to him it sounded childish and huffy.

She didn't answer.

The dog started to scratch violently. They sat listening to the whirring of claws on skin. At last, when it seemed the air between them must crack, a clock took breath and struck four and released him. He stood up.

'I'd better get back. I shouldn't worry about your ex-husband. He couldn't possibly be here. If you're worried about anything, call the police.' He started for the door with the difficulty he always had when disengaging himself from her presence.

'The phone's not fixed yet,' she said.

'I'll look in tomorrow if you like.'

'Thank you very much,' she said humbly, and walked through the house with him, and the garden, to the front gate, and down to the river bank above the millpond.

'I remember a few years ago we had a particularly wet winter and this pond flooded and—'

He realized she wasn't listening and turned to see her staring at the river with horror on her face.

'What is it? What's the matter?'

She pointed at a whisky bottle in the brown oily water.

'It's his brand,' she whispered.

The bottle did indeed look a sinister emissary bobbing in the water, sucked under the massed leaves in the pond. Light had gone from the sky.

'Nonsense,' Richard told her firmly, 'nonsense, it could have floated down from anywhere.' He realized she was clutching his arm.

'Go in now, it's getting cold. I'll look in tomorrow. Why don't you get someone, a friend, to come and stay?'

'I have.'

As he left her Richard had the distinct feeling that Mrs Rossi was slightly crazy, deranged; perhaps by her divorce.

'You haven't forgotten that it's the stool-ball AGM have you?' said Janet. 'I'll be back by about ten, I expect.'

Richard had supervised the boys' bath and they were playing in the bedroom. He went up to tell them to go to bed. Mark was fooling about with a pair of plastic binoculars.

'Let's have a look,' said Richard. He hung them round his neck and went to the window.

'These could be very useful,' he said. 'For observing wild life or spying on the neighbours.' He put them to his eyes and adjusted the focus. They were surprisingly powerful and picked out the lighted panes of the village hall windows, stars and clouds in the black sky, the church spire against the moon. He raked them through the woods, up to the Mill House. Light shone in the sitting room and two upstairs windows. He looked beyond the house up river. From the black mass of the river bank rose a thin twist of grey smoke. Realization kicked him in the stomach. Someone was in the pillbox, watching the Mill House, waiting. Rossi.

'Come on, Daddy, let's have a go!'

Richard handed back the glasses, feeling sick, and sat on the bed. His immediate impulse was to rush out, up to the Mill House. Janet was out, he would have to wait until the boys were asleep. He hustled them into bed and kissed each tenderly, with the fear that he might not see them again, and went downstairs, put on coat and gloves, and waited. The thought came to him that it would be wiser to call the police, but he dismissed it. He had never in his life been called on to do anything even slightly frightening or dangerous; he was an eater of meals on time, a sleeper in soft beds, wearer of slippers. His only brush with fear was when Janet went into hospital to have the boys. He crept upstairs and removed the book from Gary's sleeping hand and straightened the Action Man on Mark's pillow. He checked the central heating and closed the front door quietly behind him.

He walked quickly through the village, meeting no one, and ran across the wet field and into the wood. Sharp stones pierced the soles of his shoes as he ran. Pain in his lungs bent him double on the front door-step as he pressed the bell. It drilled through the house. The dog was barking frantically. He rang again and again, desperately. Then realizing why she wouldn't answer, sensing her terror in the locked house, poked open the letter box to call through it.

Iron choked his voice, his head swelled like a black balloon. He tried to claw the fingers from his throat, then swung his foot back and kicked hard where he sensed his attacker's legs were. It struck home, and Richard fell back against the door as the grip loosened. Rossi was rolling on the ground, a knife beside him. Richard grabbed it and threw it in a weak shoulder-wrenching underarm. A splash sounded. Rossi was rising. Richard pulled back his fist, shutting his eyes, and cracked it on to his jaw, and again. Pain jarred up his arm. He took off his glove to suck his knuckle, and realized that Rossi had been overcome not just by his blows but by the alcohol whose fumes were being pumped in reeking gusts from his panting body. He pulled himself up and stumbled through the front garden.

Richard sat on the step, wiping his glasses which he hadn't thought to remove. Rossi belched as he disappeared. This crude eructation hanging in the night sky filled Richard with rage against him and his terrorizing of Rose. He set off after him. His footsteps spurred Rossi into a lurching run. He turned not right, into the wood, but left along the lane that led to the sand quarry. For a moment Richard saw him spread-eagled against the high wire fence like an escaping prisoner, then he was over. Richard found the gate and climbed to the top, jumped and fell into soft sand. A ghostly convoy of bulldozers stood. Rossi was running across the flat towards pale mountains of sand. A high wooden building on stilts bulked against the sky. The word 'corrosive' glittered in the moonlight on a rusty tank. Richard lost Rossi in the white sandscape, his shoes were full and heavy, he stopped running and stood, air swirling round him like black ectoplasm, his heart banging, yet he was not afraid.

He realized that it was Rossi's fear, not his own that he felt, and that Rossi was very near. He knew his enemy and Rossi did not. For all he knew Richard might be a fiend from hell. Rossi stumbled round the base of a sand-hill. Richard started after him; his joints moved slickly, blood oiling his muscles. He was gaining on Rossi and could hear sawing breaths in his chest. Rossi took a despairing look over his shoulder and made for a giant crane or dinosaur whose neck stretched out some thirty feet over the highest mountain. Thick raindrops were pitting the sand. Richard reached the crane and saw Rossi climb over the cab and on to the monster's neck. The rungs must have been greasy with rain, but Rossi climbed on towards the top, where he must surely be trapped, and crawled dark and terrified against the sky.

Richard was suddenly sick of it all.

'I'm going home!' he shouted. 'Come down.'

The only words used between them. He turned to go, as if ground was falling away from his own tingling feet, arms tearing from their sockets, chest caving with the altitude. As, ground spinning under him, he turned to see if Rossi was descending, he saw him hanging, kicking wildly from the crane, kicking, struggling to hook his legs back up. His legs went still, he dangled, his fingers slowly opened out and he plummeted silently into the heart of the soft volcano. Rivers of sand ran down the sides, trickled, and stopped.

Richard stood in the rain. He looked round at the sandscape

undisturbed under the moon, the still machinery. There was nothing to be done. To reach Rossi he too must leap from the crane and suffocate in sand. Help would be too late.

He turned and ran.

While the bath was running he stood in the clouds of steam shaking every grain of sand from his socks and shoes and all his clothes into the basin. Rain without and steam within; he lay back in the water and watched the black window-pane liquefy. The rims of his nails were greenish with packed sand. He took the nail brush.

Janet's key twisted in the lock; he attempted a snatch of the *St Matthew Passion*, but his throat choked up as if with sand.

'We've been asked to a party tomorrow,' came Janet's voice.

Luckily, it was Wednesday. Rose Rossi didn't come in in the morning and the shop closed in the afternoon. Alone in the house, golden rod beckoning like false blonde women at the window, Richard saw how trees soughed and leaves fell, the church clock struck and cars passed, the world went on and the loss of one of its sons in a sandhill seemed to matter not at all. So this is all we are worth, he thought. None of us matters at all.

Married couples were jogging round the through-lounge of the party-givers' house. The host claimed Janet, and Richard moved towards the lush buffet. He became aware of a strange noise below the music, a sort of drone. He looked round and saw that all the couples were singing the words of the songs of their youth, slightly behind the record, and Janet, eyes closed, was murmuring them too, and he only wanted to be with Rose Rossi. He went through to the kitchen.

'Do you remember,' a woman was saying, 'how, at parties when we were young, someone was always sick, and someone lost a shoe?'

'And when they put the lights out, all the girls had to sit on a boy's knee and "snog", whether they wanted to or not?' said another.

'Just getting a breath of fresh air,' said Richard as he passed unnoticed through the back door.

He drove up to the Mill House, not caring any longer about his tyres, and was shocked by a strange car parked outside the gate. He was furious; he kicked its tyre. Her friend must have come. He walked round the house, wondering what excuse he could give for arriving. Outside the sitting-room window he stopped.

There, caught in the Fry's Cocoa mirror, were Rose and her friend. The friend's hair was pulled back in Rose Rossi's grasp as she kissed her mouth.

He wandered round the woods, sent stones crashing into the millpond and disturbed no one. Eventually, frozen, he drove back to the party. The smell of black coffee hit him as he walked in. Janet was in the kitchen seated on a stool with her head in her chest. He shook her shoulder, she looked up at him sideways and mumbled, 'I've lost my shoe.'

The Stained-Glass Door

Jean MacAllister's rather large white face, which had hung soft and dreamy in the steam of her drinking chocolate, hardened as she turned from the kitchen window.

'She's out there again.'

Nigel MacAllister yawned; scratching his chest, catching his finger in a grey curl.

'She's probably lonely. Bored. Anyway she'll be gone soon. You know how those people come and go ...'

'She doesn't. She's going in now, grinding out a cigarette with her foot. That lawn must be knee-deep in cigarette butts.'

'If you can call it a lawn any more.'

'It was such a lovely garden. You'd think the council ...'

Nigel yawned again; he had heard it all before – that beautiful house, the mirror image of their own, taken over by the council; the blanket looped across the window instead of curtains, the rusting cars, the broken glass, the language. He gave his wife a slap, almost too hard, as she hung the washed mugs on their hooks.

'Come on then, or we won't get up in the morning.'

They went upstairs.

'Nigel – is anything wrong?'

'I told you, I've got problems at work.'

'Actually, you didn't.'

As the sound of a plane ebbed in the darkness a rumbling came from Nigel's side of the bed and Jean's stomach gave a timid answering bleat. She could have felt sorry for those two stomachs had they lain side by side in white bloody trays in a butcher's window, which was how, for a moment, she saw them.

The following evening when Jean arrived home from her upholstery class with her little hammer, bristling with tacks, although nothing in that house needed re-upholstering – there were no children or animals to kick and claw, not even any visiting nieces and nephews – she stood for a moment looking at the sky. A jewelled insect was homing in on Gatwick through the stars. The house next door was in darkness, but the girl in the downstairs flat had neglected to pull down the blanket across the window and Jean saw her, in the light of a street lamp, asleep on a divan, hair spread out, thumb in mouth.

As on almost every morning, Jean stood at the head of the stairs, restored and reassured by her house; the morning sunshine filtering through the stained-glass door, throwing pale pink and green and yellow bars and diamonds and lozenges of light on to the carpet, gilding the hall table, the flowers in the iridescent glass; the empty rooms unfolding quietly from the hall. Several brown envelopes lay on the mat; they were all that seemed to come nowadays. She hardly glanced at them as she threw them on to the sideboard.

Boring bills. She left all that side of things to Nigel.

Later, although it was not yet ten o'clock, in her cotton dress and sandals, she was beaded with sweat by the time she reached the High Street. Outside the baker's she bumped into a woman and looked into her powdered face, a red slick of lipstick or jam in icing sugar, and realized that this oozing doughnut had been driven, at this early hour, to pound the hot pavements to the off-licence; tell-tale bottles clashed glassily in her bag. Jean turned with relief to the wholesome shiny sticks of bread.

Later again that morning she saw, through a fine pink mist of Windowlene, the girl from next door with her baby on her hip, a plastic bag of washing on the seat of the pushchair, setting off for the launderette. Really, there would seem nothing to connect those two, the skinny blonde girl and the unarguably coffee-coloured baby; except that the tiny brown hand was tangled in the lank hair like a baby animal's clinging on to its mother's fur. As she rubbed the window clear it blurred unaccountably.

With a heavy hand she sliced slabs of French bread for the bread and cheese lunch she was holding, the proceeds from which were to go to Oxfam. Her friends pecked like starlings with greasy beaks; her bread hovered in the air as first Nigel, then the girl next door, superimposed themselves on the chatter about children's O-level options, a topic of very limited interest to Jean.

She sighed and smeared her bread with butter and pickle.

'I'm starving,' she remarked through a mouthful of piercing crust. 'Let's take our coffee on to the patio,' she suggested, but the sunny stones were splintered by pop music from a radio next door.

'Will you turn that bloody thing down!' She suddenly erupted in a brown geyser of hot coffee. Her friends mopped and soothed, but all at once realized how time had flown and that so must they.

The MacAllisters had brought their friends, Peter and Mary, back to supper after a concert at the Fairfield Halls. Blue skeins of cigar smoke wound over the coffee cups, binding them, still softened by music and golden-bellied wood, together. The doorbell burst blue ropes, shattered golden wood. Jean returned from answering it.

'It was that girl from next door. Mandy. She wanted to use the telephone. I told her to use the call-box on the corner.' Her voice rose.

'It was for her own good. These people have got to stand on their own two feet. That's the trouble with the welfare state, it makes people lazy. Apathetic. Soft. I mean, Nigel's worked damned hard for everything we've got!'

She stalked into the kitchen, clashing bowls, leaving Nigel and Mary to rekindle a cigar and prod a candle with a dead match, dropping ugly black specks into the rosy wax. Peter followed with a couple of spoons.

'I wish she'd go!' Jean burst out. 'I'm sick of her. Always looming. Intruding. Imposing her miserable life on mine. I mean ...' above the thunderous tap, wrenching pink rubber gloves on to her fingers, 'it's not my fault ...'

Peter side-stepped the spray as the water hit a fork, and turned off the tap.

'Of course, it's not your fault. Your trouble is, you care too much about other people. You're too sensitive.'

The next morning Mary telephoned. 'Have you been in the copse lately?'

'No. Why?'

'There are masses of blackberries there. Beauties. Come and have a bite of lunch after yoga and we'll go blackberrying.'

'If you like.'

The receiver gave a squawk, almost a hurt sound, as she put it down on her friend's voice.

She had not intended to bulge in her leotard and black tights that morning, her head achy with too much wine the night before, and Mary's wholemeal pizza would undo any benefit the exercise might give; but the half-empty freezer groaned like a threatening ice floe for the soft fruit and she had made no jam yet. The afternoon found them in the copse armed with

Tupperware containers. Jean felt the knots that yoga had failed to untie dissolve in the sun and bird song as she gazed at a branch that bore bud, white flower, hard green berry, solid jelly brushed with red and the rich black culmination; on a single stem. Mary grabbed her arm.

'What's that noise?'

A blackbird shrieked. Over their banging hearts a steady shuffling sound came nearer. The middle-aged women clutched each other among spilled berries. It came towards them.

A baby broke through the undergrowth. It crawled, laughing through lips juicy with squashed blackberries. Mandy strode up and scooped the baby, who kicked its legs in delight, under her arm and was gone, but not before they had seen her face, streaked with tears and dirt where an earthy hand had brushed them away.

Although they continued to pick greedily, the gloss was gone from the afternoon. As Jean hurried past the house next door, through the smell of a blocked drain, it seemed to lunge at her; her own house in a distorting mirror.

It seemed that she had lost the art of making jam. She boiled and boiled; the house was filled with the smell of apples and blackberries but the jam would not set.

Hot uneasy nights when she and Nigel sweated separately in bed followed hot days when Jean could do nothing but lie on the grass. The sprinkler on the lawn brought a cool damp hour on some evenings, then she did the ironing, alone in the house; through a glaze of gin. She ceased to notice the light falling through the stained-glass door; the stems of the flowers on the hall table swelled and stank; the pile of unopened brown envelopes on the dusty sideboard grew higher.

She woke one night, whimpering; her silky nightdress clinging like a rag. Unhappy noises came from the hot cages next door. Someone was shouting, the baby was crying, glass smashed.

'Nigel,' she whispered in the darkness of her life grown rotten, 'Nigel.'

With a groan, he fell on her; she felt a tear fall on to her neck and burn the hollow of her collarbone.

Tomorrow she would clean the house, cook a wonderful meal, and over it get Nigel to tell her what was wrong. Together they would tackle and beat the foe, whatever it was. She nestled against the dear body that had been given into her care and moaned softly to think that he had not been able to trust himself to her.

It was afternoon by the time she was able to get on to the patio with the *Telegraph* crossword. In the gleaming house were flowers and such beautiful still lifes of fruit and vegetables that she would be reluctant to put them to the knife. She twirled the pen in her fingers; the sun struck its transparent plastic facets, threw revolving rainbows on the newsprint. Something dropped to the grass. A pear had fallen from the tree in next door's garden. The tree was heavy with golden fruit against the blue; ripe, heavy, going to waste. A bird even had its beak in one. She looked at the house. The family upstairs was out. The drug addicts in the middle flat were either asleep or dead. Mandy's radio was silent.

She was on the wall almost before she knew it. The pears fell into her hands and spread skirt. Scented flesh broke against her teeth. Suddenly, in a cracking of branches, Mandy's face thrust through the leaves. Jean jumped, breaking twigs, grazing the backs of her thighs on the wall and landed heavily on all fours. She looked up over her shoulder, like a dog. Mandy was standing on the wall, gigantic against the sky, hurling pears at her, shouting,

'You want it all, don't you? You want the lot! Well, go on then, take it! Have the bloody pears!'

Jean caught a pear as she fled inside. It lay in her hand, gilded, wormy.

By six o'clock the shameful incident, marinated all afternoon in her mind, was sufficiently tenderized and trimmed to be offered as an amusing anecdote to Nigel when he came home. But he did not come home.

Jean woke on the sofa to a smell of burning from the oven and to find that someone had drunk all the wine. She lifted the receiver to ring the police and let it fall. She knew that he had left her. Days and nights passed. Someone. There must be someone. Not her friends. There was only Mandy. Fellow sufferer. Betrayed. But golden pears blocked her path. Jean seized two withered apples from the fruit bowl, smiling in anticipation of Mandy's face as she understood the peace offering. There was a light behind the blanket, and music. Jean pressed and pressed the broken bell.

'There'll be a heartache tonight, heartache tonight . . .' came thumping through the cracked stained glass.

Later she realized that she had been sitting for a long time in the skeleton of a chair. She had forgotten all about her upholstery class. She went to the telephone.

'Peter. How are you? It's Jean. Is Mary there?'

'Jean! Are you all right?'

'Of course, I'm all right. I merely wanted to ask Mary if she had any of that red Dralon left. Why shouldn't I be all right?'

'It's just that it's three o'clock in the morning . . .'

Jean was woken by an unfamiliar noise from next door. Laughter. Feet were going up and down the path. She threw back the duvet and ran to the window.

Mandy was leaving in a taxi.

Jean struggled with the window and forced it open. She wanted to say something, make everything all right. She clawed through the wardrobe and pulled out a bag. 'Mandy!' The car back-fired a contemptuous burst of grey smoke at her. Mandy was gone. Escaped. Victorious. Jean hurled the bag through the window. It burst, spilling spurned, never-needed baby clothes over the road.

Mary might have telephoned her, but she would not have got through, because that morning the phone was cut off.

The man in the social security office gave Jean a funny look as she sat down in the peeling grey and yellow room. She knew she looked all right; she had checked in the 'ladies' in the pub.

'How was Brittany?' she asked brightly. He stared. 'Don't you remember? I came in a year or so ago about my holiday insurance and we discovered that we were going to the same place.' Evidently he did not remember.

The weather became colder. Jean lay shivering in the aftermath of a dream in which she and Nigel were putting up the tent on a campsite and Nigel had started to hammer the tent-peg into her head. She realized that it was more than a year since he had gone. She could still hear the hammering. A man was fixing a 'For sale' sign to the fence. She remembered the face of a woman outside the baker's, whom she had despised as a doughnut. Now it was she who lay on the edge of a bed grown too vast; a white soggy meringue left on the side of someone's plate.

Surely she had had most need of blessing? Jean came down the church aisle more unsteadily than was possible from the mouthful of wine, although she had not risen from the altar rail after receiving the sacrament. She had stretched out her hands again for the cup, but the blue glassy eyes of the vicar had cut them and passed over her.

If afterwards, in the porch, his white sleeve billowed for a moment like the sail of a rescue ship, it was at once drowned by a wave of eager young faces. A woman's voice called her name tentatively as she stumbled over the hump-backed gravestones, grey whales and basking sharks with granite teeth, that reared under her feet. She cursed herself for putting those two pound notes in the collection. Much good it had done her. Her heart was already thumping with the beginnings of shame. There was only one way, impossible now, to soothe it. Let soft seas of alcohol lap over the brain. She walked into the terrible yawning dry jaws of afternoon.

Something made her stop and look in her purse. She pulled out two pound notes. The miraculous green paper shook in her fingers. She must have put a pawn ticket in the collection bag.

'Thank you, God,' she said as she went into the off-licence.

Tired, and buffeted by Christmas shoppers, Jean was thankful to get home. How pretty the holly wreath looked, festive against the stained glass. Nigel must have done it to surprise her. She knelt to kiss its berries; the cold prickles grazed her face. Her key wouldn't fit. She rattled and rattled. Tears burst from her eyes as she put her mouth to the letter box, smearing the polished brass.

'Nigel,' she called. 'Nigel! I can't open the door!'

He opened it in a rush of spicy air. But it wasn't Nigel. A boy stood staring at her.

'Mum,' he shouted, 'Mu-um!'

She scrambled up. The holly had scratched her lip. With the metallic taste of blood she remembered. She turned back up the slushy path and into the house next door.

She kicked off her shoes and lit the fire and sat down to see what she had bought. A Bird's Trifle. How odd. Still, there was a little milk; it wouldn't matter if it had gone off slightly. Her coat fell open and she confronted a thigh; she must have forgotten to put her skirt on. She sat in her leotard stroking in pity the poor white flesh marbled with cold. The light went out. The gas fire went out.

In the light, from the street lamp, falling through the blanket looped across the window she turned to the trifle. The Dream Topping. The hundreds and thousands melting in rainbow drizzle.

Starlight Blaze and Pepperpot

Annette and I were not really friends at school. We were classmates, in the 1950s, in our last year at a girls' primary school in a small country town, which I left years ago. Annette was one of the horsey set, an exclusive group who wore their hair braided or in ponytails and whinnied round the playground, jumping invisible hurdles. They could ride horses, they could draw horses, they *were* horses, or at least young centaurs, half girl, half horse. Once, when our form mistress, Miss Steele, asked her a question in class, Annette tossed her head and answered 'Nei-ei-eigh!' Miss Steele was in a good mood that day, and decided to laugh with the rest of us but another time it might have earned Annette a crack on the head with the register, which brought tears to the eyes and left you feeling dizzy and sick. My mother, who always saw the best in people, had told me that Miss Steele was probably so bad-tempered because her fiancé had been killed in the war. Miss Steele shared a cottage with a teacher at another school who, it was said, had lost her fiancé too.

Annette was the undisputed leader of the horsey girls. It was she who gave them their names. Annette was Starlight Blaze, and Jilly, her small lieutenant, was called Pepperpot, because of her freckles. Pepperpot was like one of those miniature ponies who are put in a racehorse's stable to keep it company. Oddly enough, it was Pepperpot Jilly who went on to make the Olympic dressage team and to own a famous racing stables, while Starlight Blaze, along with Midnight, Lucky, Toffee, Candyfloss *et al.*, having cleared the grammar school gates, cantered into obscurity, as far as I was concerned, at least.

But there was one incident for which, as much as for rocking the classroom with laughter on a grey winter's day, I never forgot Annette. Maria Cattini was the sort of girl nobody – teachers or pupils – took much notice of. Her school blouses were dingy, and she could have been the girl whose mum didn't use Persil, in the advertisement. The only interesting thing about Maria, apart from being half-foreign, was that her father drove an ice-cream van. It didn't come down our road, but I'd seen the van and it was beautiful, decorated with giant cornets and knickerbocker glories, plangently chiming some Neapolitan love song. *Antonio's Italian Ices* was painted on the side. Maria had enjoyed a brief popularity one summer, when her father turned up on sports day and handed out free ices, but she did not have a best friend, and she spent playtimes hovering on the edge of the horsey set's gymkhanas, waiting in vain to be invited to join them. Her little sister was in my brother's class in the Infants, and the two girls always walked home hand in hand. Lucky beggars, we said, I bet they have ice-cream every day.

Then, suddenly, this unremarkable girl became notorious. It was all over the local paper. My mother tried to hide it from me but I'd seen the headline: ICE CREAM MAN GAOLED.

Maria's father had been sent to prison for luring little girls into the back of his van with choc ices.

'What's goaled?' asked my brother. Nobody answered, and Bobby probably thought it was something to do with football.

'Best stick to Wallsy ices in the future,' said my dad, and started to sing '*Oh! Oh! Antonio*'.

'This will be dreadful for Maria,' my mother said. 'You must ask her to tea, Hazel.'

On the day Maria returned to school, the horses were lined up by the wall and the rest of us milling around nearby when she walked in the gate. A hush fell over the playground.

'My mum says I'm not allowed to play with her,' said Jilly.

'Nor am I.'

'Me neither,' said several others.

'How about you, Hazel?' Elizabeth, my best friend, asked.

'Same here,' I muttered.

I heard again my mother's words, and I stood there in the crowd. Three sharp blasts of the whistle should have sounded then, to summon us in, but there was silence.

Annette's voice broke it. 'Maria!' she shouted, 'Over here!'

Maria flinched. We held our breath. What was Annette going to do to her? Hit her? Humiliate her in some way?

Annette reached under her gymslip and fumbled in the pocket of her navy-blue knickers.

'Here, Vanilla,' she called, holding out her hand. A sugar lump lay on her outstretched palm. Maria sidled towards her with her head down, her eyes on the asphalt. It took her ages to cross the playground.

'Well, come on then, you dopey horse. Don't you want it?'

Maria bent her head and nuzzled the sugar lump from Annette's hand. Her hair fell forward, hiding her face.

'Walk on, Vanilla,' said Annette, giving her a little push towards the other horses.

I have no idea what became of Maria, but I have often wondered about her, what that prison sentence did to her family – and about Annette. My own life has been full, with happiness and sorrow; I have been married and widowed, and I have a wonderful daughter, Tansy, a lovely son-in-law, and an adorable grandson. I've got my own business, a flower shop called *Amaryllis* – I did the flowers, with sprays of tiny scarlet berries, for Tansy's winter wedding.

It's usually in the small hours when I'm lying awake, fretting over some tricky decision – you can't afford to be sentimental in business – that Annette pops into my head. I sometimes imagined running into her again. Then, a couple of years ago, I did.

The Hampton Court Flower Show is an annual treat I share with Tansy, and we were there, inside one of the marquees, with Callum, my grandson. Callum, who was five, was fascinated by a display of carnivorous plants, sundews and Venus flytraps, and had to be restrained from opening the lids of all the pitcher plants in the hope of seeing some insect prey meeting a sticky end. I was prising his fingers from a nepenthe when I caught the eye of a woman next to me. She gave me a rueful smile, and in its flicker, I knew her. It was Annette, taller, with her mane now silver, caught back from her face by the sunglasses on top of her head. I got an impression of a moonstone-coloured shirt, a flash of jewellery.

I was about to say her name when I saw a stocky figure approaching, a hint of racing silks in a cerise and emerald blouse, salt-and-pepper hair. Pepperpot. Starlight Blaze and Pepperpot. So they had stayed friends for all these years.

I followed Tansy and Callum who were drifting away, and as I did, half-turned to see Annette and Jilly looking towards me, as if speculating whether I was somebody they knew. It was very unlikely that they would have recognized me, I thought, or that I was imprinted on their memories as they were on mine. After all, I had done nothing to distinguish myself during our acquaintance. They would have no reason to recall a child who had played no part in their lives, except to be a witness to a moment of grace in a school playground half a century ago, back when they were horses.

Tansy and Callum had stopped in front of a stand of bonsai trees. I started to explain the principle of bonsai to Callum, pointing out the perfection in miniature of the leaves and tiny trunks, when, taking me completely by surprise, my spectacles blurred. I had to get away from those stunted oaks, beeches, and cedars rooted in bowls, from all the thwarted forest. My throat prickled, as if I'd swallowed a cactus. I took Callum's hand, holding on tightly as he led me towards the ice-cream booth, and carrying in my mind a snapshot of Annette and Jilly, standing there like two calm horses looking out over a stable gate into the late afternoon.

Where the Carpet Ends

The Blair Atholl Hotel was berthed like a great decaying liner on the coast at Eastbourne; if it had flown a standard from one of its stained turrets it would have been some raffish flag of convenience hoisted by its absentee owner, flapping the disreputable colours of the Republic of Malpractice and Illegality.

The front windows had a view of the Carpet Gardens and the pier, but the back of the hotel, where Miss Agnew lived, gave on to the drain-pipes and portholes of another hotel and a row of dustbins where seagulls and starlings squabbled over the kitchen refuse. Miss Agnew, compelled by the vicissitudes of life to book a cabin on this voyage to nowhere, was one of the off-season tenants who occupied a room at a reduced rate at the top of the hotel, where the carpet had ended. These people of reduced circumstances were required to vacate their rooms just before Easter when the season started, or pay the inflated price required of summer holiday-makers. After the third floor, the mismatched red and black and orange carpets gave way to cracked linoleum and, in places, bare boards. A terrifying lift, a sealed cage behind a temperamental iron zigzag door, carried them up to their lodgings, separated from each other by false plywood walls which divided what had once been one room into two compartments. One floor above them, huddled precariously like gulls, perched a colony of homeless families, placed there by the council in bed-and-breakfast accommodation, whose misery filled the pockets of the landlord and his manager.

If, as Le Corbusier had said, a house was a machine for living in, the Blair Atholl, thought Miss Agnew, was a machine for dying in; but at least there, unlike the occupants of the many old people's rest homes in the town, they were doing it on their own terms. The residents of the fourth floor formed a little community in exile, rescuing each other when the lift stuck, knocking on a door if someone had not been seen about, purchasing small sliced loaves for the sick and Cup-a-Soup and tins of beans to be heated on the lukewarm electric rings, and braving doctors' receptionists, in the smelly telephone booth, to beg for a home visit but dreading above all an admission to hospital, from which one so seldom returned. They met in the conservatory at the back of the hotel in the evenings for a rubber of bridge or to watch a programme on the television – a reject from the lounge, whose horizontal hold had gone – and they formed a little human bulwark against the sound of the sea and the approaching night. It did not do to think too much, Miss Agnew had decided; to dwell on people and cats and dogs and houses in the past was to inspire one to board the next bus to Beachy Head, but sometimes she could not resist stopping to speak to a cat or a dog in the street, and the hard furry head and soft ears under her hand evoked lost happiness so painfully that she strode away berating herself for laying herself open to such pangs, her red mackintosh flapping like the wings of a scarlet ibis startled into flight.

She did not know why antagonism had flared up between herself and the manager, Mr Metalious. She paid the rent on time and she was surely no more bizarre than any of her fellow residents, such as the Crosbie twins, seventy-year-old identical schoolboys who dressed on alternate days in beige and blue pullovers they knitted themselves, and grey flannel trousers and blazers. She felt sure they would have affected caps with badges if they had dared; they did wear khaki shorts in the summer and long socks firmly gartered under their wrinkled knees. Or than the transvestite known as 'the Albanian', a smooth-haired shoe salesman who by night flitted from the hotel, a gauzy exotic moth, to sip the secret nectar of the Eastbourne night. Or than Miss Fitzgerald who left a trail of mothballs and worse in her wake and cruised the litter-bins of the town and rifled the black plastic sacks her fellow tenants left outside their doors on dustbin day. Or than Mr Johnson and Mr Macfarlane who spent their days philosophizing in the station buffet. Or than the Colonel whose patriotism embraced British sherry. Or than silent Mr Cable. Or Mrs MacConochie.

Miss Agnew thought that perhaps she reminded Mr Metalious of some teacher who had shamed him in front of the class, or a librarian who had berated him for defacing a book. She had followed both these professions in her time, but she was not interested very much in his psyche, and anyway videos were more in his line than books. Perhaps she had alienated him when, on moving into the hotel, she had asked him to carry her box of books to her room. He had acquiesced with a very bad grace, telling her that his duties did not include those of a hall porter: perhaps her decision that he would have been offended by a tip had been the wrong one. Whatever the cause, and even before she had overheard him refer to her as a stuck-up old cow, she knew he did not like her.

'Nothing today, Miss Agnew,' he would call out as she passed her empty pigeonhole beside his desk.

'I wasn't expecting anything,' she told him truthfully, but he was determined to regard the lack of post as a confirmation of her low status and as a triumph for himself.

Anyone less bovine than Miss Agnew would have been hard to imagine; she was more ovine, as befitted her name which she believed to derive from the French, with her long mournful face framed by a fleece of off-white curls. Now that it didn't matter any more, she was thinner than she had ever hoped to be. The most she had hoped for in this town, which she had more than once heard referred to as 'God's Waiting Room', was anonymity. She was desirous to be known only as Miss Agnew and she expected nothing more of her pigeonhole than dust or a cata-logue for thermal underwear, and why he picked on her for this particular humiliation she did not know. None of the residents got much post, except the Albanian who received thin cob-webbed envelopes addressed in a spidery hand, and the Crosbie twins who corresponded copiously with each other in the course of each of their infrequent quarrels.

It was lunch-time and Miss Agnew was seated at a table in the window of Betty Boop's, a small vegetarian restaurant that suited her herbivorous taste, ruminating over a piece of leek flan. She had managed, by taking very small mouthfuls and laying down her knife and fork between each bite, to prolong her meal for twenty minutes or so, when she saw Miss Fitzgerald pass, head bowed against the wind to avoid a spume of salty vinegar being blown back into her face by the northeaster, from what was undoubtedly someone else's discarded bag of chips.

Since a recent survey had condemned Eastbourne as a town of guzzlers, Miss Agnew had become aware of the habit of the populace of snacking out of paper bags; the precinct was sugary with half-eaten doughnuts, meaty with burgers and strewn with the polystyrene shells that had held pizza and baked potatoes. The toddlers under the transparent hoods of their striped bug-gies clutched buns and crisps and tubes of sweets; and now there went Miss Fitzgerald conforming, for once, to a local custom.

Miss Agnew was thinking about Beachy Head; it was comforting to know that it was there. When she had walked there
in the summer she had been dazzled by the colour of the sea –
opal and sapphire as in Hardy's poem 'Beeny Cliff' – and she
had felt a melancholy empathy for the writer because for her, as
for him, 'the woman was elsewhere . . .' and nor knew nor cared
for Beeny or Beachy Head and would go there nevermore. Miss
Agnew had felt a powerful force pulling her to the cliff's edge,
and only the thought that she would probably plummet messily
on to the boiling rocks, rather than curve like a shining bird
through the sky into the iridescent sea, had propelled her backwards on the turf. The Crosbie twins had told her that many
more bodies were recovered than were reported; the local police
and press had a policy of suppressing such information, *pour
décourager les autres*. She wondered how largely Beachy Head
loomed in the minds of her fellow residents.

Now she gulped down her elderberry wine, paid the bill, and
succumbed to an impulse to follow Miss Fitzgerald, feeling
amused at herself and more than slightly ridiculous as she turned
up the collar of her mac like that of the trench coat of one of the
private eyes in the detective stories she used as a drug against
insomnia when she lay awake in the night and felt the hotel slip
from its stone moorings and nose towards oblivion. She tracked
her quarry past the pier that strode on shivery legs into a sea of
gun-metal silk edged with flounces of creamy lace, like the expensive lingerie she had loved once. Now she was glad of her thermal
vest and her hair blew about her head as brittle and dry as the
wind-bitten tamarisk and southernwood bushes.

Hotel gossip had it that Miss Fitzgerald, despite her rags and carrier bags, was very rich. Any discussion of her eccentricities
would include, at some point, the refrain, 'She comes of a very
good family, you know.' The black sheep driven from some

half-ruined Anglo-Irish castle, Miss Agnew surmised, as she hurried along, merging into the wall when Miss Fitzgerald stopped to investigate a litter-bin, muttering furiously as newspapers and polystyrene foam cups and boxes showered the pavement. The few people she encountered made wide curves around her, swerving into the road as she marched on, with the tail and paws of a long-deceased animal around her neck lashing the wind. Were there sheep in Ireland? Miss Agnew wondered. Pigs and chickens certainly, and grey geese in Kilnevin: perhaps St Patrick had rid the Emerald Isle of sheep along with the snakes.

She reflected that she was getting sillier and sillier every day that she spent at the Blair Atholl; it was because she had nothing to think about. Perhaps she was manifesting early symptoms of Alzheimer's disease, brought on by the gallons of tea she had poured over the years from the aluminium teapot; aluminium found in quantities in tea, she had read recently, was a contributory factor to the disease, and that friendly familiar teapot, like a battered silver ball reflecting the fire-light in the facets of its dented sides, must have made her an almost inevitable candidate for premature senility. Why else would she be following Miss Fitzgerald's erratic and litter-strewn progress, playing detective in the icy wind? The teapot had belonged to Pat, the friend she had lived with for thirty-three years. The lease of the flat had been in Pat's name too, and when it had expired Miss Agnew had neither the means nor the desire to renew it. She hoped that Pat was not watching now, and feeling that her friend's purposeless life negated the years they had spent together, but the brightness and laughter and strength that had been Pat was a heap of ash in a plastic urn, so of course she couldn't see her.

Miss Fitzgerald struck up a side road and Miss Agnew followed her past the guest houses with hanging baskets and gnomes and cards in the windows advertising vacancies, whose names, the Glens and the Blairs and the Lochs and the Braes, suggested that they were passing through a settlement of Scots in exile. They emerged into the long road called Seaside and Miss Agnew found herself studying a green plaster rabbit and a set of ruby-red plastic tumblers on the deck of a broken radiogram in the window of a junk shop, while Miss Fitzgerald contracted some business with its proprietor. A sign stuck to the glass said: *Lloyd Loom Chairs Wanted Any Condition. Good Prices Paid.* How odd, thought Miss Agnew, that those prosaic wicker chairs should have become collectors' items; if you waited long enough everything came back into fashion, but she knew that she would not. Not yet antique, and certainly unfashionable, she stepped into an adjacent shop doorway as Miss Fitzgerald emerged still talking volubly and stuffing something into one of her plastic carriers. Miss Agnew remembered that there was a creaking circle of green wicker chairs in the Blair Atholl conservatory, which she felt suddenly sure were genuine Lloyd Looms. Miss Fitzgerald crossed the road and stood at the bus stop, but Miss Agnew decided to walk on a little before retreating to the Blair Atholl, although a heavy shower had started to fall.

This part of town seemed to be called Roselands; there was a men's club of that name, and a café; the name shimmered softly in tremulous green leaves and pink blowzy petals, the name of a ballroom or dance hall in a film, where the lost and lonely waltzed away their afternoons, reflected in mirrors full of echoes and regret.

Miss Agnew opted for the Rosie Lee Café, which seemed cheerful and steamy, where memory would not draw up a chair at her table and sit down, but as she pushed open the door she saw a fellow resident of the Blair Atholl, Mr Cable, a redundant bachelor late of the now-defunct Bird's Eye factory, seated there smoothing out the creases from a very black-looking newspaper prior to applying himself to the Quizword. She retreated.

The shower had spent itself now. All the bright and garish gardens she passed, the tubs and window boxes of the terraced houses, and the flowers in the interstices of the paving stones, the shining windows and letter boxes had a desperate air, as if neatness could stave off desolation; a cold salt wind was blowing off the sea and a palm tree rattled behind a closed gate. Tall pampas grass was lashing the houses with canes, softening the blows with hanks of dirty candy-floss, and punishing again. There was too much sky in Eastbourne, Miss Agnew thought – she found its pearly vastness terrifying; gold light poured from the Downs gilding bleakly the cold glass panes of a Victorian red-brick church and blazing in puddles on the road and pavement. Mothers with prams and pushchairs on their way to collect older children from school seemed unaware of, or immune to, all this gold that rolled from the spokes of their wheels, drenched them and turned their baby carriages to chariots of gold.

Miss Agnew had to pause to snatch her breath from the wind outside a low building set back from the pavement; it was a newly refurbished home for the terminally old. A large yellow van with *Sleepeezee* on its side was parked in the drive and a mattress was being carried in. Then, through a window, Miss Agnew saw a girl in a white uniform bounce up towards the ceiling, and as she came down a young man bounced up. Up and down they went, trampolining, bouncing up, bouncing down, laughing, until for a second they were in mid-air in each other's arms before tumbling down in an embrace on the new mattress; the living larking about on a deathbed.

Miss Agnew was at once elated and distressed. An image came into her mind of her parents, long ago tucked up in their marble double bed with a quilt of green marble chippings to keep them warm. She caught a bus back to the town centre, and as she sat on its upper deck, she decided that it was right that the young should embrace in the face of death, and closed her ears to the profanities of a bunch of smoking schoolchildren sprawling about the back of the bus; their harsh cries sounded as sad as the voices of sea birds on a deserted beach at dusk.

As she stepped out of the lift on the fourth floor she noticed a pram, belonging to one of the bed-and-breakfast families, wedged across the narrow stair that led to their quarters, and saw the disappearing draggled hem of a sari above a pair of men's socks. She shook the raindrops from her mac and hung it up and made herself a cup of soup and a piece of toast. Later that evening she went down to the conservatory to watch the nine o'clock news.

'Pull the door to, would you?' said Mrs MacConochie. 'There's a draught.' The wind was buffeting the glass panes, the television picture shivered.

'I don't want to be part of this,' Miss Agnew said to herself, looking around, at the Crosbie twins counting stitches, the defeated fan of playing cards in Mrs MacConochie's hand, Mr Cable clawing his winnings, a pile of one-pence pieces, across the baize table whose legs were criss-crossed with black insulating tape. Wicker creaked under old bones, the horizontal hold slipped and Miss Fitzgerald mumbled under a cashmere shawl. I don't want to be a drinker of Cup-a-Soup in a decaying hotel room, whose only post is a catalogue for thermal underwear, thought Miss Agnew, just as I do not want to join the respectable army of pensioners in their regimental issue beige and aqua raincoats, whose hair is teased, at a reduced rate on Wednesdays, into white sausages that reveal the vulnerable pink scalps beneath, and who are driven to luncheon clubs in church halls by cheerful volunteers. I am not nearly ready to sleep easy on a Sleepeezee mattress. Something's got to happen.

The weather forecast ended.

'Have you put on your stove?' Mrs MacConochie asked Mr Cable. He had. It was Mrs MacConochie's colonial past that made her refer thus to the dangerous little electric circles with frayed flexes, which failed to heat the residents' rooms; her own room was almost filled by a Benares brass table with folding beaded legs, and burnished peacocks with coloured inlaid tails, and a parade of black elephants with broken tusks; herds of such elephants trumpeted silently in the junk shops and jumble sales of Eastbourne.

The Albanian paused outside the conservatory, then stuck her head around the door.

'Good evening, everybody.'

There was a murmur at this diversion; they glimpsed tangerine chiffon and a dusting of glitter on the blue-black plumes of her hair. She smiled, like a dutiful daughter, round the circle of her surrogate family, but there was nobody there to tell her to take care and not to be home late, and she melted away into the mysterious night.

'Pull the door to, would you?' called Mrs MacConochie, wrapping her tartan rug tighter around her knees. 'There's a draught.'

'Something must happen,' said Miss Agnew to herself again as she prepared herself for bed. 'Something will change.'

In the morning nothing had changed. A seagull laughed long and bitterly outside her window. Mr Metalious still disliked her; there was nothing in her pigeonhole. A grey rain was slashing the street. As she crossed the foyer, she passed the Albanian, a poor broken moth caught by the morning, dragging dripping wings of tangerine gauze across the dusty carpet, blue-jawed and sooty-eyed in the fluorescent light.

The only thing which was different, she noticed as she

entered the conservatory, was that all the Lloyd Loom chairs had gone, and Miss Fitzgerald was standing under a paper parasol in the rain, watching a van pull away from the back entrance of the hotel.

Windfalls

It was Martinmas, the eleventh of November, and in the front room of the house called Fernybank the morning sun of a St Martin's summer – the halcyon days which sometimes occur at this time of year – was diffused with shadows of leaves through the three green panes at the top of the window. A *Fatsia japonica* grew close to the house, always unclenching new green hands to knock on the window, and a rockery, thickly embedded with plants, among them the eponymous ferns, and divided by a crazy-paving path, sloped down to a low wall. The play of light on the foliage outside and the house plants gave the room the aspect of a botanical glasshouse; it was a green faded room with bookshelves either side of the tiled fireplace, racks of LPs, tapes and CDs, a music stand and a clarinet. On the mantelpiece stood a mahogany-cased clock and a Newton's cradle tick-tocking from a recent encounter with a duster. Martin Elgin, sixty-three-year-old orphan, widower and housewife, had lived in Fernybank, one of a pair of semi-detached villas, for several years without redecorating anywhere. He had never heard of Martinmas until his wife Shirley told him about it, or a St Martin's summer.

After Shirley died, Martin had sold his share in their electrical repair business to his partner and moved from London to this town some twenty miles away, to be nearer their married son, Danny, and his family. His retirement freed him to not practise his clarinet, to not do up the house or redesign the garden or play any of the language tapes he had been given as presents, or join any clubs or make new friends, or do any of the things expected of him. It had, however, given him endless leisure to brood on his parents' last years and his wife's last months and conclude that he had made a botched job of every emotional emergency call-out. He knew that he could not go on like this indefinitely, and filed inside the latest Robert Goddard novel from the library was an application form from B&Q, who were taking on older staff.

This morning he was pleased he wasn't at work and he was getting ready to go out, because his daughter-in-law had asked him to collect his grandson, Noah, from school. Noah, who was not five yet, was in his first term in the Infants, mornings only, and it was difficult sometimes for Megan, a trainee IT consultant, to pick him up. Danny commuted to London where he worked as a systems analyst.

Martin was wearing a black waistcoat unbuttoned over a dark grey flannel shirt with a yellow tie, graphite-coloured cords and black suede boots. He looked what he was, an amateur jazz musician. Martin took the train to London once a month to play with his old mates, staying the night with his brother and visiting his wife's grave in Norwood Cemetery the following day. He put on his jacket, with the two poppies intertwined in the buttonhole: a white peace poppy in protest at the illegal war in Iraq and the red poppy he would not renounce. The white poppy, bought in a local bookshop, reminded him of a little white-haired lady who used to stand outside the tube station in all weathers when he was young, calling out in a whispery voice, 'Pacifist papers, pacifist papers.' Martin never bought one. And he would never have expected to join the beard-and-sandals brigade, yet he had boarded the coach to London with a local contingent to swell the massive anti-war march of 2003. He had always been Mr In-Between, too busy with his work and music to get involved in anything else. Which was possibly why he would never be a first-rate musician.

Shirley, a CND veteran, was the political one. She had cried with joy when Labour won the 1997 election. Sometimes he thought it was good that she didn't know what was happening to their country – the bus and tube bombings, accusations of witchcraft, more guns and knives on the streets, the police shooting of an innocent 'terror suspect', all the loony legislation and nonsense about ID cards, the list went on and on. Don't even get him started on Transport for London or South West Trains. Thing was though, Shirley would have tried to do something about it.

To be fair, there were no sandals among his lot on the march but loads of trainers, several beards, and fleeces, woolly hats and gilets galore. Danny had cried off at the last minute. Megan had a migraine. The shouting and banging drums and shrilling whistles as they marched through the streets deafened and embarrassed Martin until he could bear it no longer and slipped down a side street where he spotted a pub. Fortified, he made his own way to Hyde Park. His contingent was lost for ever and he found himself entering the park in a phalanx of black-clad Muslim women holding banners in a language he couldn't understand. The freezing mud of Hyde Park, penetrating his boots as he listened to Shirley's hero, Tony Benn, gave Martin his first attack of rheumatism. And what had the march achieved, apart from Martin's brief experience of being at one with a crowd and satisfaction that for once he'd spoken out?

Martin, born towards the end of the Second World War, had grown up despising the ordinary Germans who knew what was going on and did nothing. He lived lately in a constant state of unease about atrocities and injustices about which he did nothing. He had never questioned the fundamental decency and innate sense of fair play of the British, but now information was coming to light about an abomination known as the London Cage where prisoners of war had been tortured, and secret interrogation camps in Germany after the war. Holocaust deniers were springing up all over the place and every time you turned on the radio you heard about Guantánamo Bay and Abu Ghraib prison, you heard the word 'torture' bandied about, and discussions as to whether its use could ever be justified. If Martin were to count, he must have lived through, and hardly paid attention to, almost as many conflicts as there were pages in his boyhood stamp album. His granddaughter, Lily, had shown only a brief polite interest in his prized collection of flimsy, magical oblongs, squares and triangles – stamps, like cigarette cards, played no part in her world.

Armistice Day was affecting him more this year than he remembered it having done before, perhaps because he had more time to watch the local news. He had woken to the early morning news on the radio announcing that four soldiers from his father's regiment had been killed in Basra and a dozen police recruits had been blown up in a separate suicide attack. Somebody's boys. The old cliché would never lose its power to hurt. Both his grandfathers had been in the first war but he couldn't remember them talking about it, and Martin's father had never spoken about his time in the army. Martin and his brother had wondered lately if that was because Dad had not 'had a good war'. National Service had been abolished by the time the Elgin boys reached conscription age and so military matters had never impinged on their family, beyond the Forces' requests on *Two-Way Family Favourites* at Sunday lunch-times. Martin would have preferred to observe the two minutes' silence alone with his radio but now he would have to do his shopping before picking up Noah, and the eleventh hour of the eleventh day of the eleventh month would find him on the hoof.

It was too warm for an overcoat and Martin wound a scarf round his neck before going through to the kitchen to lock the back door. He was distracted by the window; the leaves were late in falling this year, but the chestnut was almost bare and the sun turned its bellied trunk and branches to a brass chandelier. Elsewhere in his garden and beyond the trees were hung with green, yellow and russet flounces. Martin had come to enjoy, as much as he felt entitled to enjoy anything Shirley could not share, this house and garden with its visitors, the night people, the moths and rats, badgers, foxes and hedgehogs; he tolerated the slugs and snails who always left a little mesh of glitter in the space between the back door and skirting board, and most of all he enjoyed observing the sky and tree people whom he was privileged to have as neighbours. He kept a pair of binoculars on the draining board to catch their performances.

There was a sunny smell of toast in the kitchen and a countertenor singing like a fallen angel on the radio as two squirrels chased each other through the branches of the oak tree; first one, followed by the other, leapt in an arc the seemingly impossible distance through the empty air to a hazel tree, just catching a bunch of twigs almost too frail for their weight, swinging wildly before dashing on to a bough of bleached, ivy-girdled dead tree slanting across a tall willow. The squirrels sat side by side on a branch, in silver jackets opening on to white shirt fronts, and one of them appeared to put an arm around the other. Then, sensing that somebody was trying to capture that tender gesture in the twin round eyes of binoculars through a kitchen window, the marvellous acrobats were gone.

When Martin was a boy there had been a WANTED poster of a grey squirrel in the post office. The reward offered was 'A

Shilling a Tail'. Squirrels, like pigeons and any other wild life to which mankind took a dislike, had become 'fair game' again. Martin had read about restaurants putting roast squirrel on the menu. In the prevailing climate of cruelty people had become shameless in their gluttony, while the more hypocritical claimed that by eating these long-established immigrants they were helping the cause of the red squirrel and our little native songbirds. For his part Martin decided that what the birds and animals did to get by was none of his business and he forgave the squirrels in advance for the bulbs they would dig up before the spring. He had watched one of them, it was grey with a reddish stripe running from the back of its head to the tip of its plumed tail, sitting on the stone step holding a dug-up crocus, green and white, and nibbling it as we might eat a spring onion. The thing about squirrels, they really seemed to enjoy life.

Although Martinmas was such a benign, blue-skied, scarlet-berried day as Martin set out, there had been high winds and rain during the night. Remembrance Sunday a few days earlier had been characteristically grey with a bitter wind stirring the medals and cockades, buffeting the flags and banners and the poppy wreaths pooling on the granite steps of the war memorial, watering the eyes and hanging dewdrops on the noses of some participants, the heroes in black and camel overcoats and anoraks who had survived ordeals that Martin had never been called upon to face. Martin had watched the measured tread of the wreath-layers, white gulls wheeling above the bugler sounding the Last Post, bareheaded men weeping and the marching girls and boys in the uniforms of youth organizations. Although he always bought a poppy, he had not attended any such ceremony since he was a boy, but when he went out for his newspaper, he found himself walking from the newsagents to join the gathering in the civic park, to be caught in the melancholy grace of the occasion. What, he wondered, was passing through the mind of the lone survivor of the First World War, huddled under a blanket in a wheelchair, paying his respects perhaps for the last time to his fallen comrades, boys dead for almost ninety years? And of course Martin had to ask himself, not for the first time, how would I have measured up, would I have had a good war? He became aware of a smell of old face flannels and fried chicken coming from someone standing near him and stepped away.

When he got home his heart was so heavy he didn't know what to do with himself. He went into the garden to plant, belatedly, the snowdrop bulbs Megan had given him for his birthday. Each thrust of the trowel into the cold wet clay hurt his hand. It was a duty discharged; he didn't give a monkey's if the little blighters came up or not.

As he walked to the shops Martin noticed that the road and the pavement were strewn with smashed rowan berries, crab-apples, split conker cases, all sorts of red, yellow and purple ornamental fruits; winged seeds and nut shells cracked beneath his boots. Nature's bounty. They must have been brought down in the night. His way took him past drives and front gardens where drifts of leaves and apples lay under the trees. A wealth of fruit that people couldn't be bothered to harvest.

At the small shopping precinct, Martin's heartbeat quickened at the thought of looking through the window of Gemini, Unisex Hair Salon, and the possibility of seeing the proprietor, Valerie, at her work. He had encountered Valerie twice, when he had taken Lily to have her hair cut. Lily was ten and walked the short distance home from school with a friend. Martin would look after her and Noah until Megan got back. He had thought a lot about Valerie, whether he could, or should, try to get to know her better. He was half disappointed, half relieved, when Megan had taken Lily herself last time; it was Megan, the old hand, who explained that Gemini was one of the 'air signs. Although Gemini was unisex, Martin felt he could not go there on his own account. He always went to Jimmy's, the barber where Danny and Noah had their hair cut, to maintain his neat grey fuzz. He wondered if he had the energy to even begin a friendship with another woman. Too much baggage, as they say. Valerie was somewhere in her forties; she would either be married, or divorced with problem children and dependent parents, or living with an abusive partner — there she was, with her great legs in sheer tights and kitten heels, wielding a hair-dryer, dressed in a white blouse, with a discreetly deep cleavage, cinched into her black pencil skirt with a broad patent leather belt, and over it an unbuttoned black gown with the sleeves rolled to the elbow, making her look a devastating combination of academic and factory girl. Her blonde hair was swept up and held at the back in a big shiny black clip.

The thing about Valerie was, she had the quality of kindness. Valerie was one of those women who, as they go about their daily business, do more good in the world than many who set themselves up as professionals or charge around emblazoned with charitable logos, wearing their hearts on their t-shirts. The first time Martin had taken Lily to Gemini he had sat intrigued, watching the stylists, all in black and white, and the black-gowned customers reflected in the bevelled deco mirrors which could reproduce somebody to infinity or capture passers-by outside and make them walk the wrong way until they disappeared into the looking glass. The silver and black and white choreography of this salon of mirrors was like a gelatin print and deserved, he thought, a Busby Berkeley soundtrack, rather than the local radio station banging on in the background. He watched Lily's wet rats' tails blooming into soft curls under the dryer and falling in snippets round her chair, and he watched Valerie, presiding over her kingdom. An old lady had come in to have her hair done for her husband's funeral, and when it was time to pay, she found she'd forgotten her purse. 'It's on the house, my love,' Valerie said, putting her arm round her. The whole salon was in tears.

Martin gave Valerie a smile and wave as he walked on. Her face lit up and she acknowledged him with a pair of scissors, but he wasn't entirely sure that she knew who he was. Then he remembered with a jolt of shame a dreadful thing which had almost happened to him. Something he had been just saved from. It had happened the week before, in Haggerty's, the town's remaining department store. Martin had been travelling up the escalator to the second floor when he saw the naked polystyrene torso of a woman on a pedestal just within reach. He gave a sort of groan, a sigh, yearning towards her, stretching out to embrace her – and snatched his hands back in horror when he realized what he was doing. He looked round. Nobody had seen him. But the disgrace if they had. How could he have done such a thing? Suppose some woman had screamed. He saw himself escorted from the premises by a security guard. And that would have been getting off lightly. How could he have faced the family ever again? It was a spontaneous gesture of tenderness, but what an inexplicable, seedy, shabby assault it would have seemed to them. Did the figure even have a face? He couldn't remember now. It was a sort of caryatid, waiting to display some garment.

He had to go to Woolworths for light bulbs, and while there decided to buy some sweets for the children. He was by the confectionery, noting gloomily that the shelves were full of Christmas chocolates already, when he thought to check his watch. One minute past eleven. When it seemed as though the two minutes' silence must have elapsed, the music from the CD counter stopped and loud giggling came through a PA speaker; a girl's voice could be heard saying, 'Get off me! No *way* am I doing it! You'll have to. It ain't *my* job.' Martin caught the affronted eye of a woman standing to attention near him. She hurried towards the doors with her head bowed as, over the dull clang of something falling in a scuffle, a young man's voice, bursting with suppressed laughter, announced that as a mark of respect the staff and customers of Woolworths would now observe a two minutes' silence. Martin focused on the Pic'n'Mix, the multi-coloured assortments of sweets in perspex cages, pastels and stripes and shiny jellified shapes which carried the warning that they contained pork and bovine gelatine. He was struck by the inherent loneliness of the Pic'n'Mix. It reminded him of lying in bed in the dark with too many radio stations to choose from and the display of his DAB radio shining like one of those blue fluorescent insect killers in a butcher's shop. Spoilt for choice, he left without sweets or light bulbs. This meant that he had to go to Robilliard and Daughters General Stores.

The light bulbs were to be found between the pet food, obscure brands with foreign labels, and sacks of biscuits and bird food and a pungent box of dried pigs' ears, and the knitting wool. Martin found what he needed and took them to the counter, where a pile of rodent glue traps lay beside an animal charity collection tin. One of the Robilliard daughters was in conversation with a customer. She almost spat the words, 'Do you know what I think they ought to do? They should build prisons under the sea! That would solve the problem for good and all.'

On Martin went, past Slots-Of-Fun, a cosy-looking little Technicolored gambling den, and the charity shop where the bloke he knew as Jeff was standing in the doorway chowing on a Ginster, and past Tanya Hyde Sunbeds and Nail Parlour to the newsagents where, as was his habit, he adjusted a couple of the worst red-tops, turning their faces, and the rest, to the wall. What sort of message were newspapers and top-shelf magazines giving to his grandchildren and all the other kids who came into this shop? A headline flashed into his mind: GRANDAD ON

MANNEQUIN GROPE CHARGE. He bought his paper and a packet of liquorice Rizlas, a couple of samosas and two Crunchies.

He reached the school with minutes to spare and stood in the infants' playground with a handful of mums accompanied by babies and crazy toddlers careering about, uttering shrieks that their mothers seemed quite impervious to as they chatted. Noah was released at last, carrying an awful lot of stuff for a little boy who was only part-time at school, and flung himself into Martin's arms, dropping half of it. Martin sorted him out and they walked the short distance to Noah's house hand in hand.

'How was your morning?'

'Foine.'

Noah looked worn out, white faced, and his hair, which was no particular colour until the sun highlighted all sorts of subtle tones in it, was sticky with some sort of yogurt or glue, which had also globbed on to his blue school sweatshirt.

'What shall we play, Grandad?'

'It's such a lovely day I think we'll just muck about in the garden after we've had some lunch.'

'I'll show you my latest tricks on the trampoline.'

The garden, with its double swing and trampoline, had a cidery smell, from the large misshapen cooking apples lying on the grass. Martin rolled a cigarette as Noah bounced, trying to invent tricks to impress his grandad, delighted to have him to himself. His sweatshirt and t-shirt rode up exposing his white tummy and as he turned a somersault Martin experienced with such clarity a memory of his son Danny as a boy that he choked on his cigarette. It was Danny, in his last year at primary school, playing the lead in *The Shirt of a Happy Man*. Danny, his bare chest white above baggy black trousers, his dark eyes shining, somersaulting and handspringing across the stage. He had loved doing it, the audience had loved him, Martin and Shirley had wept through their laughter. It was as though a camera transfixed him mid-leap from his childhood into the future, and a black-and-white photograph was imprinted on Martin's heart while time moved on.

'Noah, did your daddy ever tell you the story of the king who wanted to wear the shirt of a happy man?'

'No.'

'Well, once upon a time there was a king who had everything his heart could desire, a beautiful queen, a palace, servants, jewels, but still he was not happy. He grew ill with sadness and nothing could make him laugh. People came from far and wide to try to cheer him up but the king grew sadder and sadder until one day a wise man told him that he would only be happy if he could wear the shirt of a happy man. So he sent his servants all over the kingdom to find a happy man and bring the king his shirt, but they all came back to say that they couldn't find anybody who was perfectly happy. The king grew sadder still until he almost died of sadness until at last . . .'

'I'm bored of this king.'

'Anyway the point is, the only man in the whole kingdom who was happy was this man who had no shirt, and the king laughed and laughed and they all lived happily ever after.'

'Why didn't the king have any children?' Noah was slashing the air with a plastic sword.

'Mind that sword. Why don't you play in the sand-pit for a bit?'

'It's not a sword, it's a Lightsaber, only it doesn't flash any more.'

Martin lifted the lid off the sand-pit to find that the greyish sand was full of half-buried toys. He pulled out a dead football, buckets and spades, various dinosaurs and grotesque humanoid robotic figures.

'"I shall find him, never fear. I shall find my grenadier,"' he said, holding up a soldier from no recognizable regiment.

'He's a baddie. He's Hitler.'

'Hitler?'

'Da guy what made World War One!'

'Two, and I wouldn't exactly call him a guy. It wasn't like *Star Wars*, you know! Hitler ... look at all these apples going to waste.' He flicked one with the toe of his boot.

'They've got maggots.'

'Yeah, they might have now but they didn't always have. Come on, help me to pick them up. They're called windfalls.'

'I don't like the brown bits.'

'We can cut those out. How would you like to make an apple pie?'

Some apples were beyond use, turned to mush or stippled with circular patterns of white mildew. Noah unearthed a doll's head, which he brought to his grandad like little Peterkin presenting old Kaspar with the skull in the poem, thought Martin, feeling as defeated by attempting to explain Hitler to Noah as old Kaspar had been by the Battle of Blenheim. And should he try? Kids today had enough on their plates already, with wars and famine, climate change and endangered species thrust down their throats, as it were, before they could even speak. When he was a boy, aliens and mutants dressed in weird robes or aluminium foil, with goldfish bowls on their heads, were always intercepting our spacecraft, pleading 'Our planet is dying. You must save us!', but now the boot was on the other foot. What kind of useless punctured football of a world would Noah's children inherit?

By the time the apples were peeled and cored, Lily had arrived home and wanted to help make the pastry.

'Fine bread-crumbs, mind,' said Martin. 'Make it like the sand in your sand-pit.'

As he watched the children working, Martin suddenly thought, I'm happy I'm as happy as a sand-boy. As happy as

Larry. And a little dog, a bright-eyed, grinning fox terrier sort of dog, jumped into his mind.

'Hey, supposing Grandad got a dog? A little dog called Larry?'

Can you see me, Shirley? I'm making this pie with the grandchildren, with Noah who you never got to meet.

They heard Megan's key in the lock just as the pie, golden, glazed with egg and decorated with pastry leaves, was lifted out of the oven. Perfect timing. The children ran to meet her. Megan stood in the kitchen doorway with her black laptop case, in her grey suit and pink shirt, staring at the state of the kitchen. Mud, sand, flour, scraps of pastry and apple peel on the floor.

'We were just going to clear up, weren't we, kids? Only we got a bit side-tracked,' said Martin.

'No, that's fine. Lily, why haven't you changed out of your school uniform? Come on, Noah. Into the bath with you, I think.'

'But Mummy, we made you a pie! Out of the apples from the garden!'

'So I see. It looks lovely. I'll put it in the freezer as soon as it cools down.'

'Why can't we eat it?' said Lily.

'We will. One day. I've already planned tonight's dessert.'

Noah burst into tears. Lily ran out into the garden. Martin could see her through the window on the swing pushing herself higher and higher.

'Look, Megan, I'm sorry.'

'No, I'm sorry. It's just that I'm utterly, totally, exhausted. It's just that some of us don't have the time to go grubbing about for rotten apples in the garden!'

'I'd better be going then. I'll go out the back way and say goodbye to Lily.'

'Aren't you staying for supper?'

Two samosas and a can of beans at Fernybank, or waiting here till Danny gets home?

'I don't think I will. I've already planned my supper. Where's my shopping bag? Oh, here's a couple of Crunchies for a rainy day. Noah, have you got a kiss for grandad? Give my love to Daddy, and ask him if he remembers *The Shirt of a Happy Man*.'

First publication/reading details

Awesome Day	BBC Radio 4, 2013
Babushka in the Blue Bus	*Times Literary Supplement*,1988, *Times Literary Supplement Short Stories*, 2003
The Day of the Gecko	*The Worlds* [sic] *Smallest Unicorn and Other Stories*, Cape, 1998
Electric-Blue Damsels	*Dreams of Dead Women's Handbags*, Heinemann, 1987
Ennui	BBC Radio 4
Family Service	*Babies in Rhinestones and Other Stories*, Heinemann, 1983
Glass	*Femme de Siècle*, (ed. Joan Smith), Chatto & Windus, 1992
Grasshopper Green	*Black Middens, New Writing Scotland*, 2013
Heron Cottage	*Seduction*, (ed. Tony Peake), Serpent's Tail, 1994
The Last Sand Dance	*The Worlds Smallest Unicorn and Other Stories*, Cape, 1998
The Late Wasp	*Babies in Rhinestones and Other Stories*, Heinemann, 1983

The Laughing Academy	*The Laughing Academy*, Heinemann, 1993
A Mine of Serpents	BBC Radio 4, 1991
The New Year Boy	BBC Radio 4, 1991
Pigs in Blankets	BBC Radio 4
Pink Cigarettes	*Babies in Rhinestones and Other Stories*, Heinemann, 1983
Pumpkin Soup	*S Magazine, Sunday Express*, 2010
Radio Gannet	BBC Radio 4, 2007
The Running of the Deer	*Park Stories*, 2009
Shinty	*The Laughing Academy*, Heinemann, 1993
Shooting Stars	*S Magazine, Sunday Express*, 2008
A Silly Gigolo	BBC Radio 4
A Silver Summer	*The Worlds Smallest Unicorn and Other Stories*, Cape, 1998
Slaves to the Mushroom	*Dreams of Dead Women's Handbags*, Heinemann, 1987
Soft Volcano	*New Review*, 1974
The Stained Glass Door	BBC Radio 3, 1980, and *Encounter Magazine*, 1981
Starlight Blaze and Pepperpot	*Good Housekeeping*
Where the Carpet Ends	*Dreams of Dead Women's Handbags*, Heinemann, 1987
Windfalls	*The Atmospheric Railway*, Cape, 2008